THE ROOT OF ALL EVIL

BY

PHILIP B. COULTER, PhD

DORRANCE
PUBLISHING CO
EST. 1920
PITTSBURGH, PENNSYLVANIA 15238

The contents of this work, including, but not limited to, the accuracy of events, people, and places depicted; opinions expressed; permission to use previously published materials included; and any advice given or actions advocated are solely the responsibility of the author, who assumes all liability for said work and indemnifies the publisher against any claims stemming from publication of the work.

All Rights Reserved
Copyright © 2015 by Philip B. Coulter, PhD

No part of this book may be reproduced or transmitted, downloaded, distributed, reverse engineered, or stored in or introduced into any information storage and retrieval system, in any form or by any means, including photocopying and recording, whether electronic or mechanical, now known or hereinafter invented without permission in writing from the publisher.

Dorrance Publishing Co
585 Alpha Drive
Suite 103
Pittsburgh, PA 15238
Visit our website at *www.dorrancebookstore.com*

ISBN: 978-1-4809-1303-5
eISBN: 978-1-4809-1625-8

Acknowledgments

Many people have generously contributed to the writing of this novel. It was extraordinary good fortune to work with and learn from numerous mentors, colleagues, and supervisors in several universities where I studied or taught over almost a half-century.

More recently, several members of the Frisco Lakes Writers Group, namely Jan Angelley, Whit Gentry, Barbara Levell, Carol McCoy, Sandra Robertson, Patrick Simons, and Gerry Woods read and commented on various chapters of the manuscript. Their comments and criticisms were always positive and helpful.

Dorothy and Dr. Carl Westerfield, who have spent most of their adult lives living and serving in universities, carefully read the entire manuscript and made numerous detailed criticisms and recommendations regarding virtually every aspect of this work of fiction, including technical editing, character development, plot, dialogue, consistency, etc. To have two close friends with such extraordinary literary intelligence who are so very generous with their time and talent is unbelievable good fortune. I am also grateful to another good friend and neighbor, Susan Bonner, for technical advice and tutoring in some computer applications that were essential in completing the manuscript.

It was my good fortune to work directly with two excellent professionals at Dorrance Publishing: Alexander Rigby and Ashley Austgen. They helped the book fulfill its potential and kept in on a tight production schedule. I am grateful to them and their colleagues at Dorrance Publishing.

Finally, I thank my wife, Mignon, who has been a source of strength and joy in my life for over a half-century. She, too, worked in universities for many years so when I asked her about characters, scenes, dialogues, or plot, her responses always helped to make the story better—either more realistic or more imaginative, whichever it needed. When I became weary of writing, reading, and revising, she provided the necessary encouragement to continue. I gratefully dedicate this book to Mignon, with love.

1 Thirty minutes before the bell in Riedel Tower sounded its eight sonorous gongs on the morning of Monday, June 3, a knock on the door of Alpha State University President R. Steven Faust caused him to lay aside the *Wall Street Journal*. Ms. McInerny, his executive assistant, the repository of the University's rules and regulations and most of its ancient secrets and current gossip, had informed him earlier this morning that Margaret Benedict had an eight o'clock appointment to brief him on today's press conference. As Vice President for Public Information, Margaret Benedict had earned a strong reputation for enhancing the University's public image. In addition to her master's degree in marketing and twenty years of experience with a large firm in Chicago, she was blonde, svelte, charming, and, as usual, looked stylish in her light grey and blue Yves St. Laurent pants suit.

"Come in," Faust said in a morning voice. Margaret entered, carrying a folder of press releases on expensive paper featuring Alpha State's letterhead in black and gold, and its iconic seal depicting a sunrise, with the caption '*Illuminare Humanitas*.'

"Good morning, Mr. President," she said. "Are you ready to announce the appointment of our new Provost and Executive Vice President for Academic Affairs?"

"I guess," he responded, standing tall and handsome behind his large executive-style desk, in his tailored, navy, three-piece suit. "I still don't know why I let you talk me into a press conference. Just issuing a statement to the media would suffice."

"Now, Steve," she said, wincing and flashing her dark brown eyes, "you told me when you hired me that you wanted a plan to make the ASU brand a household name in our region and in the whole country for everything in

1

higher education, not just football. This press conference is part of our plan."

"Okay, what is supposed to happen at this press conference?" Faust asked, looking over his glasses and still not hiding his reluctance.

"Here's the format. I will call us to order at nine, state our purpose and summarize the highlights of our new provost's record. Then I will introduce five people who served on the search committee. First, you. Then, Alex Wolfe as chairman of the Board of Trustees. Then Melinda Osterman as chair of the Faculty Senate. Next, Harry Parcells will speak as president of the Student Government Association, and last comes Sarah Marshall, president of the Alumni Association. I asked each of them to represent his or her constituency and to state, in less than three minutes, two reasons why he or she thinks Andrew Cameron will be a wonderful executive VP. After that, I'll introduce Dr. Cameron, who will take five minutes or so to say he's really glad to be at Alpha State, great things are going to happen, and . . ."

"Cameron has to catch a flight to Prague at twelve noon," President Faust interrupted, "so this thing can't go on and on. Ms. McInerny has arranged for Isaac Brown to take him to the airport no later than 9:30 AM, in a university car."

Somewhat taken aback, Margaret continued, "Then, when we gather in the anteroom to go on stage I will make sure everybody knows not to take more than three minutes each."

"Well, Margaret, I hope this press conference idea works. It seems risky to me. Building up big expectations when maybe we should start a little more low-key," Faust retorted.

"Steve," Margaret said with feigned impatience, "three years ago when you hired a new football coach; you arranged for him to address a joint session of the state legislature! A quick press conference for our new second-in-command of the whole university is the least we can do. Otherwise, a lot of people will think we don't care about academics."

"Okay, Margaret, okay, we're committed. Get over there to Alumni House and hope the media give us good coverage. I'll be there a few minutes before nine."

As she walked toward the door, Margaret Benedict asked, "By the way, Steve, why is our new provost taking off for Europe on the first day of his new job at Alpha State?"

"He's at the end of his first year of a research and consulting contract with a European drug research agency. It's renewable and worth up to two million dollars a year for us. I've told him he can stay on as principal investigator of the contract, but this fall he's got to turn over the actual work to faculty members at Alpha State. To get renewed, he has to meet in person with several of the drug agency execs in Prague starting Wednesday morning."

"Who's going to take over the work from Dr. Cameron?" Margaret asked.

"I'll pull a team from the Med School and Public Health. Of course I'll get Wolfe-Otis Pharmaceuticals involved. They've been generous to us, and we can return the favor."

As she exited, Margaret said, "I smell great PR and maybe a congressional set-aside."

"Margaret, great idea about a legislative set-aside. I like the way you think," he said with a smile. "Now go charm the media. I'll be there."

At 7:50 AM, as the door closed behind Margaret Benedict, President Faust answered the buzz from Ms. McInerny. "President Faust," she said, "the Chairman of the Board of Trustees is on the line. He wants to ask you something about the press conference."

"Okay, put him through," Faust responded. "Good morning, Alex. What's on your mind?"

"Steve, do I have to show up at this meeting at nine, you know, to announce your new VP?"

Alexander Wolfe was President and CEO of Wolfe-Otis Pharmaceuticals, Inc., one of a dozen Fortune 500 companies headquartered in New Cambridge and one of the largest pharmaceutical corporations in the U.S. Faust counted on the support of his long-time friend.

"Alex, we need you there. What's the problem?"

"I'm tied up with our lawyers in a contract dispute with a supplier, and the union rep is threatening to call in his heavy artillery from their national office with some bullshit charges about unfair working conditions at the plant. No way in hell can I make it this morning," Wolfe said.

"But Alex, we need you for only thirty minutes. That's all. I promise. Margaret Benedict has it all arranged."

"It's damned hard to say no to her," Wolfe said.

"So you'll come and make a brief statement about why you think the new VP will be great for the University? We need our Board chairman's blessing."

"Damn, Steve," Wolfe said, "don't you remember that I never supported him on the search committee? And half the Board still agrees with me. I told you before, what we need a VP for is to keep the faculty in line so we can get some things done for a change. We need a kick-ass guy, and he just ain't it."

Several seconds of embarrassing silence passed before President Faust cleared his throat and continued, "Alex, I forgot to tell you, he's bringing an open-ended, sole-source contract with him, worth about $2 million per year. Renewable. It's with," glancing again at the letterhead on his desk, "the 'European Drugs Policy Centre', and ASU will subcontract with Wolfe-Otis Pharmaceuticals for about a million a year, for several years, for the R and D. Does that help to ease the pain of a quick trip to campus?"

"Damn, Steve, you drive a hard bargain." Then, after a pause, "Alright, I'll be there."

"Great, see you there," Faust said, and hung up the phone.

Outside, across campus, virtual silence reigned except for the almost orchestral production of a lone mockingbird, performing a complicated melody from his perch on a limb of the large oak tree between the Admin Building and Blackburn Alumni Center. He continued his symphony even though Riedel Tower slowly chimed eight somber tones, allowing his melodies to be heard only between gongs. Almost nobody heard the mockingbird's aria or Riedel Tower's gongs. The quadrangle was empty. No clusters of students scurried along the sidewalks between classes. Faculty offices and classrooms were dark. June 3 falls between the end of the spring semester and the beginning of summer school. Almost all of the thirty-five thousand students and two thousand faculty members of this complex brain factory, charged with co-producing the three Rs - reading, writing, and 'rithmetic - were away from campus pursuing three other Rs - relaxation, rejuvenation, and retooling.

Soon after the eighth gong, several stylish SUVs, whose sides were covered with station call letters or newspaper logos, pulled into the parking spaces in front of Blackburn Alumni Center. As the reporters left their cars and walked up the sidewalk to the front door, a few gray clouds had begun to gather high in the otherwise sunny, blue sky. This early in June and this early in the day, the weather was quite pleasant in New Cambridge.

The pungent aroma of a dark roast filled the conference room of Blackburn Alumni Center. Media field reporters share many characteristics, one of them being caffeine addiction, especially at a press conference scheduled for what they consider such an "early" hour as nine o'clock in the morning. As soon as they filed into the large conference room, filled their cups with Costa Rican Tarrazu from a silver urn, and tasted the fresh European-style pastry, they began to awaken. Several reporters and camera operators from local network television stations began identifying electric power outlets in which to plug their lights and cameras to record today's unusual press conference. The cameramen were young, dressed in scruffy jeans and T-shirts, and appeared to be indifferent to today's event as they set up their equipment in the ample space between the first row of theatre-style seats and the elevated podium dominating the north end of the room. As they finished, each of the on-camera reporters, all of whom were female, thirty-something, perky, attractive, chatty, and dressed in expensive business attire from the waist up, posed in her camera's lights and articulated "testing, testing, one, two, three, four" for

4

her operator, who signaled approval.

Sidling up to his reporter, the tall expressionless cameraman for WDJD-TV frowned and whispered, "Mona, what the hell are we doing here, anyway? School's out. There's nobody on campus but us."

"How should I know?" Mona said. "The boss called me early this morning on my cell and said to get you and get over here for a nine o'clock press conference. Nice digs here, by the way. My first visit. Anyway, something about President Faust making some kind of big announcement."

Meanwhile, the education reporters from the *New Cambridge Morning News*, the major newspaper in the state, and another daily from the state capitol entered the large conference room. They chatted for a while, coffee and croissants in hand, beneath the middle of the five very large, tall windows dominating the east side of the conference room, each of which was framed with gorgeous gold drapes, trimmed in black. The morning sun radiated through the windows, producing shadowy figures on the floor beneath the media representatives as they walked around the room. Soon, journalists from WSLS, the local NPR station, came in.

With minutes to go, the 120-seat conference room was filling with faculty and staff on twelve-month contracts, students employed for the summer as assistants in a library or laboratory, several Trustees and alumni, and administrators, most of whom sampled the coffee and croissants. Backstage, five members of the Academic VP search committee and Margaret Benedict conversed with their new recruit.

Margaret looked at her watch and announced, "It's two before nine, ladies and gentlemen — show time. We have a standing-room-only audience and lots of media." The group strolled from offstage to the podium and took their seats and the audience grew quiet. Each of the nine gongs from the Riedel Tower resonated louder than usual this morning, due to the effects of a blue sky, mild temperature, low humidity, and a gentle breeze. Margaret stood alone behind the microphone at mid-table.

"Good morning, and welcome to Alpha State University," she said with a clear voice and charming smile, as TV cameras recorded her introduction and reporters scribbled notes. "We are here to announce that Dr. Andrew Cameron has joined the ASU family as our new Executive Vice President for Academic Affairs and Provost, effective today." Applause arose, first from the students but quickly spread to other members of the audience.

Margaret Benedict continued, "I am glad to see that you are as enthusiastic about Dr. Cameron as we are. But please, bridle your zeal until we finish our presentation. He has to catch an international flight at noon today so he cannot be late. Those of you in the media, please note the press releases on the table in the back of the room."

Sometime between the ninth gong from Riedel Tower and the beginning of Margaret Benedict's brief summary of Dr. Cameron's experience, the mockingbird ceased to sing and disappeared from his perch on the lower limb of the oak that stood just outside the five large, two-story windows on the east side of Blackburn Alumni Center.

As planned, Margaret summarized the highpoints of the University's eighteen-month search to find a new Executive VP: big executive recruitment firm; potential candidates from all over the world; winnowed the list to the fifty best; background searches; letters of reference; airport interviews; months of search committee deliberation; university-wide and alumni input; more deliberation; committee recommendations to President Faust; five candidates' campus visits; Faust's decision; Dr. Cameron is our choice. More applause.

Accelerating even more, Margaret summarized Cameron's academic background: doctorate in public policy from Berkeley; two-year post-doc at the National Institute of Drug Abuse in Washington; faculty appointments at University of Rochester, then at Albany University; ten years as dean of Rockefeller College at Albany; teaching, research, and service; five books published; teaching awards, research awards, and administration awards.

Breathless from her rapid-fire recitation of the new provost's record, she pivoted to see if President Faust was ready. "Now, here is Alpha State University's President, Steve Faust."

Faust walked to the mike at mid-table, stood tall behind the podium, flashed his charming smile and seemed to make personal eye contact with everyone in the audience. "I haven't heard spontaneous applause and cheers like we just heard since last January when Alpha State scored the touchdown that won the conference championship." More applause and cheers.

"With the appointment of Dr. Cameron," he continued, "Alpha State will be at the top of her game, so there's no reason a press conference can't also be a pep rally. What impressed me most is that Dr. Cameron understands and supports the time-honored and most fundamental purposes of the university and yet is a modern reformer at the same time. He knows what the contemporary university must do and he is committed to adopting new and productive ways to do it. He has pledged to modernize Alpha State's curricula, to partner with organizations that share our interests, and to lead us into the elite top thirty academic ranking among American public universities. So, I think he will have a lot of fans among faculty and students. He is our academic leader and has my complete confidence to represent the University at the state capitol, in Washington, in missions abroad, and to provide stable leadership on campus when I am away. Margaret?" More applause.

Margaret stepped behind the mike as the President returned to his chair. "Next, ladies and gentlemen," she said, "we will hear from Mr. Alexander Wolfe, chairman of the University Board of Trustees and president and CEO of Wolfe-Otis Pharmaceuticals."

The five sunny, still-life pictures framed by the windows on the east side of the conference room were becoming animated, as occasional gusts of wind moved the limbs of the giant oak against a background of fast-moving grey clouds in a darkening sky. TV camera operators adjusted their lighting.

"If there is anything I have learned about success as a CEO, it's that you've got to keep your bottom line growing. To do that, you've got to be more efficient and increase your market share. To do that, you've got to keep costs down and turn out a product that satisfies your customers. If you do that, your shareholders will get a good return on their investment and stick with you. Getting good people into your top management positions is the key to making this happen. We all wish Cameron well in fulfilling this mission."

The smattering of applause following Wolfe's remarks did not hide the growing sound of more gusty winds, sheets of rain drumming into the windows, and tympanic rumbles of distant thunder.

As she returned to the mike, Margaret looked out the large windows and paused as if immobilized for a moment by nature's surprising turn. Reestablishing audience contact, she said, "Thank you, Chairman Wolfe. Now, it's my pleasure to introduce the president of Alpha State's Student Government Association, a senior this fall, Harry Parcells." Then came more applause and even cheers from his fellow students, as he positioned himself behind the microphone. He was tall and muscular, resembling a basketball player. He wore a navy suit, a blue dress shirt with a button-down collar, and a rep tie, reflecting the contemporary version of the traditional Ivy League look.

He began, "When President Faust told me he had picked Dr. Cameron for our new VP, I was, like, this is great! I mean, ya know, he's just what we need, okay? He will work hard to get the funding we need to build, like, a new and larger student center on campus, complete with a concierge service and a modern fitness and recreation center." With this announcement, the students present raised a boisterous cheer, after which he continued, "Look. Dr. Cameron'll be to the university what Facebook, Twitter, blogging, and YouTube combined are to our life on campus. I pledge to work with him in any way I can, representing my constituents and voters. Welcome, Dr. Cameron!"

Margaret, calm as ever, announced, "Next, may I introduce Sarah Marshall, president of the Alpha State University's Alumni Association."

Sarah Marshall hadn't changed much in the twenty-five or so years since she had served on ASU's cheerleading squad. "I am really excited by the standing room only turnout to greet our new executive vice president. This is like having Lady Gaga, Kanye West, Kim Kardashian, and Oprah all visit our campus on the same day." These introductory comments prompted both cheers and jeers, and she went on. "First, Dr. Cameron is committed to internationalizing the university. That means we will get an international travel program for alumni. Second, he likes for students to get practical experience with their classroom study, which includes bringing sort of real-world practitioners into the classroom. He likes bringing famous musicians, actors, writers and so on to campus to give lectures and conduct mastery classes in the arts." The dean of the College of Fine Arts, seated on the fourth row, rolled his eyes and gritted his teeth at Sarah Marshall's use of the word "mastery" instead of the correct word, "master" classes. "So, I am pretty sure that when these celebrities are on campus, Dr. Cameron will find a way to make them available to the Alumni Association for a fundraiser. I'm positively thrilled! We're so lucky! Margaret?"

Margaret Benedict next called on Melinda Osterman, a senior sociology professor and current president of the Faculty Senate. She was widely known as a champion of faculty rights and an opponent of the administration. In fact, President Faust and Margaret Benedict had had two serious conversations about whether to invite her to speak on behalf of the faculty at the press conference, and finally decided to do it, hoping that Dr. Osterman would interpret the invitation as an olive branch, and temper her remarks.

As she approached the microphone, she smiled at President Faust and the sky grew darker. Margaret Benedict's assistant, standing backstage, turned up the conference room's overhead lights to full power. By this time, the wind was blowing sheets of rain sideways into the tall windows. "Well, is it something I haven't even said yet?" Osterman asked and glared at the ominous storm in a dramatic Glenn Close-style, to which the audience reacted with worried grins and muted laughter.

With the interior lights now illuminating the otherwise dark room and a state-of-the-art stereo sound system amplifying her voice, she continued, "The proletariat always knows that they have a chance to survive and prosper only if they are united. Within the constraints of the search process we were forced to follow, which only muted the real class struggle within this university, we got lucky. Class collaboration is normally to be avoided, but in this case the faculty came to a decision that agrees with both the corporate elite and the student bourgeoisie – Andrew Cameron is capable of doing the job we need here."

Many in the audience shuffled their feet or coughed at the radical nature of Osterman's introductory remarks. Some whispered to each other. Several students giggled and smiled knowingly. The rain continued to pelt the windows. "The faculty needs an advocate. The provost is the university's chief academic officer. He can help us make life at this university decent for faculty and students alike by hiring more faculty, and especially women and minorities. That would enable us to reduce teaching loads to a bearable level, offer smaller classes, and spend more time counseling students outside class, all of which improve the quality of education. He has indicated support for curricular reform. That would give us a chance to rid the curriculum of racism, sexism, classism, homophobia, and three hours of academic credit for courses such as 'canoeing for jocks.' And, he could champion the same principles in a reform of our discriminatory and exploitative system of faculty hiring, promotion, and salaries."

The audience remained silent. President Faust squinted, looking straight ahead, growing angry at Osterman's political diatribe. Margaret Benedict's pulse rate increased when she glanced at her watch. "And furthermore," Osterman continued, "maybe he can figure out a way to put the brakes on Alpha State's follow-the-money obsession. Instead of developing our teaching programs to meet students' intellectual and career needs, and our research programs to solve society's most serious problems, we behave in whatever ways will bring in the most money. We strive to develop whatever programs wealthy alumni, corporations, and congressional pork barrel set-asides will support. That must change." Members of the audience seemed to be holding their breath, as the only sounds in the auditorium were Osterman's stormy rhetoric and the stormy wind and rain slamming against the tall windows. She returned to her seat on the dais to robust but brief applause.

Margaret Benedict replaced Osterman at the microphone and glanced at President Faust, then into the lights of the TV cameras. She cleared her throat and said, "Finally, let's welcome Alpha State University's new Executive Vice President and Provost, Dr. Andrew Cameron." She took her seat.

Cameron positioned himself at the mike and waited for the applause to end. "Thank you. I am flattered by your positive reception. Thanks to all of you here on the podium for your very generous remarks. I can't live up to such elevated expectations, but I promise you, I will do my best.

"Alpha State University, in the twenty-first century, follows in the footsteps of the ancient Greek tradition of higher education founded by three philosophers: Socrates, who taught Plato in the Ancient Agora; Plato, who taught Aristotle in the Academy; and Aristotle who taught Alexander the Great in the Lyceum. Their scientific and humanistic legacy still teaches all who want to learn. The primary mission they established for a university hasn't changed:

to develop in each of our students the facility and habit of ethical, critical thinking and the skills of responsible productivity in their careers - how to live and how to make a living. You may recall that Socrates did that rather well, but the leaders in ancient Athens charged him with corrupting the youth and disrespecting the gods." Cameron paused and scanned his audience.

"At his trial, Socrates refused to recant his teachings or to admit wrongdoing, so the Athenian authorities ordered him put to death by drinking hemlock, which he did with regret at leaving this earth but with eagerness to learn what happens in the afterlife." The audience was totally silent, not a cough, no shuffling of feet, not even thoughts about the heavy wind and rain against the windows, which all but drowned out ten gongs from Riedel Tower.

"My contemporary interpretation of 'corrupting the youth' is equipping them with the tools of independent, objective, critical analysis and encouraging them to think for themselves. Today, 'disrespecting the gods' means questioning the legitimacy of whatever idols people deify and worship – for example, money, power, celebrity." Even the older, more experienced journalists seated in the press area had quit taking notes and sat motionless, astonished by Cameron's inspired rhetorical skill and sensing the potential for controversy in his remarks. Tired of competition from the wind and rain, Margaret Benedict turned up the volume of the sound system.

Wind and rain continued to bluster; cameras continued to roll; audience members continued to listen and wonder. Some felt uncomfortable. Cameron continued with a short recitation of the "fundamental changes" that Alpha State must undertake if it is to fulfill its mission. Each change would seriously affect the interests and practices of one or more university groups – faculty, staff, students, administrators, alumni, donors, Trustees, and contractors. Eyes narrowed or brightened. Some throats tightened. Pulse rates accelerated.

"To conclude, I am grateful to you all for the opportunity to . . ." Boom! A blinding bolt of lightning, accompanied by a deafening thunderclap, struck the giant oak just outside the tall windows. Several seconds passed as a large limb emitted a loud *crraaacking* noise at its base, broke from its trunk and came crashing through the middle window, swatting glass into the conference room and freeing the wrathful wind to blow rain and shards of glass on several rows of frightened people. The interior lights flickered for several seconds, then came back on, revealing that the limb, which measured almost two feet thick at its base and over twenty feet in length, had stabbed through one of the large, beautiful, two-story windows. The stub of the limb on the oak's trunk burst into flame despite the blowing rain and produced swirls of grey smoke. Odors of charred oak and ozone electricity filled the conference room, adding more sensory confusion to an already strange event.

President Faust stood and looked down the table at Margaret Benedict as if to order her to do something, then at Dr. Cameron as if to claim no responsibility for anything that had just occurred. He yelled into a dead microphone, "Let's come back to order, everybody. Just keep your seats. Don't panic!" as if trying to regain control of his meeting from the forces of nature. At the same time, many in the shocked audience gasped or screamed. Those seated nearest the crashed window brushed slivers of glass from their hair and clothing. Finally, he yelled, "Margaret?!"

Margaret had already grabbed her cell phone from her purse and was calling both the University Police and maintenance to report the damage. Within three minutes, both were there, inside and outside the building, with tarps and other equipment, and quickly restored a drier order to the proceedings.

With a plane to catch and the storm's intervention, Cameron decided the press conference was finished. He shook hands with President Faust and the others on the podium. Faust took him aside and said, "Something else I forgot to tell you, Drew. Real quick. Three weeks ago, during final exams, one of our students was found dead in her dorm room. It was ruled death by natural causes. Her family took it hard, as you'd expect. Just wanted you to know in case somebody asked you about it."

"I'm so sorry to hear that, Steve. Is there anything I can do when I get back from Prague? Maybe contact the family and see if we can do anything more for them?"

"No. It's all taken care of. Just one of those terrible things that happens on a campus. Okay, Drew, there's your ride."

Cameron turned to see Sgt. Isaac Brown in police uniform. "Sir, I'm Sgt. Brown. Let's get you to the airport. Your luggage is in the car." With a final hurried handshake and expressions of farewell to his new boss, he followed Sgt. Brown out the side exit from the stage and into the waiting police vehicle.

As the University Police car left Blackburn Alumni Center, Cameron asked, "Sergeant, the storm we just had. Is that typical of this area?"

"No, sir. We usually get at least a twenty-four hour notice on a storm like that. This was a strange one. From sunny and quiet to a bad storm in about ten minutes, and a few minutes later it's sunny again. Go figure."

Turning left from the Alumni Center service entrance onto the four-lane Sycamore Boulevard, east toward Interstate 87 to the airport, Sgt. Brown steered the car around several large limbs blown into the street. "Do you think we can make it in time to catch my flight," Cameron inquired.

"No question about it, sir."

"Well, if we don't, there's probably a later flight," Cameron responded," trying to sound relaxed.

"No, sir. I called the airport. There is no later flight today that will get you to Frankfort. All the other flights are booked up. But my job is to get you there on time, and that's what I'm gonna do."

Cameron loosened his tie and leaned back in the seat, aware that not arriving in Prague until Thursday morning would cause him to miss the critical Wednesday meeting with the European Drugs Policy Centre executive committee. Wednesday afternoon would be the only opportunity to present a summary of his progress during the past year, and his plan of work for next year, and to negotiate a budget. Missing that could mean a significant reduction in the scope of work or even a cancellation of the research contract. He looked at his watch and asked again, "So you think we can make it in time, Sergeant?"

"Yes, sir. President Faust asked me to get you to the airport on time. When he asks me to do something, it gets done. Period. If a storm gets in the way, I pity the storm." At that point, Sgt. Brown entered I-87, accelerated from forty to eighty-five miles per hour, and turned on the siren and police lights, creating feelings of both uneasiness and hope in Cameron.

"How long have you been at Alpha State, Sergeant?" Cameron asked.

"President Faust brought me with him from Faust-Ingersoll Equities in New York City when he took over at the University. At Faust-Ingersoll I was deputy chief of security so I had to make a few fast trips from mid-city to JFK, Newark, and LaGuardia."

In a few minutes, they took the airport exit with squealing tires. The international terminal was in sight, which brought some relief to Cameron. Sgt. Brown picked up his cell phone and announced, "Officer Ramirez, Sgt. Brown of ASU. The departing package is two minutes from terminal C, going to gate eleven. Are you ready?"

As they pulled up to the terminal, Officer Ramirez was waiting and said, "Good to see you Brownie. Gimme his ticket." They exchanged high fives and Ramirez grabbed the two suitcases and went behind the street-side check-in counter.

"Have a nice flight, sir," Sgt. Brown said, as he extended his hand. Cameron shook his hand and thanked him, and the Sgt. got back into his car and was gone. Officer Carlos Ramirez hustled Cameron into the terminal and straight to the TSA inspection station where the agents were inspecting and admitting passengers from the five lines waiting to board a later flight. Holding his left hand aloft, Officer Ramirez guided Cameron to a small office next to the long TSA lines. A TSA officer stepped into the room, nodded to Officer Ramirez, and gave Cameron a cursory wave of the electronic wand. He did not ask him to empty his pockets, remove his shoes or belt, nor walk through the full-body X-ray machine. He simply looked at his ticket and said, "They're through boarding. You better hurry!" and motioned him toward gate eleven, about thirty yards away. Cameron thanked both Officer Ramirez and the TSA official and then sprinted from TSA inspection to gate C-11.

As Cameron approached the ticket inspector, she was speaking into her phone, "Only one seat unaccounted for; you're free to taxi out." Seeing Cameron appear before her, ticket in hand, she corrected herself, "Ursula, wait! Tell the captain to wait. We have the final passenger for you."

In seconds, Cameron was shuffling down the aisle toward row 35, heart still pounding but relieved. He took his aisle seat, put his briefcase under the seat in front of him, buckled in, leaned back, took a deep breath, closed his eyes, and, at 11:57 AM, thought to himself, *What a morning this has been.* The big jet taxied to its appointed runway and awaited further direction from flight control. Five minutes later, *Zentralen Europaischen Luftverkehr* flight 50 streaked down runway four and left the ground for *Frankfurt am Main*, Germany, nine hours and fifty minutes away. *All's well that ends well*, he thought, and he began to relax.

As soon as they were airborne, the senior flight attendant explained, over the speaker system, various safety features and procedures for the aircraft, emphasized the use of seatbelts, announced that lunch would be served in about one hour, and thanked everyone for flying with ZEL. Then, she repeated it in German. Soon, the captain welcomed all passengers aboard in English then in German. Cameron checked his ticket and saw that he was scheduled to arrive in Frankfurt at 4:50 AM and in Prague at 8:20 AM local time. He calculated that by the time he landed, proceeded through Czech Customs, and collected his luggage, it would be well after one o'clock in the morning in his head, and hoped that he could get some sleep between now and then.

In the economy seating section of the plane, five small video screens were suspended at equal distances above the middle column of seats and were also visible to passengers in the two outer columns of seats. All the interior lights of the plane were turned on by a central switch, and brightly illuminated the plane's interior. Conversations in English, German and other languages were audible all around. Soon, flight attendants were pushing carts up the aisle and serving drinks and snacks. Later, when another flight attendant asked each passenger, "*Roastbeef oder Backhendl?*" and "Beef or chicken?" Cameron ordered the chicken and a glass of water, even though he really wanted the beef and a glass of Cabernet. In just over an hour, they served lunch and returned with empty carts to collect the remnants and refill glasses. The flight attendants were humorless but efficient. Soon, the aroma of coffee permeated the plane. Again, exercising his staunchest self-discipline, Cameron declined the offer of a cup of coffee.

As the flight attendants gathered the last of the coffee cups into their carts, two hours after take-off, the interior lights of the plane went dark. Several passengers turned on the lights above their seats, creating random shafts of illumination throughout the plane. Soon seatbacks began to recline as passengers settled back to read, watch the movie, listen to music through headphones, or sleep. The only sounds were the dull, background roar of the jet engines, an occasional flutter of shuffling cards, and a baby's muffled cry.

With only gentle white noise as a background, Cameron's thoughts drifted to the events of the day. *Quite a stormy introduction this morning at the press conference. That storm blew out that gorgeous middle window in the conference room. Just as I am about to conclude my remarks, accept the position, boom. Chaos. But they got me to the airport on time. Steve Faust and his staff seem really on top of things.*

• • •

"And, Ms. McInerney, no calls, no interruptions," President Faust said as two guests entered and he closed his office door. "Doug, Rita, sit. This has to be brief," he said to his two guests, Doug Wood, who had just retired as ASU police chief, and Rita Kamens, Vice President for Student Affairs. "Okay, let's share the information we have so far. Doug, what do you have?

"Not much new," former chief Wood began. "In the three weeks since the incident and my resignation, I have been working the case full time, undercover, as you asked. Strictly on the QT. All the lab work has come back. That, plus the medical examiner's report, which you've both seen, pretty much tell the story. Death by asphyxiation due to someone smothering her with a pillow. Pictures at the crime scene and the four of us who first saw the body verified that."

"So it was a murder, for sure?" Rita Kamens asked.

"Yeah, just as we thought," Doug Wood said.

"That's all you can tell us?" Kamens asked. "I can't believe we found an attractive, nineteen year old coed, naked from the waist down, dead for two days, lying on the floor of her dorm room and . . ."

"Hold the phone, Rita. There is more," Doug Wood said. "When the lab people examined her body and cleaned her up, they looked for additional evidence, as they always do. The lab report identifies the substance on her left leg as semen."

"So, it was a rape-murder," an angry Kamens said. "I knew it!"

"Now we all know, Rita," Faust said, trying to control his anger.

"The lab's report confirms rape. That's the bad news. The good news is that with modern DNA techniques, we might be able to identify the source of the semen, in other words, the perpetrator," Doug Wood said.

"So it wasn't death due to natural causes as we told her parents and the media, it was murder. And it wasn't just murder, it was rape-murder. Don't you think we've got to . . ."

"Don't jump to any conclusions, Rita." Faust interrupted. "We will find a way to deal with it. What else, Doug?"

The former chief continued, "The dorm counselor got a couple of calls from the victim's friends on that Tuesday claiming she'd missed two final exams, one on Monday and one on Tuesday. So he went to her room to check on her and found the body at about 5:00 PM on Tuesday and then called you, Rita. The medical examiner estimated time of death as about eleven-thirty on the previous Sunday. Her dorm is completely covered by motion-sensitive security cameras, so I reviewed the images recorded several hours before and several hours after the estimated time of death, including all dorm entrances and the fourth floor hallways."

"Get to the bottom line, Doug. Do you have anything or not? Faust demanded.

"I have good images of a male who entered the dorm at about eleven, walked the stairs up to the fourth floor, and entered her room. He used a key. Here, Rita," Doug said, as he handed her an envelope. "Here are several good images of the suspect. You can look at the photo records in Student Affairs and see if he is one of our students, now or in the past."

"Okay, that's progress. Good work, Doug. Rita, see if that surveillance photo matches one of our students. Go back a year or two if you have to. When you have an answer, let me know ASAP. I want to put this thing to rest. Okay, that's all for now," President Faust said, and his two visitors left.

2 After passing through Customs and Security in Frankfort, Cameron still had time to enjoy a cup of German coffee and read some of the *International Herald Tribune* before queuing up to the Czech Airlines ticket counter and boarding his flight to Prague. Two hours later he exchanged some dollars for Euros and stepped out of the airport into his first day ever in the Czech Republic - a sunny day with light wind and an expected high temperature in the mid-sixties. At about one o'clock in the morning in his head, eight in the morning Prague time, his taxi arrived at the Betlem Square Hotel on the south side of Old Town Prague.

The hotel clerk spoke excellent English and check-in was quick. Cameron soon found himself riding up to the third floor in a very small elevator. His room included an exquisite view of Betlem Square. Satisfied with his accommodations, he took stock of his physical and mental state after the long flight. Even though he felt tired, he knew that the best course of action for the rest of the day was a brisk walk, a light dinner, and a good night's sleep. That would give him all of tomorrow morning to prepare for his presentation. So he brushed his teeth and took another ride on the diminutive elevator down to the lobby. Curious about his new surroundings, Cameron took advantage of the clerk's English proficiency and asked, "Excuse me, can you tell me something about the hotel? Do you know when it was built?"

"Oh, yes, sir. It was built in the thirteenth century. It has been reconstructed several times over the centuries. The last time was 1989 after the Soviet Union left. But the original Gothic foundation and cellar are still in place."

"Amazing. I had no idea it was such an old landmark. I have some time to walk around the neighborhood. Is there anything else I should see nearby?

"Oh, yes. Directly across the Square is *Betlemska Kaple* or Bethlehem Chapel, completed in the late fourteenth century. It is the church where the Catholic theologian, Jan Hus, delivered sermons criticizing the leaders of the Catholic religion."

"I guess that was pretty unusual in those days. What did he say?"

"He said the *Bible* should be published in many languages so that everybody could read it and that the Pope had too much power. Later, church officials chained him to the wall in a prison for almost a year and then in 1415 burned him at the stake for heresy. He said he was trying to get the church to think about its people rather than about the church hierarchy."

Cameron grimaced and said, "Thanks for the history lesson - an expensive lesson for Jan Hus."

City map in hand, he left Betlemska Square and followed the narrow streets generally west toward the Vltava River that wanders through the middle of Prague. He noticed three distinct physical features of this ancient city. The narrow, curving, streets in and around the Square are made of cobblestone, the sidewalks are made of mosaic and the weather can change in just a few minutes. He noticed the temperature drop as a grey overcast sky replaced the sunny blue, and a mist began to fall. As he turned north on to the busy and larger street that runs parallel to the Vltava River, he forgot his jet lag. By this time in the late afternoon, more streetcars and autos crowded the darkening streets and more pedestrians jammed the sidewalks and cross-walks at red lights.

Waiting to cross *Smetanovo náb eží* at the stoplight by the Charles Bridge, Cameron heard what, at first, sounded like a distant trumpet playing a higher note then a lower note over and over. He soon discovered it was the two-note siren of a Prague police car, the two notes forming a fifth interval, repeating G-C, G-C, G-C in rhythm, about a block behind him. As the police car came closer, the alternating notes grew louder. As it approached Cameron, it became almost deafening and the interval changed to a harsh, disharmonious diminished fifth, F#-C, F#-C, F#-C. As it sped away, the interval reverted to the original fifth and its volume declined. For the first time since his college days, he remembered something his professor talked about in a music appreciation course — *Diabolus in Musica*, the Devil in Music. The medieval Catholic Church banned the use of this dissonant diminished fifth in all of its church music because they believed it would conjure the devil. Even contemporary musicologists classify the sound of that interval as evoking visions of impending evil and feelings of fear. Hearing the Devil's interval, while walking alone down a dark street in a misty rain, jet-lagged, in a strange city, conjured a combination of fear and confusion in Cameron.

The Devil's interval was soon replaced by the ear-piercing screech of a streetcar's steel wheels as it ground to a stop at the red light only a few yards from Cameron. He stepped into the entrance of what appeared to be an apartment building to retreat from the chaos. In thirty seconds, with bells clanging and its engine moaning, the streetcar crossed the intersection and went on to the next. He realized at that time that jet lag had begun to take its toll.

What Cameron began as pleasurable sightseeing had become miserable discomfort, so he opted to return straight to the hotel. To save time, he decided to improvise the shortest way back rather than to return as he had come. Away from the main streets, the frantic rush-hour noise gave way to quiet, and the glaring street lights were replaced by dim lighting from inside buildings on the narrow streets. As he continued his journey into silent darkness, his street curved away from the Vltava river and split into two even smaller one-way streets, the more southern of which he carefully followed. The virtual absence of sound and light in this labyrinth of small streets and alleys brought to mind his exposure in college to the Czech novelist, Franz Kafka. He remembered that most of Kafka's novels were set in a mysterious and macabre Prague. Cameron thought, *Well, I hope this evening in Kafka's hometown doesn't get any worse. But now I know what a little bug feels like crawling through a complex network of tiny tunnels. And my strange feelings . . . must be alienation, disorientation, and hopelessness.* With those thoughts, he had pretty much exhausted his recollection of Kafka's literary themes.

After another twenty minutes of studying his wet map in the dim light from the occasional shopkeeper's window, wandering down one street and up another, his heart pounding with anxiety and impatience, tired and wet, he finally emerged onto *Betlemske Namesti* and saw his hotel at the other end of the square. He ducked into the first café he saw, rain water dripping from the tip of his nose, took a seat and ordered a dinner of pork, dumplings, and sauerkraut. By the time he had finished and paid his bill, he began to feel the full weight of two long days with very little sleep. *One hour ago, I was wet, lost, tired, tense, and hungry*, he thought, as he crossed the street to the Betlem Square Hotel. *Now I'm just wet and tired.*

He asked the clerk for a 6 AM wakeup call, went to his room, tossed his wet clothes into a laundry bag, and stepped into a steaming hot shower. Exhausted by his two days with little sleep and benumbed by his macabre walk around Old Town, he decided not to unpack but to go straight to bed. As he pulled the covers back, he saw the piece of mail given to him by the hotel clerk when he first checked in. He opened it to find the program for the drug policy conference he was attending for the rest of the week and a handwritten note from an Axel Dekker, assistant to the Prorector for International Relations at

Charles University in Prague. Dekker's note indicated that he would meet Cameron in the lobby of the Betlem Square Hotel for breakfast at around 7:45 in the morning unless Cameron called him to make other arrangements. *Fair enough*, he thought. With that, he slipped between the covers, turned off the bedside lamp, and fell asleep.

Promptly at six o'clock, as requested, an automated hotel wakeup call roused Cameron from a deep sleep. He soon felt rested and energetic despite having had so little sleep for the past two days and being seven hours ahead of his own time zone. He showered, shaved, and dressed, knowing he needed about an hour of serious review of the research paper he was presenting later this morning to the European Drug Policy Conference, but he was determined to do it with coffee in hand even though the hotel café did not open until seven. Moments later, as he approached the morning clerk at the registration desk, he observed that she was sipping a cup of steaming, black coffee. He said, "Good morning. Could I get a cup of coffee to take up to my room?"

"The Cellar Café opens at seven o'clock. Breakfast with coffee there is quite good," she said, implying her refusal to honor his request. After a brief, somewhat embarrassing pause, she did pour him a cup as well, but with an expression of pique, as if his request were quite irregular. He placed three Euros on the registration desk, thinking that should be enough for a cup of coffee and a tip. She didn't refuse the offering.

He spent the next hour in his room, drinking coffee and reviewing his paper. At the request of the European Drug Policy Council, Cameron had prepared an analysis of the changing marijuana control policies in the U.S. Satisfied that he was ready for the presentation; he put the necessary materials in his briefcase and took the mini-elevator to the lobby to meet the Prorector's assistant for breakfast. As soon as he entered the lobby, he spotted a man about forty seated in one of the leather chairs reading a Czech newspaper.

The man rose with his hand extended. "You are Dr. Cameron, I presume?" he asked.

"Yes. Are you Axel Dekker?"

"Yes, sir," Dekker said, as they shook hands. "Welcome to Prague. It is a pleasure to meet you."

"The pleasure is mine. I got your note and the Council program last night. Thank you for that. Let's get breakfast in the Cellar Café. The clerk said breakfast there is very good." With these words, Cameron winked at the clerk, evoking a more or less friendly smile from her.

"Sir," she said, "to get to Cellar Café, take corridor to right, past elevator, then first door on right down stairs. Please enjoy breakfast," no doubt extending this last courteous wish as an apology for her earlier discourtesy. Cameron thought, *She was trained for her job during the Soviet Communist domination and still occasionally struggles with the transition from bureaucratic indifference to pleasing the customer with a pleasant attitude and good service.*

Affixed to the walls of the corridor leading to the Cellar Café were various medieval weapons of war - swords, axes, rapiers, clubs, knives, machetes, even pistols — a motif that continued through the large, cave-like door and down the long, narrow, winding stairs deep into the cellar. The walls and ceiling of the dark, cavernous stairway were constructed of large grey and brown stones.

"So this is the original cellar from the old Gothic building," Cameron remarked. "And very well preserved, don't you think?"

"One of the reasons I like Prague so much," Dekker said, "is that it always reminds me of the importance of history."

They proceeded to a room with two long tables offering a large variety of breakfast food and drink. *Fit for a Gothic king*, Cameron thought. They chatted as they filled their plates and returned to the main dining room, where they took the first table on the right and began eating.

"So, you are the assistant to Prorector Havlicek?" Cameron asked.

"In truth, I don't have a rank yet. I am between final approval of my dissertation a few weeks ago and formally receiving a doctoral degree in early fall. Charles University hired me to assist with some of the tactical operations in their International Relations Office.

"Good for you. Congratulations! What is your field?"

"Statistics."

"You shouldn't have any trouble getting a good job, with all the emphasis on research and development. Every corporate or government R and D unit has to have at least one PhD-level statistician to keep them honest."

"I hope you are right. But I haven't entered the job market yet."

"Your accent sounds European but not Czech. Is that right?

"That's correct. I am Dutch. I was born in The Hague and lived in Holland through my college years at the University of Leiden."

"Pardon me for asking so many questions, but I am curious. I hope it's okay," and Cameron paused until he received a nod of affirmation from Dekker. "What did you do between college at Leiden and graduate school at Charles?"

"For twenty years, I served in an administrative agency under the joint command of the European Union and NATO. I was deployed first as a clerk but ended as director of data management. That's where I got my interest in statistics. For the last several years of my career with the Joint Task Force, I was assigned to the Prague office, so I took advantage of Charles University's doctoral program."

"That's great. What's next for you?"

"I think Prorector Havlicek will make my temporary position permanent as soon as I receive my degree. The International Relations Office serves as command and control for all of the University's joint operations with other countries."

"So what is your ultimate career goal - research, teaching, or administration?"

"To start, I have applied for a two-year post-doctoral fellowship in higher education administration funded by the European Union. It can be used at any accredited university that wants the administrative services, but the EU hasn't announced the winners yet. I hope the fellowship will be my safe house until I can find a permanent mission."

"Then I hope you get the offer," Cameron said, and they finished their breakfast and poured themselves a second cup of coffee. Cameron realized that he had been asking a lot of questions but he was curious about Dekker, who presented a study in contrasts. He was ruggedly handsome, despite a jagged scar etched above his left eye. And for someone in his early forties who had spent the last twenty-some years as a sedentary bureaucrat and then in a computer lab as a geeky graduate student in statistics, Dekker looked young, fit, and strong.

"Let's talk about the rest of the day and the rest of the week. Fill me in on what you and the Prorector have planned."

"Because the Prorector deployed me to serve as your handler during your visit to Prague, with your approval, of course, I took the liberty of drafting a proposed schedule. Please feel free to change any of it." With that, he handed Cameron a copy of the schedule. "For the rest of the morning, I propose to show you around Old Town Square. It is a marvelous example of historic Czech culture and architecture."

"That sounds perfect." As Cameron answered, he hoped that today's tour would erase the disconcerting memories of last night's experience with Prague's Old Town.

"Excellent. We shall do it. You present your paper this afternoon. For the evening, Prorector Havlicek has arranged dinner at a fine Czech restaurant overlooking the Vltava River. Mrs. Havlicek will accompany him, and my partner, Anna Zezulka will accompany me. I am sorry Mrs. Cameron can't join us."

"Me, too, Axel. Maybe another time."

"So, that takes us through tonight. All day Thursday you are scheduled to meet with various Drug Council managers, so I'll leave you in their hands. Friday morning, I suggest we take a walking tour from Charles Bridge, across the Vltava River to New Town Prague, to Prague Palace and St. Vitus Cathedral."

"Both of those are high on my list of things to see, Axel. Very good. Can we see both of them in one morning?"

Dekker smiled. "No, but we will do our best," and paused. "Then Friday afternoon, you get your briefing by five Council officials on the results of this past year's work in over a dozen major research projects on drugs and addiction. That briefing will be held in Seminar Room 303 in the Charles University Faculty of Philosophy and Arts. That will finish by zero-six-hundred hours."

"They have a lot of ground to cover," Cameron said. "But if it takes longer, that's fine. I feel honored to be chosen as the academic liaison between the European Drug Council and the U.S. Office of National Drug Control Policy."

"After that," Dekker continued, "if you like, you and I can have dinner in Old Town and then attend a concert nearby in St. Climent's Cathedral. The Prague Chamber Orchestra will perform several pieces by Czech composers such as Smetana and Dvorak, plus some Bach, Vivaldi, Mozart, and others. And, the cathedral is as beautiful as the music."

"What a way to end my last night in Prague. That's perfect, just as you planned it, Axel."

"Then, you can still get a good night of sleep and I will pick you up at zero-five-thirty hours Saturday morning for a trip to the airport. It takes only about twenty minutes at that time of day."

Cameron thanked Dekker for the offer, but resisted, arguing that it was much too early to rouse Dekker out of bed on a Saturday morning and that he could easily order a cab. Dekker countered that neither Czech nor Dutch protocol would allow asking an honored guest to take a taxi to the airport. Cameron felt his cultural legs being taken right out from under him, so he gratefully agreed.

They left the Cellar Café at half past eight, walking down several narrow, winding, cobblestone streets toward Old Town Square. The charm of the morning's sunny stroll presented quite a contrast with last night's frightening walk in the dark, in the rain, down haunted streets and alleys, lost in a Kafkaesque state of panic, feeling trapped in the Middle Ages. The purity of sunlight and the security of Dekker's expert guidance made a significant difference. They soon emerged onto Old Town Square. "Now this is a town square!" exclaimed Cameron.

"Old Town Square has been the center of Prague since the tenth century," Dekker said.

The open four-acre square was filled with vendors of traditional Slavic foods and crafts and surrounded by original Gothic and Romanesque architecture. The bottom floors of the buildings housed retail store and small shops catering to both tourists and residents. Upper floors contained offices and living quarters of various kinds. Each colorful building was constructed in the style of its period and looked dazzling in the morning sunlight.

Dekker pointed toward the northwest side of the Square and said, "There is St. Nicholas Church, built in the Baroque period." Turning toward the south side of the Square, he pointed toward another imposing old building with a tower. Looking at the large clock on the north face of the tower, which showed twenty minutes to nine, he urged, "Come on. Let's hurry. Maybe we can get a good seat and a cup of coffee at the Grand Hotel Café for the show." Although Cameron was a little confused about what his guide meant by "the show," he followed Dekker at a fast pace.

To reach the Grand Hotel across the square, they had to weave their way around several large clusters of tourists, all listening through headsets to their professional tour guides who discussed the history and beauty of Old Town Square in various languages. They got a table on the outer edge of the Grand Hotel's street-side café, directly across from the front of the old building with the tower. Cameron's eyes widened and he said, "Now I know why you wanted coffee here. That's the old Astronomical Clock on the Town Hall Tower. Right there! I've read about it. And we have an incredible view for the 'show'."

Dekker agreed. "At zero-nine-hundred hours, we will see and hear quite a show." Cameron learned from Dekker's quick description that the colorful clock was constructed in 1410 and that it has three parts. At the top is an astronomical dial that represents the position of the sun and moon and displays various astronomical details. Below that is the 'Walk of the Apostles', which features statues of the Twelve Apostles and other small mechanical figures that come out of the tower and march around the outside of the clock. Under that is a calendar dial with twelve large circular medals representing the twelve months of the year.

Right before the hour, a virtual sea of tourists stood between the outdoor section of the Grand Hotel Café and the clock, waiting for the display of medieval mechanics and eternal aesthetics. At nine o'clock, the action and gongs began, and in about nine seconds, it was over. The spellbound international crowd gasped and murmured as they shot I-phone videos.

For the remainder of the morning, Executive Vice President for Academic Affairs and Provost Andrew Cameron and soon-to-be Dr. Axel Dekker wandered around Prague's Old Town Square, each becoming better acquainted with the other as Dekker provided commentary on the various charming features of the square. Cameron was fascinated by the horse-drawn carriages available to tourists for a journey around the area. The driver of each carriage wore a black uniform with a cape, and his two horses were adorned with bright red and blue headdresses and red diapers.

Scattered around the Square were numerous large kiosks from which vendors sold food or crafts. Some prepared meat-filled crepes in a large black metal pan in large open ovens perched on metal stands above a wood fire right on the cobblestone street, essentially large, portable fireplaces. Other vendors grilled meats on spits turning above the fire. Adding to the pungent mixture of cooking aromas filling the square were vendors preparing pancakes, waffles, and donut-like pastries rolled in sugar and cinnamon on long rotating spits, each cooking over an open fire. Needless to say, the fragrances, optics, and sounds on the square created a rare sensory experience. The craft stands included vendors selling hand-made leather goods, and Czech dolls. A blacksmith pumped air into his fire to make bells, swords, jewelry, and other metal items, which he crafted by hand. Cameron and Dekker strolled around the Square, sampled the pastry, and spent some time in the Franz Kafka Museum, located in the house where the writer of macabre novels had lived for most of his life.

"The morning has slipped away," Dekker said, "and I have a staff meeting at the University that I must attend. I suggest you eat a quick lunch so that you can get to your panel session, and I will meet you at the end of it, about half past five, and give you any last minute details about the rest of the evening. Is that satisfactory, sir?"

"Of course. That's good."

"If you walk two blocks down this street, toward Charles University, you will see a nice café on the corner. I recommend it. And if you want to take some gifts back home to your family, you will see, also on your left, side by side, two stores I recommend. They both sell various kinds of Czech products, of high quality but at reasonable prices."

"Good," Cameron concluded, "I'll see you at five-thirty. And thanks for a great tour of Old Town Square."

"You are welcome, Dr. Cameron."

"Please. Can we dispense with the formality? No 'sir' and no 'Dr'. Please call me Drew." Dekker agreed, and with that, they shook hands and parted company. The morning had been a very pleasant and informative experience, and Cameron wished his wife and children could have been with him.

After lunch, Cameron ducked into both of the stores that Dekker had recommended and bought cashmere pashminas for his wife, daughter, and executive assistant in his office back at the University at Albany, and a ceramic, hand-painted coffee mug featuring scenes from Old Town Prague for his son. He arrived ten minutes early at the conference room that Charles University had allocated to the drug conference session on the topic "Cannabis: Criminalize or Legalize?" Academic researchers from five European countries and Cameron from the U.S. presented the findings from their countries to answer the question. Each supported his or her presentation with graphs, tables, and coefficients displayed on a large video screen.

The moderator finally called a halt to the panelists' Q and A discussion with audience members and summarized their apparent consensus: rigorously enforced prohibitionist policies against the use of marijuana do not reduce use or illegal behavior but they do cost the taxpayers more money for law enforcement and incarceration. Several panelists and members of the audience commended Cameron's research and expressed the wish that U.S. authorities would see the wisdom of it.

Cameron left the panelist table to join Axel Dekker whom he spotted standing near the door in the back of the room. Dekker announced, "The Prorector requires me now in a rather important meeting with the Czech Minister of Industry and Trade and representatives of Nordic Computer Electronics. Will you mind it if I leave you alone?"

"That's fine, Axel. Sounds like duty calls."

Dekker smiled, handed Cameron a sheet of paper, and said, "Here are the restaurant's name and address and directions to get there from the Betlem Square Hotel. It is an easy walk. We will see you there at zero-seven-thirty hours?"

"Seven thirty it is. Now, go. You've got important work to do. I'll be fine."

Dekker disappeared out a side door, so Cameron stretched his legs and began the walk back to Betlem Square. But this time, he negotiated the maze of narrow, curving, cobblestone streets with more confidence than last night. Soon he was greeted by the hotel clerk, who informed him that the walk to the Vltava Restaurant would take about fifteen minutes, so he took the small elevator up to his room to watch CNN International in English.

At about seven, he began his walk to the restaurant. As he waited for the red light to change by the Charles Bridge, Cameron was struck by the thought that each block in Old Town Prague, large or small, seemed packed with buildings, four to six stories tall, each containing rooms of various sizes, housing commercial offices and living quarters. That seemed typical of big cities almost anywhere. Yet, when he looked through the walkway into the interior of a building, he discovered that it was mostly hollow, resembling an old western fort. This open interior space, from ground level to sky, was large and occupied more than half of the square feet of the total block footprint. It was hidden from street view unless entered through one of the doors, some sized for pedestrians, some large enough for trucks.

Walking several more blocks, he discovered that each of the entry ways leads into a large, open, well-lighted interior space. Sometimes, the space was warm, quiet, and inviting, e.g., a restaurant, coffee shop, or bar with walls decorated with stone carvings, paintings, banners, and statues celebrating Czech history, sports, life in general. But with no ceiling. Quiet conversation and laughter rose from the patrons, who wore anything from business attire to jeans and T-shirts, and sat at tables covered with colorful cloths. The aroma of kava, pils, spicy goulash, and other Czech foods permeated the night air. Other entry ways were for trucks and led to stark stone and concrete cells, also open to the elements above, efficient for delivering goods and supplies, and for collecting trash. In every block he investigated, Cameron found that the outside of a block, in full view, was only a stark concrete wall. But the open space inside, hidden from view, embraced the good life of eating, drinking, and socializing. *How ironic*, Cameron thought.

His exploration ended when he discovered that he had only a few minutes to meet the dinner party, so he walked toward the restaurant. From a distance of half a block, he spotted Dekker and the other guests just entering and seconds later he followed them in. Dekker introduced him to Prorector and Mrs. Havlicek, then to his companion, Anna Zezulka, then to two senior faculty members, one the chairman of political science and one a biologist, accompanied by their wives.

Prorector Havlicek was a large man, in his late sixties, with grey hair and piercing blue eyes. His wife, also tall, projected the demeanor of a once glamorous younger woman who now listens rather than talks. As the conversation got underway, it was clear that speaking English was uncomfortable for her. In contrast, when Dekker introduced his companion, Anna, it was clear that her English was excellent. She was in her late thirties, tall, with brownish-blond hair, attractive, and confident. The political scientist and biologist's expressions varied between seriousness and indifference. They were friendly and spoke English well. Their wives were cheerful but not facile in English. The nine of them chatted as they followed a waiter from the front door to their seats at a table near the large picture window with a splendid view of the Vltava flowing under the *Manesuv* Bridge. Once seated and even before the waiters could hand menus to everyone, the Prorector said to the nearest waiter, "*Prineste nam lahev vychlazeneho Becherovka, prosim.*"

Seeing Cameron's puzzled expression, Dekker whispered, "The Prorector just ordered a bottle of chilled *Becherovka*."

"Okay. What is that?" Cameron asked.

"It is a Czech liquor, similar to the Dutch *jenever* or German *schnapps*. Most people drink it chilled, straight. I hope you like it."

In a moment, the waiter returned with a tray carrying two green one-liter bottles of *Becherovka* and nine glasses, each resembling a three-inch-tall beer stein, and proceeded to fill each little stein. Prorector Havlicek then held his glass aloft and announced in English, with a heavy Slavic accent, "I will now propose a toast to our distinguished guest, Dr. Andrew Cameron, Vice President of the Alpha State University in the United States of America. Welcome, sir, to the Czech Republic, to Prague, and to Charles University. You honor us by your presence. We, at Charles University, look forward to a long and beneficial friendship between Charles and Alpha." Whereupon, he consumed his *Becherovka* in one gulp and replaced his glass on the table. Cameron followed the other guests as they did the same. He thought to himself, *Not sweet at all. Tastes a little like kerosene would taste, I think. Could be worse, I suppose.*

As Cameron mentally improvised a response to the Prorector's kind words of welcome, the waiter refilled each glass. Cameron stood, raised his *Becherovka*, glanced around the table at each guest, ending with a steady gaze on his host, and began his response. "On behalf of Alpha State University, may I express my gratitude for your very warm welcome, Prorector Havlicek, and for hosting me during my stay in Prague. I am honored by your generosity. I wish that my stay could be longer and that my wife were also here to meet each of you."

On an impulse, Cameron decided to assume that those present understand the nuances of the English language and American humor. He continued, "To be honest, I am amazed that the administration, faculty, and students of Charles University have ever accomplished anything important." Here, he paused and surveyed the faces of his dinner companions as their eyes widened in shock. Then he added, "Because the beauty of the *Vltava* and Prague's architecture is more than enough to distract anyone from serious academic pursuits." He paused again to be sure that his statement had been understood. Eyes relaxed and mouths broadened into smiles of appreciation and even giggles.

"In the future, if you envision any way in which Alpha State University can collaborate with you in your work to provide enlightenment to the Czech Republic, to Europe, and to the world, please consider us as eager partners. Your mission is our mission." Whereupon Cameron downed his *Becherovka* in one swallow. The Prorector and all the others stood, looked at Cameron, drank their *Becherovka* and plopped their glasses back down on the table in unison with a loud whacking noise. Prorector Havlicek and Vice President Cameron shook hands with considerable enthusiasm.

Formalities finished, they began several conversations about their two universities. One waiter distributed platters of beef *tartare* and buffalo mozzarella around the table for starters, one poured more *Becherovka*, while another waiter began taking dinner orders. The evening was going well.

The menu included English translations and Cameron found many entrées that he would like, but his first choice was a Greek salad and one-half a roast duck with yeast and potato dumplings, white and red cabbage. He found Czech cuisine to be delicious and filling and the dinner to be most enjoyable. The duck was tender, tasty, flavored with spices he could not identify. He had never tasted anything like the dumplings and cabbage, two dishes relegated to the category of "farm food" in the United States, but which were exotic when prepared as traditional Czech accompaniments to game dishes. Toward the end of their entrées, the various conversations about unrelated topics ended, as if on cue. Prorector Havlicek said, "Vice President Cameron, are you interested in international student exchange programs?" The group had definitely entered the "new business" section of its agenda

Cameron answered "yes" and mentioned the academic and social benefits that study abroad had afforded some of his own students. Their subsequent conversation revealed that they agreed on the parameters of a good exchange program. Others at the table listened but remained quiet.

Then, as if changing channels on a television set, Anna Zezulka assumed leadership of the conversation. Earlier in the evening, she had revealed a quick wit, considerable knowledge of international economics, and excellent English. She was also direct. "Dr. Cameron, it has come to our attention that the city of your university is planning for some years the building of tram or street car transportation system in the central business district with the possibility of adding light rail to connect with your nearby towns. Will you agree to organize a discussion of this topic between New Cambridge officials and Czech officials?"

Anna's question caught Cameron off-guard, and for a moment he was overcome by his instincts to stay within his authority as Alpha State's vice president. He knew almost nothing about New Cambridge's streetcar plans. Stalling for time, he asked, "First, Anna, I need to understand your interest in this topic. Are you offering consulting services to help New Cambridge with their project?"

"Moravian Motor Works near Prague manufactures heavy duty trams, including the engine, the chassis, and the body, and exports them all over Europe and to Canada. Prague's own streetcar system, made up of MMW technology, is one of the longest in the world and it works quite well for many years. We can work with your city engineers and government leaders to supply you with the trams you need at a very attractive price." Cameron was impressed with Anna's terse but convincing opening lines.

"Anna, I should tell you, first, that I don't live in New Cambridge, yet. My wife and I will move there later this summer. So, I don't know anyone in authority in city government. Decisions about acquiring large transportation assets from abroad are not part of my responsibility at Alpha State. But I do like the idea of working with the Czech Republic to take advantage of your expertise and, maybe, your products. By the way, what is your interest in the idea?"

"I am assistant director of trade missions in the Czech Ministry of Trade, Dr. Cameron. Could not you arrange a meeting of the officials who make decisions about such matters?" she asked, again going straight to the point.

"I will certainly inquire about it, Anna. Do you have a business card?" Cameron wrote "streetcars," on the back of her card, and when he looked at the front, he noticed that it read "Anna Zezulka, MBA." Anna smiled and nodded.

By this time, the waiters had cleared away the entrée dishes and were serving dessert and coffee. Though he had eaten a lot, Cameron realized he must rise to the occasion when the waiter placed a plate of hot plums in rum before him. With the first bite, even before he had swallowed, this dessert seemed to stimulate the release of endorphins in his brain, and he felt ecstatic. Then, as if on cue, Dr. Pavel Holzer, chairman of the Institute of Political Science, and Dr. Petr Dedek, professor of biology, both leaned over to catch Cameron's eye. Dr. Holzer spoke first, repeated their titles at the university, and asked point-blank, "If our students can benefit from study at your university and your students can benefit from study at our university, why cannot our professors benefit from working for a time at the other university?"

Cameron quickly responded by rephrasing the question, "If student exchanges are good, so are faculty exchanges?"

"Correct," the biologist Dedek affirmed.

"I like the idea," Cameron conceded. "It expands faculty experience and that enriches their teaching and research. There is no reason I know of why we can't explore that possibility between our institutions. Would either of you like to spend a semester or year at Alpha State University?"

The biologist and the political scientist looked at each other, then at Cameron, and answered in unison, "Yes."

Dedek continued, "Both of us serve on the council to arrange faculty exchanges between Charles University and other universities in the European Union. We intend to expand to North America, Asia, and Africa."

"Your plan to globalize your faculty exchanges is a good one," Cameron said. "As soon as I start my new position at Alpha State, in a few weeks, I will explore this possibility with the relevant parties. To be honest, I am fairly sure we can develop such a program." Holzer and Dedek seemed satisfied with Cameron's reaction and retreated from the conversation almost as fast as they had initiated it.

During the discussions about student and faculty exchanges and the possibility of importing Czech street cars for use in metropolitan New Cambridge, Cameron had noticed that Axel Dekker appeared to be taking notes. *Maybe he keeps a log of his boss's activities outside the office*, Cameron thought to himself. In any case, everyone seemed to finish his or her last sip of the robust Czech *kava* at about the same time, and Prorector Havlicek signed the check for the evening's dining. As he rose, so did the other diners, signaling that the meeting is adjourned.

As they left, Cameron found himself thanking his hosts and exchanging kisses on both cheeks with each of the four women, and vigorous handshakes with each of the four men. Everything had gone well and all the Czechs emphasized how much they enjoyed meeting Cameron and how good they felt about a future of collaboration between their respective universities. As the diners moved toward the front door of the restaurant, Dekker asked Cameron and Havlicek to wait for a moment and then said, "If I may, I want to suggest that we meet at zero-eight-hundred hours tomorrow in your office, sir," looking at his boss. "During dinner I took notes on your points of agreement concerning student exchanges, so it would be no trouble for me, later tonight, to turn these into a draft of a formal agreement between our universities. Tomorrow morning, each of you could examine the draft and modify it, or, if you both agree, sign the document. If there is not mutual agreement, no harm is done. If there is mutual agreement, then . . . ." They agreed to meet at eight in the morning.

They departed the restaurant and went their separate ways. Unlike last night, Cameron knew two different routes to Betlem Square, and he proceeded to walk briskly beside the Vltava to his hotel. It had been an enjoyable day, and he missed his wife and children back in upstate New York. He asked the hotel clerk for a wakeup call at six and was asleep by ten-thirty in his quiet room.

• • •

The time was approximately three-thirty in the afternoon in New Cambridge as President Faust informed Ms. McInerney, "I'm going to take a walk around campus in the fresh air and clear my mind. I'll be back in fifteen or twenty minutes. Call my cell if you need me."

"Very well. Enjoy your walk."

Faust walked the stairs down to the first floor and headed past Riedel Tower toward the commons. He was virtually alone, because summer school had not yet started. He took a seat on the bench in the far corner of the commons. Within a couple of minutes, former ASU police chief Doug Wood walked from behind a classroom building and took a seat beside Faust. In less than a minute, Rita Kamens joined them.

"Okay, Rita, this has to be quick. Do your records in Student Affairs show the suspect to be one of our students or not?" Faust asked.

"A former full-time student," Kamens answered. Charles M. Lemon, age twenty-three. His last known address is 1022 Cranston Place, a private rental apartment near campus." Doug Wood copied the information on a small pad.

"Okay, Doug. Stay on this one. Find out if he still lives there. If not, where? But don't let him know we're onto him," Faust ordered.

"Matching the photos will get us an arrest," former chief Wood responded. "We've got semen from the crime scene, so as soon as he's in custody, we can get his DNA from his blood or hair to make the match. Then it's a done deal."

"Why don't we arrest him right away?" Kamens asked.

"Yeah. He could disappear to anywhere," Wood added.

"No, Doug. Stick to the plan," Faust ordered. "We are working this out as we planned. We are doing what is best for all parties concerned in the long run, the parents and the University. I have told you before, if we reveal this information now, several hundred freshmen, who have paid ASU their tuition and fees and board for this fall will not show up. And, their parents will demand their money back."

"He's right, Doug," Rita added. "That's happened at other schools."

"And that results in a huge loss of revenue each semester for several years to come. Besides, give her parents time to grieve in peace. Do you think they are any better off if the media get this story now? Doug, just follow him around, get the necessary evidence. Get back to me when you do. Now, I've got to go."

"But what about the dead girl's dorm counselor, Steve. Is he still part of the problem?" Kamens asked.

"He was a doctoral student who just finished his PhD. He was working as a dorm counselor to pay off what he owed for student loans while he wrote his dissertation. I got his debt taken care of. And I had a talk with him a couple of weeks ago and made a call to the president of one of the schools he had applied to for a teaching position. Last week he got a generous offer from that school and accepted. He has already left ASU and is at his new job. He understands our efforts here and his responsibility. Now, let's get back to work."

3 It was good to be back home. As soon as Cameron closed the door behind him, he smelled the fragrance of a vase of spring flowers on the kitchen table. The note said, "Welcome Home! Love, Vanessa, Char and Tom." A separate note apologized for not being able to pick him up at the airport and offered more love and welcome. Although he was tired from the long flight from Prague, he felt like a million bucks to be home with his family. A radiant noontime sun shone through the sliding glass doors to the patio, unusual for upstate New York in June, so he opened them and welcomed a mild breeze into the house. It was noon on this beautiful afternoon in Albany, but seven o'clock in the evening in his head, so to satisfy his hunger for dinner he prepared a triple-decker peanut butter and blueberry jam sandwich and opened a diet soda.

After unpacking, he made several phone calls, the first of which was to the home of his administrative assistant in his current position as dean of a college at the university. Relieved that the college ran smoothly in his absence, he walked out on the patio to breathe in the spring air to counter the effects of sleep deprivation of the last twenty-four hours. His back yard was beautiful with several varieties of tulips and other flowers just coming up and the grass becoming green again after a hard upstate winter. Returning to his desk inside, he finished making notes on the Prague trip and items he should attend to as a result. He also made himself a cup of strong coffee to help ward off his drowsiness, and listened to a CD of two of his favorite high-energy jazz musicians, J. J. Johnson and Kai Winding, as he worked.

Soon he heard the front door open and close and daughter Char squeal, "Daddy, you're home!" as she bounded around the corner from the front hallway into his study. As early as third grade, it was clear that she was cute with

32

her auburn hair and freckles and destined to be athletic with her natural quick-ness and coordination. Now, at age nineteen, when she steps onto the court for the Cornell tennis team, she gets "oohs" and "aahs" from the spectators both for her drop-dead good looks and for her ferocious backhand.

"Char! I'm so glad to see you," Cameron responded, amid hugs and high fives.

"I'm so glad you got the new job, Daddy! Did your meetings in Prague go okay?"

"Thank you. The Prague trip went well."

"Great! Tell me about Charles University. Is it, like, Soviet still?"

"Not at all. It's the Czech Republic's flagship university, very old and dis-tinguished, large, and academically strong. Now, how have you been this week? Still humiliating all competitors with your hundred-and-twenty-mile-per-hour serves?"

"Only my first serve," she said with an impish grin, as she struck a cute, braggart pose with thumbs tucked under imaginary suspenders. She had a summer job teaching tennis at the Albany Country Club. "Wait. I think I just heard a car in the driveway. Tom or Mom?" They both scurried toward the front door.

"He's home! The *Zhuyao ren* is home from Prague!" Tom said as he burst through the door. "Welcome home, Dad. We missed you."

Like his sister, Tom had his mother's auburn hair, dark brown eyes, and above average height. Unlike his sister, he had always been studious, neither exhibiting nor desiring an athletic physique. He had just finished his junior year at Cornell as an honors student majoring in Asian Studies, thus the greet-ing to his father as "*Zhuyao ren*," Mandarin for "main man." His Chinese was good already, especially after six semesters of language study at Cornell and a study-abroad semester at Beijing Language and Culture University. Entering his senior year in the coming fall meant he would soon have to choose the graduate programs to which he would apply. So far, his favorites were Berkeley, where Cameron had done his doctoral work, Michigan, and Columbia.

Char smiled broadly as her father and brother exchanged vigorous hugs. She had, since she was very young and before she could really remember much, loved and admired them both, and in the last couple of years she had looked at each of them as a role model almost as much as she looked to her mother. Tom said, "So, Dad, did you have a great trip? How did your presentation go?"

"Very well, thank you. The whole drug conference was well organized and they are almost certain to renew my research contract for another year. We can discuss the trip more when your Mom gets home. How have you been this past week? Do you have good students to work with?"

"Another day, another *yuan*, as we Camp Fennimore staffers say." Tom had a summer job teaching Asian history, culture, language, and contemporary affairs at a summer honors camp for advanced high school students on a lake in the Adirondack Mountains, north of Albany. "The students are really bright but need a lot of direction in subjects they don't know much about."

When Tom and Char left to put their things away in their rooms, leaving Cameron alone momentarily, he realized how tired he was, and how happy he was to be home with his family. At least two out of three so far, and soon the third would arrive. It was almost five o'clock on Saturday afternoon but midnight to Cameron.

A few minutes after he and the kids sat down in the den to talk more, they heard the garage door opening, then the slam of a car door. All three Camerons, led by Drew, fled from the den to the kitchen door to meet Vanessa Cameron — wife, mother, and soon-to-be unemployed attorney.

As she entered the kitchen, Cameron and Vanessa kissed and embraced before either of them spoke. "I missed you, Drew," Vanessa said quietly.

"I missed you, too," Cameron echoed, "and I wished for you, all of you, a thousand times." He then stepped back so that his kids and wife could also greet each other with an appropriate hug, after which he put his arm around Vanessa's shoulder as they walked into the den. "Before I forget," he continued, "let me give you your Czech presents." As they took their seats in the den, he pulled the sack of gifts from his briefcase, and announced, "For you, Vanessa, a scarf. For you, Tom, a coffee mug. For you Char, a scarf. All made in the Czech Republic and all purchased in Old Town Prague."

Char spoke first, "Thank you, and let me tell you something? It's a scarf, generically, but the real name is 'pashmina,' and all the fashionistas are wearing them. What do you think, Mom?"

"It is perfect. Have you ever seen anything made of cashmere that isn't perfect?!" Vanessa said, with head motions and body language portraying dramatic flair, and gave her husband a big hug. "Char, show me how the fashion models drape pashminas around their necks and tie them."

"While you two are outside shivering in the sub-freezing cold with your pashminas," Tom interrupted with his nose in the air, "I shall be inside, warm and comfortable, enjoying a hot dark roast in my colorful, decorative, hand-crafted, ceramic Czech mug. Thanks, Dad. I love it."

After she showed her mother the stylish ways to wear a pashmina, Char continued the long practice of verbal jousting with her brother. "Chillax, Tommy boy, Mom and I will be warm and elegant in our pashminas, I'll have you know, but you will be full of poisonous caffeine."

To which Tom responded, with feigned sarcasm, "Whatever."

With a wry grin, Cameron shook his head and said, "Is it good to be home or what?!", and gave one more quick hug to each of his family members.

"Let me propose a plan, "Vanessa said. "Tom and Char both have dates tonight. You need some rest, above all, Drew. Why don't I prepare a light dinner right away, Tom and Char can get ready to go on their dates, and you watch a little CNN, until dinner is ready — pizza and a salad. Then, we'll get you to bed early, and I'll put the finishing touch on today's legal work. Is that agreeable with everybody?"

All agreed, and Cameron said, "I meant to ask you, how did the negotiations go today? Will you be in court Monday?"

"The negotiations went well, and we are due in court Monday morning. The lawyers from Borden, Atkins, and Crowley were agreeable, and we pretty much got our way on most issues. So it looks like I will be able to finish this case several days before we leave for New Cambridge. Given that you are home, Drew, and my last case in New York State looks like an almost certain victory, shall I pour us some wine?"

"Honestly, Vanessa," Cameron said, "one glass for me and I wouldn't be able to tie my shoes. I'm beat. Let's all celebrate together with wine tomorrow. You go ahead and have a glass tonight. You've earned it."

The dinner and clean-up afterward went fast, the kids left for their social evenings, Cameron took a hot shower and went straight to bed, and, by ten o'clock, Vanessa had written up the legal agreement that the two teams of attorneys had negotiated earlier today. She slipped into bed beside Cameron, careful not to wake him, and soon fell asleep.

The next morning, bright and early, Cameron awoke rested but, as usual, in desperate need of a cup of coffee. He dressed and crept from the bedroom into the kitchen to put on a pot of French roast. Then he fetched the Sunday edition of the *Times-Union* and pursued one of his favorite pastimes, reading the newspaper and drinking coffee. He had, for unknown reasons, been interested in public affairs since childhood. But when the American Education Press, Inc., awarded him the Charles Palmer Davis Medal for excellence in the study of current events when he was in the seventh grade, things accelerated. The award generated considerable praise from his teachers; one of them called him a "news junkie." It became clear that he enjoyed learning about public affairs, and understood its importance better than his classmates. Many years later he had realized that the award had defined a convenient pathway for the rest of his life. Thirteen years later, he received his doctorate and entered a career in higher education.

Cameron awoke from his daydream when Vanessa, with tousled hair and still clad in pajamas and a light blue terrycloth robe, tiptoed into the room behind him, placed her hands on either side of his face, and surprised him with a big kiss on the top of his head, as she had many times before. She said, "Good morning. I have some strange news to report while we are alone. It might be nothing, but I think it's something you should know — about some major players at ASU."

Vanessa took a seat on the couch. "Drew, I'll tell you everything I can, but I'm sworn to secrecy on some matters unless the judge tells me I can reveal facts that are not in the public domain. It concerns a case I've been working on. The firm is representing a hospital in New York City that alleges that the pharmaceutical company committed fraud in the clinical trials of their new asthma drug. Empire Pharmaceuticals, Inc. was headquartered in New York City at the time. One of my colleagues on the case noticed that Empire later moved its corporate headquarters to New Cambridge and changed its name to Wolfe-Otis Pharmaceuticals, Inc., about ten years ago. Now it starts to get interesting; the CEO of Empire Pharmaceuticals then is CEO of Wolfe-Otis now. And the current chairman of Alpha State University's Board of Trustees."

"Alexander Wolfe?" Cameron asked. "Are you sure?"

"My colleague came across several references to the suits against Empire in various documents we obtained. In reviewing the documents and the judge's ruling, I discovered something curious. The judge had ordered the record of testimony and other evidence sealed. It is the same Alexander Wolfe."

"Stranger than fiction."

"Let me tell you the rest," Vanessa continued. "Hofstadter McManus, Inc. managed Empire's investments, which were over a billion dollars. The Hofstadter McManus VP who handled their account was also implicated in some way in the now-sealed fraud suit. His name was . . . is . . . Stephen Faust."

"Weird coincidence?" Cameron asked.

"Sorry, but no. It's the same R. Stephen Faust who is now president of Alpha State University. That's all I am legally allowed to say. It's about all I know."

They both sat in early morning silence, until Cameron put his coffee cup down and said, "It could mean nothing. There was probably a good reason for the judge to seal the files. You know, preserving market competition or something like that. President Faust seems to have an excellent reputation among a lot of very important people at ASU and in New Cambridge and statewide, so that's all I need to know. But thanks for the information, Vanessa."

During the next two weeks, as they prepared to leave their home in Albany for a new life in Bedford and New Cambridge, Cameron tried, without much success, not to worry about the story Vanessa had told him. Moving to a new job in a distant part of the country already involves enough emotional volatility and long lists of things to do and worry about. He, Vanessa and the kids stayed on an even keel by working hard each day to take care of business. Packing, making lists and phone calls, attending three going-away parties, getting both cars ready for the long trip, finalizing their work at the University and the law firm, and spending as much time as possible together as a family, got them through.

Saying goodbye to Tom and Char and leaving them in Albany to live with friends for the rest of the summer was hard for all four of them, but they did what they had to do, including formulating a plan to get both kids to Bedford for a week or so at the end of summer. Meanwhile, Tom and Char would be fully occupied in their summer jobs. But the farewell wasn't easy, and Cameron and Vanessa had three days of driving from Albany to New Cambridge in separate cars to think about it.

They met the moving van early on the fourth morning and watched as the crew moved all their earthly possessions into a nice home in a quiet neighborhood about twelve miles from downtown New Cambridge and the ASU campus. The movers did an outstanding job in packing and unloading, for which Cameron tipped them well, signed the necessary papers, and bid them adieu.

Suddenly it was very quiet. They called both kids at work in Albany, reported that they were in their new home, promised to send pictures of the new home via I-phone, and then said their melancholy goodbyes. During that week they met several pleasant neighbors, got their computer, television, stereo, and telephones connected, sent and answered numerous email messages, called Cameron's new office at Alpha State to report their arrival and new home phone number, subscribed to the *New Cambridge Morning News* – the metropolitan daily paper, finalized insurance on the house and cars, and completed other chores necessary when moving to a new town. On the weekend, they discovered a small arts theatre in Bedford and enjoyed a French film with English subtitles.

At six-thirty on Monday morning, Cameron pulled out of his driveway. A neighbor had warned him that going into New Cambridge from suburban Bedford during the week any later than 7:00 a.m. could take almost twice as long. He also learned that rapidly growing New Cambridge was surrounding Bedford and its numerous suburbs and suburbanizing previously rural areas in surrounding counties. The only way to know you had crossed the line from suburban Bedford into the city was the sign saying "Welcome to New Cambridge, pop. 1,545,022." The greater metropolitan area, including New Cambridge and seven surrounding counties, was home to over four million people.

Following the directions of his GPS, he turned from Bedford's sedate Willow Avenue onto the entrance ramp up to the interstate. The names and design of the streets, the six or eight-lane interstate highway, the faster speed limits, the transitions from residential to commercial to industrial, the larger scale of everything, and even the kinds of vehicles he saw differed from those in the smaller Albany-Schenectady-Troy metropolis in upstate New York, where he had traveled for years. *How would I ever learn my way to work without Athena?* he asked himself. He had named the female voice in his GPS Athena after the Greek goddess of wisdom. *If only there were a GPS for negotiating my way through my new job as Executive Vice President. Well, anyway, let's see what's up with Steve and René this morning.* He turned on the car radio and slowly searched the lowest FM dial numbers until he found NPR's *Morning Edition*.

He glanced at the speedometer, which indicated well over eighty miles per hour. *Oh, nice, Drew. Get a speeding ticket on your first day!* He slowed down to seventy and was reassured via the rearview mirror that no police car was in pursuit. As he passed the interstate sign proclaiming "University Boulevard 2½ miles," he focused his thoughts on the practical matter of walking into his office as Executive VP for the first time and getting to know his office staff of over twenty people. He had looked forward to this first occasion, and prepared for it by almost memorizing the short bios of each of them. And of course, his executive assistant, Holly Nabisco, with whom he had met twice during his interviews for the job and concluded that she is competent, dedicated, discreet, and tireless. He took the University Boulevard exit off the interstate and slowed to forty for the last leg of his first journey to work.

During the next three miles down University Boulevard, the neighborhood ambience changed from commercial to high-end, gated-and-guarded communities of newer homes that appeared to be worth at least a million dollars each, many worth much more. The residential environs on the south side of the university provided shelter for some very wealthy people, Cameron concluded – probably bankers, attorneys, surgeons, corporate CEOs. Then, nearer to the university, typical campus commercial establishments appeared — restaurants and fast food chains, a large grocery store, service stations, a hair salon, several sports bars, a book store, small office buildings for professionals, print shops, and others. Arrayed around him in the half-mile to Riedel Tower in the center of campus stood office buildings, labs, classroom buildings, athletic practice fields, the basketball arena, a large performance hall, structures housing research institutes, etc. Cameron paused for a city bus to pass, then turned left into the parking lot. Cameron assumed he would get a good space this early in the morning — Riedel Tower was chiming seven gongs just across the street almost as if to announce his arrival. To his surprise, near the rear entrance to Admin, a parking space was marked, in large black letters on a gold background, "RESERVED – EXECUTIVE VICE PRESIDENT." Athena announced, "You have reached your destination." Cameron felt equal parts pride and pressure as he parked in his own personal parking space, entered the building, and took the elevator to the third floor where both he and President Faust had office suites.

As he exited the elevator and turned right down the corridor toward his office, he spotted Holly Nabisco standing half in the office doorway and half in the corridor waiting for him. It was evident from her facial expression that if this were his new administrative assistant's way of welcoming him on his first day at the office, it was certainly a serious greeting. As soon as he was within earshot, she blurted out, in a frantic run-on sentence, "Dr.-Cameron-Dean-Ackerman-died-last-night-you-need-to-appoint-an-acting-dean-for-the-College-of-Liberal-Arts-as-soon-as-possible-okay-what-do-you-want-me-to-do-first?"

"That's dreadful news, Holly. How did he die?"

"Heart attack is what the doctor thinks, but there's nothing official yet, about 8:30 Sunday night, last night," Holly said in a less rapid cadence as they walked from the corridor into the Executive Vice President's office.

"Does President Faust know?"

"I don't know. According to an e-mail on Friday from Helen McInerny, he's been in Washington for three days and she expected him back Saturday afternoon late but not in the office, so he might not know about it. Maybe they called him, too."

"Who is 'they'? How did we find out?"

"His son-in-law called us earlier this morning. He's a colonel in the Air Force and said he was reporting this incident to his father-in-law's immediate superior, or something like that."

"Holly, that sounds like we might be the only office in the university that has been informed of his death. Other than President Faust, is there anybody else we should notify?" Cameron asked, partly as a test of Holly's sense of protocol.

As they walked by Holly's desk, she picked up a steno pad and pencil, and they continued through her office and into Cameron's private office, where he sat on the edge of his desk. Holly took a straight chair near the desk as she considered his question and said, "I believe we should call all the Liberal Arts department chairs and the office of every college dean and let them know what happened. If we can't reach any of them personally, we can leave a message with their assistant, or her assistants. It's only 7:10 AM. We can just keep trying until we get them. And I also have all their cell phone numbers. We could call their cell phones if you want to."

Coming from a broken home, Holly had found it necessary to pay most of her own expenses when she attended ASU, so she had worked one or two jobs during her matriculation as a fulltime undergraduate student in the College of Business Administration. Despite the heavy work load, she narrowly missed the 'honors' designation and finished in only four and one-half years largely due to her adroit scheduling of a lot of night, weekend, and online classes, persistence, hard work, native intelligence, and no social life. The printing firm she had worked for half-time, for two years while a student, hired her as a secretary about a week after her mid-year graduation, but within a year the College of Journalism hired her as the dean's administrative assistant. For the past nineteen years, she had been a competent, loyal, and well-paid ASU staff employee. She had been administrative assistant to the EVP for three years. Her academic training and her work experience in the university had given her an astute sense of what is proper and improper when the guidelines are not clear. Supporting all that was her survival, even triumph, over a very difficult early family life of strife and poverty.

"Okay, Holly. Good suggestions. Here's what we will do. First, call the president's office to make sure he knows. Tell Ms. McInerny that we are notifying the deans and liberal arts chairs by phone this morning. Find out if President Faust wants to issue a press release from his office or if he wants us to do it, or a joint release. If he wants me to do it, who in this office normally does things like that? Do you do it? Who is our public relations officer?"

Holly was taking notes, expressionless, all business. "Got it," she says. "I sometimes write up the first draft of a press release, run it by one of the associate or assistant vice presidents, redraft, then submit it to the EVP . . . uh, that's you, executive vice president, for final approval or changes before getting the go-ahead to release it."

"Good. Let's do that if the president wants a press release from our office. Your idea about notifying the deans and chairs is good. Get that done, too. It's now 7:20 AM, Holly. We need this underway by 8, as soon as our colleagues arrive. Can we do that?"

"Of course. And, please let me say how glad I am you are here, Dr. Cameron. Welcome to ASU. Sorry we couldn't start you off on a more cheerful note. Oh, by the way, can you wait here just a minute?" Holly disappeared into the outer office. Seconds later she reappeared with a cup of coffee in her hand and said, "Here is your first coffee, black with one sugar, as you like it. I remember from your interview. Normally I make the first pot of coffee in this office in the morning but I don't serve it - except this first time, to welcome you."

"Thanks, Holly. I'm glad you are here, too." And with those words, at 7:25 AM, several of the EVP staff members could be heard talking as they entered the outer office. Cameron went out to say hello to his new colleagues and Holly went to organize them to solve the problem at hand. By 8:30, the problem was solved. He was also pleased that Holly had not scheduled any appointments for him until ten o'clock, in order to give him a little time to become more acclimated to the office. He spent the next hour reading through a huge accumulation of his postal mail, email, and inter-office memos to get up to speed on current activities.

At 9:50 AM, he noticed that the first item on his agenda was a meeting with two faculty members. Holly had given him a file containing the necessary information — purpose of their visit and copies of their resumes — which he proceeded to review. At ten, Holly knocked on his door, opened it, and said, "Your ten o'clock is here — Dr. Braxton van Landingham and Dr. Deborah Kahn."

"Please come in," Cameron said, "It's a pleasure to meet you both."

As if on cue, speaking for the pair of them, van Landingham responded in a distinct southern accent, "Thank you, Dr. Cameron, for agreeing to see us this morning. And we welcome you, sir, to Alpha State. We are so glad to have you as our new provost."

Van Landingham's southern drawl was followed by Kahn's New York City accent. "Yes, we couldn't be happier that you are here. This place really needs some academic leadership and the whole university is eager to get started."

"Permit us, if you will," van Landingham continued, "to introduce ourselves. I am now a Research Professor of American History with a PhD from the University of Virginia. I specialize in the Civil War, which I still prefer to call the 'War of Northern Aggression.' I have published three critically acclaimed books and countless articles in professional journals on various aspects of that important subject. As a University Research Professor this year, I have been completing the definitive history of Massey Point, Virginia, home to three Confederate generals."

During the next several minutes, van Landingham punctuated the delivery of his self-promotional speech with such odd body language that Cameron all but lost track of its content. The southern historian resembled a comedic character, dressed as he was in a navy blazer, light gray slacks, white dress shirt, red suspenders, and red bow tie. But as he spoke, he hooked his thumbs behind his red suspenders, then gestured to Cameron with one arm outstretched, then straightened his bow tie with both hands, then crossed his arms on his chest. Then he repeated these motions in the same order for as long as he continued to hold forth. Cameron chuckled to himself as he wondered if van Landingham did this in every class he taught. As the historian finished his pompous presentation accentuated by clownish choreography, he ended in the arms-across-chest position with a self-confident smile. He seemed to have no awareness that his gyrations were odd, to say the least, nor did his colleague, Dr. Kahn.

Cameron remembered from the résumé that van Landingham's books were published by vanity presses and that most of his articles appeared not in professional history journals but in unrefereed tourist magazines, state economic development brochures, and as guest editorials in southern newspapers. In the spirit of academic diplomacy, when van Landingham finished, Cameron commented, "You've had quite a career."

Without a second's pause, Dr. Kahn asserted, "I am a Research Professor in the Department of English, and I am a well-known expert in comparative literature, with a specialty in eighteenth century French dramatists. I studied at NYU and the Sorbonne and I took my doctorate at Yale University. I have published several books and many journal articles in my field, and I have won several awards for the importance of my research. This past year, as a Research Professor, I have been working on Voltaire's architectonic transition from universalism to French nationalism in the decade of the 1730s. Until now, nobody has ever been able to account for this incredible transformation, which has had such a profound influence on western literature. I spent this past year at the Sorbonne, analyzing Voltaire's private papers, and I have solved the mystery. It was during that decade that his outlook toward Shakespeare changed from admiration to animosity. I know that this is going to be a very, very big deal in literature."

During Dr. Kahn's self-adulatory speech, Cameron had two thoughts. He remembered that her résumé listed only one book published by a university press, one by a vanity press, and one was self-published on the internet. So, in two out of three manuscripts, she avoided the time-honored tradition of anonymous peer review and took the easy, some say dishonorable, way out. And he had to quit counting Kahn's emphatic use of the word "I" when she reached double figures early. "So you like to solve international mysteries," Cameron said.

At that point his petitioners quickly transitioned to a lengthy narrative about their appointments to the position of Research Professor a little over a year ago for one academic year and a summer. "And so that brings us to why," Dr. van Landingham concluded, "we have come to you today. Both of us need a one-semester extension of our Research Professorships. We have strong research records and merit the university's support."

Dr. Kahn added, "I . . . we need more time to complete two very important projects. And it is an opportunity for you, very early in your tenure here, to show your strong support for research and scholarship. You can send a message."

"You see, don't you, that both Dr. Kahn and I cannot finish these important breakthrough projects without additional time and financial support. I can do my research only in Massey Point, the Museum of the Confederacy in Richmond, and the Library of Congress in Washington. She can finish her work only in Paris. And our research is expensive to conduct."

"Both of us have spent our entire careers at Alpha State University," Dr. Kahn said, "building up our respective departments from rather obscure to large and competitive, even though both of us have had dozens of very lucrative offers from very prestigious universities back east and in California. Am I right, Brax?" Dr. van Landingham nodded his serious assent.

"But, Mr. Provost, it is not just the money," Dr. van Landingham argued, "it is also the timing. This very day, Haslett at Princeton has two of his doctoral students in Massey Point working on the same problem. If the University doesn't allow me to finish my project in a timely manner, they will finish their dissertations, and Haslett will get a book out of it before I do, and I might never have the chance I deserve."

"In my case," Dr. Khan asserted, "doctoral students and faculty members in four different academic disciplines are now involved in conducting research into the Voltaire-Shakespeare split — scholars in English and French literature, Francophone studies, and drama. So if I don't get this finished very soon, my book won't come out first, and Alpha State and I will not get the credit we deserve."

By this time, Cameron recognized the theatrical structure of their visit. In act one, they welcomed him to Alpha State. In act two, they delivered monologues emphasizing what important scholars they are. In act three, the script called for demanding more money and time to conduct research — all in a friendly but self-praising manner. He also remembered Holly's memo in the agenda file about this appointment. She had said, *They want to meet with you about their Research Professorships. They probably want another semester or year. Current policy says they are eligible for another one after five years. Dr. Madden, the previous EVP, and the committee awarded all of the RPs for the academic year way back in February and there's no money left. But it's your call.* And Holly had been right.

"If I granted your requests," Cameron began, "I would stand in violation of university policy, not to mention that the previous provost and his committee awarded all the money for Research Professorships for next year way back in the winter. So, there is no funding left. I'm afraid your requests just can't be honored."

"Well, if word gets out that you don't support serious research by your best and most senior professors," Dr. Kahn said, "the faculty is going to be very upset."

"These Research Professorships were designed and awarded to do exactly that," Cameron countered, "but the supply is limited." He noticed that the emotional tenor of their dialogue had now changed from gracious to defensive.

Dr. van Landingham interjected, "If you will check your records, Mr. Provost, you will see that this office did, in fact, award a Research Professorship to Melvin Corsair, the biologist, for three semesters and a summer.

We wonder why the natural sciences get favorable treatment not available to the humanities."

As he responded, Cameron sensed that the conversation had moved into a hostile act four, introduced by a scene of unfriendly confrontation. "Even if that were true, and it is not, I am bound by university regulations," he said, "and if those need to be changed, we have to go through the correct process and change the formal rule."

Both Dr. van Landingham and Dr. Kahn stood to leave, and she added, "The faculty will not be happy when they hear your rigid policy on research," to which Dr. van Landingham nodded and frowned his agreement. Both marched out of the office, their expressions and body language exhibiting considerable pique, no doubt as their script called for in the event of dramatic failure. Neither one said goodbye.

Holly knocked and came in immediately, saying, "You have a ten-thirty with Ms. Hernandez, HR Director, to fill out some more forms to make you a legal employee. It's upstairs in four-sixteen. Your eleven o'clock is back here with the officers of the Graduate Student Association. Here's a draft of a press release about…the late Dean Ackerman. President Faust said if you approve it, we should send it out in his name. He stayed in Washington over the weekend and is flying home right now."

The meeting with Human Resources took only a few minutes, and Cameron was back in his office by eleven. He read the press release Holly had prepared about Dean Ackerman and found it to be a compassionate statement of the dean's passing, his professional achievements at Alpha State and elsewhere, his family, and information about funeral arrangements. As Holly shepherded the students into his office, Cameron gave her back the draft of the press release and said, "Get this out to the media as it is. No changes. Excellent job, Holly. Thanks." With no change of expression, she took the draft and closed the door behind her, then stood outside the door for several seconds, smiling.

As soon as Cameron finished his meeting with the four officers of the Graduate Student Association, Holly popped into his office and closed the door. "Dr. Cameron," she said through clenched teeth, "Dr. Kahn called once and came here to the office once while you were with the grad students. She . . . demanded another meeting with you. Only five minutes, she says, maybe less. I told her I would let you know what she said. But you are supposed to be at a luncheon meeting of the New Cambridge Civic Association in the Concordia Plaza Hotel at noon as their guest. They are going to welcome you and introduce you to a lot of the business and professional leaders in town. You're not scheduled to be back here until four, which is pushing it. But Dr. Kahn says she has to deliver a 'very important' lecture to the New Cambridge Ladies' Theatre Auxiliary at four. For you to get to your noon meeting, you need to leave right now!" she all but commanded.

"The English Department is close by, isn't it?" Cameron asked.

"Yes, about five minutes away."

"Okay. Call Dr. Kahn and tell her I'm available at eleven fifty-five for five minutes. That gives her," looking at his watch, "ten minutes to get here. She is one persistent . . . woman. Interrupt us if she hasn't left by noon."

One minute early, Holly knocked and brought in a disheveled and out-of-breath Voltaire expert who, without introduction, began another shameless soliloquy designed to persuade Cameron to extend her Research Professorship. "Jeff and I should not have come here together. It was too much to ask. But it's different for me. My dear friend Jeff works in just one discipline, history and his research is so parochial. My research is multi-disciplinary and universal in scope. It applies the perspectives and methods of literature, theatre, and history — with a touch of philosophy, as well. It's harder to do and, when done, better as a result. Believe me; the struggle for women's rights is not over on this campus by any stretch of the imagination. Women on this campus would be impressed if you reached out to a disadvantaged minority by extending my Research Professorship. If you are actually out of money, you could skip the research award. Just give me my regular salary and time off from teaching. Jeff wouldn't even have to know. I'd just be at the Sorbonne conducting research on my own."

Cameron remained silent through Dr. Kahn's testimonial and observed that she became more dramatic and agitated. Her face grew flushed, her eyes narrowed, she left her chair, moved toward Cameron's desk, and shook her finger at him as she began the women's rights argument. Her New York accent became even more pronounced and spittle sprayed from her mouth when she articulated sibilant sounds and the stop-consonant "t" and her hands shook with nervous anger. *What an audacious, egomaniacal, back-stabber*, Cameron thought to himself. *And, she called van Landingham her dear friend!*

"Dr. Kahn," he responded, "I can only repeat what I already said: the length of a Research Professorship is one academic year plus a summer, and you are eligible for another one in five years. Teaching loads are determined by department chairs in consultation with their deans. My answer must be 'no'."

Cameron's response evoked a scene that needed only a rainstorm with heavy winds to resemble the dramatic denouement of a Shakespearian tragedy. There stood Dr. Kahn, in the middle of Cameron's office, channeling King Lear as she flailed her arms above her head — aggrieved, bitter, bawling. She screeched out, "How could you do this to me?! What am I going to do?! You will regret this!" in an artful blend of anger and sadness. He handed her a box of tissues and she blew her nose and dabbed her eyes as her tears created tiny rivulets of cosmetics on her cheeks. Holly's knock provided the cue that it was time for Cameron to go to his next meeting downtown, somewhat late. As he passed Holly he whispered, "Keep an eye on Dr. Kahn until she leaves the office. Help her if she needs help. You have my cell number if you need me. See you later." Holly rolled her eyes, handed him his schedule and said, "Of course. Remember that you have a four o'clock with the associate vice presidents and me to work on the deanship vacancy in Liberal Arts."

Other than the inevitable conclusion that Dr. Kahn is one arrogant, self-centered, and decidedly uncollegial colleague, Cameron tried not to think of the bizarre scene just acted out in his office. Rather he focused on the next task, attending his first monthly meeting of an organization usually referred to by the acronym, BHEF — Business-Higher Education Forum. All he knew is that its purpose is to provide opportunities for about thirty university leaders and thirty local business leaders to develop mutually beneficial relationships. As soon as he entered the meeting room in the hotel, he spotted his boss, who had come straight from the airport to the meeting. President Faust greeted him with a hearty handshake and began introducing him to many of the business leaders who stood nearby.

"Please be seated for lunch," the presiding officer intoned over the PA system. Members and guests took their seats at one of the round tables in an elegant banquet room of one of New Cambridge's fancier hotels and were soon served a delicious lunch.

After lunch, the agenda centered on "Preserving the Bayh-Dole Act," a piece of congressional legislation signed by President Regan in 1980. Before the BHEF presiding officer made his introductory remarks about the topic, he introduced Cameron as ASU's new executive vice president for academic affairs and offered a warm welcome on behalf of BHEF.

Next, the presiding officer called on a patent attorney from a large law firm in town to discuss the Bayh-Dole Act. The lawyer described how it changed the law on intellectual property to allow universities, rather than the federal government, to take ownership of an invention or discovery made in the completion of research funded by the federal government. Ownership includes the right to apply for patent protection, to form a corporation to produce the new technology, to promote and commercialize it, and to collect all royalties and other fees except where these are shared with the inventor or chief researcher(s) by previous contractual agreement. It was clear that the term 'invention' refers to any number of new discoveries, many with important commercial value. The speaker clicked the next slide which listed stem cells and pharmaceuticals and medical devices designed to prevent, cure or ameliorate illness and disease. Next came chemicals and materials, and then electronics and optics. Like most other large universities, Alpha State, several years ago set up its own Office of Technology Transfer to accelerate entry of their federally funded inventions into a lucrative market.

Next, the presiding officer introduced Congressman Reiner, who presented an after-lunch speech about the virtues of the Bayh-Dole Act. He discussed a strategy to protect it from modification by the federal judge in a pending court case, and then answered questions from the audience. The applause was substantial as he left the podium, whereupon the presiding officer called for motions from the floor. One of the members rose and offered a motion to authorize the BHEF treasurer to allocate up to $100,000 for lobbying efforts to ensure that the state's congressional delegation would protect Bayh-Dole against any effort to weaken it. A quick second was followed by unanimous approval and, at three-ten, adjournment. Cameron spoke again with President Wolfe, met several more people, and felt welcomed as a new member of BHEF.

Back in his office, he shuffled through about twenty small pink slips on which Holly had noted either a phone message or visitor. Nothing looked urgent, but one message stood out. It was from an old friend and former classmate at Berkeley, Randy Randolph, whom Cameron hadn't seen since he last attended the American Public Policy Association meeting in Seattle, three years prior. Randolph was now a senior professor at the University of Washington. Cameron called the number Holly had written on the pink notice and waited.

"Hello. This is Professor Randolph."

"Randy! Drew Cameron. How in the world are you?"

"I am great, Drew, and it's great to hear your voice! Thanks for calling me back, Professor-Doctor-Executive-Vice-President-Provost Cameron! I just read in the *Chronicle* that you left Albany and now work at Alpha State. Onward and upward, are we?"

"We shall see. It's my first day on the job, so I almost have a clue. How's the family?"

"Drew, I have an Administrative Law class to teach in ten minutes, so I'll have to be brief. Remember little Susie, my daughter? She starts her senior year in high school this fall. Can you believe it? She's an honors student so far and wants to major in music, vocal or piano she thinks. She and I plan to visit several universities around the country and see if one fits her better. Alpha State's Music School has a strong reputation, so we want to visit ASU if you advise it."

"Randy, that's wonderful! And you should stay with Vanessa and me when you're here. Of course, I don't participate in admission decisions, but it doesn't sound like she needs a recommendation from me. When are you coming?"

"We will let you know as soon as we can get it on the calendar. I think she'll be competitive for a scholarship almost anywhere. She is a much better high school student than I ever was, so all I need from you is your confirmation that ASU's Music School is as good as its reputation. Or that it isn't."

"I think it is, Randy – both classical and jazz. They get SRO crowds when they perform. And they do several CDs every year. She should contact our Admissions and Records Office — Dr. Zachary Kilgore is the VP — and get all the information and application forms," Cameron said.

Following a lengthy silence, Randy asked, "Zachary Kilgore? Dr. Zachary Kilgore?"

"Yeah, that's right."

"Thanks, Drew. I gotta run to class. Literally run. I will get back to you about this. I think there may be a problem. So long for now."

Cameron had accessed the ASU Admissions Office website on his computer to get the phone number for Randy Randolph and, just as he hung up, he noticed the icon for Kilgore's bio. He clicked the icon and began reading Kilgore's credentials, including master's degree and doctorate in computer science, when Holly knocked and entered, saying, "We're here for the meeting." She was followed by the five assistant and associate vice presidents responsible for academic affairs — the teaching, research, and service functions.

Holly stayed on after the meeting to tell Cameron something about his final event for the day. "You are to have cocktails with President Faust and the state legislators representing New Cambridge and the surrounding counties. All you have to do, according to Ms. McInerny, is to put in an appearance, let President Faust make the introduction, have a cocktail, schmooze as long as you like, then you are free to go. No business will be transacted, just socializing."

"Okay, will do." Cameron responded.

After Cameron bade her goodbye and left for the six o'clock meeting with legislators, Holly stayed on for another half hour to get some business items primed for the next day, writing notes to herself, and finalizing his agenda for tomorrow. She felt good about his first day and enjoyed the feeling.

Cameron met the legislators and had a good discussion with Steve Faust, who seemed to be an easy-going and reasonable boss. The legislators seem to like him. So, after one drink and forty-five minutes of schmoozing, Cameron drove back home to suburban Bedford. He and Vanessa discussed the day, his and hers, over a nice dinner she had prepared - made-from-scratch lasagna, a big salad, and a bottle of Chianti *classico*.

4 Cameron's first day as Alpha State University's new Executive Vice President and Provost was one of the busiest days of that first summer. After that, he had only a few more twelve-hour days, no unexpected deaths of key administrative officers, and no more melodramatic scenes with self-centered faculty.

He had immediate access to President Faust in addition to their weekly meetings, scheduled for Monday mornings at seven-thirty. Faust seemed easy to work with, open to new ideas, in command of every facet of his university, and well-respected by university staff, government officials, and the business community. He encouraged Cameron to take initiatives and to keep him informed. He said, on at least two occasions, "You handle the academics, and I'll handle the fundraising. Call me if you need me."

Summer school proceeded as planned. Professors professed, students studied, exams were given and graded, and grades were mailed to students. Students and professors went home. Campus life modulated from somewhat busy to silent. Virtually all faculty members, even those on twelve-month contracts, and many administrators and staff took the vacations their contracts allowed. Viewed from above, the campus resembled an ant hill from late August to early July, with students ambling or scurrying along the connecting paths, most carrying backpacks, singly, in pairs, and in clusters, day and night, among dorms, classrooms, cafeterias, bookstores, the library, parking lots, the arena, the coliseum, and numerous eateries and beer joints just off campus. During dead time, the period between the end of summer school and the beginning of the fall semester, even the area around Riedel Bell Tower, in the center of campus, was mostly the quiet province of birds and squirrels, except when campus lawn care crews buzzed through —mowing, edging, clipping, replanting, seeding, and fertilizing.

During that hot, late-summer period, the Camerons had time in the evenings and most weekends to meet neighbors for grilling steaks, an impromptu glass of wine or beer in the late afternoon, and the occasional game of bridge. Vanessa stayed busy studying for the state bar exam, either at home or at the ASU law library, redecorating parts of their new home, making friends with more neighbors, and shopping for new furniture in anticipation of taking some of their current furniture to a consignment store.

One late afternoon after work, as Cameron entered his home, Vanessa greeted him with a kiss and a question: "What do you know about Emerson, Fineman, and Murray?"

"Nothing, I think. Is it one of the big law firms downtown?"

"Yes, and their managing partner, Jeffrey Kaufman, called me today to ask if I am planning to take the state bar. I told him I am studying for it now and would probably take it in late fall. He asked me to call him when I get the results back. One of their senior attorneys who specializes in health care law just retired, effective at the end of the year, so they need somebody to replace her."

"And that somebody could be you! Are you interested?" Cameron asked.

"If the conditions are right and the other attorneys are decent, I'd definitely be interested," Vanessa said, "but I never thought a firm would be initiating the inquiry, especially since I've been in town only a few weeks. And I haven't even taken the bar exam yet. Maybe one of my former colleagues in the Albany firm called them about me."

They conveyed this information and other news to Tom and Char when the kids called to say they would arrive in Bedford in about a few days and stay a week before going back to Cornell for the fall semester. Both were enjoying their summer jobs in Albany, missing their parents, and looking forward to seeing them and Bedford.

In the couple of weeks between August 1 and the start of the fall semester, Cameron received hundreds of phone calls, two of which would have important repercussions in the next few months. At exactly eight o'clock on a Tuesday morning, he answered a buzz from Holly, who said, "I have a long-distance call from a man in the Czech Republic named," and she paused, "Ox L. Decker, I think it is. He's from Charles University."

"His first name is Axel with an 'ah', Holly. Thanks, put him through."

"Hello, Axel. How are you?"

"I am fine, sir. I mean Drew. I am fine. It is good to speak with you again. How is your summer going in your new position?"

"Very well, thank you. A bit warmer than I am accustomed to but pleasant enough. How is life in the Prorector's Office?"

"Quite pleasant. Prorector Havlicek sends his regards. The reason I called, Drew, is to let you know that I have formally received my doctoral degree from Charles University. Plus the EU gave me an administrative post-doc for two years."

"That's wonderful news, Axel. Good for you. And you can take the fellowship to any university, in any country?"

"Any accredited university that offers both undergraduate and graduate degrees as long as I am assigned to an administrative office, not just teaching or research. I have several in mind, two in Europe and two in the U.S. One of them is Alpha State University. The fellowship pays quite well, so I will need no additional compensation."

"Axel, you'd have to submit the regular paperwork along with your credentials and come here for interviews, but the final decision on an appointment like this is mine. I'm sure everyone here would appreciate your work skills and we need your help, especially in planning and international matters. I encourage you to get your paperwork here as soon as possible. When are you available?"

"Prorector Havlicek has hired me in a permanent position in the Office of International Relations but has allowed me to leave in late December if I elect to take the EU fellowship starting in January."

"We could start you in January. Get your paperwork in and then let's get you here for interviews ASAP," Cameron said.

"Very well, Drew. I am pleased. Also, Anna sends her greetings."

"Give her my best, Axel. Will she go with you, wherever you go"?

"Yes. We are, as you say in the States, a 'committed couple.'"

"Great. I look forward to seeing you both here."

"Thank you for your confidence in my ability. I will send the paperwork as an email attachment and post the originals by regular mail." They promised to stay in touch regardless of the outcome of this particular possibility.

Later that week, on a Thursday night soon after dinner, Cameron received a phone call at home from his friend Randy Randolph at the University of Washington. They exchanged the jocular greetings of old friends and set a time for Randolph and his daughter to visit Alpha State University in mid-fall to see if she might want to become an undergraduate student there next year.

Randy's tone changed abruptly from friendly to serious as he said, "Cameron, can we go off the record? Just two old friends having a talk?"

"Sure, Randy," Cameron agreed. "What is it?"

"You remember when we talked last, you told me to have my daughter contact the office of Alpha State's VP for Admissions and Records . . . to get information about applying there?"

"Right."

"You referred to him as Dr. Zachary Kilgore. As does Alpha State's admissions website. Drew, Kilgore was a graduate student here in Computer Science about twenty years ago and helped my department set up our new computer lab. After I saw that he was in administration at ASU, I mentioned him to Bart Engstrom. Bart's a good friend of mine and was Kilgore's graduate advisor in Computer Science. He told me that Kilgore never finished, that he just dropped out. He was in the MS program for a couple of years and then enrolled in the doctoral program for a couple of years but never finished either program. Contrary to what his website bio says, he does not have his master's or doctorate in Computer Science from Washington. I called our records office to make sure and they verified it. He just doesn't have either degree, Drew. Not from here."

Cameron was dumfounded. "Randy, that doesn't sound like good news, so I will look into it right away. There must be a typo or misunderstanding or something like that. Maybe the person who set up our Admissions and Records website made a mistake. Anyway, I will get to the bottom of this and let you know what I learn. Falsification of a resume to get a job is . . . not a good thing."

"Don't shoot the messenger, Drew."

"Not a chance. I'm saving a bottle of expensive Cabernet for when you and your daughter arrive. So you'd better get here. I'm anxious to see little Susie all grown up."

After the call, Cameron made a mental note to look into Randy's allegation first thing the next morning. But his old friend wouldn't say it unless he was convinced it is a fact. There must be some mistake here, Cameron reasoned. Maybe Kilgore got a doctorate somewhere else later. Anyway, he hoped a quick review of the records or a phone call would clear things up.

Admissions and Records was one of those large, administrative and clerical bureaucracies in a university that nobody pays much attention to unless applications or admissions decline. As far as Cameron knew, that office had been performing its core functions quite well: organizing and supervising the undergraduate admissions process and managing the collection and storage of all student and employee records.

As he greeted Holly in her outer office the next morning, Cameron decided first to call Steve Faust to alert him to Randy Randolph's information about Kilgore and to get any advice he might offer. Then he would discuss the matter with Kilgore and take whatever action seemed appropriate.

"President Faust called about ten minutes ago, but he didn't say what it's about," Holly said. "Do you want me to call him back right now?"

"Sure, let's start the day with the president."

The phone was ringing in his office even before he could hang his sports coat on the elegant wooden rack by the matching built-in bookcase behind his desk. "Good morning, Steve. How are you?"

"Couldn't be better, Drew. What's new with you?"

"It's quiet and we intend to get caught up and ready for the faculty and students to get back."

"Good. Good. Just two quick things, Drew. The legislators really liked you the other night. They were impressed. Several of them told me so. You might not have realized it, but one of them was Shelby Clements, the speaker of the house in the state legislature. He's very powerful in the state. Shelby helps us a lot with state funding and uses his clout with our congressional delegation to help us there, too. He's a good man. The other thing is, I got a letter from a man named Havlicek at Charles University in Prague with a copy of a student and faculty exchange agreement between Charles and Alpha State. That is great work! How did you pull it off so fast?"

"They were eager to collaborate and had done their homework on Alpha State. When the subject came up, I supported it. So, we put the agreement together. Glad you like it."

"Globalization is here to stay, so we need to make it work for us. Your agreement with Charles will be our platform into eastern European markets. There have to be at least a dozen high tech, engineering and pharmaceutical firms in this state, including some of Alpha State's start-ups, that would love to market their products and services in Eastern Europe. Prague is an opening. Good work, Drew. I have to go now. I'm due at the airport in less than an hour. The annual meeting of higher ed CEOs is in Colorado Springs, at the Broadmoor Hotel this year. I'm taking my tennis racquet and golf clubs. See you next …"

"Steve, one second more, please," Cameron interrupted. "I might have identified a problem, and I need your advice before I look into it. I have a report from an old friend on the faculty at Washington in Seattle that Zachary Kilgore never finished either his master's or doctoral degree there. He even checked with their records office. As you probably know, Kilgore's résumé and his bio on our Admissions website list both degrees as completed at Washington. Our formal requirements to fill the position included a doctorate just to be considered. Am I missing something here?"

Faust's failure to respond for several seconds created an embarrassing silence. Finally, "Of course, there must be some confusion in the records or something. Zach does a great job for us. He got rid of all the paper records, and we're all digital now. We never hear a complaint against him or anyone in his shop. But I will look into it and let you know, whatever. In the meantime, you work on the real problems, Cameron. See you when I get back." Then, click.

Cameron found two of President Faust's remarks troubling. First, he seemed not to be the least bit concerned that one of his VPs might have obtained his position through fraud. And, he seemed to see international academic study solely as a means for state businesses to increase their profits, with no appreciation for increasing students' opportunities to strengthen their critical thinking skills and experience other parts of the world. He made a mental note to revisit the Kilgore situation early next week.

In two hours, he was scheduled to meet with Susan Deutsch, director of ASU's Office of Technology Transfer or OTT. Holly had arranged the meeting at his request because he wanted to get up to speed on what Alpha State's OTT does. He had at least three hours of communications — reports, emails, memos, letters, and phone messages — to read and answer before then. And in one day, the faculty would arrive back on campus. Then life in the Office of the EVP would start to get very busy, according to Holly.

Cameron recalled Vice President Susan Deutsch's biography as he drove across campus to her office. After earning both a law degree and an MBA at the University of Wisconsin about twenty-five years ago, she had worked in the Patent and Trademark Office in the U.S. Department of Commerce. President Faust had recruited her away from Washington, D.C. with a big salary and carte blanche to organize Alpha State's Office of Technology Transfer. Her responsibilities as Vice President for Research and Economic Development now also included managing a growing research and technology park with a business incubator and a sizeable venture capital fund. According to Holly and two of his AVPs, Deutsch had a great eye for scientific and technological innovations with practical applications, an impressive mastery of intellectual property law, the competence and charm to deal with faculty research scientists and corporate executives, and the complete confidence of President Faust. They also said that OTT operated a lot like the Athletic Department and that Susan Deutsch operated a lot like the football coach — independent, successful, pampered, and powerful. Under her leadership, Alpha State had made impressive progress toward breaking into the top thirty research universities with respect to total annual federal research funding.

Cameron arrived two minutes early and was ushered straight into Deutsch's large, plush office. At exactly 10 AM she walked in through a side door and greeted him warmly. "Dr. Cameron, good morning and welcome to Alpha State. You probably don't remember, but when you were here for your first interviews almost a year ago, I was out of town except for one meeting. When you met with the law school faculty, I had rushed in from the airport so I could sit with them and see you and hear your discussion. I'm so glad you're here."

"Thanks, I'm happy to be here, and please call me Drew."

"And I'm Susan," she reciprocated, as she laid her briefcase on the desk and pushed her sunglasses back on top of her head. "Please sit. How can I help you?"

"I am here, Susan, to get a quick briefing on Alpha State's activities in the area of tech transfer, and you are recommended as the one person in command of that information. And some more information about the Bayh-Dole Act. I heard a little about it at a recent BHEF meeting."

"You flatter me, Drew, and I love it," she said in an almost coquettish style and smiled. "Tech transfer is in my DNA. But to be thorough, I must mention three related areas of our work. Here's a little brochure I give to our potential clients when they want to know if we can help them." To Cameron, the attractive, thirty-page magazine resembled a very slick corporate promotional document, not a university publication.

"Let me start with Bayh-Dole. It was adopted by Congress in 1980 and regulates what happens to inventions that result from a university's fulfillment of a federal research grant. Alpha State must have a written agreement with the principal faculty investigator regarding assignment of ownership of an invention. We are required to inform the feds about the invention and whether the university wants to retain title to it. If we don't retain title, the feds take it. If we retain title, we have to file for a patent. If we get the patent, we share any earned revenue with the inventor. We have to use that revenue for education and research. All this protects intellectual property rights - patents, copyrights, and trademarks."

"So," Cameron asked, "tech transfer is the process of converting one of our faculty member's inventions, discovered while conducting research supported by a federal grant, into a practical product that can be patented and that has commercial value?"

"Exactly, Drew. That's why ASU has the Division of Innovation and Economic Development, DIED," she spelled with a smile. "Don't be fooled. It's alive and well. The Technology Transfer Office is one of three offices in the ASU Research Park. The other two are the Business Incubator and the Venture Capital Fund. Our Business Incubator provides space, some supplies, logistics, and assistance to innovative entrepreneurs, mostly outside the University, who want to develop new ideas and technologies but who might not have the resources to do it at first. Our Venture Capital Fund is an account we can use to provide financial resources to someone who wants to start up a new small business to design or sell commercially attractive new technologies. Of course, when we provide an innovative start-up business with either space or financial assistance, our contract calls for profit-sharing with ASU. So, we are careful to provide those resources only to promising new ventures. Then we can use our share of the revenue to support university research and education."

Cameron was amazed at ASU's record in tech transfer. Deutsch mentioned several of ASU's recent success stories in facilitating federal research grants from which faculty researchers discovered or invented new technologies. ASU had placed entrepreneurial businesspeople in one of the incubator offices, arranged to have the technologies patented, and set them up in new business ventures or spin-offs from large corporations. As a result, the University reaped continuing revenues, which it used to generate new grants, inventions, patents, and more profits. And these activities were spread among numerous new technologies, including computer software, chemical processes, pharmaceuticals, computer animation, knee and hip replacement mechanisms, and even one copyright on a musical composition. As he listened, Cameron couldn't help but respect the results in terms of state and regional economic development. But another part of him wondered if a not-for-profit public university, an institution funded by state taxes and tuition, should be allowed, even encouraged to amass such profits by declaring the results of their federal taxpayer-funded research as proprietary and protecting their profits with patents.

"So that's the short version of what we do here, Drew," Susan Deutsch said. "Is that what you had in mind?"

"Yes, thank you, Susan. It's much clearer now. And very impressive. I want us to open the lines of communication between Academic Affairs and DIED, between you and me, so we can help each other accomplish University goals."

"Sounds good to me, Drew," Deutsch said and they shook hands goodbye. As he walked down the long corridor to leave, the interior of the building reminded him more of a new Wall Street bank than a university building. He felt certain that Susan Deutsch and the Division of Innovation and Economic Development would require close attention.

It was just before bedtime that night that Cameron finally had a chance to review the agenda that Holly had handed him as he left the office at a little after six that Friday evening. Most of Monday would be consumed by a dozen thirty-minute interviews with various Liberal Arts professors concerning selection of a new permanent dean, curricular reform, and strategic planning. Many faculty members are so conditioned by their jobs and egos, he knew, that they assume that every social interaction requires them to deliver an uninterrupted, fifty-minute lecture, so Holly's management help would be critical to keeping on schedule. The twelve Liberal Arts faculty he was to interview were chosen by his AVPs as a purposive sample to represent junior and senior ranks, six different departments, all three of the divisions within the College

— humanities, social sciences, arts — and the disparate points of view among and within the departments. Monday would be interesting and, he hoped, useful as a way to learn more about his new university.

The mid-August dead period between summer school and fall semester ended that weekend and on Monday ASU took on once again the characteristics of a disturbed ant colony. About 35,000 students, 13,000 non-teaching employees, and 2,000 faculty were back. At 8 AM, President Faust answered his private cell phone to hear an excited former ASU police chief Wood say, "We've got to meet. You and me and Rita Kamens. I have everything we need to … you know …."

"Three things, Doug. First, send me a bill for all your days on the job, expenses, etc., so I can get you paid. Second, ASAP get me the original and one copy of all relevant documentation and shred everything else on this case. You have done an excellent job. And I won't forget it. I have a bonus in mind for you, later. Third, I'll take care of the rest of this matter, and we're done. I'll inform Rita. Okay?"

"As you wish. As you wish," Doug Wood responded.

As soon as they hung up, Faust dialed Rita Kamens' private line in Student Affairs. "Rita, Steve Faust. I'm calling about the terrible uh … dormitory incident of last June. Here's how we proceed. I'm sending you copies of everything we have on the case. Read it and shred it. The official copies stay in my office. Pretty soon they can make an arrest and we can tell our story to the public. That we have kept it secret from a media storm to protect the parents; we did the investigation; we caught the guilty party."

"Fine with me, Steve. I'll be glad to be done with it."

"Okay, Rita. We're on the same page. See you later. Gotta run."

Just down the hall of Admin, Cameron sat in his office, sipping coffee and answering email inquiries before Holly escorted Dr. Milton Quigley, senior professor of English, into his office. "Thanks for coming in this morning, Milton. I'm pleased to meet you. Given our brief time today and the list of important topics we need to discuss, let's get right to it."

"Sounds good to me, Andrew. And I'm also glad to meet you. Welcome to Alpha State."

"Alpha State has suffered some, I'm told, because we have not developed and implemented a strategic plan. Similarly, we have been criticized, from inside the university and outside, for maintaining a somewhat outdated curriculum. This fall we have to begin the process of hiring a new permanent dean for your college. What can you tell me about the English Department that will help us create a long-term planning process, reform the curriculum, and hire a new dean for Liberal Arts?"

As Cameron spoke, Professor Quigley's facial expression and body language conveyed sincerity and openness and curiosity. Then his expression changed. This expert on the British romantic poets — Byron, Wordsworth, Shelley, and especially Keats — lowered his eyebrows, tensed his chin and lips, clenched his teeth, and squinted his eyes. His transformation reminded Cameron of the memorable scenes in every film director's version of the Jekyll and Hyde mystery — dramatic and a little spooky, to say the least.

Quigley's voice was hoarse but intense. "There will not be an English Department in a few years unless you hire a new dean who will appoint a new department chairman who will quit recruiting faculty who haven't a clue about what English literature is, but who insist on turning the whole department into a cauldron of radical, tribal in-fighting and bastardizing the curriculum so that it becomes an instrument of their political and cultural self-glorification and 'empowerment,'" he said, in a long and caustic sentence.

"That sounds serious, Milton," Cameron responded, "but I'm not sure I understand, exactly. Could you clarify that for me?"

"It means that most of the faculty hired in the past ten or fifteen years are replacing the literary canon with pure, unadulterated nonsense and worse. They have no respect for anyone from Homer through Joyce and certainly not for any of America's great twentieth-century authors. They make fun of Poe, Hawthorne, Dickenson, Melville, all of them. We have a sacred and historic obligation to teach truth and beauty to our students, and the canonical literature contains all the truth and beauty that we know."

"So, the younger faculty," Cameron interrupted, "are changing the literature curriculum? Away from teaching the works in the canon?" Cameron asked, as he continued jotting down notes on a legal pad.

"Exactly," Quigley hissed.

"What are they teaching, then?"

"We are supposed to teach literature courses to 'educate' all our students. But they design their courses only to 'empower' certain groups. Want to hear some examples? We now have scores of courses on gay literature, lesbian literature, Chicano literature, African-American literature, literature and disability, and then we have several specific, advanced undergraduate courses in each of these ridiculous so-called genres. The theme is always the same: counter-revolution against the oppressive hegemony of white heterosexual males."

"So you think the English Department has gone too far in this direction?" asked Cameron.

"One inch is far too far. Oh, to be sure, we still teach a few courses on the classic periods of literature and on particular authors of works in the canon. But when these young so-called 'postmodernists' teach those courses, they deconstruct everything into some ideological morass. To them, neither a single word nor an entire novel means what the experts have always said it means. They preach that it could mean any number of things or nothing, or we don't know and probably cannot ever know what it means. It's all deconstructionist egotism and ideology. For example," Quigley continued, as his face grew redder, "when they teach a course on Hemingway, they hardly even mention that his work is the best literary account available of how people who faced the death and destruction of World War I became detached and cynical, the 'Lost Generation', and how they coped with it. Rather, they interpret it as the literary documentation of twentieth century American sexism and the enslavement of women."

"Maybe we need to talk again, Milton. Our time has about run out for now. Thanks for your input."

"You're welcome, Andrew. Good luck with curriculum reform. We really need it, and I think you understand that now." Dr. Milton Quigley rose with a confident smile, and left Cameron's office at 8:29 AM.

Your eight-thirty, Dr. Rasmussen, was here but he left just a moment ago to visit the restroom. He should be right back."

"Good, I need another cup of coffee anyway. But, Holly, don't let me have another cup of coffee with each appointment. That would be eight cups for the morning, way over even my limit." As Cameron returned to his office from the coffee room moments later, mug in hand, Dr. Robert Rasmussen, a new associate professor of political science, a specialist in voting behavior and political dynamics, hurried into the office. Holly made the introduction, and Rasmussen refused her offer of coffee as they took their seats. Rasmussen who seemed young for a new associate professor, was only twenty-nine, according to his curriculum *vitae*. He spoke in nervous bursts, seldom smiled, and seemed anxious to leave even though he had just arrived.

"Congratulations, Robert," Cameron began, "I saw on your *vitae* that you received tenure and promotion to associate professor last spring."

Rasmussen said, "Seven articles in leading journals, one monograph published, and a second one under contract."

Cameron had seen a few young hot-shots in academe before - some angry, some arrogant, some both, even before tenure and especially after. Most were intelligent, hard-working high achievers, usually with their doctorates from large departments in large universities, self-absorbed, and with little or no respect for their senior colleagues. They found their students and teaching a little boring. They felt that something or somebody was always wrong. Cameron suppressed his feeling of disappointment and said, "That's a good record. I hope you keep it up your whole career. You will make some important contributions to your field and help a lot of students."

"I have my doubts about whether that will ever happen at Alpha State," the young political scientist said. "The old guard runs the department and they won't let us teach a graduate seminar unless we have tenure and associate rank. I'll have to wait until next spring before I get to teach a seminar, and it's not even in my specialty, and doesn't include doctoral students. *They* always insist on teaching the doctoral students."

"I guess that's why they call it 'paying your dues.' Nobody likes a seniority system until he or she gets seniority."

Rasmussen grew visibly impatient. "They protect their outmoded mid-twentieth-century curriculum like it's the Holy Grail. The required seminars for the master's and doctoral programs are simply not political science. They are an embarrassing amalgamation of history, normative philosophy, and strict-constructionist legalism. Their idea of modern political science is early behavioralism – stuff that Eulau, Dahl, Deutsch, and Easton were doing six decades ago. They don't measure variables, they don't model anything, they don't collect data, and they don't understand experimental research! They wouldn't know an ARIMA model or a Solomon four-group design if they found it in their soup."

"So we have a methodology problem in the political science curriculum?" Cameron asked, as he realized that Rasmussen was unaware that he, Cameron, had a doctorate in policy analysis and was familiar with these research techniques.

"We certainly do have a methodology problem," Rasmussen continued. "But since you asked, the problem is not just *what* we teach. It's also *who* teaches *how much*. The younger faculty members have to teach more than the old guard, especially freshman intro courses. And it is the younger faculty who are getting all the research published. Most of the old faculty members haven't published in years. Yet each year, it is the old faculty who get the big pay raises."

"Have you discussed any of these problems with your chair?" Cameron asked.

Rasmussen dismissed the question with a thinly veiled challenge: "Things have to change or you will lose your Department of Political Science. I can assure you, the good people will leave. And no doctoral students will want to study here."

"You have shared your observations with me, and I appreciate your candor. We might have to meet again on this topic, because our time this morning has slipped away. Thanks for coming in, and keep up the good work, Robert."

Cameron continued to remain neutral, objective, and in a learning mode throughout the remainder of the interviews. He heard eight more half-hour testimonials about curriculum reform, choosing a new dean, and planning, plus a few other extraneous issues that morning. He ate a quick take-out deli lunch that Holly and ordered for him, then heard four more spiels by three o'clock. He took copious notes, drank only one additional cup of coffee, and learned a great deal about ASU's College of Liberal Arts. It seemed that his plan to diagnose the general health of an entire college by talking with just twelve of its professors worked fairly well. Although he did anticipate that his probes about curriculum and leadership would reveal many of the standard academic conflicts along the continua of age, methodology, tenure, workload, and ideology, he had not thought that just two interviews would suggest that these conflicts are so mutually reinforcing. Arrayed on one side he found the younger, pre-tenure, methodologically more sophisticated, faculty with more recent PhDs, assigned to undergraduate courses rather than graduate seminars. They also teach more and publish more research, but receive smaller salaries and annual raises. On the other side were the older, tenured faculty, decades away from their graduate training, espousing somewhat out-of-date methods, publishing little or no research, teaching the graduate seminars and teaching fewer courses, for which they receive larger salaries and raises.

When it was all over, Cameron cleared his mind with a brisk, ten minute walk once around the Riedel Bell Tower and back. Holly seemed more serious and soft-spoken than usual as she briefed him on business he had deferred during his meetings with Liberal Arts faculty. "I hope I am not out of line by asking, but are you planning to replace me?" she asked.

Cameron thought she was joking. "Not today, I think."

"Well, you just received an email application from Axel Dekker for the position of 'administrative assistant' to the EVP for Academic Affairs and he is available to come to campus for interviews at your convenience." She handed him the file.

"Holly! How could you think that? Your job is very secure. Axel Dekker is a new PhD from Charles University who just received a two year post-doc from the European Union. To study and practice higher ed administration as a participant-observer. The EU pays him a salary wherever he goes. I think I'd like to hire him, but we shall see what others, including you, think when he comes for interviews. As soon as he has learned the ropes here, he could help both of us do our jobs. Life should get a little easier. Given the pace of work in this office, I think we could use him. So, do not, I repeat, do not even think about being replaced. You do a wonderful job. I am glad to have you here."

"Thank you, Dr. Cameron," Holly said, her face revealing relief at hearing the good news. "I'm happy to be here."

"Show me we have sealed the deal, then," Cameron said, as he raised his hand high above his shoulder in preparation for a 'high-five' expression of mutual agreement. Holly reciprocated, whereupon both smiled and went back to work.

As he read through his notes on the Liberal Arts interviews, the pattern of disagreements within each discipline that Cameron had suspected earlier became undeniable. Paired with Milton Quigley, senior professor of English and thoroughgoing defender of the literary canon taught as truth and beauty, came new assistant professor Victoria Ashcroft, radical feminist/lesbian/deconstructionist supreme, who attributed all of this world's problems to the evils of bourgeois, white male hegemony, especially the likes of Sophocles, Shakespeare, Keats, Hawthorne, Twain, Hemingway, Arthur Miller, and scores of others. Sporting tri-colored hair cut short, several visible tattoos and piercings but no traditional make-up, dressed in boots, fatigues and braless in a T-shirt, an angry Ashcroft spit out each word she had spoken about the absolute necessity to teach and write literature to empower women, African-Americans, Hispanics, native Americans, the LGBT community, the disabled, and the proletariat in general.

Coleman Williams, a senior professor of political science, provided the virtual polar opposite of the young Robert Rasmussen. Whereas Rasmussen called for a curriculum based on mathematical modeling and an inversion of the seniority pyramid, Williams found such ideas "amusing but dangerous" and praised the eternal wisdom of the revered statesmen and the instructional value of uniqueness in every case study ever done in political science. He chided the newer young political scientists as "barbarians at the gate" because "they equate knowledge about governing wisely with mathematical equations."

The advice given by the two music professors also struck a dissonant chord. The music theorist spoke ill of "those untrained jazz musicians who are no better than street musicians" and "don't know Mozart from Tchaikovsky." Just four interviews later, a professor of jazz studies, a pianist, broke what had seemed like a curse when he suggested to Cameron that at least the first four semesters of course work for music performance majors, both classical and jazz, should be the same. He argued that the curriculum at that level should push them to develop mastery of their instrument or voice and enable them to become facile with the technical and aesthetic aspects of music, any music. He also argued that classical students could benefit a lot from some training in improvisation, and the jazz students need more work in the European foundations and sight-reading. "First, you educate musicians, then you help them develop into whatever type of musician they want to be — classical, jazz, R and B, heck, I don't care, even rap as long as they're serious." *Finally*, Cameron thought to himself, *someone who appreciates the contributions of others in his department, not just his own.*

Both of the historians, on the other hand, provided more mutual disrespect than civility. The first, a full professor, was a traditionalist convinced of the superiority of early American history over that of any other time and place. He seemed to see the product of historians as very esoteric, arcane, and precious, appreciated by only a few of the finest intellects, and above all 'revealed" knowledge that must be protected by legions of impenetrable footnotes. His counterpart, a young, untenured Latin American historian, described himself as a "post-colonial liberationist" who believed that history is for the people. Footnotes misdirect attention, he argued, and besides, the only legitimate purpose of history is to inspire the contemporary underclass to throw off the chains that U.S. national government, U.S. multinational corporations, and traditionalist elites in Latin American countries use to exploit them. For a moment, Cameron thought of the old adage, "He who doesn't study history is doomed to relive it," and entertained the notion that maybe reliving it is not as bad as studying it, if either of these two historians is correct.

Although the two sociology professors disagreed, they did so without being disagreeable. One of them, although a fairly radical Marxist-feminist, was soft-spoken, dressed fairly conservatively, displayed no tattoos or piercings, and listened with respect when Cameron spoke. She was articulate and spoke in long sentences and complete paragraphs. Her requirements for curriculum reform were modest, concerned with exposing students to sophisticated ideas and theories about forms of social organization and their implications.

But, she moved from moderation to almost rage as she, on her own initiative, changed the topic to ASU's Riggs School of Business and the Law School. "But, Dr. Cameron, I don't think the University's big problems are within my department or any other department. The big problem is inequity *between* colleges in the University," she enunciated with more volume. "For example, take a look at business and law. Last year, I confronted an acquaintance in finance about his salary and mine, and here's what I learned," she announced as she retrieved a sheet of paper from her pocket.

"We both earned Big Ten doctorates and came to Alpha State the same year. I have published eighteen refereed journal articles and two academic books; he has eleven articles, no books, and about a dozen unpublished reports maintained as privileged by his corporate funders, so nobody else can read them. I don't know what the student evaluations of his teaching are, that's private information, too, but I know I have received two teaching awards since I came to Alpha State sixteen years ago, and he doesn't list any teaching awards on his résumé. I teach two courses per semester; he teaches one or two, depending on his 'other commitments'," and she used two hooked fingers of each hand to supply sarcastic quotation marks around the finance professor's explanation of his teaching load. "In the last five years, the average size of my undergraduate classes has been fifty-six students. His," and here she paused for dramatic effect, "thirty-nine. Do you think price is a function of supply and demand in this case? He consults with big corporations for money and the University places no limit on how much he can earn in extra income. Ever since I received tenure," and here she raised her volume enough to be heard through the walls into the outer office, "I have worked an average of ten hours per week, according to their records, for the New Cambridge Civil Liberties Union helping to investigate complaints of minority-group residents against government agencies or officials. I started as an intake interviewer, and now I serve on the executive board — for nothing."

"Sounds to me like your record would stack up quite well against any academic, here or elsewhere," Cameron said.

"Damn right," she said. "The university currently pays me $88,500 per academic year. They currently pay him $153,000 per academic year, according to the university's public records in the library. When I asked him why they pay him so much more than me, when my record is better than his, here is what the capitalist plutocrat said: 'They have to pay me more; otherwise they know I'd leave the university and go work for a bank or brokerage firm.' With a straight face, he said that!"

Cameron was familiar with salary differentials among academic departments, but he had never heard it illustrated with such verve.

"Is he so naïve," she continued, "that he thinks there is no difference in the job requirements of a professor of finance and a corporate financial analyst? If he worked for a corporation, he'd have no job security like tenure, he'd have to do whatever his boss tells him to do, and his hours on the job would double. But noooooo. At the university he gets it all — job security, fewer hours, freedom to set his own work agenda *and* a salary to compensate him as if he *didn't* have job security, fewer hours, and academic freedom. But the University pays him more with a smile. Plus he is allowed to consult for big bucks, with all of his 'free time'! And the same goes for that band of shysters in the School of Law. Let 'em join a big firm and find out what eighty-hour work weeks are like if they want the big money."

The Marxist-feminist gave Cameron much to think about. The other sociologist, three interviews later, had little or nothing intelligible to say. At the very beginning, when Cameron asked questions about curriculum reform, leadership, and planning, for each topic the sociological theorist responded with some variant of "That depends on your perspective."

"So what is your perspective on curriculum reform?" Cameron queried.

"Under some conditions, functionalism provides an optimal perspective, although Parsons did not always agree with Durkheim on ontological, epistemological, or metaphysical assumptions. It's been trendy since the sixties to rely on a conflict methodology, but despite Du Bois' contributions, no one has been able to theoretically integrate Fanon with the more traditional Marxist doctrines. On the other hand, it can be useful to conceptualize a curriculum as a site around which to construct a paradigmatic-interactionist perspective, but not everybody agrees that Blumer took us much beyond Mead in that respect. In any case, Tönnies has shown us that the latent functions of a curriculum, in any *Gesellschaft*, probably neutralize the best intentions of the curriculum designers."

After that response, Cameron drew the discussion to as quick a conclusion as civil discourse would permit, thanked the sociologist, and felt a great sense of relief when he exited. He also had a much clearer understanding of the idea that there is no such thing as a one-armed sociologist, because if you ask a sociologist a simple question, you always get, "Well, on one hand it is . . . but on the other hand you have . . . ."

Many scholars argue that, if somehow we were able to rank all of the academic disciplines with respect to their generalizability and usefulness, i.e., how well their principles apply and how useful they are to our practical understanding of the world, two disciplines would tie for first place: philosophy and physics. Some argue that in their upper reaches, these two disciplines are really only one, the study of the principles governing time, space, matter, and behavior. What is the nature of man and the universe? Whereas once these were very popular disciplines with crowded courses and many majors, both had fallen on relatively hard times. Because philosophy is concerned only with the general search for truth, which it considers a public good and, therefore, once discovered, must be free and available to everybody, it doesn't have great commercial value. But when philosophy is transformed into ideology and used in pursuit of self-interest, it becomes partisanship and power, investments and profits. Physics is similar in that regard. Transformed into technology and engineering, it produces material products that enhance the addictive qualities of consumerism and produce enormous revenue streams. For philosophy and physics, purity has brought them an aura of irrelevance. Theologians tell a story, only half in jest, that just might be true. When someday philosophers and physicists have studied everything and learned everything there is to know about time, space, matter, and behavior, when they remove the last impediment to human omniscience, they will find an impatient God sitting there, and he will say, "Well, it certainly took you guys long enough!"

Cameron wasn't sure what to expect from either philosopher that morning. What he discovered was that the discipline at Alpha State was rather deeply divided between traditionalists and modernists. The traditionalists saw man's salvation in the serious study of the philosophical texts from Plato and the Greeks through the nineteenth century European thinkers. The modernists favored the study and use of critical thinking, symbolic logic (a subfield of both mathematics and computer science), and empirical data to analyze a problem and to determine appropriate action relative to the problem. Each point of view calls for a different curriculum. Not much practical help there.

"Holly, put this in a confidential file, my eyes only, and yours if you're interested. If some of this were ever to get out, fistfights would follow," Cameron said, as he handed her a folder containing his extensive notes on the many interviews.

"Did you learn anything useful?" Holly asked.

Cameron paused to gather his thoughts. "Yes. Each department has its serious disagreements about what to study and teach and how to study and teach it. That's healthy. What's not so healthy is the way so many disciplines allow ego and commercial self-interest to dominate what and how they teach." With that, he started toward the door.

"Dr. Cameron, you asked me to remind you about some things you wanted to do this week," Holly said, looking at a list. "Set up a new scholarship fund for next year. Return a call from your friend at the University of Washington. Arrange for Axel Dekker to come to campus for interviews. Select members of the strategic planning committee and the curriculum reform committee. Plus numerous meetings have already been set for the next week — ASU alumni executive committee, you and President Faust are meeting with the officers of the New Cambridge Chamber of Commerce, the board of directors of the New Cambridge World Affairs Council, and several others."

As he walked back to his office from a late lunch at the cafeteria, he could hear the university marching band rehearsing on the soccer field. The first game would be a week from tomorrow, and local and national media had been on campus reporting and editorializing about every aspect of ASU football. Last year's team lost by a field goal in the national championship game, and only three starters had played out their eligibility and left the team. Most sports analysts had picked ASU as a pre-season top ten in the country. The buzz across campus had been about almost nothing else, as was always the case in early September. Cameron had enjoyed his brief meeting with Coach Paul

Sylvester earlier in the summer and had wished him well in the upcoming season, but he had not seen him since. That is why it was ironic, when Cameron entered his outer office, that Holly said to him, with a distressed look on her face, "Coach Sylvester's office called. He wants to see you right away. This afternoon. It's very important. You could do it at four."

"Okay, call him and arrange it."

Promptly at four, Holly escorted into Cameron's office not Coach Sylvester but defensive line coach Rudolph Greene, who announced in a deep voice, "Coach couldn't make it. Something came up and he sent me. I'm Coach Greene. We have a problem."

"I'm pleased to meet you Coach Greene. Have a seat. What's the problem? How can I help?"

Coach Greene, a handsome African-American who, at about age forty, stood at least five inches above Cameron's six feet, weighed right under three hundred pounds, and looked as if he could still play the game. His pecs and biceps stretched his XXXX-large ASU Eagles Football T-shirt. He sported a shiny, clean-shaven head and a demeanor somewhere between serious and hostile. In his college years, he was selected to the All-America Team. In his professional years, he made the All-Pro team because he was a quick, strong, ferocious tackler. After his pro career, he returned to ASU as the defensive line coach.

He fumbled with something in his pocket, and then pulled out a piece of paper. "Coach got this yesterday afternoon. He wants you to put a stop to it right now. It's insubordination. And when stuff like this gets out, it hurts us. The media can't resist this kind of," and here he paused, searching for a noun other than an expletive, "insubordination." He handed Cameron the paper and took a seat.

It was a memo under the letterhead of ASU's Department of Kinesiology, College of Education, addressed to Coach Paul Sylvester. Cameron read it to himself.

Dear Coach Sylvester,

Congratulations on your impressive accomplishments last year and good luck to you and the team as you begin another season. I join the thousands of people all over the state and nation in eagerly anticipating another sterling season of ASU football under your leadership. We continue, with considerable pride, to have several of your players majoring in exercise science and health promotion.

I write to ask a favor. Although I have just moved to New Cambridge to assume the position of chair of the Department of Kinesiology, I am aware of the cooperative relationship that has existed between your football program and our department. I know that when the game is close, referees sometimes use their discretion in calling penalties, mainly in order to keep the game under control and in the interest of promoting the greater good of the game – sportsmanship and honor. In the past, your assistant coaches have made that argument when they occasionally asked a professor in my department to reexamine a failing grade he or she had given to a football player to determine if it is really in the best interest of the player and the university. They have offered arguments in support of their requests such as, 'He's really a good kid,' and 'He works very hard,' and 'He gives us no trouble whatsoever,' and 'He comes from a poor, broken family, and just needs someone to give him a chance,' and 'He's destined for big things,' and 'How could it harm anybody?' and so forth. The evidence I have examined indicates that we have cooperated with your requests in several cases. Our cooperation has enabled players to stay in school, to remain eligible, and to win football games. Unfortunately, it has rarely enabled them to graduate.

Because you have asked for many such favors, and we have granted quite a few, I in turn, am asking you for one small favor. Taylor Banfield, one of our fourth-year seniors will graduate next May with majors in both teacher education and mathematics. It's too early to know for sure now, with two semesters to go, but he has a pretty good chance of finishing in the top ten percent of his class. He has decided to pursue a career of teaching math in junior or senior high school because he wants to help kids learn math and to help his country reestablish its credentials in math, science, technology and engineering so it can compete well in the world economy. He has received university awards in both math and education. He has a tuition scholarship from the University and has paid for his room and board and books and so forth by working in one of our dormitory cafeterias and tutoring at a couple of the local high schools. He is a really great kid, only twenty years old, from a large family.

He is also the fourth-string quarterback on your football team this season. You may not remember him. He has made the team every year but never played in a game. So the favor I ask is this: would you let him play quarterback a week from Saturday in the game against Western Kentucky University? Not the whole game, just the first quarter. He will give you his absolute best. His parents would love it. And it would mean so much to him. What harm could it do? WKU isn't in our conference. Bending a rule for the greater good is justified in this case. And what an inspiration it would be to thousands of ASU students whose genetics preordained them to be too small, too short, too thin, too weak, or too slow to earn a position on your team but who attend ASU anyway and earn degrees. So could you please give Banfield a break Saturday? He's number eleven.

If you think my request is really strange, you could turn this letter over to the local media in order to embarrass me. Or, I suppose I could turn this letter over to the local media along with documentation regarding favors you have asked for and we have granted. Or I suppose you could let Banfield play the first quarter against WKU. He's a really good student, a good Christian, and a fine young man.

The letter was signed, "Most sincerely yours, Wendell Conaway, Professor and Chair, Department of Kinesiology." Cameron managed to repress his urge to laugh and looked up at assistant coach Greene waiting for his comments. Greene stared back with almost angry concentration, as if waiting for the snap before charging through the line to maul an opposing quarterback.

"Coach Greene, tell Coach Sylvester that I will look into the matter, as you have requested. I will talk with Dr. Conaway and see if he can enlighten me a little about what this means." Here, Cameron paused to allow Coach Greene to speak. When he did not, Cameron asked, "Is there anything else you want to tell me about this letter?"

"There's nothing to it. It's all a bunch of baloney. You make sure this guy doesn't cause trouble just as we are starting the season. Who does he think he is?" Greene stood and began walking toward the door, without offering to shake hands or to say 'goodbye,' but stopped as he touched the door handle and turned toward Cameron. "Ya know what really gets me? These guys that do nothing but prance around in their classrooms and labs all day, get lifetime job guarantees, never break a sweat, never break a bone, never even get a bruise, and sure as hell couldn't, oh, sorry, sure couldn't attract a hundred thousand people to the campus six times every fall or get on national TV every time they play, or win bowl games, or bring fame and a fortune to ASU year after year and . . . ." Greene trailed off, then turned and ordered, "Coach says, 'Just take care of it so nobody gets hurt.'"

"As I said, Coach Greene, I will look into it and get back to you. But I have to ask you, again, are Dr. Conaway's allegations about his department doing favors for the football program true?"

"Not a word of it is true. Not one word. He's a trouble maker." With that, he opened the door and disappeared.

"Holly, could you get Dr. Conaway in Kinesiology, on the phone? And find out for me how much Coach Greene makes in annual salary. I'm curious."

In a few minutes, Holly responded, "Dr. Conaway is giving an all-day workshop at the annual meeting of the National Association of Collegiate Kinesiology in Chicago, but he will be back in town tomorrow. His secretary gave me his hotel room number, so I left a phone message at his hotel to have him call you at home tonight. Coach Greene's annual salary is $555,000."

"Fine, Holly. Thanks. And Holly, it's too late now, but first thing Monday morning, call Axel Dekker in Prague and find out when he can spend two full days here interviewing for that post-doc, and get him scheduled. Get him a room at the New Century. I'll supply you with a list of people who should meet with him so you can set up a schedule of interviews. Also, get me an appointment with the VP for Development early next week, to discuss setting up the new scholarship fund. And, I noticed that Chief Redden is on my schedule first thing after the meeting with Steve Faust on Monday morning. What's on his mind?"

"He said he just wants to pay his respects to the new EVP and to answer any questions you might have about campus security. He's at nine on Monday."

"Thanks, Holly. Sounds good. By the way, it's now six-thirty on Friday evening. I'm going home. Why don't you do the same?"

"Soon," she said, "I just have a few things to finish."

5 The fragrance of a strong Arabica blend seized Cameron for a moment as he exited the elevator on the third floor and walked to the right, down the thickly carpeted hall to President Faust's office for the regular Monday morning executive committee meeting. *Where does he get his coffee?* Cameron wondered to himself. *I must tell Holly to find out and get some for our office.* Despite having attended scores of academic meetings, some of which he chaired and some of which he simply attended, Cameron felt a little nervous going into this one.

"Its seven-thirty, people," announced President Faust, with Mrs. McInerny at his side ready to take notes, "so let's get started."

Committee members took their seats around the large, fine walnut conference table that must have weighed a ton. Four of the eleven vice presidents were women, three of whom had been appointed by President Faust. Eight of the eleven vice presidents had MBAs, the primary academic credential of business management, not PhDs, the terminal academic degree. The exception was the director of athletics, who had only an undergraduate degree from Boston College, where he had been a star quarterback and later the football coach. Gossip around the provost's office indicated that the athletic director's typical work day included eighteen holes of golf with friends, then lunch, then several rounds of drinks at the Nineteenth Hole, followed by a nap at home.

Just as Cameron noticed the absence of Zachary Kilgore, VP for Admissions and Records, but before he could evaluate the implications of that fact, he heard President Faust saying, "I am very pleased to formally introduce Drew Cameron, our new Executive Vice President for Academic Affairs and Provost. I hope all of you have had a chance to get to know him better in the past few weeks, because he is exactly the man we need to provide academic leadership to this university."

The entire group, including Faust and even the prim and proper Ms. McInerny, applauded and smiled their approval. Cameron was a little embarrassed by it all but appreciated the welcome from this important group. Faust continued, "Two of his primary goals this year are to organize a strong planning process for the university and to restructure the curriculum so that, as we turn our consumers into products, the labor market will value them highly. Drew, as you develop your strategy, keep this group informed. Their feedback is invaluable."

With that, Faust moved to the next item on his agenda. "I spent the past week in Colorado Springs at the annual meeting of the American University President's Association. I want to share with you three ideas we discussed there and get your input on them. We have talked about all three of them right here at this table before, but I think this year and next will be the time when the forward-thinking higher ed leaders around the country make their mark with some innovations. The first idea is identity branding, which got a lot of attention at the meeting this year. Margaret Benedict and I have talked about this a lot. Margaret, why don't you lay out the basics for us."

"In the field of public relations," Margaret began, "we have been concerned about identity branding for a long time. I have been nagging Steve about conducting a soup-to-nuts brand audit for well over a year. That's where I think we should begin — a thorough analysis of all our external and internal communications, some sample surveys of each of our different constituencies to determine their knowledge, attitudes, and practices regarding Alpha State, and several focus groups to dig deeper into how we could strengthen our image and our shareholders' identification with the Alpha State brand."

"I want you to think outside the box on this one, people. It's important," President Faust interjected.

"Crucial," Margaret agreed. "If the Alpha brand is to gain traction in the national and international higher ed markets, it has to be powerful and subtle at the same time."

The VP for Finance and Administration spoke up, "If we don't grow, we don't survive. So to expand market share, we have to increase the number of consumers of our products. That means not just more students but more demand for more of our goods and services of whatever kind. So how does identity branding do that?"

"It helps us make ASU synonymous with college education state-wide and even nationally," Margaret answered. "Think of what Xerox did. They made their name synonymous with the verb, "to copy". Think of Kleenex. Think of

Band-Aid. They made their corporate names the generic names for their products and have dominated the market."

"Margaret is on target," Faust added, "and as she can tell you in detail, our plan is not only to make ASU synonymous with college education but with sports, entertainment, apparel, patriotism, progress, and their personal identities – not just for our students, but for our alumni and everybody in the state and beyond. We've got to move on. Keep identity branding in mind. Margaret will touch base with you periodically as we initiate our campaign. Next topic —strategic partnering, which lies mainly in Innovation and Economic Development, so Susan Deutsch will start us off."

"Forming a mutually beneficial, strategic alliance with a corporation or business organization in pursuit of a shared goal — that's partnering," Deutsch instructed. "The key words are 'strategic' and 'shared goal', both of which mean the same thing. 'Strategic' refers to why we do what we do, not how we do it. 'Shared goal' refers to net benefit when we do what we do, measured anyway you wish, but the standard measure of our net benefit is, of course, profit in U.S. dollars."

"And how do we get partner buy-in?" asked the handsome VP for Information Technology from New Delhi in his British-accented English. His vice presidential colleagues occasionally said, behind his back, that he thinks and sometimes speaks in asymptotes and algorithms rather than words and sentences. "I have discussed this idea with CEOs and managers of several software companies and they don't seem to understand." It was true that his Cal Tech doctoral training in computer science sometimes made it difficult for him to engage in conventional conversations with normal people, even normal computer software people.

"Subodh, you can't get them interested in partnering if you talk in polynomials and vectors," Deutsch said, which brought respectful laughter from her colleagues, including Subodh. "You have to talk to them about the commercial application of technologies and how they can improve their bottom line if they work with us," Susan Deutsch stated. "If they partner with us, we create synergy. And profit. And enhance our brand identity. My office will set up some workshops on partnering for all of you. We'll send you an email."

"Partnering requires a paradigm change for us," President Faust said. "Historically, most public universities taught undergraduates, conducted research, gave away the results as a public good, and often served the mainly underserved segments of society for free. Okay, let's finish with a brief discussion of rightsizing – the art and science of reducing personnel costs but continuing to provide the promised service. Most of the presidents I talked to at the conference really like the way ASU's uses casual faculty — graduate students, post-docs, temporary part-time lecturers, adjunct professors, and other non-tenure track teachers. It meets classroom demand at a lower cost. I also told them that we make sure we still have plenty of the right kind of tenured and tenure-track faculty in those departments that get a lot of big research contracts, from industry and the feds, and produce big overhead funds."

Subodh raised his hand again, and President Faust said, "Go ahead, Subodh."

"We must not forget the important role that courseware and distance education can play in reducing costs and increasing profits. The technical people in Continuing Ed can work with a professor to produce an entire course on line — lectures, discussions, tutoring, tests, scoring tests, final grade, everything. These on-line courses can be offered to students all over the world for years, with only small modifications over time, for the same fee that a regular on-campus course earns. It is very profitable."

"You are exactly right, Subodh. Why don't you say a few words about that newest kind of on-line course you're developing. What's it called?

"It is called 'MOOC,' President Faust. MOOC stands for a massive, open, on-line course," Subodh answered. It's offered to anyone with a computer, anywhere on earth, and it is free. It's the next big thing in on-line courses."

After a moment of thoughtful silence, Susan Deutsch asked, "How does a MOOC make any money if it's free?"

"Excellent question, Susan. Access to an ASU MOOC will be free to about 100,000 people in Asia. However, if one of those students wants a certificate or credential saying he completed or passed the MOOC, it will cost him, say, $50 to $100. Initial studies show that seventy-two to eighty-four percent of the students who complete a MOOC want to receive the credential. Also, we charge companies that want to hire employees for matching their needs with our MOOC students. And, we can sell the names of our MOOC students who do not do so well to for-profit universities so they can try to recruit them as students for their on-line offerings. Plus, we can charge our better MOOC students for extras, such as awarding them actual academic credit for a MOOC. We can also sell access to any of our MOOC courses to small colleges and universities."

"Thanks, Subodh," Faust said. "Last year I asked Subodh to develop this MOOC idea ASAP. About a year ago I had lunch with the CEO of Dynamic Electronics in New York, and he went on and on about how much they had increased their profits by outsourcing to India. So we are going to do the same thing with our MOOC. We can pay Indian educators and technologists about fifteen percent of what we have to pay Americans to do the same work, to develop our MOOC products."

"And they do it very well," Subodh joined in. "The market is large and growing, and our profits will grow, too."

"Oh, we must talk, Subodh," exclaimed an enthusiastic Susan Deutsch. "What an incredible idea!"

"Okay," President Faust interrupted. "Subodh, Susan, I am charging you two with co-chairing Alpha State's effort to get into the MOOC business ASAP and big time. We will talk later to come up with three more people to serve on a committee with you to operationalize this idea pronto."

An enthusiastic discussion of opportunities to increase profits via branding, partnering, rightsizing, and MOOC continued for several more minutes. President Faust adjourned the meeting at eight-thirty, and the participants promptly gathered their notebooks and papers and left for their own offices. Cameron felt uneasy about the tone of the meeting. In all his years in academic life, he had never heard a long discussion of academic policy expressed completely in terms of corporate profit and totally devoid of any reference to ways to serve the students and society more effectively. *Is it just ASU or are other universities becoming this way now? Does it have to be this way?* he asked himself. As soon as the other VPs had gone, Cameron approached Faust and said, "Thanks for your very flattering introduction, Steve. Got time for one quick question?"

"Of course, Drew. What's on your mind?"

"I couldn't help noticing that Zachary Kilgore wasn't at the meeting this morning. I wanted to talk with him about this apparent mix-up with his résumé. We need to get it cleared up as soon as possible. One way or another."

"He and his family are on vacation, Drew. They always take a couple of weeks in early September. That's when his work is slack, so he gets out of town for a while. Ms. McInerny can tell you when he gets back, I don't remember. So let's just put this résumé thing on hold until we can get him back to clear it up. Okay?"

"Sure. Will do."

As soon as Cameron walked into his own outer office from the corridor, he saw ASU Police Chief Charles Redden sitting in the waiting area near Holly's desk. She rose and moved toward her boss to explain that the chief is here to see him.

Redden, a much-decorated career law enforcement officer, started as a rookie in the New Cambridge Department of Police, worked his way up to the rank of captain and served as one of three deputy chiefs during his last five years on the force. Many people said he would have made a great chief, but his rigid, no-nonsense approach to the job and his unwillingness to play politics alienated some of the city council members. He had retired from the New Cambridge force last year at the age of sixty-two. When ASU's chief of police resigned only a couple of weeks before Cameron was announced as the new EVP, the New Cambridge chief recommended Redden for the vacant position.

President Faust and a committee selected Redden as ASU's new chief in late June, about the time Cameron joined ASU.

"It's good to meet you," Cameron said as they shook hands.

"Thank you, uh, Vice President Cameron. Same here. Or should I call you Provost Cameron?" the campus police chief asked.

"Neither. How about Drew?"

"Of course, and I'm Charlie."

"Good," Cameron responded, as Holly closed the door behind her. "What's on your mind this morning, Charlie?"

"The reason I'm here looks like a serious matter, and I have come to you for advice on how to proceed. May we go . . . off the record?"

Cameron was surprised by Chief Redden's request but said, "Yes. We are off the record. Now, what's the problem, Charlie?"

The chief continued, "Since I was eighteen, I have been in uniform, either in the U.S. Army or the New Cambridge Police Department or at Alpha State. While I was in the Army in Germany, I earned a college degree through the University of Maryland extension program. I am a very firm believer in following the chain of command. The University organization chart says I report to you. So here I am."

Redden cleared his throat and continued, "When I first became chief here, a few weeks ago, I had several long briefing sessions with each of my senior staff in the department. Sgt. Lovell, our chief data person, said she suspected that someone was tampering with campus crime statistics that the ASU Police Department collects. She said for the last few years the ASU crime stats that appear in the media, especially in the *American News Weekly* magazine annual college edition, are always lower than the stats she tabulates in the department and reports to the University Records Office. She compared last year's crime stats on our hard drive to former chief Doug Wood's handwritten report, which is based on tabulating officer's incident reports. We still have the hard-copy originals locked in a file. His hand-tabulated report matches the individual officer's incident reports. Sgt. Lovell said the figures on our hard drive do not match the former chief's own handwritten report, but they did match the figures that appeared in the media reports."

Cameron refrained from asking any of the half-dozen questions that came to mind. Rather, he waited for a few seconds until the Chief paused, and then said, "Please go on."

"I knew something was wrong. I've been a cop for over forty years, so I think like a cop."

"Cops and scientists think a lot alike, don't they? Both want to know what the problem is and how it can be solved," Cameron added, now becoming more comfortable with Redden's credibility.

"I guess so, Drew. The problem, as you say, was the difference between the two sets of figures — the former chief's calculations and the data reported in the media. All I could figure is that somebody had altered the figures. For several years, Alpha State has had only one person on the force who does all our data entry, Sgt. Sylvia Lovell, and she's also certified as a beat cop. She's one of us."

"Did you talk with her?"

"I did. I am convinced that she entered the actual crime incident data that the previous chief had given her from his original tabulation just as he instructed — the real figures for the real cases we processed in the Department. Only Sgt. Lovell and I have the password to enter data on our computer system."

"Then who altered the figures?"

"This is where I need your assurance that we are speaking in strictest confidence, Dr. Cameron . . . Drew. I don't know who altered the figures but I know how to find out. Sgt. Lovell has some training in computer programming, but not enough to do the computer forensics we need to find out who falsified that information."

"So who can?

"I already called in a favor from an old friend, a retired FBI computer forensics specialist, now working for a private security firm in New Cambridge. This is all off the record."

Another long pause ensued. "Charlie, does this story have a happy ending?"

"I'm not sure," the University Chief of Police said, shaking his head.

"Why not? It sounds like you already have a solution to the problem," Cameron said, hoping to reassure the Chief.

"It's the possible solution that worries me."

"How so?" Cameron asked, by this time suspended between spellbound and impatient.

"My computer forensics friend was able to determine that the data on the Police Department hard drive was altered, but not by someone using one of the computers in our office. It was altered by . . . ." and Chief Redden stopped speaking and stared at the floor for several seconds. "Someone, using a computer registered to the University Office of Admissions and Records, hacked into the Police Department computer system and altered last year's official record of campus crime statistics. That action took place late at night on October 20. Earlier that same morning, my office had sent the crime data to Records as an attachment to an email, as we do every year. The crime stats we originally entered on our permanent record, the accurate ones, are higher for every felony crime than the data the University reported to the media and, even more important, to the FBI. That's a violation of the Clery Act," Chief Redden said with shame in his voice.

"Remind me of what's in the Clery Act?"

"It's a federal law passed back in the early 1990s requiring college campuses to report all felony offenses to the FBI each year, in a timely fashion. All campuses also have to provide this information to the media. And, it authorizes the Department of Education to levy a $27,500 fine, per violation, per year, on any college that doesn't comply and to take away all of their federal student financial aid."

"Okay, Charlie, where do we go from here?"

"We know which desk-top in Records was used to alter the Police Department stats. It's still in operation there, and we know the date and time it was done. I have a plan that I want you to consider, Drew. It might, just maybe, lead us to the perpetrator," the Chief said, returning to his more professional conversational style.

"Please go on," Cameron said.

"The normal date on which the Police Department has reported campus crime stats to Records for the last several years is October 20, two weeks from tomorrow. Let's assume that the person or persons who falsified the crime data on the Police Department hard drive from a desk-top in Records last year does it again this year, late on the night of the day we report to Records. We can set up an electronic stake-out in advance and, if history repeats itself, catch him or her in the act. My FBI friend has never done this kind of digital surveillance for a university, but he has done it in the private sector many times and will do it for us if we request it."

Encouraged, Cameron said, "I like the plan. It just might work. I will authorize it under one condition — that we keep it on a strict need-to-know basis until we have results. You, me, your FBI forensics friend, and the sergeant you mentioned, that's it. Agreed?"

"Yes, sir," stated Chief Redden, in a voice reflecting a lifetime of military and police discipline.

"Okay. Set it up and keep me informed."

As Chief Redden left the office, Cameron tried to relax despite the unexpected dynamics of their conversation for the past half hour. First came the low of learning about ASU's falsified crime statistics. Then the high of Chief Redden's excellent work in determining that his Police Department computer system had been hacked. Then the low of learning the location of the hacker's computer – Admissions and Records. Then the high of Chief Redden's plan to catch the perpetrator. Then the low of anticipating what person, with access to computers in Admissions and Records, might be the perpetrator, and why. Cameron reasoned that in two weeks, they would either know the identity of the perpetrator or they wouldn't, but he was not sure which he preferred. He knew that sometimes an action taken to solve a problem does solve the problem, but has unintended, unexpected, undesirable consequences. Sometimes these "uncons" constitute another problem worse than the original. Success becomes a nightmare. He had two weeks before Redden would implement his sting operation and time to get some other important things done.

The next morning, Holly almost accosted him at the outer door with good news. "We received an email from Dr. Dekker in Prague very early this morning, regarding his visit to interview for the administrative assistant position. He will arrive on Tuesday, November 29 and depart on Saturday, December 3. He is booked to stay at the Colonial. I'll set up interviews with the people whose names you gave me, and arrange for his pick-up and delivery at the airport. Anything else on Dekker?"

"Perfect, Holly. Nothing else that I can think of right now. Thanks, again."

"Between now and then, your calendar is already getting crowded."

"Business is good," Cameron said, and then winced as he remembered the business terminology in the Executive Committee's discussion of partnering, right-sizing, identity-branding and MOOCs yesterday, which reminded him of President Faust's apparent lack of concern about Vice President Kilgore's résumé.

He turned to Holly and said, "Prepare a letter, for my signature, to the official in charge of academic records at the University of Washington in Seattle asking for verification of all degrees awarded to Zachary Kilgore."

"Two more things, Dr. Cameron. We need to schedule times for you to interview the four finalists for the new Westerveldt Chair in Intellectual Leadership. You know, the 'super chair.'"

"Remind me again who they are, Holly."

"They're from History, English, Finance, and Engineering."

"Okay. Set them up, one hour each, on separate days, during the morning," Cameron requested, as he started to walk toward his office. Then he stopped, and asked, "What's the other thing, Holly?" with mock impatience.

"Your meeting with President Faust and the Chamber of Commerce officials has been moved. It was supposed to occur next month, but now it's Friday at noon."

"Great. Tell Ms. McInerny that I'll be happy to drive if President Faust wants a ride."

Cameron intended to spend the rest of the afternoon catching up on communications – phone, email, and postal. After an uninterrupted hour, for which he was grateful, Holly buzzed him with a message. "I have Music on the phone, Jazz Studies director Carson Mitchell. He says it's urgent."

"Put him through," Cameron said.

"Dr. Cameron? It's Carson Mitchell in Music. How are you?"

"Fine, Carson. And how are you?" Cameron said, even though he could not remember ever meeting Carson Mitchell.

"Great. I'm sorry to bother you. I know you're busy. But I have an offer for you and your wife, if you're available and interested. You might not have heard, but Friday night, Ellis Marsalis is playing a gig in our concert hall, and I thought you might like to hear him. Somebody told us you like jazz so maybe you have heard of Ellis Marsalis?"

After recovering from his initial surprise, Cameron answered, "I'm a big fan of his. In fact, I have several of his CDs. He's one of my favorite jazz pianists," and paused again before adding, "and I think we are free on Friday night. Thanks for the heads up. What time is the concert?"

"It's at eight. And we have reserved two complimentary tickets for you, right down front, as a way to welcome you to ASU. If you're interested, we'll set aside season tickets for you and your wife for any concerts we or visiting musicians do for the rest of the year. Just give us a day's notice if you can't make it. And by the way, we hope you both can come to a small reception afterwards. You can meet Mr. Marsalis in person."

"Thank you very much Carson. We will be there."

How nice of them, Cameron thought, as his mood shifted from frenetic problem-solving to melodic improvisation around a theme of happy anticipation. He dug back into his work with renewed vigor, up-tempo and straight ahead.

On the following day at mid-morning, he studied the résumé of Alexander Robertson in anticipation of an interview with the first candidate for the "super chair." When a private donor gives the university money to endow a chair, the funds are invested in secure stocks and bonds. The University uses the annual interest income to supplement an already large full professor salary and to provide various perks to attract a big name in whatever academic field the donor had specified. Perks can include a travel budget, funds for equipment and books, and so forth. President Faust had agreed to the donor's stipulation that the first Westervelt Chair would go to someone already on the ASU faculty. When invested well, the three million dollar gift would generate over one hundred thousand more to supplement the chair. This could mean an annual income of two to three hundred thousand dollars for an occupant of the chair, depending on the occupant's academic field.

Cameron had never met Alexander Robertson. Robertson already had a limited teaching schedule, which allowed him to be away from campus more than his colleagues in the Department of History. His résumé indicated that he had come to Alpha State directly from Princeton University, where he had earned a doctorate in history. His rather lengthy dissertation, *Roosevelt, Eisenhower, and*

Reagan: Profiles in Modern American Leadership, had been published by a major commercial publisher as a three-volume series, which had won a prestigious national award. As a result, he transcended some of the ASU and state rules governing the granting of tenure and promotions and, only six years later at the relatively tender age of thirty-two, was promoted to full professor with tenure, a rare event in the academic profession. His scholarly output was very impressive. His books were praised in scholarly history journals and in the *New York Review of Books.* His critics claimed that his work was short on footnotes and rather too "imaginative" in connecting and explaining events or actions while presenting little relevant evidence. His fans, on the other hand, argued that his analysis was clear, as much for the educated layperson as for the professional historian, and stressed human interest in historical detail. Regardless of who was right, several of his books had risen to the top ten on the *New York Times'* non-fiction bestseller list. Some of his critics, indeed some of his colleagues in Alpha State's Department of History, argued that his work could more appropriately appear on the *New York Times'* bestseller list for works of fiction.

Writing a book that gets into the top ten of the *New York Times* bestseller list generates considerable income, additional publishers' offers of large advances, well-paid book-signing tours and lectures, and reviews of the books in popular magazines and newspapers - in short, wealth and fame. Cameron saw from examining Robertson's almost book-length résumé the progression from occasional interviews on New Cambridge radio and TV stations to frequent NPR and PBS invitations to appear on one of their shows to discuss his latest book. Then came invitations from many of the national electronic media to grant interviews to be aired on their nightly news casts or to appear on their Sunday morning TV news shows as an expert commentator. Many of those who knew him at ASU sometimes wondered how he managed to publish a new book every two years and travel so much to appear on radio and TV. Some of his colleagues resented that the media now consult him, and that he agreed to appear, as an expert commentator on trends and events far beyond his certified credentials in contemporary U.S. political history. Some even alleged that he operated a clandestine research firm, in or near Washington, D.C., whose employees were young, all-but-dissertation historians who actually conducted the basic research and wrote the first drafts of his books. There also had been a plagiarism charge brought against him in a law suit by another author who claimed that Robertson had quoted a lengthy passage of his work without proper citation. Because the judge sealed the records and ordered both authors to maintain silence about the decision, no one outside the suit knew what had happened for sure. All that Cameron knew was that, although Dr. Alexander

Robertson, Professor of History, was relatively young, he had a very strong record as a candidate for the Westerveldt Chair in Intellectual Leadership — and that Steve Faust had praised him for all the favorable publicity his TV and radio appearances had brought to ASU.

As he closed the résumé file, he heard Holly's knock on his door, whereupon she escorted the handsome, blond, blue-eyed, historian into the office. He was dressed in an expensive, tailored navy blue suit, light blue dress shirt, and a red, black, and grey rep tie. His tanned, Hollywood-handsome face featured perfectly white teeth and a confident smile that, in combination with his intense blue eyes, exuded both charm and a need to be somewhere else soon.

He looked straight at Cameron, extended his hand, and said, "Alexander Robertson, Provost, Alexander Robertson. I am so glad to meet you, so very glad. I have wanted stronger academic leadership in this office for some years and you … are … the right man for this job."

"Thanks for coming to see me. I have been looking forward to meeting you ever since arriving at ASU," Cameron said. "Please sit, be comfortable, and let's talk about the Westerveldt Chair. My role in this process is to interview each of the finalists selected by the faculty committee and then to make a final choice. Your résumé is impressive."

"Two very important items are missing from the publications section," Robertson replied. "After seeing the prospectus, Knobbs-Baldwin Publishers awarded me a handsome advance for another book, entitled *Innocents Abroad: American Military Misadventures from Viet Nam to Libya*. After reading the prospectus and a chapter, Herbert Minton at Yale called it 'patriotic criticism' of modern U.S. military policy. Second, Colt and Middleton Publishers just last week gave me a sizeable advance for another manuscript, almost finished, that I'm calling *To Have and To Have Not: Wealth and Poverty in Twenty-first Century America*."

"How do you turn out so many books year after year?"

"Jon Stewart asked me the same question on *The Daily Show*. Get up early, know what's important, analyze it better, work harder and longer, say it with more clarity," the Westerveldt Chair nominee answered. And as he asserted each of his tenets of high-level academic productivity, he inched forward in his chair, widened his deep blue eyes, and stared straight at Cameron. With his last assertion about saying it better, he sat on the edge of his overstuffed leather chair as if poised to defend in case of disagreement.

"Words to the wise, I'm sure," Cameron said, and began to understand why a one-hour conversation with an arrogant braggart seems much longer. "In your *vitae*, you call yourself a 'public intellectual.' What is a 'public intellectual,' and how does it relate to the Westerveldt Chair?"

"Gwen Ifill first called me a public intellectual when she interviewed me on PBS *News Hour*. A public intellectual provides unbiased interpretation of current affairs – the important trends, events, personalities, etc. – for the people in the society he serves. It's a role that used to be played by leaders mainly in government, religion, and journalism, but now, only higher education can do it, for two reasons. First, government, religion, and journalism have sold out. Government leaders have become slaves to partisan ideologies and self-interest. Religious leaders have become captives of dogma, cover-ups, and bitter sectarian distrust. Journalists now work for media owned by just a few large multinational corporations; they focus on celebrity personalities and sensationalism and seldom analyze events in proper historical time or social space. Second, we now live in the digital age — radio, television, the computer, I-pads and I-phones. The public intellectual now must master not only the techniques of analysis and writing but of oral and visual presentation. The few with good analytical and writing skills have squeaky voices, or can't answer a simple yes-or-no interview question in fewer than three minutes, or don't know how to dress for visual media, or don't know how to look at the camera, or they need a teleprompter to discuss an issue, or, forgive me, they are just plain physically unattractive. Fortunately, there are a few of us in higher education who can do the job of the public intellectual."

"I see," Cameron answered. What he saw was a self-obsessed, self-promoting, ambitious and probably brilliant historian. *Despite that, can he fulfill the obligations of a super-chair holder?* Cameron wondered. "If you become the new Westerveldt Chair occupant, what is the first thing you would do?"

"I'd call my friend, Chuck Todd, to let him know, and soon I'd be on *Meet the Press*, again. And I'd get calls right away from Diane Rehm and Michele Norris to tape a segment for their NPR shows, and probably from Mika Brzezinski on MSNBC. Since the day I said some nice things about her book on women in America, she has called me twice to appear on their morning show. Her dad introduced me to her."

"So you know Zbigniew Brzezinski?" Cameron asked, wondering whether to be impressed with Robertson's connections or appalled at his shameless namedropping.

"Sure. Last year, when we were both waiting to appear on MSNBC's *Morning Joe*, he asked me how I liked living in New Cambridge and working at ASU. And why I wasn't 'back East where I belonged' as he put it. And a few months ago I got a feeler from Johns Hopkins, where Brzezinski works, asking me if I'd be interested in their full professor vacancy. So, I have that and an almost sure thing at Emory to fall back on if this doesn't work out."

"Are you considering leaving ASU?" Cameron asked.

"To be honest, I am in the best position to make this Westerveldt Chair and ASU world renowned. In fact, I am already doing it. Do you realize how many times NPR, the three major TV networks, CNN, PBS, and numerous print media come to our campus to interview me, electronically or in person? It's in my résumé. I attract more good students to ASU than winning football does," he said with apparent scorn. "In the last two years, I have gotten more media time for ASU than Sabato, Kearns Goodwin, Harris-Perry, Toobin, or any of the others have gotten for their schools. And I publish books and do some teaching, too. Even undergraduate teaching."

"I see your point, Alexander. Anything else I should consider in making a decision on the Westerveldt Chair?"

"Yes. Just remember, universities have the primary responsibility to seek the common good through factual knowledge. That cannot be done with more tales of love and tragedy, or more techniques for the money changers to fortify the temple, or better alchemy for the pharmacorp robber-barons."

With that statement, they stood and shook hands, and Robertson left. It was some time later that Cameron grasped the meaning of Robertson's final statement. With "tales of love and tragedy" he referred to fiction — writing novels. "Money changers" referred to Wall Street bankers. "Better alchemy" referred to pharmaceutical corporations that monopolize the market with their high-priced drugs by legally preventing the sale of generics that are just as effective but cheaper. One of Robertson's three competitors for the Westerveldt Chair was a novelist in the English Department who had published a dozen or so romantic novels set during or right after World War II. Another candidate was a financial economist in the School of Business who developed the mathematics underlying securitized credit derivatives that Wall Street bankers use and which contributed to the 2008 recession. Third was a biochemical engineer who had generated millions in funding to conduct proprietary research under contracts with pharmaceutical corporations that sometimes prohibited publication of the results but allowed awarding patents to one of their off-shore subsidiaries. Robertson's final statement had been a slightly disguised knife in the back of each of his three competitors for the Westerveldt chair.

Somewhat bewildered by "public intellectual" Alexander Robertson's combination of brilliance and brazenness, Cameron turned to his computer to respond to any important email messages that had come in since noon. Before he had finished answering the second email, Holly knocked and entered.

"Dr. Cameron, I have a five-fifteen dental appointment, so if it's okay I'll take off now."

"Sure, Holly. See you tomorrow."

An hour later, he was half way home on the interstate when it occurred to him that his purpose in coming to Alpha State University was to "drain the swamp," figuratively speaking, but he had soon found himself "neck-deep in alligators" and had forgotten the real purpose of his mission. He resolved to refocus on his main goals as he turned into his driveway.

At home, he found Vanessa in a comfortable chair on the patio, looking through a stack of mail. "Do I have news for you," he said as he came up behind her and gave her a kiss on top of her head. We have a pair of tickets to the Ellis Marsalis concert at the University, tomorrow night. And we are going to dinner before the concert. How does that sound?"

"Just wonderful, my dear. Perfect. It's time we did something fun in our new town, something besides work. And I have news for you. Today I realized that back in June, I signed up to take the state bar exam for a date this fall. Guess what? That date is next Tuesday morning. I hope I'm ready."

"Great. You're ready. You will knock the top off," Cameron said.

They continued discussing the bar exam while they enjoyed a glass of Cabernet and prepared dinner. Cameron grilled hamburgers on the patio and Vanessa readied tomatoes, pickles, onions, ketchup for him, mustard for her, and iced tea. It was almost seven when they sat down to eat. Then, a quick clean-up of dinner dishes, an hour of work, the news on TV, then off to bed for a restful sleep to prepare for tomorrow's challenges.

"You've already had several important calls this morning, Dr. Cameron," Holly announced as he stepped from the hallway into his outer office. "And good morning."

"And good morning to you, Holly. Who called?"

"Ms. McInerny called to say that President Faust has another meeting downtown after today's meeting with the Chamber of Commerce, so he'll be taking his own car. She emailed you a copy of the Chamber's agenda. It's on your desk. He sends his apology and will see you at the meeting. Chief Redden called to say that the plan you and he agreed to is now fully operational," she quoted from her telephone notes, "and he says to let him know if you want to join him to observe the results. Music called to say that all your season tickets will be at the will-call window tonight. The rest of the messages are either on your desk, or I already took care of them."

"Good. How's your tooth?"

"I'm the proud owner of a new crown, my third," Holly answered. "Thank you for asking."

Cameron sat at his desk and began reading the agenda for the Chamber of Commerce meeting. The first several items were the standard protocol for most formal meetings — call to order, recognition of any special guests, approval of last meeting's minutes, treasurer's report, old business, new business. The subheadings under "old business" included partnership with Alpha State University — STEM research, investment, and economic development. He immediately recognized the meaning of the acronym, STEM – science, technology, engineering, and math.

He was surprised when he saw two of the items under new business. First was a report from Alpha State University's new Executive Vice President on academic reform and strategic planning. Cameron wondered why Faust hadn't warned him that he would be on the agenda to discuss curriculum and planning. The meeting was to begin in a little over three hours, and he was not prepared to make a formal presentation to the entire Chamber.

The second agenda item that startled him, but in a positive way, was listed as "New Cambridge Transit Authority". This item jogged Cameron's memory of his time in Prague when Anna Zelzulka asked him to arrange for her to meet with Transit Authority officials and to propose that the Czech company supply the street cars for the New Cambridge transit system. He wondered what had happened to that idea since he had sent the letter to NCTA suggesting that they consider it and contact Anna Zezulka.

But he had no more time to think about these two matters because he had to preside over two important meetings, back to back — a shorter one in the provost's conference room with his own staff concerning the distribution of responsibility for academic matters in the various colleges among his assistant vice presidents and a longer one with the whole faculty of the College of Natural Sciences on design of their new classroom and lab building.

At noon, when he emerged from the elevator on the twelfth floor of the luxurious downtown hotel, Cameron was surrounded by Chamber members — corporate CEOs, attorneys, industry managers, downtown business executives, bankers, real estate executives, and a few state and local government leaders. When he heard someone call his name he turned and saw Steve Faust in a brisk walk toward him.

"Drew, hi. Sorry I couldn't take you up on your offer of a ride, but my plans got changed. Let me introduce you to a few people you need to know." For the next ten minutes, Cameron shook hands, exchanged introductory greetings and talked ASU football with a dozen or more people with impressive titles on their business cards. Then, as if on cue, the members began taking their seats.

"Drew, are you going straight back to campus after this meeting?" President Faust asked.

"Yes. I hope to get some paperwork done and cut out a little early. Vanessa and I have reservations for an early dinner at *Le Jardin*, then to the Ellis Marsalis concert on campus."

"Splendid. *Le Jardin*, huh? I'll make a call and get René to take good care of you. Sounds like a wonderful evening. Good food, good music. When you get back to campus, I want you to make a call for me. I promised Michele Murray you'd call her this afternoon to schedule an appointment. She's an engineer. She's very intellectual and says she wants to support academic programs, nothing else. We haven't discussed any details yet — how much or for what. Here's her private number at Murray Robotics. See what you can work out with her. It's time for you to get involved with fundraising."

"Of course. I'll let you know how the conversation goes."

While dessert was being served, the Chamber president rapped three times to call the meeting to order. Cameron rose to a robust round of applause when the president welcomed him as the new Executive Vice President at Alpha State and the "new go-to man at ASU when Steve Faust is out of town." Cameron found the reception a little embarrassing.

U.S. Senator Earl Broadbent walked in late, shook a few hands, and flashed a broad smile as he walked to a seat, guided by a Chamber staff member. The senator, a life-long resident of New Cambridge, was a senior member of the powerful Senate Committee on Appropriations, so he was a popular and powerful celebrity in the state. The presiding officer acknowledged his presence as the members applauded.

The program continued to move along as dishes were cleared from the tables. When his time came, Steve Faust gave a brief but impressive report on ASU's continuing efforts in support of state and regional economic development. He concluded with two major points. "First, you should know that the university is placing much greater emphasis on innovative but practical STEM research - science, technology, engineering, and math - which is most relevant to local, state, and regional economic development. Second, our Division of Innovation and Economic Development is prepared to help you convert your innovative ideas into proposals, patents, and profits. I am also happy to report that we are very close," and here he paused to look straight at Cameron, "to being ranked by *American News Weekly* as one of the top thirty public universities in America." Again the meeting erupted into applause for Faust and ASU.

Next came several committee reports, one of which concerned plans for a new metropolitan streetcar and high-speed rail system. Then, Cameron provided a brief summary of preliminary work accomplished to date on curriculum reform and a planning process, and sat down to polite applause. The meeting adjourned at 1:40 PM, and Cameron spent another ten minutes meeting members, including several ASU alums, as they sought him out to introduce themselves and to wish him luck in his new position. Steve Faust, standing behind the semi-circle of members talking with Cameron, said in an exaggerated stage whisper, "I'm off to another meeting, see you next week, Drew." So as not to interrupt the conversation of any of his new acquaintances, Cameron merely winked and nodded a slight bow toward Faust. Faust nodded and left.

Later, as Cameron was leaving, a younger man walked beside him and, in a quiet voice, said, "Dr. Cameron, I'm Charlie Kempton, chief of engineering for the City of New Cambridge. Do you have a minute?"

"Of course, Charlie. I'm pleased to meet you."

"I want to let you know what has happened to the information you brought back from Prague this summer. Mayor DelVecchio, a month or so ago, appointed me to chair a small committee of transportation engineers and management people. Our orders are to select three firms that build streetcars, give them our preliminary specs for the city's new streetcar system, and request proposals to supply our first twenty or so cars in a few months."

"Great to hear that the city is making progress, Charlie. I don't know anything about building a good streetcar system — I'm no engineer — but I was impressed with the Czech government official who told me about their streetcar manufacturing company."

"We are moving fast now, Dr. Cameron. Based on your recommendation, we did some serious research on Moravian Motorworks in the Czech Republic, and they look good. So I'm pretty sure we will ask them to submit a bid. Three of us will be making a site inspection in Prague next week, so we will know for sure then."

Both surprised and pleased, Cameron said, "Thanks for keeping me informed, Charlie. I wish you luck in choosing three good firms. Public transit will be a boon to New Cambridge, so I hope you get the best. As soon as it can be public information, let me know what you and the committee think about Moravian Motorworks."

"That's up to Mayor DelVecchio and the city attorney, but we can probably tell you, Dr. Cameron." Glancing at his watch, Charlie Kempton frowned and said, "But right now, I gotta get back to work. Pleasure meeting you, sir, and thanks for the tip about Moravian."

Ten minutes later, Cameron stood at the valet parking booth, waiting for the return of his car and thinking about how nice it would be if both Alpha State's new exchange agreement with Charles University and the purchase of new streetcars from Moravian Motorworks were to work out well. As he drove from the hotel onto the boulevard east toward the Interstate, his mind transitioned from Chamber of Commerce business to tonight's dinner and jazz concert that he and Vanessa would enjoy, so he listened to his *Ellis Marsalis Trio* CD for the rest of his trip back to campus.

Another trio was comfortably seated in large, overstuffed leather chairs in the plush library of the Renaissance House on the twentieth floor of the New Cambridge World Trade Center. Renaissance House was no doubt New Cambridge's most exclusive private club. There the trio planned their forthcoming performance in quiet tones. But instead of playing a score with legatos in F major sevenths, they composed a scheme based on stealth and strategy. Alex Wolfe, CEO of Wolfe-Otis Pharmaceuticals and chairman of ASU's Board of Trustees, raised his hand to draw the attention of a tuxedoed server, who soon delivered three glasses of sherry from his silver tray to their table.

"Those Chamber meetings," Wolfe complained, "are becoming more and more like a trip to the dentist, except nothing useful ever gets done there."

"That's why we're here, gentlemen. Here we can make good things happen," Senator Earl Broadbent consoled.

"Plus here at Renaissance, unlike our own offices, we have peace, quiet, and privacy, not to mention the decent surroundings," President Faust said, admiring the large stone fireplace that rose a full twenty feet to the ceiling. The ASU Board of Trustees paid for Steve Faust's membership, Wolfe-Otis Pharmaceuticals, Inc. paid for Alex Wolfe's, and a person, corporation, interest group, or political action committee paid for Senator Broadbent's membership. The large picture window framed a panoramic view of downtown New Cambridge.

"I don't have much time," the senator announced, "so let's see if we are all on the same page with this venture. Alex, what's been happening, how close are you to announcing the new drug results?"

"PDR has finished all the clinical trials and my R and D staff is reviewing them now, so we should have a final report in about a week. Very successful trials, by the way. They show that the new drug, which we're calling 'propacricin', controls both type-I and type II diabetes quite well. It makes life just about normal and extends life expectancy for years. With no daily injections, just a weekly pill. Steve, is your Dr. Novak on board to be principal investigator of record?" Wolfe asked Faust.

"He's fine with it. He's done it before. In fact . . ."

"Who exactly is Dr. Novak?" the senator interrupted as he turned to Steve Faust.

"He's perfect for the job, Earl. He's the editor of a medical research journal, he's published tons of research himself for years, and he's a senior physician-researcher in ASU's med school, with a big reputation in the field. All he wants is to see the write-up of the clinical trials that PDR did for Wolfe-Otis, and if he finds everything in order, he will sign on as principal investigator of the study and Wolfe-Otis staff people will be listed as co-investigators."

"He'd better find everything in order," Wolfe said. "We paid PDR a bundle to do the clinical trials. Some of my R and D people will redraft it in the Wolfe-Otis format. And, Senator, Wolfe-Otis is guaranteeing Dr. Novak at least five opportunities per year, for five years, to make speeches at any of our national or regional pharmaceutical meetings for $35,000 a pop, plus a small interest in the patent of propacricin, to show our gratitude for his help,"

"That should take care of him," Senator Broadbent added with a grin. "By the way, I'd look for another name for your 'pro-pack-it-in' or whatever you call the new drug. Nobody will ever be able to pronounce it. Or remember it."

"Don't worry, Earl, our marketing people will come up with a simple commercial name that every diabetic will remember and nag their physicians to prescribe," Wolfe assured the senator.

Turning to President Faust, Wolfe continued, "So, in the next several weeks, Steve, you and I should schedule a joint press conference to announce the new drug breakthrough. But first, right now is the time for you to use some of the money in the ASU Foundation account to buy Wolfe-Otis stock. Our stock prices will jump big-time right after the announcement. Later, you can keep it in Wolfe-Otis or move it elsewhere, whatever your people prefer."

"How much are we talking?" Faust asked.

"I'd recommend about twenty-five million in there, at least, and think of it as an early opening of your capital campaign," Wolfe answered. "You'll make a bundle. Can you do that?"

"Yeah, I think so," Faust responded. "The Foundation is doing pretty well with uncommitted funds, and we need to sell off some less profitable stocks anyway."

All three men paused for a moment to sip the last of their sherry and to glance at their Rolexes. Then the senator said to Steve Faust, "While you were in Colorado, Alex and I worked out some more logistics for ASU and Wolfe-Otis. Alex and his board of directors have decided that they need a new home office building for Wolfe-Otis. The current one is too small for their new status as one of the world's leading pharmaceutical firms. So, Alex and I have made some arrangements to get them into new facilities."

"Wait till you hear this, Steve," Alex said. "If you agree, here's the plan. Wolfe-Otis gives ASU its current headquarters facilities for use as a satellite campus on the south side of New Cambridge. The good senator has arranged to include a big congressional set-aside for state economic development in the next fiscal year budget, a chunk of which will go to ASU to pay for converting the facility to its needs . . .you know… classrooms, labs, administrative offices, and so on — economic development."

"And," Earl Broadbent added, "I persuaded the New Cambridge mayor and council to use their power of eminent domain to 'acquire' some prime real estate to offer to Wolfe-Otis Pharmaceuticals to lure them into locating their new head-quarters there. So, Wolfe-Otis will have a great new HQ and research facility on the corner of Pemberton and Highway 324, near the interstate, the airport, and, in a few years, a station of the new rapid transit line. Right now, the only things on that property are some dilapidated apartment buildings and a lot of drug dealing."

"And," Steve Wolfe added, "he convinced the mayor and the state legisla-tors from the New Cambridge area to pledge no property taxes for ten years."

"That all sounds . . . incredible," Faust admitted, "but Alex, you weren't planning to move your HQ out of New Cambridge . . . were you?"

"No, no. But we will say we have to, to remain competitive. The media will pick it up and then you and Earl will step in and save the day with this deal, and I'll agree to it. What do you think?"

Faust pondered for a moment, and then said, "Everything seems to be in place for a grand *coup* except FDA approval for propacricin." Then he paused. "But," he continued, raising his eyebrows and smiling at Earl Broadbent, "be-cause our senator chairs the Senate Appropriations Subcommittee on Health and Human Services, he just might have a few friends at FDA.

"It's win-win-win-win, my friends," the senator said with a grin. "ASU, Wolfe-Otis, the state, and diabetics will benefit from this arrangement." Al-though unspoken, Broadbent knew that he, too, would win re-election to the U.S. Senate in part because of this deal. It would guarantee major contribu-tions to his next campaign.

"Anything else, gents?" Wolfe asked, signaling that the meeting was near its end. In agreement, the three men left the Renaissance House for their re-spective offices across town, satisfied that they had put a good plan into motion.

The ASU Admin Building seemed quieter than usual, even for a Friday after-noon, as Cameron returned from the Chamber meeting. When he entered his outer office, the first thing he saw was six large wall clocks spaced evenly around the waiting room. Each was labeled with the name of one of the world's great cities and its hands set to that city's present time. He had asked Holly to order and install them over a month ago. What better way to symbolize to all visitors to his office that education at ASU is and must be global, international, cross-national, comparative. He noticed Holly standing beneath the clock la-beled "Prague" and indicating eleven o'clock.

"Holly, how nice! They look great."

"I hope you like the cities I picked, Dr. Cameron. If not, I can change the signs and reset the clocks." Along with Prague, the clocks had labels and the correct time for New Cambridge, Mumbai, Lima, Moscow, and Mexico City.

"We can change them every six months or so, but your first choices seem just right for now," Cameron responded. "Also," handing Holly the piece of paper with Michelle Murray's telephone number on it, "could you get Michele Murray's assistant on the phone and arrange a meeting for the two of us. She's the CEO of Murray Robotics."

"Will do. And I'm glad you like the way I put up the clocks. I knew you'd want one of them to be Prague. I think you had a really good idea to put them up in our office. Oh, by the way, Dr. Conaway from the College of Education is waiting in your office. He seemed anxious to see you and promised it wouldn't take long. Your next fifteen minutes is free. I told him that's all he can have."

Wendell Conaway was a tall, lanky, man in his mid-forties with a ruddy complexion and red hair. As Cameron entered his office, Conaway, who was standing in the middle of the floor admiring the pictures, awards, and other memorabilia hanging on the Provost's walls, pivoted and extended his hand. After exchanging the usual pleasantries, Conaway, true to his word, said, "Dr. Cameron, I am here without an appointment, and I thank you for seeing me on … really no notice at all. I will take up only a couple of minutes. It's late on a Friday afternoon, anyway."

"No problem, Wendell. I assume you are here about your letter to Coach Sylvester."

"That's correct. I apologize if it has caused you any trouble, Dr. Cameron, but my patience and tolerance were so strained by the football people that my sense of humor got the better of me and I dashed off that letter in a fit of . . . I'm not sure what. It is tongue-in-cheek, of course, but on the other hand, I am so tired of Sylvester sending his people over to Education, and other colleges, to beg for a change of grade, almost to the point of a threat, if his player-in-academic-trouble-*de-jour* isn't given at least a C or D, and if not, an incomplete, so he can play in some game or become eligible, or whatever. I have documented seven cases of that in my department alone, and I've been at Alpha State only one year."

"I can see you're a little perturbed by it all, Wendell, and well you should be. Admittedly, scholarshipped athletes have a very busy and hard schedule. I enjoy and respect sports, but we do have the integrity of our primary mission to maintain."

"It's hard to play a sport and complete your academic requirements," Wendell admitted. I ran track at Purdue for four years on scholarship and finished my undergraduate degree in four years plus one summer. It was hard, but it taught me something about time management, in addition to running a faster mile and knowing a lot about physiology and health education."

"Congratulations, Wendell, scholar-athletes are pretty rare. I will speak to the Athletic Director and tell him that all of his coaches should use an ounce of prevention, for example, better athlete-selection and better and more tutoring, rather than trying *ex post facto* to change grades already earned."

"Thanks, Dr. Cameron. That's all I wanted to hear. We are pretty touchy about that topic. All academics are. Thanks for meeting with me, and you have a good weekend."

"You, too, Wendell. Nice to meet you."

Soon, though it seemed like hours to Cameron, he and Vanessa were babbling like teenagers in the car as they traveled into downtown New Cambridge for dinner. At a few minutes before six, they pulled into valet parking and entered *Le Jardin*. A tall *maître d*, who looked very much at home in his tuxedo, greeted them, "*Bonsoir et bienvenue dans Le Jardin. Avez-vous une réservation?*"

Cameron spoke no French, but before he could respond in English, Vanessa used her six semesters of college French, reinforced by helping both kids through high school French, to answer, "*Bonsoir. Les Camerons a six.*" she said.

Continuing in English, but with a tantalizing French accent, the *maître d* said, "President Faust of Alpha State University has requested that you agree to be seated at table nine, in the section served by René. With your permission, René will take special care to see that you have a wonderful dining experience tonight and whenever you return to *Le Jardin*."

"*Oui, merci beaucoup,*" Vanessa answered, with a proud smile, "*table neuf et Rene sere excellent,*" and the *maître d* escorted them to table nine.

"Incredible, Vanessa! You sound like a native speaker. Can I hire you to work in our French Department, madam?"

"Only if they need an English-speaking attorney," she retorted. "I have worked too hard studying for the state bar exam, which is coming up on Tuesday. Besides, I think I just told the *maitre'd* everything I know in French."

The next ninety minutes was heaven on earth. René was the perfect server with courtly manners, almost magic efficiency, impressive knowledge of the chef's preparation of any item on *le menu Le Jardin*, and confidential advice if you are undecided between two entrées or which wine would best match your entrée. The food was equally delicious. Vanessa followed Rene's advice and ordered the chicken Clemenceau with Lyonnaise potatoes and the salad maison with Roquefort dressing. Cameron had no trouble singling out the broiled black drum with lightly steamed asparagus featuring only a hint of butter and lime juice, and the Romaine salad with classic vinaigrette. The bottle of Chablis Champs Royeaux, as recommended by René, was very tasty. But, because time did not stand still during their enchanted experience, they realized the need to hurry through desert and coffee, pay the tab, including a handsome gratuity, and retrieve their car from valet parking in order to get seated at the concert by eight o'clock.

They picked up an envelope of tickets at the will-call window and found their seats in ASU's Jeffrey Knox Concert Hall, named after a former chair of the Music Department. Their seats were located on row six in the middle section on the aisle — as good as it gets. At eight, the lights dimmed and the crowd hushed, as a young woman holding a mike appeared on stage-left and announced in a resonant alto voice, "Ladies and Gentlemen . . . please welcome . . . Mr. Ellis Marsalis."

To thunderous applause as the curtain opened, Marsalis entered the stage from the right, walked to center stage, placed one hand on the grand piano, faced the audience, smiled, and nodded his head once in approximation of a bow. Then he took his seat at the piano bench and adjusted its height as the applause died and the concert hall grew dark except for the spotlight illuminating him at the piano. He stared at the keyboard for about thirty seconds. Cameron and Vanessa looked at each other thinking, *Is something wrong?*

Then the renowned modern jazz pianist played several notes in slow succession with his right hand. Then he repeated the six notes in a different order. He seemed to be trying to begin a simple tune but couldn't quite remember how it starts. Then, the fourth time, he played these six notes in an order and rhythm, over a diminished seventh chord in the left hand, that made them recognizable as *Do You Know What It Means to Miss New Orleans?* The audience gasped and was transported to the birthplace of jazz and Marsalis. His slow, sentimental, modern interpretation included seven minutes of beautiful melodic improvisation, which led back to a restatement of the melody and a sentimental, bluesy ending. Then silence. The spellbound audience finally awoke from its reverie and burst into unrestrained applause. Marsalis waited until it stopped, slowly turned his head toward the audience and smiled, almost as if to say *Gotcha!* Then, without saying a word, he continued with an up-tempo rendition of a Thelonious Monk composition.

And so went the rest of the evening for Drew and Vanessa, a night in perfect harmony. For the first time since June, when they had moved from upstate New York to New Cambridge, they forgot about leaving so many old and dear friends and their home in Albany, missing their kids far away in college, learning a new and challenging job for Drew, and preparing to pass the state bar exam and finding a new job for Vanessa. They were happy.

The last thing Cameron heard before falling into a deep slumber at about midnight was Vanessa's barely audible reminder, "Don't forget to thank Steve Faust . . . for arranging our very own server . . . René . . . *Le Jardin*."

• • •

Having been awakened by a 2 AM call from Lieutenant Reginald Jackson in the New Cambridge police department, ASU's Chief Redden, in full uniform, sped down the interstate toward campus to the Beta Mu Omicron fraternity house, which Lieutenant Jackson had referred to as a crime scene. The Friday night fraternity party had become a little wild, somebody called the New Cambridge Police Department, and when they arrived they discovered that cocaine was involved. That's all Chief Redden knew as he pulled up to the Beta Mu Omicron house on the edge of campus and parked beside four other police cars with lights flashing. Several dozen students milled about inside the fraternity house, and on the large front porch, in the chilly autumn air, appearing distressed, some being questioned by uniformed officers in private rooms, the others being carefully guarded inside while they awaited interrogation.

As Redden walked toward the house, he spied Lieutenant Jackson, an old friend from the days when they both had served on the New Cambridge force. Jackson spotted him and said, "Charlie, glad you're here. I called you as soon as we got the call at HQ."

"Thanks for the call, Reg. What do we know so far?"

"We got a call from," and he glanced at his notes, "a Mr. James Moody a little after one. I am second shift exec all month, so I dispatched six officers and came along by myself. Bernie is running the incident investigation," news that brought the slightest hint of a frown to Chief Redden's face, "so let's see what he's got so far."

Bernie was almost invisible as he stood in the dark under one of the large maple trees in the fraternity house's front yard talking on his cell phone. When he saw his supervisor and the university chief approaching, he said a few more words, pressed the off button, and replaced the phone in his pocket. "What can you report, Bernie?"

"Lieutenant, Chief Redden. In a nutshell: numerous underage students intoxicated, alcohol everywhere; evidence of cocaine and marijuana possession — numerous joints in evidence, suspicious powder in several places. Right now we're questioning the students while we wait for Officer Underwood to come back to the scene with a warrant to search for cocaine and to get urine samples from the students. Some of them have already lawyered up and won't give us anything but their names. I called ADA Cooper and he said he'd get the night court judge, tonight it's Abernathy, I think he said, to issue a warrant. Underwood went to Judicial Square to pick it up. He should be back right away."

Chief Redden knew he should report this incident to his superior, Executive Vice President Cameron, but given the hour, he decided it could wait until a few more facts were known. What he did not know or suspect was that ADA Cooper had called G. Bennett Douglas at home to inform him of the facts so far. Douglas was the University's senior attorney and reported to President Faust. He was respected, feared and very well connected with the main law firms in town and around the state, the New Cambridge Police Department, local, state, and national politicos, the top corporate leaders in the state, and was an Alpha State alumnus. He had asked for an informal "heads up" from the District Attorney's office whenever ASU interests appeared about to be threatened in any kind of legal situation, and the ADA obliged.

• • •

Several miles away in the coffee room on the fifth floor of Wolfe-Otis Pharmaceuticals, three tired men in white lab coats sat at a table on which the original and the only copy of twenty-four reports rested in two neat stacks. "So we're agreed guys?" the tall, older director of research and development asked. "We make experimental trials seven, fourteen, fifteen, and twenty-six go away, change the numbers on the other trials to make the numerical sequence correct, rewrite the intro and summary to reflect the fact that we ran twenty trials instead of twenty-four, and reproduce however many copies we need."

The second man in a lab coat carefully collected the four rejected trial folders and walked across the room. "Don't forget we gotta get Dr. Novak from ASU over here soon for a show and tell. I'll take care of the four rejects — originals, and copies." Soon the shredder whirred.

The third lab scientist, a computer programmer, nodded to the two pharmacologists and volunteered, "I'll delete the four bad trials on disc and in memory, and renumber the twenty good trials to get them in the correct sequence. Plus, I'll take care of all the other sequential numbering and so on."

The lab director concluded, "Okay, good. I'll do the final editing, get the twenty trial reports bound into a single volume, and put in the call to Novak first thing Monday. I want you both here when we meet with him."

At 1:45 AM, all three lab scientists turned off the lights and left via the elevator at the rear of the building. At 2 AM, one of the three armed security guards stationed in the large, first-floor lobby at the main entrance of Wolfe-Otis, Inc., began his periodic nightly trek up and down the hallways and staircases of each floor to ensure that everything was in proper order in the corporate headquarters. As soon as he finished his rounds, he rejoined his two colleagues seated in the lobby. He pulled up a large leather swivel chair on wheels, propped his feet on the side of the front desk, and resumed reading the sports section of the *New Cambridge Morning News*. A second security guard asked, "All the mad scientists gone for the night, Chuck?"

"Yeah. All's quiet. And the *News* picks ASU to win by two touchdowns this afternoon."

6 When the phone rang at 6 AM on that Saturday morning in October, the cloudy nighttime darkness still resisted the sun's effort to deliver light. On the fourth ring, Cameron grasped the phone on his bedside table in a warm room, further darkened by pulled draperies, and noticed that Vanessa was not beside him.

"Hello," he said, feigning a cheerful 'I'm wide awake' greeting.

"Dr. Cameron, Charlie Redden. I'm very sorry to bother you early on a Saturday morning, sir, but we have a problem."

"If you think I should know about it, Charlie, then I need to know," he responded, swinging his legs around to the side of the bed and his feet on the floor. "What's up?"

"Last night, the BMO house had a party that got out of control. A Mr. James Moody called it in to New Cambridge Police, and they called us as a courtesy. Apparently, Mr. Calloway's daughter had been at the party earlier and complained to her dad. There was a lot of alcohol being consumed, and most of the students were under age. There was also evidence of controlled substances on the premises, including a white powdery substance on two silver serving trays on a table in the downstairs rec room. We got a warrant to search the premises and one to require urine samples from everybody there. We searched the whole fraternity house, starting at about 2:30 this morning."

Vanessa entered the bedroom and placed a hot mug of dark roast and today's *New Cambridge Morning News* on the bedside table next to him. His smile and nod to Vanessa revealed his gratitude but failed to conceal his trepidation about possible felony offenses at the BMO house last night.

"Go on, Charlie. Did you find cocaine?"

"We found about a quarter kilo. We took urine samples, copied their driver licenses, took their statements, took their pictures, and the usual. Some of them wouldn't answer questions. They've seen too many police shows on TV. Of course, nobody would admit anything about the coke, so we arrested four of the five officers of the fraternity; one was out of town. They were taken to central lock-up in New Cambridge but their parents bailed them out in less than two hours. All of them, a total of seventy-two, were instructed not to leave New Cambridge."

Even though Vanessa did not know who 'Charlie' was and gained no understanding of Charlie's message from hearing only Cameron, with her attorney's instincts she knew from his tone and body language that the call was bad news.

"One more fact you might be interested in. Two of them were not ASU students or BMO members — two males who live in a posh neighborhood on the north side of New Cambridge. Neither one claimed to work anywhere, but they drove to the fraternity party in a big Mercedes. We have their house staked out until we get to the bottom of this. The rest were members, pledges, and dates."

"So you think the two non-students may be suppliers?" Cameron asked.

"We'll find out."

"Okay, Charlie. What happens next?"

The lab will run tests on the urine samples as fast as they can. Then we'll know what to do. Monday, the ADA will schedule court dates for those who test positive. That's about it."

"Charlie, thank you for keeping me informed. Did you call President Faust?"

"No, sir. My chain of command goes directly to you. Do you want me to call him?"

"No. That's Okay. I'll call him. He needs to know. Thanks again, Charlie. Keep me informed as this develops. You have my cell phone number, don't you?" Cameron asked.

"You're welcome, and I do. By the way, before we hang up. Are you ready for Monday night? You know, our sting operation?"

For the last two weeks, Cameron had moved to the back of his mind all conscious thoughts of Redden's plan to set a trap for a possible computer hacker trying to erase or change the official data files of ASU's crime statistics for the past year. Remembering it in the context of tonight's fraternity party gone wild made him a little depressed about the state of civil society on his campus, and his mind drifted for several seconds as he gripped the phone.

"Dr. Cameron? Are you still there?"

"Yes, Charlie. I'm here," Cameron said slowly, recovering his self-control. "I will be there Monday night. It's on my calendar."

First, Cameron called President Faust at home and at his office but reached an answering machine at each number. He left messages on the events of last night, but refused to allow the topic to dominate his breakfast conversation with Vanessa. Rather, he insisted, "I want to hear your reviews of the culinary arts at *Le Jardin* and the piano styling of Ellis Marsalis."

When they compared notes on the food and music of last night, both confessed that it was the best night out since they had moved to Bedford, and maybe their favorite date in years. Vanessa concluded their discussion with, "Char would probably say something like, 'The Bard of Avon put it best: 'If music be the food of love, play on', except she would get the quote right, word for word."

"And," Cameron added, "she would give us the name of the play, act and scene numbers, and the name of the character who said it." He paused, shook his head, and said, "Damn, I miss Char and Tom."

"Me, too. Let's call them," Vanessa said, and Cameron agreed.

Because Vanessa would be taking the state part of the bar examination in a few days, they had decided to stay at home the entire weekend. Late that afternoon, they went for a five-mile, out-and-back jog and enjoyed the cool autumn day. She felt good and knew she could fall asleep and rest well the whole night. On Sunday, she would spend an hour or so reviewing some of the materials on their new state's legal system, go out for another run, and get another good night's rest. On Monday, she would rest. Tuesday, she'd be ready. Their light dinner at about six on that Saturday evening was interrupted by a phone call. As soon as Cameron answered, he heard, "Steve Faust, here, Drew. Returning your call. I'm about to go out to a big cocktail party, dinner, and gala at the Coronado Plaza. I hope you and your lovely wife have a similar plan. What's the urgent matter you called about?"

"Thanks for calling me back, Steve. You have plans so I'll be brief. Sometime after midnight, early this morning, the New Cambridge Police and ASU Police were called to the BMO house to break up an unruly party. They found . . . . Did anyone call you about this already?"

"Yes, Drew, but I appreciate your heads up on it. The New Cambridge chief, Tom Benton, called this morning, right before I left for a meeting at the statehouse. I think everything is under control. It seems there were a couple of uninvited guests who caused the problem. Tom said he would get back to me as soon as he gets it sorted out."

Cameron felt confused by his boss's rather nonchalant assessment of the situation. "So you're not too worried about it?"

"No, not really," Faust admitted. "On a large university campus, in the twenty-first century, you are going to get incidents like this. It goes with the territory. Think about it, Drew. We want to establish a distinguished center of learning to create, disseminate, and apply the knowledge and values of science, the arts, the professions, etc. So what do we do? We assemble thirty-five thousand male and female teenagers, put them in what amounts to several dozen upper-middle class hotels in very close proximity, with no chaperones, like their own city. Then we surround them by liquor stores and drug dealers. The whole idea is ludicrous, but it does seem to work out in the long run."

For several seconds, Cameron could not respond. He thought that Faust expected him to chuckle at this ironic and cynical interpretation of the contemporary university, but Cameron's sense of humor did not stretch far enough to find the police raid of an ASU institution funny.

"I've been in touch with Chief Redden since early this morning, and I'll continue to monitor the situation as the police establish more facts," Cameron offered. "It could be serious."

"You worry too much, Drew. We'll take care of it. You'll see. Let's talk Monday and see where we are then. Gotta run. Ruth's waiting."

Although he dreaded going in to work on Monday morning, he arrived at the office just before seven and even a few minutes before Holly. He was looking over his weekly schedule on the computer when she quietly appeared in his office doorway with a hardcopy of Monday's schedule of meetings, deadlines, calls to make, reports to write, and other activities. When she stood unnoticed for a full minute, she sensed that something was wrong.

"Dr. Cameron, good morning," she said, and studied her boss for a clue about what might be the matter.

"Good morning, Holly. Have a good weekend?"

"Yes I did. I planted about eighty tulip bulbs, and I have high hopes for some beautiful spring flowers."

"Congratulations. I didn't know you were a tulip farmer. By the way, do you remember writing the University of Washington personnel office to ask if and when they awarded Zachary Kilgore a graduate degree?"

"I do. They responded several weeks ago, and I put their letter, unopened, in the safe next to my desk, as you asked."

"Okay, Holly. Now is the time for me to take a look at it."

Holly retrieved the unopened letter and handed it to Cameron. Cameron felt uneasy about what he might find inside but realized that Zachary Kilgore either falsified his resume to get a vice presidential job at Alpha State or he hadn't.

Using a silver letter opener emblazoned with "ASU Eagles," he slit open the envelope and read it.

Dear Executive Vice President Cameron:

We recently received your request for information about Mr. Zachary Kilgore, one of your employees, concerning his matriculation in our graduate programs at the University of Washington. We are happy to comply. Mr. Kilgore enrolled in the master's degree program in Computer Science in fall, 1987 and pursued that degree through spring, 1989. He then dropped out of the master's program without completing that degree and enrolled in the doctoral program in Computer Science in fall 1989 and continued taking courses in that program through spring, 1991. He left the University of Washington after spring, 1991, having completed neither the M.S. nor the Ph.D.

I hope this answers your question satisfactorily. If not, please contact us again and we will respond. In the meantime, all the best to you and your colleagues at Alpha State University.

Most sincerely yours,

Angela Clinton-Ackerman, Ph.D.
Vice President for Admissions and Records

At seven-forty in the morning, he sat alone in the quiet of his office, lit by a single reading lamp on his desk and the glow of the screen saver on his computer. He replaced the letter in its envelope and put it in his out box. *First,* Cameron thought, *I tell Steve Faust the news and get his response. Second, I go to see Kilgore, this morning if possible, to tell him what the University of Washington's official record indicates. If he didn't get a doctorate somewhere else, I'll ask him to resign, and fire him if he doesn't. Third, I need to consult with Faust and some other administrators and appoint an interim VP for Admissions and Records. Fourth, assembling a search committee can wait until early next spring. An interim VP will run the show until then.*

"Holly, get President Faust on the phone. It's urgent."

Holly came through his door saying, "Ms. McInerney said he's not in yet, maybe in the car on the way. She is calling him on his cell phone to ask him to call you here."

"Okay. Put this letter back in the locked file. Kilgore has no degrees from Washington. Keep that between us for now."

Before Holly could react, Cameron's private phone rang. "Office of the Provost," Holly answered, listened briefly, and said, "Just a moment, sir," and handed the phone to Cameron.

"Steve, sorry to trouble you even before you get here, but we have a problem. I got an official letter from the VP for Admissions and Records at the University of Washington telling me that Zachary Kilgore did not receive an M.S. or Ph.D. degree there. He's deceived us, Steve, and it's clear what has to happen next."

After a long silence, Faust responded, "He has done such a good job for us, Drew. I'd sure hate to lose him. I just can't believe it. Are you sure?" Another long pause. "I guess the letter from Washington is … . What do you propose to do, Drew?"

The words gushed from Cameron's mouth, "Kilgore did not have, does not have the credentials he said he had when he took the job, credentials which are required for the job he occupies. It was stated in our recruitment ads. We are committed. He makes $250,000 a year in salary. ASU passed over numerous candidates who did have earned doctorates and other excellent qualifications, and hired one who faked his qualifications. He cannot be trusted after that, even if he has done a good job, as you say." Cameron worried for a moment that his desire to make an emphatic statement to Faust had, instead, produced a harsh response, so he paused.

"Drew, I know all that. What do you propose to do?"

Suddenly a new thought flashed in Cameron's mind. "Steve, I'm going to sit on it for twenty-four hours. Let's keep it confidential for now and let the shock of it recede and see what to think of it tomorrow. Then I'll talk with him."

"Sounds like a good plan, Drew. We can both cool off and make a better decision tomorrow. Maybe we can find a way around it. Keep me informed."

"Of course. In the meantime, business as usual," Cameron added, as they said their goodbyes and hung up.

Cameron's quick decision to delay any reaction to the fact that Kilgore had defrauded the university was not, contrary to President Faust's assumption, designed to allow a "cooling-off" period or an opportunity to cover it up. Rather, it followed from a sudden suspicion that two of his problems shared similar physical, organizational, and electronic origins. *Maybe it's just coincidence*, he mused to himself, *but, if time permits, having more good information is better than having less. How many times have I said that in a classroom lecture?* It occurred to him that there is a chance that two of his current problems have the same solution. Zachary Kilgore falsified his resume to get the job as VP for Admissions and Records. Chief Redden and his FBI computer forensics friend had determined that the computer used to hack into the ASU Police Department crime files one year ago was located in the Office of Admissions and Records. Tonight is the last night before Admissions and Records must by law report campus crime data to the U.S. Department of Education. Cameron was scheduled to join Chief Redden and his friend in the ASU Chief's office, where the computer forensics specialist, aided by the appropriate electronic technology, could catch a computer hacker in the act. *Why not wait*, Cameron asked himself, *for one more day to see if there is a connection, to see if one of Kilgore's people is also involved in hacking into the police computer files.*

Holly entered and handed him four files. "You have only four appointments scheduled today, but one of them is downtown for a one o'clock lunch with Ms. Murray of Murray Robotics, and I thought you might want some prep time for that one. The rest are here in the office, pretty straightforward."

"Thanks, Holly. What do we do first?"

"You are free until nine. While you were on the phone with Chief Redden, you had a call from somebody you met during lunch on Friday." Holly paused and squinted, as if uncertain about what to say next. Then she added, "He said he would call back at exactly nine o'clock if you are free then. He said he needs to tell you something 'private, personal, and very important' — that's a direct quote — something about the Moravians, I think he said. I hope you know what he means. He wouldn't tell me anything else. Do you want to talk with him . . . about Moravians?"

Cameron thought for several seconds before he remembered. "Holly, at Friday's Chamber of Commerce lunch I met the young chief engineer for the City of New Cambridge, who told me that the city council would probably include the Czech Republic's Moravian Motorworks as one of three bidders to supply streetcars for the new public transit line. I wonder why his call is 'personal and private.' Make sure I'm free for his call on the main line at nine. It shouldn't take long."

"Then at eleven, you have Melinda Osterman from Sociology. She wants to talk about curriculum reform. At one you're due downtown with Ms. Murray to discuss a gift to the university, and at three-thirty, you are interviewing another candidate for the super-chair — Dr. Emile Kupchinski in the College of Business, Department of Economics and Finance. Add to that the half-dozen surprises we always get on Monday."

"Okay. Did President Faust send over anything about Ms. Murray and her gift, and what do we have on Dr. Kupchinski's academic record?"

"Both files are in your left hand, Dr. Cameron," Holly said.

"Of course they are, Holly. And my face is red. Or should be," evoking from Holly only a fleeting smile of modest pride as she returned to her desk having pleased her boss.

At exactly nine o'clock, Cameron's phone rang and Holly said, in a very businesslike tone, "Your nine-o'clock is on line two."

"Hello."

"Dr. Cameron, this is Charlie Kempton, New Cambridge chief of engineering. We met at the Chamber lunch this past Friday, and talked about getting bids from three manufacturers for our new streetcars?" he said with a raised pitch at the end of each statement, implying "Do you remember?"

"Sure, Charlie. My assistant said you mentioned Moravian Motorworks."

"Yes, sir. Here's the deal. I'll tell you what I know, but first you have to promise me that you will never tell anybody that I told you. Please?" Kempton said.

After several uncertain moments, Cameron said, "As you wish. No problem."

"Remember I told you that the expert committee had recommended three streetcar manufacturing companies to ask for bids for our new line? And the mayor and council approved them? Well, I found out something else, something I don't approve of at all. I was working late Friday night and by accident overheard a conversation in the hallway outside my office between Mayor DelVecchio and Ed Dinwiddie, the CEO of Urban RailTech here in New Cambridge. Please don't ever repeat this, Dr. Cameron, or I will get fired so fast you wouldn't believe it."

"Okay, Charlie. It's our secret," Cameron said, beginning to feel a little impatient.

"Mayor DelVecchio and the council agreed to request bids from the three companies we recommended — American Streetcar, Pioneer Transit, both in the U.S., and Moravian Motorworks in the Czech Republic. But he never intended to give the bids from Pioneer and Moravian serious consideration. The fix is in for American Streetcar."

"What do you mean, 'the fix is in' for American Streetcar?" Cameron asked.

"The mayor and council, early on, picked Mr. Dinwiddie's firm to lay and maintain the tracks for the new line. Their official justification is that his firm is a good one and a local business, so the contract would provide a lot of local jobs. That's a good thing. But I found out that the real reason is that Dinwiddie owns a lot of shares of American Streetcar, almost twenty percent, and American has promised him a big kickback if they get the contract to supply the cars. And Dinwiddie has promised the mayor a big contribution to his next campaign for office. The mayor's planning a run for governor. No way is this fair," Kempton said, his anger beginning to surface.

"This kind of behavior on the part of public officials is old school at best, illegal at worst," Cameron said, reluctant to commit himself at this point. "So what's your prescription?"

"There isn't anything I can do. You know what happens to whistle-blowers. But, I have an idea. You could make it happen," Kempton said, shifting the responsibility to Cameron.

"And?" Cameron answered, beginning to feel impatient.

"Could you get someone in authority, either in Moravian Motorworks or the Czech government or both, to come to New Cambridge and put a hard sell on the mayor and council? Frankly, Moravian is my favorite if you consider quality of product engineering, price, and corporate stability. Moravian sold a lot of streetcars to two Canadian cities years ago and the engineers in both cities tell me they are very pleased with the results. If you can arrange for the Czechs to visit, I'm pretty sure it will force the mayor and council to give Moravian a fair look. Dr. Cameron, I've got to go. Sorry. I'm at a pay phone in the bus station. Guarantees privacy. Thanks for listening," and then "click" as chief city engineer Kempton hung up the phone.

Cameron pushed aside the negative thoughts that flooded his mind, such as, *Why does something or somebody have to screw up every opportunity that comes along?* He also remembered the words emblazoned above the U.S. Supreme Court building in Washington: *Eternal vigilance is the price of liberty*. Then he repeated to himself his modified version of that motto: *Eternal vigilance is the price of everything that's any good*.

"Holly, could you get Anna Zezulka on the phone. She's in Prague. I gave you her business card."

Holly glanced up at one of the international clocks in the Provost's outer office and said, "It's four-fifteen in Prague, Dr. Cameron I think we can get her."

With typical efficiency, Holly had Anna Zezulka on the phone in less than fifteen minutes, even though she had to get her pulled out of a meeting with the EU Commission on Industrial Strategy. Cameron was impressed with the familiarity and warmth in her voice. He requested that she and a couple of Moravian engineers should come to New Cambridge to see the city personally and answer any additional questions New Cambridge officials might have. After a brief discussion, she agreed and promised to let Cameron know as arrangements were made. Both sincerely expressed pleasure at the prospects of seeing each other again.

"Holly, get me Avery Gibbs on the phone," which she did right away.

"Avery, Drew Cameron. Good morning. Did the market open way up this morning?" he asked tongue in cheek.

"Good morning, Drew," the ASU Foundation President said. "No, the market crashed this morning and the Foundation is broke, and you and I will not get paid for several years. Other than pain and misery, what can I do for you today?"

"You may be an investment wizard, Avery, but you are also a rascal. All I need to know is what sort of paperwork I should complete to move that eight million dollars from uncommitted Foundation funds to the new scholarship fund that Steve Faust and I agreed to."

As Avery Gibbs responded, his mood seemed to change. "I . . . I'm not . . . uh . . . . What you need to do . . . is talk with Steve about this. The Foundation is in the middle of some changes in investment strategy and, uh, restructuring some of our commitments to better protect our assets in this weird global economy, and the Board members are thrashing about more than usual. So, we've uh ... I'm not sure, uh, what else I can tell you now, Drew."

Sensing something strange but having no idea what it might be, Cameron simply responded, "Good enough, Avery. I'll talk with Steve and see when we can get this scholarship show on the road. We can do the paperwork later, no problem. Take care."

Cameron had read his letter of offer many times and remembered well that Faust had promised to make available eight million dollars from the foundation account, by the end of Cameron's first semester, to set up an interest-bearing scholarship fund to award to low-income students of exceptional academic ability. He had extensive notes of their conversation that established the details. The plan was to award one hundred scholarships covering tuition, fees, and room and board, a total of two million dollars, to freshmen who began college in the fall of Cameron's second year. Then, an additional two hundred students for the next year. Then two hundred more in each of years three and four. Year one students would finish at the end of that year, freeing their scholarship monies to be newly awarded to new students in year five. However, something seemed to be going very wrong.

Cameron tried to call Faust but instead got Ms. McInerney, who promised to have the president call him as soon as possible. So, resisting frustration and confusion, he turned to other business.

First, he reviewed the file on Michele Murray, his one-o'clock. According to her bio, in the nineteen thirties, Michele Murray's father, Peter Murakov, an engineer in Kiev, fled Russia because of oppression during the Bolshevik revolution. He arrived on New York's Ellis Island, where he applied for U.S. citizenship in a new land of freedom and opportunity. In 1941, he and his Russian wife moved to New Cambridge where he established a small machine shop. They named their daughter Manya, meaning "rebellious" in Russian, because they wanted her to stand firm for individual freedom. Murakov Engineering became more and more successful, at first because of lucrative government contracts to design and produce small weapons during World War II and beginning in the 1960s, because of his wise decision to invest as much as possible in research and development in an emerging field called "robotics."

In 1962, Manya Murakov, who called herself "Michele," finished her undergraduate degree in electrical engineering and worked in her father's business. When her father died, she took over the business, and changed her name to Michele Murray and the name of her company to Murray Robotics, Inc. Now it is one of America's largest robotics engineering firms, with production facilities in New Cambridge and Korea and plans for another plant in the near future. Over the years, she had contributed over one million dollars to the University in support of engineering disciplines. She remained single.

Just then Holly knocked and announced, "Dr. Osterman is here to talk about curriculum reform."

"Hello, Drew," Osterman blurted out as she marched into the office. "I voted on the search committee to offer you the job and was glad you are here until you threw me to the lions as chair of this damned curriculum reform committee. What a bunch of . . ." and she paused, unsure whether to pepper the rest of her sentence with one or more of her favorite obscenities, for which she had earned a scarlet reputation all over campus. But, as Cameron had learned in several meetings with her and the curriculum committee, even those on campus who were offended dared not chastise her for her frequent obscenities. They knew she had a very agile intelligence and a short fuse. They had also seen her lifting weights, punishing the boxer's heavy training bag at the ASU Fitness Center and running sprints on the outdoor track. She had earned both respect and fear from her colleagues.

"But Melinda, you were the only one on campus equal to the task," Cameron said, as a tease. "Besides, what's the problem with your colleagues on the committee?"

"How many days do you have for this meeting?" she answered with caustic humor. "And, can you have Holly get me some coffee? And some for you, too."

As soon as their coffee arrived, Cameron said, "Melinda, you and the committee have had over two months to study our undergraduate curriculum. What should we do to improve it, to make it the best we can offer?"

"Okay, Drew," Osterman said, "here's my analysis." Then for the better part of an hour, the sociologist presented her analytical model of what is wrong with most university curricula, including ASU's, based on changes in American society. Her analysis was a scathing indictment of American society and its universities, based on facts and evidence, and included scores of footnotes indicating her sources. Much of her analysis was not new to Cameron. He also harbored some resentment at declines in the quality of various sectors of American society. But he was impressed with her cogent arguments relating changes in American culture to changes in American universities.

"Okay," she went on, "in summary, our undergraduate curriculum is too segmented, too specialized, and too vocational. It neglects literacy, numeracy, and critical thinking. In short, it's a mess. We need a good, tight core curriculum of well-designed general education courses and we should require it of every undergraduate student who gets a baccalaureate degree from us. And, most departments should modernize their majors and minors."

At that point, Holly's familiar buzz sounded on Cameron's phone. "Dr. Cameron, it's 12:30. You need to drive down to Murray Robotics soon, right now, to join Ms. Murray for lunch."

"Yes, Holly. Thanks. Will do."

"Melinda, Holly says I have to get downtown for my next meeting. Thanks for your hard work and this report. I appreciate your diagnosis of the main problems we have with our curriculum and your logic in making these connections. As we say in policy analysis, 'If you don't know the cause, it's hard to devise a cure'. You have my support to continue. First, let's develop that core curriculum for all students, and then require each department to revise its major. This is very important, and you are doing a splendid job. Keep it up."

With that, and a blush of gratitude from someone who almost never blushes, they shook hands and left Cameron's office. Holly handed him an umbrella. "It's raining. Don't lose it, it's mine," she admonished with a twinkle in her eye. About a month ago, he had lost her umbrella and replaced it with the new one she just handed to him. "And there's a big accident on the interstate, so you should take Atherton Boulevard all the way to Fourth Avenue, take a left, follow Fourth to Mission Street. There's an indoor parking garage at the corner of Fourth and Mission. Take the elevator up to the third floor and follow the signs to Murray Robotics." She handed him a print-out of these directions.

"Holly, you're a saint. Thanks."

"I called ahead to Ms. Murray's secretary to tell her you'd be a minute late because of the backup on the interstate and the rain," Holly announced, as Cameron hurried toward the elevator.

Atherton Boulevard, four wide lanes divided by a twelve-foot-wide grassy strip, was only three blocks from the Admin Building. Small groups of people gratefully huddled under bus stop shelters and the awnings of shops along the Boulevard to avoid the rain. No one sat on the park benches or strolled under the maples on the green dividing the boulevard. A few other cars splashed up and down the broad street.

With about twenty minutes of travel time, Cameron allowed his thoughts to focus on the probability that he would have to terminate Zachary Kilgore as VP for Admissions and Records. And tonight there is the police sting with Charlie Redden and he suspected he already knew what the outcome would be. That worry was replaced by concern about Vanessa's state bar exam tomorrow. But confidence in her intelligence and legal experience overcame his worry. She would do fine. She always did fine.

The six or eight blocks around Fourth and Mission had once been a dilapidated warehouse district, but astute planning and zoning had converted it to mixed use and now, even on a rainy, overcast day, it exhibited an almost swank, up-scale character. Cameron turned in to the corner parking garage and found a space on the third floor near the elevator and the covered walkway over Fourth Street to Murray Robotics. He refocused positive thoughts on Ms. Murray's desire to give ASU a large gift as he walked across and into her building.

Speculation in national and local news media had run rampant about the future of one of America's most successful robotics corporations. Ms. Murray was in her mid-seventies, had never been married, and had no heir. Some business analysts speculated that she would convert her operation into a publicly traded company on the stock exchange and include a proviso that made her a board member for life for a hefty annual stipend. That she had built a multi-billion-dollar enterprise required no speculation. The décor in her reception area was elaborate and futuristic in design with robotic idiography, indirect lighting, various forms of modernistic art, and twenty-foot ceilings. Most of what decorated the colorful walls reminded Cameron of artistic expressions of computer circuitry, mathematical formulae, and neural networks.

"Dr. Cameron. Welcome, sir. She's expecting you. Please go right in. Lunch will be served in just a few moments. Murray Robotics, how may I help you? Yes, I will transfer you." Cameron entered the door as instructed by the woman wearing an expensive business suit and a wireless headset. He cautioned himself to think a little harder about his perceptions and reactions or he would appear to be slow of mind. As he walked down the long corridor, with dim, indirect lighting at the ceiling and knee levels, he tried to refocus his mental and sensory powers and felt them returning.

"Come in, Dr. Cameron," he heard, as he stepped through the door labeled "M. Murray." Seated in the dimly lit room in a rocking chair near the large bay windows, Ms. Murray did not rise to greet Cameron. Rather, she said, "Thank you for coming to have lunch with me. I don't get out and about as often as I once did, and I miss scurrying around town in the wonderful clubs and restaurants," and extended her hand.

"The pleasure is mine, Ms. Murray, "gently shaking her small, frail hand. "Thank you for inviting me. It is a great pleasure to meet you, and I bring you greetings from Steve Faust. He says the two of you are good friends."

Given the information provided to him by ASU colleagues, he was surprised at Ms. Murray's demeanor. She looked older than her age of seventy five. She had covered her otherwise pale face with too much makeup in an attempt to hide a deep patchwork of wrinkles. Her eyes were sunken and red. The veins in her somewhat misshapen hands were large and blue. Her voice was weak, yet she seemed to have excellent hearing and sight.

"Yes, Steve is a darling man," she said, almost in a whisper. "Always so helpful when I need something. Please give him my regards when you see him again."

Ms. Murray changed the subject with, "So where is the stock market going next, Dr. Cameron?" He had heard a CNBC report on the subject earlier that morning and fell back on that information, feeling a little guilty that he did not footnote his source. But even before he finished, two uniformed caterers knocked and, in the next twenty-five minutes, wheeled in a series of four delicious courses, accompanied first by champagne, then water, then coffee. Finally, the puff pastry was perfect.

Then, again without any warning or transition, she announced, "Dr. Cameron. The time has come for me to make a gift to Alpha State University. My status and the status of Murray Robotics might change at any time, so now is the best time for me to help the university do something that would be valuable to your students and to the state. Something I believe in. Before you leave, I will give you a copy of my proposal," which she held in her hand. "It is only twelve pages long and documents what I want to do and why, my legacy. But I can describe it to you as we finish our coffee."

Despite being born in the U.S. and living here all her life, her speech manifested a slight Slavic accent, no doubt a remnant of her father's speech. "In brief," she continued," I want to give the university the sum of fifty million dollars," and then paused to detect Cameron's reaction.

He maintained his best poker face as he responded, "Please continue, Ms. Murray. I am very pleased and I want to know about your goals so we can think of the best ways to accomplish them with this gift."

"I want to fund several endowed chairs in American values for three million dollars each. The Murray Robotics treasurer tells me that three million is a sufficient sum to endow a chair today, even with our current low interest rates. Is that true?"

"That is correct," Cameron affirmed.

"And I want to set up an institute for the study of American values, which will support teaching, especially new courses, and research programs. The endowed chairs would be jointly housed in the institute and in their home departments."

"Do you have any preferences about which academic fields the endowed chairs should represent?" Cameron asked, struggling to conceal his excitement at the prospects.

She lifted the document from her lap, glanced at two or three pages, then looked at Cameron as she stated, "Yes. I insist that four of the chairs be in political science, history, economics, and philosophy. The university can decide what other fields are represented by the other endowed chairs, as long as they are relevant to American values."

Pleased, Cameron asked, "According to university regulations, you have naming rights of the chairs and the institute, as long as the university agrees. Do you have anything in mind? For example, your name or your company's name could be used."

Ms. Murray stared at Cameron for half a minute without speaking, suggesting to him that his question had offended her in some way and that maybe he had botched the deal. Then she said, "It is very important to me that the chairs and institute be named after John Randolph of Roanoke."

Pausing only long enough to take the final sip of her coffee, she continued, eager to get to the heart of her motivation in making the gift with that name. Cameron was grateful for the pause because he could not pull from his memory anything concrete about John Randolph. He could only assume that Randolph was from Virginia but did not know if that was even germane in this case.

Without referring to notes, Ms. Murray stated, "John Randolph was born in 1773 and lived in Roanoke, Virginia. He served his country from 1799 until his death in 1833, first in the U.S. House of Representatives and later in the U.S. Senate. He interrupted his work in Congress for a while to serve as the U.S. Ambassador to Russia. You might not be aware that my father was a Russian émigré to the U.S. As you can see," she said with a hint of a smile, "I have not spent all my time studying engineering and computer science, Dr. Cameron. I am also a devoted student of American history."

"I have only limited familiarity with John Randolph, Ms. Murray, but it's clear that he served his state and this country long and well during a critical time."

"You are right, Dr. Cameron. His biographers and the historians of that period agree on his importance in setting the course for the new American republic and on the principles he represented. When I tell you what they were, I think you will agree that America needs leaders like Randolph today more than ever." She remained silent for a moment, smiled, and then said, "His principles are simple. He defended the family. He promoted liberty. He believed in adherence to truth, revealed through scripture and tradition. He advocated for a small national government with little or no debt. He favored strong states' rights. Last, as a plantation owner, he understood the importance of the landed gentry to the stability of the republic. Those are the values that the institute and endowed professors must promote. Today, we have too many leaders in this country who, like Madison and Jefferson, don't understand or agree with Randolph, so they often conspire to defeat his ideas."

Cameron did his absolute best to hide his feelings of disappointment. He knew that no self-respecting public university could use its resources to advance right-wing ideology, even if it did so under the name of a relatively obscure early American patriot. That can never be substituted for "free inquiry" and "academic freedom." There are at least two sides to every issue, every question.

Ms. Murray continued, rescuing him from simply declining her offer. "So I want you to take my proposal," as she handed it to him, "read it with care, share it with Steve, and help make my vision a reality, to get Ambassador John Randolph's mission accomplished."

Cameron took the proposal, thanked her for lunch and the generous offer of a gift to the university, and promised to give her a quick response, all the while concealing his disappointment. Even as he bade farewell to the receptionist in the outer office and walked down the corridor, he was already thinking of ways he might redefine her proposal so that it could be accepted. As provost, he knew he could not approve the gift as Ms. Murray described it. He wondered how President Faust would react.

"You have less than ten minutes before Dr. Emile Kupchinski from the College of Business comes for his super-chair interview," Holly said, as Cameron entered the outer office. "Did everything go well at Murray Robotics?" she inquired, not expecting good news after reading Cameron's face.

"Where's Kupchinski's file? And no, not very," he said, forcing a smile. "I'll explain later."

"On your desk. Sorry. Need anything else?"

For the next eight minutes, Cameron skimmed Kupchinski's file and learned that he was born in Hungary, had a joint doctoral degree in financial economics and mathematics from NYU, had served as an officer in the New York chapter of Mensa, spent his first five years after graduate school working in a small consulting firm in New York City, then at a relatively young age became chief economist at Global Capital Securities, one of the world's largest investment banks. Many economists give him credit for developing the mathematical applications that led to interest rate derivatives, which produced untold billions in profits worldwide but then contributed to the global market collapse in 2008. He did publish the first article explaining the mathematical basis for derivatives. Rumors suggest that he made hundreds of millions of dollars himself from interest rate swaps based on his derivatives model and then retired from Global Capital Securities at the tender age of forty and took a tenured full professorship in the Riggs College of Business at ASU.

When Dr. Kupchinski walked through Cameron's door, he appeared to be the perfect combination of the American absent-minded professor and a member of the traditional European academic elite, neither of which Cameron expected. He was thin, tall, dressed in a dark tailored suit, white shirt and bow tie, had a narrow face covered by large glasses with thick lenses, and sported short brown hair parted in the middle and prematurely graying at the temples. Yet when he walked in, he glanced around the room at the windows, then the floor, then the ceiling light fixture but never at Cameron, as if he didn't know where he was.

"Are you Dr. Cameron? Of course you are. Who else would you be?" he mumbled. Although he grinned, he seemed uncomfortable as he spoke and focused his attention above and to the right of Cameron, whose expectations for a productive interview began to dissipate.

"Dr. Kupchinski, welcome. I'm glad to meet you. Please have a seat and we'll talk about the super-chair," Cameron said.

Kupchinski remained standing near the doorway. His darting eyes intimated a state of manic confusion about what to do or say next. "Can I sit over there?" he asked, pointing to the couch.

"Please do. Tell me what you could bring to the University as the occupant of the new super-chair."

Cameron's simple question seemed to catch Kupchinski off guard, because his eyes widened as if in fear as he sat there, mute. His focused his eyes first above Cameron's right shoulder and then the floor, where he stared for at least thirty seconds causing Cameron to share some of Kupchinski's apparent social discomfort.

"Teaching, research, and service," he blurted out fast, after several uncomfortable minutes of nervous silence. "Teaching, research, and service. Teaching — I'm the only one on the faculty who can teach the doctoral students about real mathematical analysis of economic theory. Research — I have over fifty papers in refereed economics and math journals, and two of them have been cited more than five thousand times each. Service — I get dozens of calls every year from big banks and corporations all over the world, asking me to be a consultant." It was clear to Cameron that Kupchinski was reciting something he had memorized.

It was only Monday mid-afternoon, and already Cameron had discovered that his VP for Admissions and Records had falsified his resume, the money President Faust promised him for scholarships was apparently unavailable, the chair of the curriculum reform committee read him a riot act of reasons why Alpha State University and its curriculum are hopeless, a billionaire wanted to give fifty million dollars to the University to support right-wing political extremism, and he was to meet with the University police chief tonight to witness an internal sting operation that he had authorized. It had been one of "those" days, and, although the awkward and not very useful interview had gone on for only about twenty minutes, Cameron could not concentrate on Kupchinski's discussion.

Then, with no warning, he heard himself saying, "Kupchinski, your claims about your superior contributions to the University are bogus. First, you are *not* the only person on the faculty who can teach mathematical economics to our doctoral students. Your senior colleague, Harvey Kleineman, is now teaching mathematical economics for a year as an invited visiting scholar on a Fulbright Professorship at Oxford. And you have one or two younger people in math econ who have excellent credentials. Second, maybe your research is cited more than that of your colleagues, but remember, your research led to billions of dollars of profit that created no value added, so for every dollar of profit gained, there was a dollar of loss. That's a draw at best. Plus, billions were lost on credit default swaps. Third, when you perform your 'service' in the private sector, you receive a huge consulting fee that becomes part of your annual income. Whether you report all of it to the University, I don't know. So I am not persuaded by your claim to deserve the super-chair because it would enable you to 'serve' the University. You'd be lining your pockets. You teach only one course per semester now. I think you might even use some of the super chair funding to pay a graduate student to teach an undergraduate econ course so you would not have to teach at all, including the doctoral seminar that 'only you can teach', but which keeps you from accepting more consulting jobs and, thus, more income."

Cameron stopped his sarcastic retort and recalled one of his favorite aphorisms: "If you speak, you must speak the truth, but sometimes, you should just listen." He realized that his role in interviewing Kupchinski was to ask relevant questions and listen and that he had just made a significant mistake in attacking this super-chair candidate.

Kupchinski had already fallen back into his earlier frenzied state of confusion and shyness, glancing from floor to ceiling, shifting his weight back and forth from left to right, twitching his nose and mouth, blinking his eyes.

"Wait. I apologize, Dr. Kupchinski." Cameron said. "I was wrong. Please forgive me. Today has been a really bad day for me, and I am upset, but that is no excuse. It was my mistake to lose my temper, and I am sorry. Please forgive me."

Staring hard at his shoes, the mathematical economist said, "It was an accident. It was an accident. Nobody is to blame. Nobody. It's time to go. Time to go." Then he left the office.

Within a few seconds, Holly, knocked, entered, and said, "It's fifteen before six, Dr. Cameron." The phone on her desk rang but she pushed a button on her cell phone to answer, "Yes, Ms. McInerney. This is Holly." She listened, raised her eyebrows, frowned at Cameron, who sat slumped in his chair, shook her head, and said, "I'll tell him. Yes. Yes, I understand."

"Dr. Cameron," Holly said as Cameron sat up straight to assume a more vice presidential position, "that was Ms. McInerney. President Faust is in a meeting with a big corporate donor and needs you there right now. In his office. It's really important, she said."

"Mine is not to reason why. Mine is just to do or die," Cameron mumbled with grim determination and grabbed his coat from the rack.

"Alfred Lord Tennyson, *Charge of the Light Brigade*," Holly said, with a straight face except for the gleam in her hazel eyes. "English 260, first semester of the American Lit sequence. I hope you're not going 'into the jaws of death.'"

"The day I've had feels a little like butchery on the battlefield. But," he said as he picked up his phone and pushed a speed-dial number, "I do need to talk to Vanessa before I go to Faust's office."

"Sweetheart," he said almost as an inquiry. "How'd the final day of cramming for the bar go?"

"We're not in New York State anymore," she said with an air of jocularity. "This state's constitutional and legal systems are newer and much less consistent and logical, but I do think I can answer some questions tomorrow. Are you on the way home, Drew? Hurry, I miss you."

Cameron explained the situation with President Faust and then gave her only the necessary facts about his meeting later with Chief Redden that might go late. "You know better than I that an all-day bar exam is a killer. Eat a light dinner and go to bed early. You'll do well, I know. I just called to let you know I won't be able to come home until I finish with Chief Redden, but I wanted to wish you luck tomorrow and tell you that I love you. I'll be quiet as a mouse when I get home." Vanessa thanked him and they again expressed their mutual affection and hung up.

"Come in, Dr. Cameron," Ms. McInerney said and ushered Cameron through President Faust's outer office and into an adjoining oak-paneled room. Eight or ten people were talking and laughing as they enjoyed the view from the president's large window overlooking the university's lighted fountain in the middle of the circular drive in front of Admin. Most sipped champagne. Cameron scanned the room for familiar faces to determine the purpose of the gathering. He saw the ASU football coach, Paul Sylvester, and the athletic director talking with President Faust and another tall man in a tailored navy blue suit whom Cameron did not know. Standing in the same circle, listening to the principals' conversation, were ASU's chief attorney, the VP for public information, the director of ASU's capital campaign, and two other men not familiar to Cameron.

"Drew! Here are some people I want you to meet," President Faust said, as he motioned Cameron into the circle and signaled the waiter to bring more champagne. "Drew Cameron, meet Price Morgan, the CEO of Universal-Lifeguard Insurance, and Robert Anderson, ULI's chief attorney. Drew is our Executive Vice President. Drew, you know Coach Sylvester and everybody else, don't you?" They exchanged greetings and everyone seemed to be in a celebratory mood, punctuated by an occasional pop of a champagne cork.

President Faust clicked his wedding ring on his champagne glass several times to get everyone's attention, and announced, "I want to propose a toast," bringing immediate silence. Raising his glass, he intoned, "To the new partnership between Universal-Lifeguard Insurance and Alpha State University. Victory is the best policy," evoking the laughter of everyone but Cameron, who had no idea what the toast meant.

"You see, Drew, tonight ASU and ULI signed an agreement to name our football field Universal-Lifeguard Insurance Field, or ULI Field for short. That's why we are celebrating and why we wanted you to celebrate with us."

On an inharmonious day of multiple unexpected shocks, Cameron was fully prepared just to continue improvising his part and play right through the *sforzando* that his boss had just directed. ASU's football stadium had been famous as Gephart-Novacek Stadium since the nineteen-forties, named after the president who got it built and the coach who brought ASU football from mediocrity to national prominence in the late thirties and early forties. *How could Faust abandon that powerful legacy, that heritage, for an insurance company?* Cameron asked himself. But he already knew the answer.

"You see, from now on, millions of TV viewers and our one hundred and five thousand ticket holders will witness the ASU Eagles meet and beat their competition on" … Faust paused for effect, "ULI Field." Price Morgan smiled with pride.

"Ideal, gentlemen. That's win-win for certain," Cameron said as he shook hands with both men. "You are to be congratulated." Yet he found it curious, indeed, that the stadium and field could have different names — ULI Field in Gephart-Novacek Stadium. A week later Cameron would learn that Jonathon Gephart, wealthy grandson of the famed ASU Coach Gephart, had finally yielded to Faust's repeated requests for a large contribution to the athletic program in order to forestall a corporate capture of both field and stadium. Grandson Gephart, now in his fifties, was financially set for life as a "trust baby" but had to get some help from his friends to produce the twenty million deemed necessary to preserve Coach Gephart's name on the stadium in perpetuity.

At that point, Ms. McInerney entered the room unnoticed, sidled up to President Faust, and whispered, "Sgt. Brown is here now, and says he should take you to the Liberty National Gala in thirty minutes."

"Tell him I'll be ready. And tell Margaret. She's going with me. It starts at eight," he responded.

Faust's reference to time caused Cameron to glance at his watch, which alerted him to the fact that the time was seven o'clock, a fact confirmed by the Riedel Tower chimes. By earlier agreement, he was due in Chief Redden's office at about seven, so he shook hands with each of the guests and excused himself. At seven fifteen, Faust walked Cameron to the door where he confided that ULI had paid ASU forty million dollars for naming rights for the football field for twenty years, the largest such deal any U.S. university had ever concluded. "The press conference to announce this to the public is tomorrow morning. Ten o'clock. Ms. McInerney left a note with your assistant. You need to be there," Faust ordered, leaving little room for doubt. "I'm sorry I haven't been available to work with you as I should but the advancement people and I have been locked in negotiations with Price Morgan and his people for days. You have some problems to discuss?"

"I do, "Cameron responded.

"Then let's get on it tomorrow."

Cameron left the celebration, deciding to walk the three blocks across campus to the ASU police station rather than drive. The uniformed officer at the reception desk stood as Cameron entered the room. "Good evening, Dr. Cameron. The Chief is expecting you. Please sign in here, sir," he said as he gave Cameron an ID badge and escorted him to room 110.

"Come in, Dr. Cameron," Chief Redden said. I want you to meet former FBI Special Agent Roland Swain, currently Rollie Swain of Swain Forensics — Rollie, this is my boss, Dr. Cameron, so be nice — and Rollie's assistant, Lyman Morris. And the technical person in ASU's Police Department, Sergeant Sylvia Lovell. All of us here are cleared for all aspects of this operation."

They exchanged greetings then talked about ASU football. It became clear to Cameron that former FBI agent Swain was not only knowledgeable about the technical world of computer forensics but also intelligent and affable. He and Redden had become friends during his term in the FBI field office in New Cambridge years ago when Redden was a lieutenant in the New Cambridge Police Department.

"Rollie, why don't you and Lyman explain to Dr. Cameron how all this is supposed to go down tonight," Redden suggested.

Swain and Morris had brought several pieces of impressive computer equipment and attached them, with numerous wires and plug-ins, to the Police Department's computer system hard drive. "The purpose of all this high tech equipment is to detect any attempt from outside to hack into the Department's system. The software we've installed is able to read and copy a hacker's software instructions without being detected by the hacker," Swain said.

Morris added, "Our software will identify the hacker's computer and record everything that occurs during the hacking transmission. And, as a safe-guard, we've made two copies on disks of the data in question, campus crime statistics by type for last year. One is locked in the Chief's personal safe and one in our safe at Swain Forensics."

Chief Redden said, "I should also tell you both," directing his remarks to Swain and Morris, "with the Provost's consent and assistance, I secured a for-mal, secret agreement with the U.S. Department of Education that they would accept ASU's crime statistics as official only from the ASU Police Department. DOE agreed to receive the data from any other source but to hold it aside for us to review and, if necessary, to use it as evidence of a crime. Now Sgt. Lovell needs to tell you about the final part of the plan. Sylvia?"

Sgt. Lovell stood up straight and reported, "Sir, I worked with Swain Forensics to arrange surveillance of Brubaker Hall, the location of the com-puter used last year to hack our system. We have installed video surveillance of all four entrances and the surrounding parking areas, plus four Swain oper-atives are on site and recording the license plates of all cars still in the sur-rounding lots after seven o'clock. When we detect someone attempting to hack into our data and ID the source computer, if it is assigned to anyone or any office in Brubaker, we will notify the four operatives stationed there. They will continue surveillance until we arrive and detain anyone trying to enter or leave the building. If the hacker is using a computer in Brubaker Hall, we have him. Or her. Any questions, sir?"

"No, Sergeant, I like your plan. Thanks for the work all of you have put into this so far," Cameron said to the group.

"Okay, we all know what to do this evening," the Chief said, indicating an end to the briefing. "Dr. Cameron, it's 7:45 PM and Sgt. Lovell, Rollie, and Lyman have already eaten. Have you?"

"I have not," Cameron replied.

"In about five minutes, I am expecting Leonardo's to deliver the large pizza I ordered. I hope you like pepperoni and onions, thin crust. I'm happy to share," Redden said.

"Offer accepted. With thanks. I'm famished," Cameron said.

As the provost and chief split a delicious pizza in the lounge and chased it with root beers, they talked about several frivolous things of no connection to the evening's activities.

When they joined the others in the computer room, they found Morris wearing a headset and monitoring the forensics equipment by listening and observing three separate screens for any evidence of a hacking attempt. Lovell was questioning Swain about technical details of the procedure and Swain enjoyed providing instruction to a very good student. Later, Swain took the monitoring responsibilities, and Morris and Lovell continued the discussion about what signals an attempt to hack into their crime data base. They were as different in persona and personality as up and down. Lovell was a tall, attractive, athletic, African-American woman with a careful smile, youngish in her early forties, unflappable, military in demeanor, quiet. Morris personified the geekish but handsome male in his mid-thirties, talkative only when discussing technical details about hardware and software, young in behavior even though by evening his five-o'clock shadow had aged his pale face. Although they had met just a few days before, the pair interacted like old friends. By nine o'clock, both Morris and Swain trusted Lovell's skill enough to allow her to take a twenty-minute solo shift of monitoring the forensic sting operation while they made a pot of coffee.

"My congratulations to you both," Cameron said to Swain and Morris. "TV police shows give the impression that coffee is always terrible in police departments. The cops always complain about it. But you two make an excellent cup of coffee."

As the sentinels drank their mugs of coffee, their moods changed from anxious anticipation to mild boredom. Conversation remained polite, to be sure, but limited to the exchange of information necessary to conduct the business at hand. Cameron and Swain sat in comfortable chairs, feet propped on stools, reading magazines. Although Lovell appeared to be reading *Newsweek*, she was focused on Morris as he sat monitoring the several screens and listening for any signal through the headphones. Redden sat near the back of the room at a long conference table catching up on office paperwork, with frequent glances at whoever was wearing the headset. No one spoke, the room was quiet. Overhead lights were off and the room was illuminated only by lamps at Morris's work station and beside each of the readers.

At about five minutes past ten, Morris sat erect, raised his right hand high into the air as he adjusted several dials on the monitoring machines with his left, and said, "We have signals!" Then he nodded his head up and down. Swain was first to his side, reading the signals on the several screens. In less than a minute, Morris started scribbling on a note pad, "ASU comp A222041-687 Bru Hall 400 Kil."

Sgt. Lovell whispered, "ASU computer, assigned to Vice President Kilgore, located in room 400 Brubaker Hall, Admissions and Records," which Chief Redden acknowledged with a nod of his head.

"Sgt. Lovell," the operation is yours, as of now. Take charge," Redden commanded.

"Yes, sir," she answered, then spoke into her cell phone, "Mr. Daily, the suspect is in room 400 Brubaker Hall on campus. ASU computer serial number Alpha dash 222041 dash 687. Secure the area. Detain anyone who tries to exit the building. We are on our way." Lovell spoke with an authoritative voice that Cameron had not heard from her before.

"Swain, Morris, you two stay here and keep monitoring. Call one of us on our cell phones the second you have evidence that our hacker is altering data," Sgt. Lovell ordered.

"Will do," Swain responded.

"You are free to come along, Dr. Cameron, if you want, but you must stay in the car until we have secured the area," Lovell commanded, and she and Chief Redden were already in the hallway scurrying toward the exit to the police parking lot. Cameron followed. As they passed the communications desk, Sgt. Lovell said, "Officer Denton, tell Peters and Kline to meet us in front of Brubaker Hall now, silent mode. Remind 'em that four Swain Forensics people are providing surveillance there." Peters and Kline were on night shift to patrol the campus.

In the forty-five seconds it took Sgt. Lovell to drive the police vehicle across campus to Brubaker Hall, running two red lights, Chief Redden accessed the architectural design of the big building on his I-pad, part of the New Cambridge public safety plan mainly for use by the Fire Department. "Okay," Redden said to Lovell, "suite 400 is on the fourth floor, right above the front door. Three exits, all into the main hallway. One straight across from the elevator and stairs. One on each end of the suite, near the elevators."

In a minute, the four campus police officers and Mr. Bailey of Swain Forensics were huddled behind a small utility building next to an unmarked Swain SUV. The only lights to be seen on the fourth floor were in the middle, around suite 400. Chief Redden said, "This is Sgt. Lovell's operation. Sergeant?"

"Mr. Daily," she addressed the Swain operative, "has anyone left or entered the building since we talked?"

"No, ma'am. No one has entered or exited the building since you called," Dailey said. "As you instructed, my men secured the building," and he continued to peer at the front door, his assignment.

Ten minutes on a cool but comfortable October night under a gorgeous starry sky often pass much too fast. On that night, however, time seemed to stand still as the officers and private security agents hid in the dim moonlight behind the white, tin-roofed utility structure. The breath from their whispers produced puffs of condensation in the air as they discussed their mission and what might happen next.

The second Sgt. Lovell felt her cell phone vibrate in her hand, she placed it to her ear and heard Rollie Swain say, "Sergeant, the suspect has just erased the data and is sending altered data back to the original file in your system. The evidence is clear."

Lovell responded, "Perfect. We're going in," and nodded to the others. Bailey informed his three Swain associates by phone and joined Lovell and Redden as they walked up the stairs and found room 400, the only room with a thin slit of light shining under its door. The chief and the sergeant nodded to one another and to Mr. Bailey. Lovell and Redden loosened the leather straps holding their weapons in their holsters. Lovell used her master key to gain entrance to 400 Brubaker Hall, not really sure what or whom they would find. The door made no sound as she pushed it open, so the person they saw seated at the computer, in rapt concentration, did not stir as the three entered. "Sir?" Lovell called out. "Dr. Kilgore?"

The suspect jerked, stood up, turned around, and lurched forward, knocking over his chair. Both officers, fifteen feet from their suspect, stepped apart and placed their hands on their weapons, part of the choreographic training of officers at the scene of a crime in progress.

"Sir, I'm ASU Police Sgt. Lovell and this is Chief Redden. Please step away from the computer. Now! We are investigating a possible criminal offense, sir, and need your cooperation. May I see some identification? The nervous suspect pulled a wallet from his left rear pants pocket, fingered it for a moment, and then handed a driver license to Sgt. Lovell, all the while remaining silent. She examined the name and picture on the license, again looked at the suspect, then handed it back to him.

"Stand over there by that bookcase, Mr. Kilgore," Lovell ordered, and nodded to Redden. She took the seat in front of the computer and looked at two screens, one of which presented the incidents of rape reported on ASU's campus last year. As the department's chief technical officer, she had tabulated the known campus incidents of every type of felony crime and had prepared the report for the U.S. Department of Education. The bottom line for rape on Kilgore's screen was four. She knew with certainty that the actual total had been eleven.

She nodded to her boss, turned to Kilgore, and said, Mr. Kilgore, you are under arrest for suspicion of violations of the Clery Act. Do you understand?" Then she placed handcuffs on the suspect.

"You don't know what you're doing," Kilgore mumbled, but showed no resistance.

Sgt. Lovell and Chief Redden walked Kilgore to their car and delivered him to central lock-up at the New Cambridge Police Department.

By cell phone, Lovell said, "Mr. Swain, you and Mr. Morris should go up to room 400 right now and collect any evidence." Then she called the squad car in which Cameron had been waiting. "Sir, we found Vice President Kilgore altering the data. We are taking him to central lockup. Do you need a ride back to your car at the station house."

"No thanks, Sgt. Lovell, I need the walk. But do me a small favor first," Cameron requested. "Could you get Chief Redden on your phone for me? I want to tell him something."

"He's right here, sir", and she handed the phone to Chief Redden.

"Charlie, I have to be the one to inform President Faust of what has happened here tonight, so don't call him. I will." After listening to the chief's response, Cameron said, "Yes, I know it's irregular, but as a courtesy to him. There may be something involved here we don't know about. When we find out, we'll act. And I want to say, you and Sgt. Lovell, your other officers and the Swain agents all conducted a first-class operation tonight. You should be proud. We'll talk tomorrow."

It was well after midnight and he was exhausted as he pulled into his garage in Bedford. He left Vanessa a brief note by the coffee pot, slipped into his pajamas in the dark, and climbed into bed. She faced a very important challenge in just eight hours and he knew her alarm clock would wake him early, too.

7 Although their alarm clock was on Cameron's side of the bed, last night before retiring Vanessa had set the alarm for 6 AM but then by force of habit had gone to sleep on her side of the bed. At about ten minutes before six, she awoke, pulled back the covers, stared for a moment into the darkness, stood up beside the bed, and then felt her way hand over hand around the foot of the bed toward the alarm clock to silence it before it rang. She pulled on her robe, stretched, and walked into the kitchen where she read Cameron's note requesting that she wake him at six-thirty. By that time, she was showered, dressed, feeling and looking good, a mug of coffee in each hand, standing over her husband's still unconscious form. "Caaaaameron. Wake uuuuuuup," she warbled, following his instructions about a wake-up call.

Both of his eyes popped open and then squinted as he lifted the covers and swung his feet around to the floor. "Good morning. Thanks for getting me up. How are you? Did you get a good night's rest?"

"I did, thanks. I didn't even wake up when you got into bed. What time did you get home?"

"About one, I think," Cameron said, as he stood and they hugged. "I'm so glad you rested well. You will knock that bar exam out of the park. I just know it. You look great, by the way. Here's to victory." He picked up his hot coffee and they clicked mugs to toast her success. His first sip stimulated his taste and smell and he could almost feel the bold dark roast begin resuscitation on the neurons in his brain.

"So, how did your police stakeout go?" Vanessa asked.

"I will tell you, even though it's supposed to remain secret, because you are not only my wife of record but my attorney of record. You know, wife-husband privilege and attorney-client privilege," which evoked a chuckle from Vanessa. "Chief Redden and his FBI forensics friend caught one of our vice presidents, Zachary Kilgore, hacking into the campus police department's file of crime stats, deleting the file, and replacing it with altered data — we think to make the university look better. And today the Police Department is scheduled to send the data to USDOE. We have a problem."

"Oh, Drew, I'm so sorry. That's a federal violation."

"Yeah, the Clery Act. But I shouldn't have told you until after the bar exam. Knowing about it may cause you to worry and throw you off your game. We can talk about it later, but please, don't worry. We'll get it taken care of."

"I'll turn it off before the exam," Vanessa promised. "Get a shower and let's eat a quick cereal and toast. I have to be in the State Appellate Court Building a little before eight. Does Faust know yet?"

"No. I've got to call him, right away"

Later in the garage, as Vanessa was about to get into her car, Cameron gave her a final hug and kiss and said, "You do not need one iota of luck, darlin,' but I wish you all the luck in the world anyway."

"Promise me, when I get this bar exam finished, you'll meet me back here around six-thirty, and you'll open the bar for me. Pass with honors or fail with ignominy, I think I'll need one of your patented vodka tonics with a twist of lime."

"And you shall have it, counselor. I promise."

When he arrived at the university, Holly followed him into his office and closed the door. "Is everything all right, Dr. Cameron?" she asked, her sixth sense telling her that her boss was troubled about something.

"No, not quite. Get me Steve Faust on the phone, wherever he is."

Cameron hung up his sport coat and took a seat behind his desk as Holly scurried to her desk. Right away, he heard the familiar buzz from his phone that only a contact from Holly's phone can produce. When he picked up, "Dr. Cameron, Ms. McInerney says he's tied up in a breakfast meeting with the CEO of TransAmerican National, something about trying to finalize a big gift to the university. She said he told her no interruptions. But she gave me his personal cell phone and said I could call him after nine-thirty. He'll be driving back to campus to preside over a press conference at ten, in the conference room in the Athletic Center. And you have to be there, too."

"Please have Ms. McInerney arrange a meeting with him right after the press conference. Tell her it is important."

"Will do. Anything else?"

"No, Holly. Thank you. I need an uninterrupted hour myself, to think through these problems."

Cameron pulled a yellow legal pad and a sharp pencil from his desk drawer. Then he listed each problem he faced and his preferred bottom-line solution on the legal pad.

Z. Kilgore — resume falsification. Terminate.

Z. Kilgore — computer hacking. Follow police protocol.

Fraternity cocaine party — follow police protocol. See M. Benedict about minimizing bad PR, notify counseling services. Ban BMO from campus for two years.

Honors scholarship funding denied — ask Faust about funding for next fall. Get firm commitment. If no for next fall, get absolute commitment for subsequent fall or else.

Murray gift — read proposal carefully. Discuss with Faust and Benedict. Reinterpret/neutralize Randolph principles? Make Murray a counter-offer?

He reviewed his five solutions and wondered how Faust would react. According to formal rules, it was the responsibility of the executive vice president to make decisions about such matters, after consultation with the president. It was also clear that his decision on such matters is a recommendation to the president, which the president can accept or reject. All large, formal organizations, he realized, must live by the admonition US President Truman displayed on a sign on his White House desk — "The buck stops here."— and in higher education, the executive vice president serves at the pleasure of the president. Although the formal authority structure is clear, it doesn't offer a clue about how to mitigate the conflict between ethical systems, which Cameron feared would occur with his and Faust's positions on several of these five problems — especially those that involve powerful interests outside the university. In those cases, it was clear to Cameron that the traditional values of the academy, preserving and expanding the enlightenment of society while maintaining its own integrity, differed from the emerging values in higher education, preserving and expanding its wealth and power. Resolution of those conflicts is usually a political decision, inside or outside the university.

Almost simultaneous with two soft knocks at his office door came Holly's welcomed interruption, "Dr. Cameron, sorry, I just talked with Ms. McInerney. The press conference starts in twenty minutes. President Faust wants you to meet him back at his office when the press conference ends so the two of you can talk."

"Thanks, Holly. Hold down the fort." Cameron put on his sport coat and picked up the legal pad listing his five problems and solutions to discuss with Faust.

The first person Cameron saw as he turned the corner into the Athletics Center conference room was TV journalist Mona Richards. She had interviewed him twice during the fall semester, once about the University's plans to expand its international curriculum and activities and once about book banning by several local school boards in the state. Of course, he supported the former, since it was his idea, and opposed the latter, since he saw no harm, only good, in high school students reading and discussing *Catcher in the Rye* or *Slaughterhouse Five* under a teacher's supervision. She had a growing reputation as a sophisticated TV journalist who sought to report and analyze important news, not to sensationalize. Cameron was surprised and pleased when Mona Richards looked up, saw him, smiled and waved. He waved back, realizing that having a friend in the media might come in handy, then took a seat on the aisle near the middle of the room.

Margaret Benedict had done her usual excellent job of organizing the press conference. The smallish conference room was packed. All the relevant media representatives were present. The podium glimmered with the familiar faces of powerful people, namely, President Faust, Athletic Director Royce Payton, Coach Paul Sylvester, Universal-Lifeguard Insurance Company CEO Price Morgan and ULI's chief attorney Robert Anderson.

Faust began the ceremony right on time, as cameras rolled. "Good morning. We are here this morning to announce and celebrate an historic event - the naming of Alpha State University's football field. To make that formal announcement, I'd like to present to you the chief executive officer of Universal-Lifeguard Insurance, Mr. Price Morgan."

As Faust sat down to polite applause, Price Morgan rose and took his place in front of the mike and TV cameras. He stood for a moment with impressive stage presence and his leading man's good looks. His address was brief and eloquent with an occasional gesture and only a hint of an upper mid-west accent from his native Chicago. "All of us at Universal-Lifeguard Insurance hold Alpha State University in high regard. We benefit from its academic strength as we hire scores of its graduates to work in our home office and regional offices around the country. We appreciate its sports programs and the way they enhance the national reputation of our community and state, and contribute to our economy. By making a small gift to the university to name its football field, we are simply saying, 'Well done, ASU. Keep up the good work.'" Then the University of Chicago graduate with a Northwestern MBA nodded respectfully to President Faust, smiled at the cameras, and said, "From all of us at Universal Lifeguard Insurance, thank you very much," and he took his seat as the audience applauded.

Coach Sylvester strolled to the mike with his perpetual, confident smile, dressed as always in his navy blue blazer with ASU stitched in gold on the vest pocket and a gold and black striped tie. His ruddy red complexion and craggy face exuded both seriousness and charm as he approached the mike. In middle age, he had added a few pounds to his six-three frame but retained the look of strength and determination that had made him an All-America selection as an ASU linebacker many years ago.

Faust was taking a chance to place Coach in front of TV cameras. At several televised gatherings where he had spoken, TV stations had found it necessary to edit his statements before airing them so that they contained no four-letter words. Coach had a colorful vocabulary. But even the moralists forgave him with excuses such as, "Oh, he is under such stress," or "He doesn't really mean anything bad, you know."

"Price Morgan is a good friend of the University," he said to the rapt audience. "He wanted to help us out, so he asked us what we needed. We told him we respect his business a lot and asked him how we could help him out. Well, we discussed it." Coach paused, smiled and said, "So, we now have become partners. Starting this coming Saturday afternoon after our pre-game dedication ceremony, ASU will play its first home football game on Universal-Lifeguard Insurance Field or ULI Field." The audience stood and cheered as the cameras rolled. "Price and ULI made it a very attractive idea. I promised him that the ASU football team will kick ass on ULI Field and make him proud."

Following another round of applause, Margaret Benedict ended the formal part of the press conference by thanking the attendees and media representatives and indicating that President Faust, Price Morgan, and Coach Sylvester would be available to the media for questions in the north end of the conference room until about ten-thirty.

Faust was obviously in a buoyant mood when a few minutes later he breezed into his inner office and said, "Hi, Drew. Sit, be comfortable." He laid his jacket on the desk, took a seat on the couch, propped his feet on the coffee table, and yelled out to Ms. McInerney, "Dr. Cameron needs coffee. And bring me one, too. Okay, Drew, what's the big problem?"

"Let's start with two problems that are connected. Zachary Kilgore faked his resume to get the VP job here and hacked into ASU's police computer system and falsified crime data, which he sent to the DOE."

"What do you recommend, Drew?" Faust shot back, making no effort to conceal the anger that reddened his face.

"First, termination for falsifying his résumé and second, criminal prosecution in federal court for hacking and sending DOE false crime data. That's a federal offence, of the Clery Act," Cameron said.

"No, it is not," Faust shot back. "Today is the day we officially send our data to DOE. And we will, as required. Valid data. If," he continued, "we had sent fraudulent data to DOE, Kilgore might have been guilty of violating the

Clery Act. But he is guilty only of thinking he wanted to help the University — misguided but not guilty of a crime."

"So what do we do about that?" Cameron asked.

"Nothing. You already decided to fire him, didn't you?"

"Yes, for résumé falsification. I have to. If I don't we will send a terrible message to our own employees and the whole world."

"Okay, we're set on those two issues. But let me say two things, Drew, before we move on. First, your arrangement with Chief Redden. I applaud your initiative. But second, never, I repeat never, go over my head or behind my back with a matter that affects the whole university community and involves important players outside the university. The consequences would be very serious. Do you understand?"

After a long, uncomfortable silence, Cameron answered, "Yes. I'll keep you posted from now on." He looked at his boss to see the reaction.

"Fine. Just remember, the impolitic, the indiscrete, the inconsiderate can sometimes have more serious implications than . . . ." Faust trailed off, feeling that he had made his point. Then said, "Go on to your next thing."

"Of course, you are aware of our agreement about funding scholarships for excellent students from low-income families? I asked Avery Gibbs in the Foundation to move the money into the right account so we could start awarding scholarships for next fall. He indicated that there is no such money and that I should talk to you."

After a lengthy pause, Faust said, "Avery's right. There is no such money in the Foundation at this time. Based on the advice of our financial managers, we decided to invest a sizeable sum in the stocks of a sound company they think is on the brink of moving up in the market. Way up. So that's where the money is now. Probably by late next spring, we will have the money to put into your scholarship program."

"Can we proceed now, as planned, or not?" Cameron said with undisguised impatience.

"You may proceed, Drew, but only with half the number of offers you proposed for year one — fifty instead of a hundred. We'll start small and then come on strong in year two."

"Fine. I will proceed. The fourth problem is that the New Cambridge Police Department was called to intervene in a party that got out of hand at the Beta Mu Omega house Friday night. They found cocaine. Chief . . ."

Faust interrupted, "That one's about gone away, Drew. The New Cambridge police chief, Al Meisner, called me Saturday and told me about it. Sorry I didn't get a chance to return your phone calls over the weekend, but I was swamped. Anyway, we took care of it."

"What do you mean, 'We took care of it'?"

"I mean that when New Cambridge was processing the names of the boys at the fraternity party, they saw that some of them were the sons of very prominent families in New Cambridge. As a courtesy, the chief let me know. We decided that the greater good was to punish the dealers, not the young college students who made an error. So, we decided to arrest and prosecute the two men who supplied the drugs and to expunge the record of those who tested positive for the coke, provided their records stay clean for one year. And we are banning BMO from any activity, any presence, on this campus for two years."

"Isn't there a good chance, Steve, that those BMO fraternity members, who come from elite families and lead privileged lives, will learn nothing out of this experience," Cameron warned, "except that they are above the law?"

"Drew, at least this way they will spend another year or two with us, living and studying on the ASU campus, under our influence and their parents' influence, rather than in some barbaric state prison, where they would learn hate and vengeance and earn a criminal record that haunts them for the rest of their lives."

"The research shows that new users with a college education benefit most from a combination of drug rehab and counseling," Cameron retorted.

"Drew, I'm not going to argue the fine points of drug research with you. It's your field, not mine. But I know you appreciate cost-benefit analysis. As an MBA student and a corporate executive for thirty years I have seen how useful it is. The solution that Allen Meisner and I worked out has the tangible benefit that it solves the immediate problem but has the intangible cost that several boys may continue to think they are above the law, at least for a few years until they grow up, get permanent jobs, get married, buy houses, have kids, and so forth. If we had solved the problem your way, we would have had a huge tangible cost right now. We would have several hostile alumni — important bankers, lawyers, insurance execs, real estate execs, corporate CEOs, and several whose work is just managing their portfolios and playing a lot of golf. I don't have to remind you of the cost of that solution — many millions in gifts for years to come, and serious deterioration of our network of alumni and friends of the University that it has taken decades to build. It was a strategic choice of being pure and poor or maximizing benefits and minimizing costs."

Realizing that the decision had already been put into place and that he could not win the argument about it, Cameron decided to finish the list and get back to his own business. "The final problem concerns Michelle Murray's tentative offer to the University. I met with her. She wants to give us fifty million dollars . . ."

"Okay, Drew! Nice work. Your very first foray into fundraising for Alpha State is an auspicious beginning," Faust interrupted.

"I appreciate your complement, Steve, but I don't think we can accept the gift as offered."

"What? You've gotta be kidding. We can't turn down fifty million dollars," Faust said, his face contorted in disbelief.

"Here's a copy of her proposal, Steve," Cameron said. "She wants to fund several endowed chairs and an institute, named after John Randolph of Roanoke. In case you haven't heard of him, he was an early nineteenth century member of Congress from Virginia, who fought against just about everything Madison and Jefferson did to ensure that this country would be a democracy. She wants the chair holders and the institute to espouse his doctrines in their teaching, research, and service."

Cameron paused for a response from Faust, but none came. Rather, Faust looked at him as if he wanted to hear more encouraging news. "But there might be a compromise solution here," Cameron said. "There's only one way we can accept the gift. In her proposal, Ms. Murray highlights six or eight of Randolph's main doctrines. Each one is the right-wing position on a particular constitutional or political principle. I think we can restate each of Randolph's right-wing assertions in rather more neutral terms, as an expression of a general challenge that American society faces. Then, we can let the chair holders and others explore all aspects of those issues over time."

"I don't follow you. What do you mean?" Faust asked, leaving Cameron wondering whether his boss liked his idea or actually preferred Murray's choice.

"Okay. One of his principles was 'defense of the family,' which for him and many people today would mean only one thing: marriage can only be between a man and woman, of the same race and religion. We could take the bias out of that idea by restating it as something like 'the family as a basic unit of society'."

As Cameron talked, Faust picked up the Murray proposal and found the page listing Randolph's principles. "What would you do with 'liberty over equality'?" he asked.

"First, I'd call it 'liberty and equality', and I'd examine alternative conditions and explanations of liberty and equality in history and what happens when there is too little of one and too much of the other. Then, I'd apply that to contemporary societies."

Faust didn't seem satisfied with that response but went ahead anyway. "Okay," reading from the proposal, "what about 'celebration of the literary and artistic inheritance of Western civilization'?"

"That one needs no tinkering," Cameron said. "It seems neutral enough."

"Number four," Faust continued, "'adherence to truth revealed through scripture and tradition'. I can see that one would get us in trouble with different religious groups and atheists."

"Then how about making it 'church and state in America'?" Cameron responded.

"I see what you're doing, Drew," Faust answered. "Very clever. John Randolph's eight principles are answers. You're converting each one into a question. What about 'states rights' superiority to national rule'?"

"Federalism in theory and practice. Political Science already has courses on that topic."

"'Small national government'. What do you do with this one?"

"Also easy. 'Size and scope of government in a changing society'."

"Okay, what about number eight, 'Opposition to debt in American government'?"

"'U.S. fiscal and economic policy'. That needs examining, don't you agree?" Cameron asked.

"Finally, 'the landed gentry's right to govern'. That one is more than a little sticky. How would you make that a neutral question instead of an answer, Drew?"

"I'd rename it 'social responsibilities of the economic elite' and deal with the tenets of *noblesse oblige*, you know, noble ancestry requires honorable behavior, privilege entails responsibility - across time and in various countries."

Faust gazed into space for several moments. "Damn, Drew. You've translated each of those two-hundred-year-old principles into a contemporary academic expression. Clever, but will it get the money? Will Murray buy it? That's the question. What's your answer to that one?"

"Maybe," Cameron ventured. "And over time, if you and I and those who replace us do our jobs well, in addition to the moderates, we will have libertarians and socialists in some of the chairs from time to time. That is, or should be, what a university is all about. Academic freedom. Exploring alternative solutions to problems. She wants the chairs and institute to bear the name of John Randolph. If we urge her to call them Michele Murray chairs and the Michele Murray Institute, to honor her charity, she might agree to it."

"I've got to hand it to you," Faust said. "My main job is to acquire and manage sufficient resources to make this university grow and be great. Your main job is to ensure that the university does the right things and with high academic standards. If it were up to me, I'd take her money and run. I think Randolph probably had some pretty good answers. But go ahead and give her a counter-proposal, dress it up, take her to dinner, see if she will bend your way. I can't help you with your counter-proposal, because if she gets pissed at the University about this, my job is to go back to her with her original proposal, smooth over her hurt feelings, and get her to fund the original package. And let me remind you, Drew, like most universities we take in a lot more alumni and corporate gifts every year for athletics than for academics, millions more. You're the academic VP. Bring in the money."

"Okay," Cameron said, as he rose to leave, not at all sure what his 'okay' meant.

"Are we finished?" Faust asked.

"We're finished," Cameron answered, and started toward the door.

"Let's stay on the same page from now on, Drew. There are several trustees who . . . let's just say, they don't always appreciate your judgment. Consult me. If I'm not available, tell Ms. McInerney it's urgent. She'll get me."

"Okay. Thank you, Steve."

Cameron strode down the hall to his own office. For the first time they seemed to be in fundamental disagreement about who should act and what should be done. He began to wonder if moving from a very comfortable deanship at an excellent smaller university to an executive VP position in a much larger institution had been such a good decision.

As he turned into his outer office, he noticed that Holly was nowhere to be seen. Then he heard the familiar, "Dr. Cameron, I have some good news!" as she came out of his office into the reception area, and handed him an envelope.

"I hope so. I could use some good news about now," he said, exhibiting a worried smile. "What is it?" The letter brought a confident smile back to his face. "The European Council for Addictive Drug Research has extended our one-year contract for up to ten years and removed the limit on how much funding we can ask for each year. Holly, we're in!"

"I thought you'd like that, Dr. Cameron. Congratulations!" Holly felt genuinely gratified by Cameron's success, because she had seen him work hard to maintain a cheery disposition while being bombarded with, and blamed for, problems that he inherited when he took the job. She had overheard the occasional whispered conversations of senior professors, even department chairs criticizing Cameron's insistence on curriculum reform. Some had said that strategic planning is just another hornet's nest of time-consuming paper work while others argued that planning is just another way for central administration to control what they do in their college (or department or classroom). Some even claimed that whenever you want the provost to do something useful for your unit, he's out of the office raising money and can't be reached, but when you need money to add a new faculty position, he says there's no money and calls a series of endless meetings that keep you from doing your job. *He's damned if he does and damned if he doesn't*, Holly thought to herself.

"Holly," Cameron said, seeming to fall back into his usual comfortable demeanor, "arrange a meeting of the Drug Studies Committee that I appointed back in August — as soon as possible, and include me. Tell them the agenda items are, 'We got the contract' and 'What do we do next?' Right now, I want to call Katie Brown in Psych to get her to chair the committee. She'll keep the research agenda balanced."

"Got it," Holly answered.

"Also, I want to arrange an appointment with Michele Murray to discuss her gift to the University." Holly started scribbling on a pad, realizing that the list of tasks might grow longer. "And prepare a letter for my signature terminating Vice President Kilgore. Make sure we offer only one reason – falsification of his resume to get the VP position. Consult with somebody in the University Attorney's Office about wording. I also want to talk with the second-in-command in Admissions and Records on the phone. What's his name?"

"He's a she. Dr. Sylvia Madrigal," Holly answered. "She joined ASU just this past summer, when you did."

"Arrange a meeting with her for tomorrow, early if possible. She's going to take over as acting VP until we can recruit a permanent VP. And I want to discuss the honors scholarship program with her, because Faust told me that we can have half the expected money, so we'll begin with that for next fall's admissions."

Holly stopped writing on her pad. "Anything else, Dr. Cameron?"

"No. It's one o'clock. I'm going to the Student Union cafeteria."

"Very good," Holly said with her usual confidence. "Wait just a minute," she said as she disappeared to one of her filing cabinets. When she returned, she handed Cameron a file and said, "Here's Dr. Madrigal's personnel file. I knew you'd want to study it while you're having lunch."

Cameron then quipped, "I would have thought of that. Wouldn't I?"

Half an hour later, when Cameron had almost finished his lunch, he had learned that Sylvia Madrigal was born in San Jose, Costa Rica and had a doctorate in educational administration, including a minor field in computer science, from the University of Costa Rica. Plus, she did a post-doc at the University of New Orleans, taught educational administration there for a couple of years, served as deputy superintendent of schools for Orleans Parish for almost ten years, then came to Alpha State in her current position of assistant VP for admissions. As Cameron swallowed his last gulp of cafeteria iced tea, his cell phone sounded its familiar ring tone from Holly.

"Dr. Cameron, I have you booked with Dr. Madrigal at nine tomorrow morning. The rest of today she's tied up giving a speech at the New Cambridge Latin American Chamber of Commerce. You're scheduled to meet with Dr.

Greene from Psychology at three today. Ms. Murray's assistant at Murray Robotics said she will be unavailable until right after Thanksgiving. She's out of town. I think it's some kind of health issue, but that wasn't clear. Anyway, I made you a tentative appointment with her on November 29. Sorry, I realize that's a month away, but that's the best they could offer us. The letter of termination for Dr., uh, I mean Vice President Kilgore, is ready for your signature. The ASU attorney said it was fine. Is all of that okay?"

"Yes, Holly. Many thanks." As he returned to his office on that cool autumn day, Cameron thought about Vanessa, in the middle of a grueling eight-hour bar exam at the federal court house and, using mental telepathy, sent her a message of love and good luck. With high hopes that she would pass the exam, he shuddered as he realized that only a bare majority of first-time takers of the bar exam pass it, and the test takers are almost all recent graduates of law schools in the state. Vanessa had studied law in California. His thoughts of Vanessa and their early years at Berkeley were suddenly disturbed by the raucous noise of a leaf blower cranking up only a few yards ahead of him on the sidewalk.

Back at the office, the letter of dismissal looked fine, so he signed it and placed it in the envelope Holly had addressed to VP Kilgore. "Holly, I'm going to deliver this letter to Kilgore in person. Give a copy to Ms. McInerney." Cameron had decided to deliver the termination letter to Kilgore in person as soon as he had learned that Kilgore was released from New Cambridge central lockup within just a few hours of his arrest. He suspected that President Faust had intervened to get Kilgore released so soon.

As Cameron entered the Office of Admissions and Records, he sensed the absence of sound in a room with half a dozen people at their desks. Bad news travels fast, Cameron figured, so the office staff must have heard something about last night's police stakeout and their boss's role in it. As Cameron approached Kilgore's administrative assistant, she spotted him and rose from her desk, cleared her throat, and said, "Dr. Cameron. What can we do for you, sir?"

I'd like to see Vice President Kilgore. It's urgent."

"Yes, sir," she said, knocked twice on Kilgore's door and escorted Cameron into her boss's office.

Kilgore was sitting in his swivel office chair, staring out the window across the campus below. He neither spoke nor turned to see who had entered his office.

"Dr. Kilgore, Dr. Cameron is here to see you," his aide said.

Kilgore swiveled his chair around. His face was pale, his hair tousled, his eyes red, his hands shaky. "I didn't expect you to show up in person," he said, looking at the floor.

"Zachary," it's my duty to deliver this letter to you. We have indisputable evidence that you falsified your resume when you applied for your position here. For that reason, I am terminating you from employment at Alpha State University, effective December 31 of this year. You must vacate your position and remove all of your possessions from the university by the end of today. If you are found in this building after five o'clock today, campus police will be called to remove you. Leave a forwarding address with your assistant so that we can mail any of your belongings to you that you leave behind. All of the conditions of your termination are explained in this letter. Do you understand?"

Kilgore raised his head to face Cameron and opened his mouth but did not speak. Cameron gave him the envelope containing the termination letter. "This letter details the situation and stipulates that the University will never submit a letter of recommendation for you. The only information we will supply to a potential employer who inquires is that you worked here and the dates of your employment."

Kilgore's face seemed to show the faintest of sad smiles, at least on one side of his mouth. Cameron asked, "Do you have any questions?" to which he replied only by shaking his head and staring at the floor. After waiting for half a minute, Cameron left this most unpleasant meeting, assured that the problem was solved.

Dr. Greene, the cognitive psychologist, was quite agreeable to chairing a committee to evaluate research proposals on drug addiction and policy and to making recommendations to Cameron about which ones to fund under his contract with the European Council for Research on Addictive Drugs. When they shook hands as she was leaving, Cameron felt confident that the committee would do a good job as a result of her leadership.

At about three o'clock, Holly entered his office and said, "Dr. Cameron, you have about a hundred unanswered emails. Want me to answer some of them? Here are some letters to sign, and a stack of snail mail that you need to read. Please mark each one for me to answer for you or send me an email with the gist of your answers and I'll prepare letters for you to sign. Here is a list of phone calls you need to answer." Holly paused for a moment, then proceeded, "As you can see, we are a little behind, but we'll catch up."

"Can't you allocate some of this to some of the associate VPs in the office?"

"Dr. Cameron, I already did. These are just the ones that need your personal attention," Holly responded

"Just put them in my box, and I will turn them around ASAP. And thanks, Holly. You stay on top of business better than anybody I know."

"There are two items I should highlight for you. Here is a copy of the email we received from Anna Zezulka in the Czech Republic," Holly said, handing Cameron the email. She and two people from Moravian Motorworks will arrive in New Cambridge on November 27 and go back to Prague on December 4. They are coming to attend a trade mission, something about the New Cambridge Transit Authority and streetcars. The other item is a call you got from the mayor's office to let you know that they will be hosting the Czech delegation to the trade conference. They want you to return the call. Also, related to the trade conference," Holly paused to catch her breath," is that Axel Dekker confirmed that he has rescheduled his trip here for the job interview to coincide with the visit by the Czech trade delegation."

"I think that's all good news, "Cameron confirmed. "And I will respond as you suggest, as soon as I can. This afternoon."

Cameron dug into the emails, letters and phone calls in part because they were important and in part to see if he could match Holly's efficiency, effectiveness, and unflappability. But in only a few minutes, his restless mind returned to Vanessa's bar exam, so he tried to live out the old adage, "Hard work keeps your mind off your troubles." Within an hour he had made major progress in moving "to do" items into the "finished" category and placed them in his outbox for Holly. By 5:30 PM, he had almost finished, so he gathered the remaining papers, stuffed them into his briefcase, and stopped at Holly's desk on his way out to give her his outbox of work.

He could see that no lights were on in his house as soon as he pulled into the driveway. He grabbed the mail on the way in, turned on the entry hall light, and realized that he was exhausted. He laid his briefcase, top coat and the mail on the hallway table, loosened his tie, and just sat for a few minutes in an easy chair in the den waiting for Vanessa and the news she would bring. Her headlights flashed through the living room windows at about six thirty, and his heart rate increased.

He stood to greet her as she opened the door. They embraced in silence for a brief while before Vanessa said, "I think I did okay. I feel pretty confident about it — better than when I took the New York bar exam, and I did okay on that one!"

"That's wonderful, Vanessa. And why am I not surprised? You aced it, you'll see. How long do we have to wait before they let you know the results?"

"Months," she said with a contrived frown. "But in the meantime, you said you would greet me with a vodka tonic with a lime wedge - win, lose, or draw," and changed her expression to a comical grin.

"Coming right up," Cameron responded. "Just sit right there." In short order, he was back in the den carrying a drink for each of them and two napkins. "Let's celebrate a job completed and, I bet the world, very well done," Cameron toasted, his wine raised.

"Thank you, dear. I hope so. I think so," Vanessa said.

Before either of them had finished their first sips, the landline telephone broke the silence of their quiet celebration. As he walked toward the phone, Cameron said, "You sit, Vanessa. I'll get rid of whoever is trying to sell us something."

"Hello," Cameron said, with equal parts boredom and impatience. "Yes." Then he listened for a moment. "Yes, she is. Just a moment." Cameron turned to Vanessa with a puzzled look on his face, covered the mouthpiece with his hand and said, "It's for you. It's a Sheldon Ackerman with the law firm, Gordon and Sharp. He's says he's the managing partner," and handed Vanessa the phone.

"Hello. Yes, this is she," Vanessa said, then listened for a while. "Right, I just finished about an hour ago," and paused to listen to Ackerman's response.

"Well, I think I did alright but I won't know for a while. The bar doesn't send the scores to the test-takers for about three months, as you no doubt remember." As she listened to Ackerman's next statements, she looked at Cameron and contorted her face to reveal anxious confusion.

"You know the risk involved in that for your firm, of course, because nothing's certain until I receive a passing score on the exam. But, I am willing to meet with you and learn more about your firm," she confessed, as her expression changed from resistance to compliance.

"Okay. Monday at ten, Trans-Am Tower, office eleven hundred. I will be there," indicating with her free hand that Cameron should help her remember the time and place of an apparent meeting. He wrote it on a pad.

She replaced the phone in its cradle, turned to her incredulous husband and said, "Where's my drink, Cameron. I think I need to be sedated!"

"Hearing only your half of the conversation, I am not sure what just happened. What did he want?" Cameron asked.

"The managing partner of one of the largest law firms in the state just asked me to come to his office next Monday morning to interview for a job in his firm. I told him that I haven't passed the state bar exam yet. He knew that I had just taken it today, but said not to worry, because I can always take it again if I don't pass it the first time. Can you believe that?"

"It's a stretch, but I suppose so," Cameron said. "But how did he even know you were taking the bar? How many people were there taking it today?"

"Hundreds, literally. Yeah, how did he know I was taking it, unless he has access to confidential state bar association records?"

By this time, Vanessa had downed her first vodka tonic and Cameron handed her another one. "Well, counselor, you have a week to do some research on, what's his name, Mr. Ackerman and the Gordon and Sharp law firm and go into the interview with some questions of your own."

138

They decided to forego a regular dinner tonight because both of them were tired and not too hungry. Rather they played the new Ellis Marsalis CD they had purchased at his concert a few weeks ago and made peanut butter and honey sandwiches for dinner. The conversation about Vanessa's mysterious phone call and what it might mean continued through their sandwiches and the clean-up afterwards. Because it was late and they were both exhausted, they went to bed early.

Cameron rose earlier than usual the next morning, rested and eager to get back into the office. Vanessa's good feeling about the bar exam and her enigmatic phone call were both on his mind as he drove into New Cambridge at six o'clock. He had decided to go to the university fitness center to work out first, shower and change into his coat and tie there, then get a quick breakfast at the Faculty Club. His plan worked well and he walked into his quiet outer office at about seven-thirty, greeted as usual by Holly.

"You need to call Chief Redden," she said. "Oh, sorry, good morning. He called a few minutes ago and wants to talk to you. He said it's urgent."

"Good morning and thank you. Get him on the phone," Cameron requested.

She speed-dialed his private extension. He answered right away and she said, "Hold for Dr. Cameron."

"Charlie, good morning," Cameron said, feeling chipper after his workout.

"Sorry to trouble you so early, Drew, but we have a possible situation," the chief said.

"Go on."

In his typically low-keyed style, Redden began, "Rollie's people at Swain Forensics have done their preliminary analysis, which they say provides airtight evidence that Vice President Kilgore hacked into our computer system and changed the data. He offered an interesting opinion. He said that he wondered why Kilgore did what he did, maybe two years in a row. Of course the answer is, 'to make the university look better.' So he thinks that because Kilgore is expert in computer systems and was in charge of an office that maintained all student records, maybe he might have been altering other records. To make the university look good."

"That would be logical," Cameron commented. "Go on."

"So, Rollie and I remembered that about two years ago the state legislature announced a big award — extra funding every year for any of the state universities that break into the top thirty public universities in America, for as long as they stay in the top thirty," Redden said.

"Yeah, Charlie, that was before I came. I learned about it in my interviews for the job."

"So we started thinking about what changes in student records might help the university most to get into the top thirty. Actually, some of Rollie's people came up with the answers. For example," and here it became apparent that Redden was reading from a prepared list, "the percent of applicants who are accepted, the percent of acceptances who attend, the average SAT or ACT scores of the entering freshmen class, the percent of freshmen who return as sophomores, and the percent of students who graduate in six years or less. Did the university have a noticeable improvement in those statistics last spring?" Redden asked.

"I don't know, Charlie, but if what you and Rollie suspect is true, it's very bad news," Cameron said.

"I'm calling to ask whether you want Rollie and me to investigate that possibility. Because, if Kilgore falsified crime data, we wondered if he might have falsified other data."

"Yes, proceed with your investigation. But keep your findings between you and me until we can discuss it. Get Swain Forensics involved, under contract, to help in any way you think necessary. I know they're expensive and your budget can't take it, but I'll find the money. Don't worry."

"Thank you, Dr. Cameron," Redden responded. "I will start today and report to you every now and then by phone."

As Cameron hung up, he realized that he had started his work day all wrong. First, he began with possibly ominous news from Chief Redden. Second, he initiated what might become a criminal investigation without even informing his superior, President Faust. Third, he began with no coffee. He was about to correct the third situation when his phone resounded with the distinctive buzz from Holly.

"Dr. Cameron, you have time for coffee before Dr. Madrigal gets here for her nine-o'clock. Can I bring you one?"

"Holly. You're a saint, but what else is new?" he said, with genuine appreciation in his voice.

Soon, Holly escorted Dr. Sylvia Madrigal into Cameron's office. Her long, dark hair, a swarthy brown complexion, and beautiful brown eyes made quite an impression. Cameron thought she looked more like a former athlete than a college professor, because of her slim but muscular figure, her confident walk, and her very firm grip as they shook hands. "Welcome, Dr. Madrigal. I'm pleased to meet you finally. We joined ASU at the same time."

Madrigal's response was cordial, relaxed, brief, and spoken with what Cameron detected as near accent-free English and a propensity to get right to the point. "Please call me Sylvia. I also am happy to meet you. How may I help you?"

"Here's how," Cameron said, following her lead of wasting no time or words. "We have a serious situation in Admissions and Records. I will be happy

to brief you on as much of the details as you want, but the point is, an immediate change of leadership is necessary. I have relieved Zachary Kilgore of his
affiliation with the University. Until we can recruit a new VP for Admissions
and Records, I want you to step into that role as acting VP, with a fifty percent
increase in your annual salary. You will have to finish teaching the course you
are teaching this semester, but you won't be able to teach in the spring term.
Do you want this in writing?" Cameron paused to gauge Madrigal's reaction.

"That isn't necessary. Your word is sufficient. I'm flattered by the offer, of
course. I will consider it. When do you want my answer?"

"Thursday by noon," Cameron answered.

She looked him straight in the eye, smiled, and said, "You will have your
answer by Thursday noon, Dr. Cameron."

"Please call me Drew. There is more, Sylvia," and Cameron explained the
honors scholarship program that he was starting for next fall. "So we have fifty
new scholarships, covering tuition, fees, books, room, and board for four years if
the student maintains his or her grades at B or better, and we add one hundred
or more each year for three years until we have a total of four hundred honors
scholars enrolled. They must have the requisite SAT scores and high school
grades of B or better and come from a low-income family. As far as I'm concerned,
if they represent one of America's minority ethnic groups – African-American,
Hispanic, or Asian, for example - that's all the better. If you take this job, I want
you to take charge of designing the program and selecting the students."

"I like that. It's an added attraction to the position. May I speak with you
again Thursday?"

"Yes." Cameron picked up the phone, buzzed Holly, and asked, "Can I
meet with Dr. Madrigal on Thursday morning? Okay. Thanks." He turned to
Dr. Madrigal and said, "You are on my calendar on Thursday morning at
11:30."

With the departure of Assistant Vice President Sylvia Madrigal, maybe
soon to be an acting vice president, Holly entered to brief Cameron on his
schedule for the rest of the day. "Your one o'clock with the University Space
Committee has been moved to one o'clock on Thursday."

Cameron replied with a comedic grin, "What's on their agenda — a Mars
landing?"

Holly grinned but resisted her natural instinct to laugh, and said, "No,
sir. Just about some classroom space reallocation they're proposing for next
fall and want you to approve." And then she continued, "And your two o'clock
has been cancelled for now. It was the New Cambridge Literary Society. They
want the University to partner with them in sponsoring an annual literary
festival, but their president, about an hour ago, had a bad reaction to some

medication her doctor prescribed, and they're probably going to put her in the hospital for observation."

"Holly, check on her tomorrow afternoon. She's an ASU grad, isn't she?"

"Yes. She got her MFA in dramatic arts here. Suzy Mills Lagrange. She married an ASU grad, too. They have both been rising stars since they left school twenty-some years ago. Word is, he turned leases on a couple of warehouses into the second biggest commercial real estate business in greater New Cambridge. And nobody knows quite how she does it, but she has strong literary connections in LA and New York City."

"Holly, you are a veritable fount of good information. Make sure we get her rescheduled as soon as she's up and around."

"What I was starting to tell you is that Dr. Carolyn Anthony from English can be available between one and three if you want me to schedule her. She's a candidate for the super-chair," Holly said.

"Sure. Get her in here. We need to have the finalist chosen in the next couple of weeks. What else, Holly?"

"You have our weekly staff meeting at three-thirty and a reporter with the *New Cambridge Morning News* at five. Then you are free. But now, Dr. Cameron, you should call your wife and see how she's doing after her bar exam yesterday."

Cameron made the call and found Vanessa rested and in good spirits. She was also planning a trip to a very expensive women's store for tomorrow to buy a new suit to wear to her job interview with Sheldon Ackerman at the Gordon and Sharp law firm on Friday.

After more paperwork and a few business calls on campus and in town, he ate lunch alone at his desk and studied the file on Dr. Carolyn Anthony, the candidate for the Westerveldt Chair in Intellectual Leadership. Her father worked for the U.S. State Department and served in several posts in Europe. She was born in Brussels, lived in several other European capitals, attended American Schools there and graduated from high school in Paris. She remained in Europe for seven more years, studying at Cambridge University, where she earned undergraduate honors in history and a doctorate in European history. She returned to the states and earned an MFA in Iowa's creative writing graduate program. When she was twenty-eight, the age at which the average academic finishes his or her one and only terminal degree, she had two.

For the next twenty years she worked at home in a small town near New Cambridge as an editor for a New York publishing firm — and wrote and wrote and wrote. In the last ten years, her seven novels and two theatrical plays earned multiple awards, including the PEN/Faulkner, a Pulitzer nomination, a Tony, and a Lewis and Clark Award for historical fiction from the American

Historical Society and occasional inclusion on the *New York Times'* Best Seller List. After her initial success as a novelist, Alpha State had asked her to teach a course in creative writing as an adjunct professor. She did so for several years and always got positive reviews from her students. Then ASU hired her as a tenured full professor in English. She had become a rare commodity — a best-selling novelist-professor whom the toughest literary critics adored.

When Holly ushered her into the office, Dr. Anthony looked a little embarrassed as she smoothed her dress, pushed back a strand of grayish hair, cleared her throat, looked straight at Cameron and said softly, in a throaty alto voice, "Good afternoon, Dr. Cameron. I am Carolyn Anthony. Thank you for seeing me."

"Carolyn, welcome. Please call me Drew. Thank you for coming in for this interview. It's good to meet you."

As she took her seat, she continued to gaze at Cameron as if expecting praise or blame but not knowing which. "I have only one main question to ask you," Cameron began, feeling somewhat uncomfortable without knowing why. "You have been nominated to a permanent chair in intellectual leadership. What do you think you would contribute to that position and to the university generally if you are selected?"

She considered the question for a moment. "May I suggest four contributions?" And without waiting for an answer, she continued, "First, as globalization continues to change the world, Alpha State remains rather parochial, if I may say so. We need to internationalize the academic experience for every student on campus. I know how to do that and I could help the university accomplish it. Second, we need more interdisciplinary study in every area of academic inquiry. The best new inventions and discoveries in science, technology, engineering, and math usually combine two or more academic disciplines. It's also true of the arts and humanities. It's true in creative writing. Hemingway told aspiring young writers, quoting Mark Twain I think, to write what they know about. College is the ideal time to get to know unknown places, topics, ideas you can write about. Third, every year I get numerous requests from universities and literary and historical societies to appear and give speeches at their meetings, usually for a nice fee. I try to avoid those speeches rather than seek them. But Alpha State's reputation could be enhanced and maybe more and better students recruited if I made more appearances and did my best to make the university look good, which it is. I would give the fees to the University. Fourth, my best novel is yet to come." She concluded with a shy smile, her eyes still focused on Cameron.

He waited for Dr. Anthony to continue but then realized she had delivered the four reasons she promised. "Those are impressive arguments, Carolyn. If you are selected for the Westerveldt Chair, how much teaching would you want to do?"

"One course each semester that meets for three hours once a week. The classroom is where scholars are obligated to stress the superiority of seeking truth and beauty rather than fame and fortune. Truth and beauty lead to the betterment of life for mankind. Fortune comes from exploiting somebody, and fame just inflates the ego." Anthony stopped, thinking that she might have expressed too strong an opinion to her provost.

"Anything else you want to add?" Cameron inquired, sorry that their hour of pleasant conversation was nearing an end.

"No, I think that's all, except, thank you for the opportunity to be considered," Carolyn Anthony said, as they shook hands and she left.

Cameron spent several minutes jotting down more notes on this candidate for the Westerveldt Chair, including some tentative conclusions, as he had done for the others. Carolyn Anthony had the documentable qualifications — a consistent record of excellent teaching and publication and a genuine interest in using her skill and fame as a novelist, with the resources of the Westerveldt Chair, to help the university achieve its mission. One more Westerveldt interview to go.

Holly knocked and entered at the same time. "There is a very distraught faculty member from Theatre in the outer office. She says she must speak with you right now about a very urgent matter. She's very upset."

"Who is it, Holly?"

"Bettina Davidson. She wouldn't tell me what it's about."

"Fine, ask her to come in."

As Holly went to get her, he recalled her name from the recommendations from her dean regarding who should receive promotion and tenure, "P and T" as it is called, and who should be denied in her college. Bettina Davidson was in what universities call the "up or out" year. If the documented evidence does not support the candidate's assertion that he or she has met the university's standards for teaching, research, and service, then the candidate is denied tenure. He or she is given a final year and then terminated. Tenure, of course, refers in reality to a lifetime contract. When a faculty member has tenure, he or she can be terminated but only for specific reasons as documented in the faculty handbook. There are few reasons, termination procedures are onerous and expensive, and the burden of proof rests on the university. Therefore, it seldom happens.

Cameron remembered reviewing the dean's recommendations from the College of Fine Arts. The Theatre and Film Department has two assistant professors in their sixth year. One they recommended for tenure and promotion; the other, Bettina Davidson, they did not. No doubt she had come to see Cameron to persuade him to overrule the decision of her department chair and the dean of her college. They both stressed that students' evaluations of her teaching were well below the departmental average. And, even more serious, her department chair had received almost two dozen unsolicited written complaints from students in several of her courses over the past four years. The chair had counseled her on two separate occasions about those complaints and the importance of good teaching but she had reacted with statements such as, "Some students just don't want to work."

As Holly opened his door to escort Bettina Davidson into his office, Cameron discovered that she is a beautiful black woman with an MFA in drama from a good university back east and that she teaches courses in dramaturgy, black theatre, and acting. During Cameron's 25 years in academic life, he had learned that the personalities and behaviors of academics from various fields differ in many ways, including speech, values, preferences, and dress. Chemists don't behave like musicians. Anthropologists don't converse or interact like computer scientists. Philosophers and journalists present quite a contrast. Engineers and poets share little or no common ground. Cameron wondered how a drama professor would act.

Holly opened the door and announced, "Ms. Davidson is here to see you," and held the door for the guest to enter. A full five seconds passed before she appeared, hair tousled, shoulders slumped, arms clutching a large bundle of file folders and notebooks, her reddened eyes radiating emotional pain, her quivering lips puckered in a petulant pout. She stepped in and surveyed the room, conveying with her expression and body language the message, *I am deeply wounded and you have to help me. Oh, please!*

"Good afternoon, Bettina. Come in and have a seat," Cameron said.

She turned, as if noticing Cameron for the first time. Her gestures and the look on her face reminded Cameron of a fawn surrounded by hungry wolves. She tilted her head and said, "Oh thank god you are here. We have a tragic situation on our hands, but together we can make something good happen."

"What's the problem?" he said, well aware of what was to come.

She appeared to be overcome with grief and began to cry. Burying her face in her hands and weeping for almost a minute, she was unable to accept the box of tissues that Cameron offered her.

"You've got to overrule those people in Theatre and Film. And that dean. They denied me tenure and promotion!" Then, as if on cue, she again broke into uncontrollable crying.

"They don't understand me. I'm an artist. The Theatre and Film Department chair, Dr. Toombs, is a specialist in 3D computer animation. He's a computer programmer, not an artist! And the dean of Fine Arts is an abstract expressionist painter. He blobs and splats! He knows less about aesthetics than a house painter."

"What was it in your teaching, performance, and service that the department and college committees and the chair and dean found lacking?" Cameron asked, trying to get her beyond tears and personal attacks and into substance.

"Nothing! They did it because they are racists. I'm African-American and proud of it. My acting in ASU Theatre Productions and in New Cambridge Actor's Theatre always gets rave reviews. My students are learning to do the same things I do. I can't overcome racism all by myself. You've got to help me!"

"I'm a little confused, Bettina," Cameron responded. "Your department chair and dean just recommended tenure and promotion for another African-American faculty member in Theatre and Film. That doesn't sound like they are racists, does it?"

"I don't think you understand. They did it because I'm a *black woman*. They can't stand it that a black woman works in Actor's Theatre more than they do, pushes her students harder than they do . . . . They're jealous and resentful!"

"I don't suppose it is a violation of University protocol," Cameron said, "if I tell you that the African-American for whom your department chair and dean just recommended tenure and promotion is also a woman. I'm sure you can deduce who she is. I think charges of racism and gender discrimination against them would be a bit weak, don't you?"

Anger began to replace hurt feelings as Bettina Davidson rose to her full height, stared straight at Cameron with glowering eyes, and spat, "Once again you don't understand. I am black. I am female. I am outspoken. I am more artistically talented then they are. They cannot tolerate that — an outspoken black woman who's a better actor then they are!"

"Bettina . . ." Cameron began, but she interrupted him.

"And if you don't understand that, maybe you are as big a racist and antifeminist as they are. I will see you in court. I will see all of you in court!", whereupon she bundled up her notebooks and stomped out of his office and through the outer waiting room in a theatrical rage, or, "exited angry, stage left" as Cameron later thought about it.

Cameron tried to follow her out to see if he could offer some consolation, but she disappeared into the hallway. "Holly, alert University Counsel that we might have a T and P racial and gender discrimination lawsuit on our hands from Bettina Davidson. Send them a copy of our file, just in case. Right now, I'm going home. I've had it."

"Go," Holly said. "By the way, your five o'clock never showed, the newspaper reporter. I never heard from him."

"Fine, I'm gone."

As he pushed the elevator button in the hall, Holley answered her phone and listened for a moment. Then, with a quizzical look, she said, "Yes, I will. Thanks." Cameron exited the elevator on the first floor as she scribbled a telephone note and placed it in his file for the next morning.

• • •

Business as usual proceeded across town in the lobby of Wolfe-Otis Pharmaceuticals, Inc. "May I see some ID?" the uniformed guard asked, more as a command than as a request. He looked at the ID, then at the visitor to confirm the picture, then at the list of names on his clipboard. "Oh, Dr. Novak. Sorry. Dr. Rayburn is expecting you in R and D, room 622. Elevators are straight back," pointing to his right and returning Dr. Novak's driver license. "Yeah, Dr. Rayburn, Dr. Novak is here. On the way up now," the guard said into the phone.

Good evenings and business-like introductions were exchanged in office 622 as four men took seats at a conference table. "So, Dr. Novak, do you have any questions?"

"No," the distinguished ASU joint professor of medicine and pharmacology responded. "It will make a big difference in controlling diabetes. FDA will approve it. Minimal side-effects except for the most elderly patients. Now, I only read the five-page summary. Can you swear to me that it is an accurate summary of the detail in your twenty experiments?"

"It's accurate. Dr. Gandolphe and I wrote the summary. It describes what's in the individual chapters."

"Why'd you stop at twenty trials," Dr. Novak asked.

"We kept replicating positive results, so we stopped the experiments to save money."

"Well, you've got a winner. Count me in as PI. When are you going public with it? And when are we meeting with FDA?"

All three Wolfe-Otis researchers beamed with gratitude at Dr. Novak's willingness to have his name appear on the report as senior principal investigator. They knew that his international reputation in medical research would help to market their new propacricin once it is on the market. What they appreciated more and took advantage of was his excessive need for constant professional praise. They knew that his sort of ego can produce the same behavior as naivety.

"Thank you. We will resubmit it to FDA probably next week and go public whenever our CEO decides," Dr. Rayburn responded. "But these new trials, especially with you as PI, will eliminate all of FDA's criticisms, so they'll probably fast-track us this time."

"Send me a complete final copy ASAP," Dr. Novak said, as he signed the original title page of the report. "To my office on campus – 3182 University Hospital on Carrington Street. Keep in touch." And he was gone.

"We're in business, friends and fellow lab rats. Business for sure, money in the bank," Rayburn said, as they congratulated themselves. "Just wait 'till we tell the boss. Wolfe's gonna love it!"

As soon as he turned onto his quiet street, Cameron could see the lights on in his house, so he knew Vanessa was already home. They shared their usual hug and kiss even before speaking. Vanessa spoke first in a tone suggesting a mixture of confusion and amazement. You won't believe my day. Sheldon Ackerman offered me a job as their senior attorney in health care litigation at Gordon and Sharp."

"Darlin'," Cameron interjected, "that is wonderful news! Isn't it?"

"I think so. I met several of the people at the firm, including two junior but very bright health care attorneys, and they all seem good. Gordon seemed sure I will have passed the bar exam. I hope I did. Anyway, he wants me to start on the first of next month and I told him I'd give him an answer by Monday. He offered me an annual salary of $150,000 until the bar examiner certifies that I passed. After that, $250,000 a year plus bonuses. I feel like Little Orphan Annie: 'I think I'm gonna like it here'!"

"Incredible! "Congratulations!" and he gave her another big hug.

"But here's the funny part, Drew. To make sure my memory is correct, after I got home I called the state bar examiner's office downtown and asked them if they release the names of people who sign up to take the bar exam to the public. She said that they keep all names of potential test-takers confidential until they have taken the exam, then they release a name only upon written request from an authorized source. So I'm wondering, how did Sheldon Ackerman even know I had signed up to take the bar one week before I took it. I hadn't told anybody. Did you tell someone?"

"Vanessa, I told only one person — Holly Nabisco — and she is an absolute model of discretion. I'm sure she did not mention it to anyone," Cameron answered.

"Oh, well. Maybe in due time I'll ask him myself. Anyway, here's an envelope addressed to you, no return address and no stamp, so I think somebody just stuck it in our mailbox."

Cameron looked briefly at the envelope and pitched it onto the coffee table as he said "later."

"Wait," Cameron said, holding his right hand aloft and speaking in the manner of a magician on stage. "I am receiving a message from the transcendental Spirit of Serendipity. He is telling me that tonight must be a night of celebration of your great achievement and that if we call *Le Jardin* and ask for a table for two, we might get lucky."

"Oh, Drew, that's a great idea! You are magnificent! You and Serendipity. Ask them to seat us at one of René's tables!"

It was pure luck at six o'clock to get an eight-thirty reservation at *Le Jardin*, even on Monday, the slowest night of the week. They had a wonderful dinner, and René, "their" server, made them feel like royalty. It was an appropriate celebratory ending to a somewhat odd day. A few days later, after discussing pros and cons, both Camerons agreed that Vanessa should take the offer, and she did.

October ended and Thanksgiving holiday neared. The pace of Vanessa's life increased considerably as she began her new job at Gordon and Sharp. In that first week, she worked hard and impressed her colleagues, which pleased her. She had missed practicing law. Cameron's friend from graduate school, Randy Randolph, brought his daughter to Alpha State for three days to visit the campus and to see if she wanted to attend ASU next fall as a freshman. He told Randy that University of Washington had confirmed his claim that VP of Admissions and Records Zachary Kilgore had never received a graduate degree there, and that the police had caught Kilgore hacking and falsifying university crime data, resulting in Cameron's decision to terminate him. He did not mention that the police were now looking into other related data falsification suspicions.

The investigation had continued and soon Chief Redden and his friend, Rollie Swain of Swain Forensics, had incontrovertible evidence that former Vice President Kilgore had also altered the last three years of data specifying the average SAT and ACT scores of entering freshmen, first-year retention rates, and six-year graduation rates. Comparing data sent to *American News Report* with the actual statistics on the same measures showed serious discrepancies. In every case, the reported data made the university look better than the actual data. For example, the reported math SAT scores were five to ten points higher than the actual in each of the three years. Discussions with Chief Redden centered not on who might have changed the data. That became somewhat irrelevant because Kilgore was gone, and disgraced, and never to get another job in any academic institution. Rather, they speculated about why he had done it — on his own or as instructed. If the latter, he must have been indebted to that someone else. The primary motivation for altering the data might have been to move ASU into the top thirty public universities in America. That move would likely result in ASU receiving the additional legislative appropriation, an enhanced reputation, more students, more tuition, more corporate and alumni gifts and endowments, etc. Their speculative trail of logic was frightening. Cameron thought, but did not say to Chief Redden, that a discrete inquiry into the whereabouts and general status of Zachary Kilgore might answer some nagging questions.

Cameron sent the correct figures to *American News Report* magazine and apologized for three years of incorrect data. However, Steve Faust was shocked and furious when Cameron told him of the discovery. Cameron could not decide at whom Faust was angry – Kilgore for falsifying the data or Cameron for detecting and reporting the fraud. Nonetheless, the incident had a corrosive effect on their relationship. Cameron worked hard to continue to be civil, but Faust grew distant.

8 The Monday after Thanksgiving was gloomy. As Cameron drove to his appointment with Michelle Murray, owner of Murray Robotics, he rehearsed his counter-proposal strategy. To get her to accept it, he had decided to emphasize two maxims of most political conservatives. First, the principle of economic efficiency: full information is necessary for a market to function efficiently because it enables each consumer to maximize his or her value for the dollar spent and ensures an appropriate amount of fair competition among producers. Second, the principle of individual liberty: When exposed to alternative solutions to a political problem, individuals must be free to choose. If that argument did not win the day, so be it. But it had to win, because if it did not, President Faust would probably sweet talk Ms. Murray into funding her original proposal. Cameron had decided that he could not live with that eventuality.

With two bound copies of his counter-proposal in hand, he approached the reception desk in the plush outer office of Murray's corporate headquarters. Before he could say "good morning" or state his name and intentions, the receptionist said, "Good morning, Dr. Cameron. Please go right in. Ms. Murray is expecting you."

As he entered, Ms. Murray rose and met him half-way across the room to shake hands. She seemed steadier in her movement and speech, and her color looked much better. "You take your coffee black, as I remember, don't you Dr. Cameron?" Without waiting for an answer, she picked up her phone and said, "Would you bring Dr. Cameron coffee, black. Tea for me. Thank you." Turning to Cameron she said, "And what do you have for me this morning? Can Murray Robotics partner with Alpha State University?

"I think so," and Cameron handed Ms. Murray her copy. "Page one presents a one-sentence statement of each of John Randolph's principles in contemporary academic terminology."

Michele Murray put on her reading glasses and examined the first page. She sat motionless with the exceptions of an occasional glance upward toward nothing in particular, and slow sips of her tea. The pause gave Cameron a chance to sip his coffee and prepare for her response.

When she appeared to finish, Cameron said, "First, following President Andrew Jackson's dictum in his farewell address to Congress, we must be vigilant against threats to liberty from anywhere, left and right, so Randolph's principles now reflect that safeguard. Page one summarizes Jackson's vigilance applied to your proposal. The second modification we propose," Cameron hurried on, "is to name the institute and the endowed chairs after you rather than John Randolph. It would be the Madeleine Murray Institute. John Randolph inspired you but it is you who inspires us and our students. You are the benefactor. It was your idea. Steve Faust and I, his executive committee, and the ASU Foundation attorneys all agree: it really must bear your name."

After a long moment, Ms. Murray smiled and said, "You know, Dr. Cameron, when a handsome younger man flatters an older woman, even one who is a computer engineer and a rather shrewd businesswoman, she is likely to believe him. Even if, in her heart, she thinks he might just be playing her."

Cameron interpreted her remark as indicating that he was at least still in the game, and in their subsequent conversation, she did ask him to have the ASU Foundation draft a contractual agreement that she and one of her corporate attorneys could review. He had ridden up the Murray Robotics elevator in an anxious state of pessimism and grim determination, aware that his counter-proposal might produce an immediate negative response. As he left, he rode down the elevator with renewed hope and even some optimism. *So far, so good*, he mused to himself.

"So, Dr. Cameron, how did it go?" Holly asked, when he returned to his office.

"Well, I think, Holly."

"Great. I have a list," Holly said in a faux-ominous tone. Whenever she said, "I have a list," it usually meant that he faced several difficult and important events or decisions in the near future.

"Okay, Holly. What's coming up?"

"Tomorrow, the Czech Trade Delegation arrives. Dr. Axel Dekker will be with them. He's set up for interviews starting Wednesday. Also, three delegates from the Czech Republic are coming on their trade mission," and Holly glanced at her I-pad to read, "Anna Zezulka, the mission chief from the Czech government, and two people from Moravian Motorworks. There's Jaroslav Doubek, a design engineer, and Dobromil Novotny, the production manager. They will go straight to the hotel. At noon they meet with representatives from the Chamber of Commerce, the City of New Cambridge, several people from the Czech consul general's office downtown, several state trade officials, and Petr Slavinska, head of the economics section of the Czech Embassy in Washington." Holly paused here and looked at Cameron for a response.

"Holly, your pronunciation of Czech names is better than mine and you've never even been there."

"The Mayor's Office is coordinating all the meetings. They sent us a tentative schedule, and said you are invited to any of the meetings you want to attend. And, thank you, I practiced on the pronunciations," Holly said, as she looked up at the office clock set to Prague time.

"This afternoon you meet with the final candidate for the Westerveldt Chair, Dr. Timothy McNathan in Biology, Chemistry, and Engineering. All three. Here's his résumé."

"Next," Holly went on, "did you get a letter at your home address from a newspaper reporter?"

Suddenly, Cameron remembered. Several days ago Vanessa had given him an unstamped envelope addressed to him that she had retrieved from their mailbox at home. "Yes, I did. But what did I do with it? Oh, it's in my briefcase. What about it?"

"He called here again asking for you. He also asked me if you were going to be in town the next two or three weeks. I told him you will. He didn't leave a number or a name."

"He's certainly persistent. If he calls again, just put him through to me if possible."

Cameron spent some time digesting Dr. Timothy McNathan's very impressive résumé. He was born and lived his first eighteen years in Far Rockaway, New York. His high school grades easily got him a scholarship to study chemical engineering at Brooklyn Polytechnic, after which he continued graduate school in his field at Princeton and, to his working class family's great pride, earned his doctorate in only three years. Then, to his family's great chagrin, in the following fall semester he enrolled in the doctoral program in biology at SUNY Stony Brook and earned another doctorate in three years. He took an assistant professorship in the Department of Biology at ASU to teach biochemistry. He had good student evaluations of his teaching, published many journal articles, did good work on university committees, and his graduate students progressed well. He discovered or created several innovative biochemical processes with direct applications in medical care, resulting in numerous awards and prizes from national scientific and medical organizations. When he was promoted to full professor in the Department of Biology, both Chemical Engineering and Chemistry asked him to accept a joint appointment. He accepted both.

When Holly brought him into the office, Dr. McNathan looked nothing like the pale, socially inept bookworm in his mid-fifties who had spent his whole life in the lab that Cameron had expected. Although his Irish-red hair was now graying at the temples and his ruddy complexion mostly freckles, his muscular, six-foot physique was trim, and he was light on his feet. When Holly completed her introduction, he smiled, shook her hand and said, "Thank you, Holly. Now I see how the Provost runs such a smooth operation." Holly wrinkled her nose and blushed.

He turned to Cameron and they shook hands as he said, "I am so glad to see you again, Dr. Cameron. We met for just a few minutes in a reception line last winter when you were here for interviews."

"The pleasure is mine. Please call me Drew, and make yourself comfortable."

McNathan unbuttoned the coat of his navy blue suit. His sky blue tie, about the color of his eyes, swung out as he took a seat below a large, colorful post-modernist painting on loan from the Department of Fine Arts. His broad, cheerful smile seemed to represent genuine pleasure at being there.

"You are the fourth and final candidate I am interviewing for the Westerveldt Chair in Intellectual Leadership. The purpose of the interview is for you to add anything you wish to your résumé that would support your appointment. So, let me ask, what do you see as your main contributions to intellectual leadership at ASU if you are selected for the Chair?" Cameron asked, laying out a general premise to allow the candidate latitude to emphasize his strong points and any less apparent qualifications, as he had done with the other candidates.

"First, thank you for the opportunity, Drew. I can tell you, I am flattered to be here."

"Timothy, your colleagues and I think you deserve to be here. And before you answer, please excuse this interruption, could you just give me a brief layperson's synopsis of what you do as a scientist, as a biochemical engineer?"

"Sure. Traditional engineers apply the principles of physics and math to the analysis, design, and manufacture of inanimate things such as tools, structures, processes. You know, like electric drills, bridges, or waste water treatment techniques — practical applications. Chemistry is the scientific study of atomic matter, anything made up of the chemical elements, and especially their interactions and reactions. It tries to uncover ways to make more complex substances from simpler ones. Biology is the scientific study of life and living organisms. Cells are the basic unit of life, and cells are made up of molecules. Am I making any sense so far?"

Cameron nodded, and said, "Clear as a bell, so far."

"So the bio-chemical engineer puts them all together to study and 'engineer' living organisms, especially as applied to problems of human health. Some people call it 'molecular engineering,' McNathan said, hopeful that his "student" understood and approved. "For example, we can grow a human trachea in the lab, or build a pacemaker for the heart. Both are examples of engineered biochemical products.

"I should sign up for your basic course. Now tell me what you would like to accomplish in the Westerveldt Chair."

"The question is, I think, how I can use what I know as a biochemical engineer to provide intellectual leadership at Alpha State." As McNathan began to answer, Cameron noticed his residual Queens accent. "Other than continuing to do what we all do — teaching, research, and service — I see three problems that need serious attention, and I think in the Westerveldt Chair, I would have a good chance at least to ameliorate them."

"What are our main problems?" Cameron asked.

"I have discussed one of them with Alice Cantrell in Philosophy. She calls it the "Hobbesian problem". In this university as in most, we live in a state of nature, which is a war of every man against every other man, as Thomas Hobbes wrote in *Leviathan.* He said that without the state to impose order and peace on a society, the people naturally live in jealousy and hostility and they always fight each other for valued resources. In a university, it's academic disciplines or departments against each other."

"That's a serious and important charge, Timothy. I suppose I represent the state if you apply Hobbes to ASU. Tell me about the jealousy and hostility," Cameron requested, smiling.

"The jealousy and hostility have turned into petty feelings of superiority and arrogance. Each discipline thinks it is the most important discipline in the university. People in each department believe that some of the other departments are also important, some are just a little important, and many are downright useless, or worse. Each department pretty well agrees on a hierarchy or pecking order of importance of all university departments, with theirs at the top. Of course, the departments disagree about this hierarchy. History looks down on Public Administration. Marketing looks down on Sociology. Physics thinks Hotel and Restaurant Management should be in a trade school. Engineering thinks Philosophy is totally irrelevant, impractical and worthless. Music thinks Marketing should be renamed 'The Department of Predatory Science', and so on."

Cameron asked, "In this university state of nature, isn't that just good natured competition, striving to be the best in the academic market?"

"It wouldn't be so bad if it were just institution-wide hubris because they are all, in fact, incorrect. There are larger, more powerful forces that agree on and give shape to the academic hierarchy and they work hard to ensure that it prevails," McNathan said.

"I'm fascinated," Cameron confessed. "What does the academic hierarchy look like?"

"Remember," McNathan said, "I have a doctorate in biology, so I believe that Charles Darwin's theories about the survival of the fittest are not only true but appropriate. In the case of universities and their departments, 'fitness' is currently defined as generating the most money in the short run. Departments and whole colleges that bring in the most money and whose graduates make the most money are defended as the most important. In the top quadrant of the fitness hierarchy are the College of Business and most of the engineering departments. Next, but lower, are professional schools such as law and medicine. Third-rank departments include other professional disciplines such as nursing, planning, agriculture and forestry, and several of the traditional physical and biological sciences. At the bottom of the hierarchy are departments in the humanities, social sciences, and education, whose faculties get the lowest salaries, the least respect, and the heaviest teaching loads."

Cameron sat spellbound, listening to this Westerveldt Chair candidate articulate ideas that he, having served as a dean then as provost, had only vaguely entertained. "Do go on. Who enforces this hierarchy?" he asked, knowing rather well the answer but wanting to hear McNathan's denouement.

"The American brand of capitalism, fueled by greed, and the American brand of culture, fueled by ignorance and sloth. Please forgive me. I don't mean to sound so hostile," McNathan answered. "It's not just Wall Street and big corporations. It's state legislatures, boards of trustees, presidents, alumni. I'm afraid they are all complicit. In his farewell speech to the country in 1961, President Eisenhower warned us about the dangerous influence of the military-industrial complex. It is alive and well and healthier than ever, but I think that if Ike were alive today, he'd feel just as uneasy about the education-industrial complex."

Cameron was struck by McNathan's critique of the university. "I'm learning a lot from you, Timothy, and we must continue this discussion later, soon I hope, but we have only about ten minutes of time left," Cameron cautioned. "Any other points you want to make about your potential contribution in the Westerveldt Chair?"

"Yes. I'll be brief," the biochemical engineer said. "We do a terrible job of teaching the required introductory science courses for non-majors. We jump too soon into technical matters of the science, biology or chemistry or physics or whatever branch of science and right into the esoteric laboratory procedures of the field. We should devote more of each of our intro courses to the creation of scientific curiosity in our students. We should also emphasize the philosophy and logic and history of science, the scientific method, critical thinking, and the benefits of scientific discovery. I think we'd actually create more science majors with that kind of intro course than the ones we teach now."

McNathan stopped a minute, as if to recall his next point, and then proceeded at his usual enthusiastic pace. "Also, I am disturbed by the contemporary growth of anti-scientific attitudes in America. Many political and religious leaders and their followers condemn indisputable scientific facts and conclusions. I am not political at all and somewhere between agnostic and atheist in religious matters, but I do understand the virtues of science. I understand climate change and man's contribution to it, for example. We need to spread a better understanding and appreciation of science among the public at-large. We are imitating the early seventeenth century. At that time, the Pope 'overruled' and condemned both Copernicus and Galileo and declared that the earth, not the sun, is the center of the universe. And sentenced Galileo to prison and banned his book. Oh, I apologize! Don't get me started. I'm sorry for carrying on so long."

"Time very well spent, Timothy. I appreciate your wisdom. Thanks for coming in. We will have a decision on the Westerveldt appointment as soon as we can, early in the second semester."

When McNathan expressed his thanks and left, Cameron realized what a very hard choice he had to make. His mind balked at the necessity to choose only one of the four. As he made extensive notes on his interview with McNathan, he realized that all four were brilliant scholars with important academic virtues and strengths but differences and weaknesses as well. He knew this decision would require a lot of thought.

"Holly, put the four Westerveldt Chair files together and schedule me some time to read and think," Cameron requested. He mused to himself, *Read and think. Things I used to do all the time. Now I have to order my assistant to schedule some time for me to do it.*

With about two weeks left before the beginning of final exams, committee reports from deans and committee chairs were pouring into his office. He had promised to attend the end-of-semester meetings of the long-term planning and curriculum reform committees and respond to their work to date. He had to deliver his semester report to the Faculty Senate, attend at least two more president's cabinet meetings, preside over another long Deans Council meeting, and tend to several other scheduled matters as well as deal with the unexpected.

Also, this semester's plans included his effort to win an acceptable gift from Madeline Murray. If he did not, his colleagues might doubt that he had the stuff for fundraising, and Steve Faust might talk Madeline Murray into funding her right-wing John Randolph of Roanoke idea. And, in just a few days, the Czech trade mission would arrive ready to convince New Cambridge to buy Czech street cars and later high-speed rail cars for their new line, a possibility he had initiated with New Cambridge at the request of Anna Zezulka. With the delegation would come Axel Dekker to interview for the two-year post-doc position. Cameron still had to outline a two-year work plan for Dekker before he arrived. There was also Steve Faust's plan, initiated and designed by chief PR officer, Margaret Benedict, to host a huge celebration for the ASU football team's perfect regular season — assuming they won the next two games. That would require Cameron's active presence most of an afternoon and much of that evening to work the well-healed crowd of corporate execs and alums for PR and fundraising purposes.

Had it not been for Vanessa's report at the end of her first two weeks as the senior health care attorney for the big downtown firm, Cameron might have succumbed to the rigors of end-of semester madness. But her reception at the firm had been friendly and professional. So many colleagues had come by her office to welcome her, invite her to coffee or lunch, and help her shelve her law books, she had almost felt guilty. Her positive beginning buoyed both their spirits. Until she was certified as having passed the bar, her boss had assigned her to work on several health care cases with junior attorneys who had passed the bar, whom she mentored, and then they would use her work to pursue the case.

As organized by the New Cambridge Mayor's office, Cameron stood in line on Tuesday morning with the mayor, representatives of the Czech Embassy and Consulate, the City Council, the state Trade Commission, and the Chamber of Commerce to greet the Czech delegation. He received a warm hug and a kiss on both cheeks from Anna Zezulka. Axel Dekker was his usual business-like self, and his eyes sparkled as he and Cameron warmly shook hands and greeted each other like old friends. Doubek and Novotny of Moravian Motorworks lacked Anna Zezulka's diplomatic skills but were fluent in English and all business. Within an hour, the Czechs checked into their hotel, soon after which they ate dinner, and retired, anticipating a long day of important discussions tomorrow.

The first day of international business negotiation was cordial but veered nowhere near a path of agreement. Although New Cambridge's engineers agreed that the Czech streetcars were as good as anybody's anywhere, price was, as usual, a sticking point. The mayor refused to budge on price, and by five o'clock on day two, when the negotiations ended for the day and the two groups adjourned to a scheduled cocktail hour, the cause seemed to be drifting at sea, maybe lost. Neither the city nor the Czech delegation reported progress, or lack thereof, to Cameron each day, for fear of appearing biased in some way. However, Charlie Kempton, New Cambridge Chief Engineer, who had confided in Cameron some months ago, did. He was involved in the discussions and in secret kept Cameron informed of everything that transpired. The mayor was just using price, Kempton claimed, as a reason to refuse the Czech offer when in fact, his real motivation was to ensure that his friend in the train and streetcar track business got the contract — a friend who had promised to fund the mayor's campaign for governor if the mayor delivered. If somebody doesn't do something dramatic to break the deadlock, Kempton worried, the deal will be lost. Cameron joined the groups after five for cocktail hour in the hotel and could tell that swift currents of frustration and distrust were already beginning to erode the determination of both sets of negotiators.

To make matters worse, he took a cell phone call from Holly at about five-thirty that added to his growing feeling of dismay. "I just got off the phone with Ms. Madeline Murray's assistant at Murray Robotics," Holly said. "She asked for you, but I told her you were unavailable. She said that, at Ms. Murray's request, she is returning your revision of her proposal by mail with a letter from Ms. Murray explaining why she is unable to fund it. And, that if you want to discuss it face-to-face, you can make an appointment and she will meet with you. But she wanted you to know right away that she could not agree to your counter-proposal."

After a lengthy and painful silence, "Okay, Holly. Thanks for letting me know."

Later that night, when he reported to Vanessa that the negotiations had run aground and that Ms. Murray had rejected his proposal, she listened, thought a minute and then asked, "Drew, do you remember me mentioning a principle of negotiation called 'separations and connections'?"

"I think so. Sort of. Remind me."

"The connections part applies to your streetcar deal. Assume two parties are negotiating, one to sell a commodity and the other to buy it, but they can't agree on price. Each is, of course, seeking to maximize net gain. The principle of connections says that you need to find a third party to enter the negotiations, someone whose participation can earn him or her a net gain but whose entry adds another commodity and/or more cash to the three-way deal sufficient to satisfy the profit needs of the party who originally would not agree in the two-party negotiations."

"I see," Cameron said. So, what are the connections I could make in this case?"

"Here is the beginning of a plan. Think about this and whether it's practical or not. Mayor DelVecchio says he wants to pay less for the Czech streetcars. Murray Robotics doesn't want to endow the institute and chairs. But, would Murray Robotics like to sell some of its technology to Moravian, to upgrade their production process with robotics? Mayor DelVecchio might enjoy the additional taxes that Murray Robotics would pay on its additional sales to the Czechs, and so would the governor's office and the state trade officials. What if you stipulate to Ms. Murray that this can happen only if she funds the institute for ASU? Would a cost-benefit analysis show that, in just a few years, she will be making huge new profits from the Czechs?" Vanessa asked.

"Whoa, lightening, slow down! The mind boggles. I think you're on to something," Cameron said.

"If the Czechs now impose a tariff on imported U.S. robotics, and I'm sure they do, maybe you could get, what's her name, Anna?, to prevail on her government to reduce or eliminate it, at least for Murray's sale to Moravian Motorworks," Vanessa added.

"I'm with you so far, I think," Cameron said. "Moravian Motorworks sells their streetcars to New Cambridge. The Czech government eliminates it's tariff on imported US robotics technology so that Murray can sell robotics to Moravian Motorworks, or whoever, at a greater profit. Ms. Murray funds the institute and chairs for ASU. DelVecchio and the whole state government get increased tax receipts annually from Murray's surge in revenues. For that, DelVecchio can't afford not to buy the streetcars at Moravian's asking price, so he agrees. Ergo, greater New Cambridge gets its rapid transit system. Is that it, counselor?"

"That's about it. I know it assumes a lot, but your job is to try to make the assumptions viable. When each of the parties to the negotiation — New Cambridge, the state, Moravian Motorworks, the Czech government, Murray Robotics, ASU — sees that this solution provides a net gain to them, they just might buy it," Vanessa answered.

"I love it," Cameron chimed in with a big grin. "It's a combination of good, old-fashioned horse-trading and rational decision making." With renewed enthusiasm he gave Vanessa a big kiss and then stayed up half the night at the computer outlining the "connections" strategy and estimating its net benefits for each set of participants. And, he found that Vanessa was right. It just might work.

Early on the morning of day three of negotiation, Cameron had conversations with the leaders of each of the parties to the negotiation. They seemed willing to entertain this new, somewhat complicated strategy if all the other parties did. By the end of day four, which included scores of phone calls among and within New Cambridge, Prague, the state capitol, and Washington,

Vanessa's "connections" had been hammered into an agreement that all parties could approve. In fact, it appeared that Murray Robotics would consider the Czech Republic's invitation to build Murray Robotics' planned production facility near Prague, rather than in Asia, and that ASU and Czech Technological University in Prague would work in partnership to provide relevant training in engineering, management, and languages, for construction and operation of the new facility.

Vanessa accompanied Cameron to the contract signing ceremony in city hall, which included a two-way video hookup with Prague. As soon as it was over, they all retreated to a private party in a nearby restaurant to drink champagne, eat a delicious dinner, and celebrate. Cameron and Vanessa slipped out soon after dinner and went home.

The four days of negotiations in city hall, and in particular the one intense day and night of making the essential "connections", had been exhausting. Anna Zezulka had worked very hard to ensure a positive outcome. During the most difficult days, Axel Dekker had been on the Alpha State campus meeting with numerous campus leaders as part of the interviewing process for the postdoctoral position in administration. Although Dekker brought his own salary and benefits as a recipient of the European Community award, Cameron had to make certain that campus leaders – both academic and administrative – supported his appointment. ASU is where Dekker wanted to work. Cameron made it clear that he wanted Dekker, but the academic ritual had to be followed, nonetheless.

Residents of the New Cambridge region had enjoyed beautiful fall weather right up to late November. Members of the Czech trade delegation commented several times about the contrast of New Cambridge weather with that of Prague in late November. Although their negotiation schedule allowed them no time to enjoy it, they had noticed the daily high temperatures in the mid-to-high sixties, skies so blue they were almost scary, trees whose leaves had turned to shades of red, yellow, orange and brown, and adequate amounts of rain that seemed to fall, Camelot-like, between midnight and six in the morning. Cameron and Vanessa had, on several occasions, compared and contrasted weather conditions in upstate New York and New Cambridge. Despite the romantic notions of *Autumn in New York*, New Cambridge autumns emerged far ahead. But on that late fall morning, as he and several of his vice presidential associates, finished interviewing Dekker at breakfast in the University Club, cold, gusty winds combined with grey skies warned that heavy coats and umbrellas would be useful.

"Finish your coffee, everybody, and let's get back to Admin before it starts raining", Cameron requested. "Any more questions for Axel? Or do you have any more questions, Axel?" Hearing no affirmative responses, Cameron declared the breakfast interview over, and amid mutual expressions of gratitude and well-wishes, the group walked from the private dining room to the lobby to return to Admin. Rain had begun to pound the campus, its sonic impact almost drowning out all but yelled conversation. Six university officials and a job candidate, all in business suits, walking fifty yards to Admin in this downpour, was out of the question. Cameron knew that from nine to ten he was free, and that Dekker was scheduled for a guided tour of the University Library. That tour could be rescheduled. He could see that the large portico outside the Faculty Club's front door sheltered the entrance and several parked cars from inclement weather. Then he thought of another useful piece of business they could conduct within one hour, and by then the storm might be over. Cameron knew that Dekker, as an applied statistician, was very interested in new computer graphics software. ASU had, in the past couple of weeks, set up a new temporary computer lab on the third floor of Miller Hall, an older building on the edge of campus that they had acquired from a small private high school, the Miller Academy. The lab's purpose was to test their new 3-D graphics and simulation software. Miller Academy had moved several months before to a new building on the other side of town. Cameron smiled as he remembered seeing delivery trucks pull up to the back of Miller Hall, under a large protective overhang above a door near the service elevator. He could use the next hour to show Dekker, a statistician, the new lab.

"Okay, colleagues, here's a suggestion," Cameron said, as they all stood in the doorway of the University Club lobby, watching torrents of water top the gutter and flow from the street onto the well-kept front lawn of the Club. "It's now eight-fifty. If this rain doesn't let up in a couple of minutes, why don't you go back inside and have another cup of coffee. I am going to commandeer that University car," he said, pointing to the black sedan with 'Alpha State University' in gold letters on the side parked under the portico, "and take Axel to Miller Hall to show him our new three-D simulation software. I have a key that will open the delivery entrance in the back, so we can park there, under their overhead shelter, and stay dry."

Cameron and Dekker secured the electronic key to the ASU vehicle from the clerk at the front desk of the Club and drove in the direction of the back door of Miller Hall. "We converted most of an auditorium on the third floor into a large classroom, Cameron said. "When we needed space to put up a small temporary lab facility, the architects recommended that we convert the elevated stage area of the auditorium into the lab. It's almost finished, but from the classroom side, you can't even tell it's there. Maintenance has put up sheetrock to wall-off the smaller lab from the larger classroom. There may be a final exam in progress in the classroom now, but we left the heavy black stage curtain up, so the sheetrock partition and the curtain make it possible to use the lab and the classroom at the same time.

As they exited the car under the Miller Hall overhang, Cameron pushed the lock button on his electronic key, causing the sedan to emit its characteristic "beep beep" and to extinguish its headlights. Gusts of wind blew cold rain on both of them as Cameron stabbed at the backdoor lock with his master key, and they entered the dark storage area of Miller Hall. "Today reminds me of a spring day in Leiden," Dekker said, referring to his hometown near the North Sea in Holland. The wind suddenly slammed the door closed, leaving them in total darkness. Dekker pushed it back open until Cameron located a light switch.

Two floors straight above them in Miller Hall, most of the fifty-nine juniors and seniors enrolled in Statistics 335: Applied Regression Analysis, had been entering classroom 305, drenched from the rain and shivering from the cold despite their raincoats, hats, and umbrellas, which they were placing on the hangers along the rear wall. Each student took a seat and began thumbing through his or her textbook and class notes in a nervous search for that last bit of information about beta weights, multicollinearity, or the standard error of the estimate. Most felt anxious. Many had been up studying most of the night for this exam. Many of them looked pale and felt weak. Several jiggled one knee up and down. Almost all of them wore jeans and sweat shirts, as if that were the ASU student uniform. Most of the women sported tousled hair and no makeup. Most of the men had scraggly beards. Many hid red eyes with sunglasses. A few were well-dressed, appeared confident, and sat near the front. Filling in for the professor was his teaching assistant, a doctoral student in statistics, who stood behind his desk at the front of the classroom, guarding copies of the exam and several packs of blue test booklets. He would neither speak nor move until the wall clock in the front of the classroom showed exactly 9 AM.

At about nine, Cameron and Dekker entered the rear door on the first floor of Miller Hall. The slight illumination revealed a large, cardboard box enclosed in a wooden frame, about five feet tall, standing against the wall where light switches should be. Cameron pushed the box aside, found the light switches and turned on the lights.

"There's the service elevator," Cameron said, pointing to the other side of the room, "that will take us up to the lab."

"I wish we had more time," Dekker said, glancing at his watch. They entered the large elevator, with its padded walls, and pushed the button for the third floor. As the large square cage, lit by a single bulb hanging mid-ceiling, began its sluggish rise, its cables squealed a dissonant soprano squawk over the grinding baritone hummed by the motor, and the floor number lights blinked its plodding upward progress. The elevator bumped to a stop at three, and the doors opened to complete darkness.

In classroom 305, raincoats hanging on the metal hooks around the walls dripped on the floor. One last student, laden with the almost mandatory backpack, entered the back door of the classroom. He took the first available seat on the back row, still wearing his baseball cap and a tattered olive drab army surplus field jacket, just as the instructor announced, "It is now nine o'clock. We will begin. Close all your books and papers and put them and all electronic devices, etc. on the floor. You will need only your pencils. No need for me to take roll. You will be counted absent unless you turn in an exam paper." Students did as they were told, and the instructor began handing to the first person seated in each column the correct number of exams and bluebooks for the number of students seated in that column of desks. The flow of exams and bluebooks down each column was followed by a wave of facial expressions and body language revealing anxiety or resignation, or, in a few cases, relief. The room became silent as the instructor took a seat on his desk and asked, "Are there any questions?"

While the instructor answered three questions, most students started to work on the exam. The last-seated student in the back rose and walked the four steps toward the back wall where the wet coats were hanging.

At the same time, Cameron and Dekker walked into the new third-floor lab and turned on the lights. "Just between you and me, Axel, I've never used 3-D simulation software. It's your field, tell me what are the most important things you have to do to develop a good package."

"To me," Dekker responded, "there are three tasks that have to be accomplished and integrated to produce a good 3-D result. The first is designing the set of simultaneous equations that . . ." Dekker broke off his technical discussion of 3-D computer graphics mid-sentence and turned to face the wall separating lab and classroom. He remained motionless for half a minute and appeared to be listening to something. He turned to Cameron without a word, raised his right hand, as if to signal "wait" and put his index finger to his lips to indicate a request for silence. Cameron remained silent, not knowing whether to feel alarmed or amused. Dekker walked to the light switch, gave the lab a quick visual scan, and then turned off the lights, causing Cameron to wonder about Dekker's strange behavior.

After they stood still in the dark for about twenty seconds, Dekker touched Cameron's shoulder and whispered, "Did you hear that, Drew? I think the classroom on the other side of the wall has a problem. Did you hear it?" Without waiting for Cameron's answer, he continued, "I heard someone say, in a loud and serious voice, 'I will kill the first person . . . .' followed by something else I couldn't understand. Stay right here."

Dekker moved across the dark lab toward the unpainted sheetrock wall that separated them from the classroom. Curiosity forced Cameron to follow despite Dekker's request that he stay where he was. They discovered that they had a good view of almost half of the classroom from the corner of the lab where the final panel of sheetrock was yet to be installed in the newly erected wall that created the lab. In addition, the old stage curtain still hung from the ceiling, as it did when the room was an auditorium, and concealed the sheetrock wall from anyone on the classroom side.

Cameron and Dekker could see unadulterated terror on the faces of scores of students. A short, stocky, white man held a pistol to the head of the instructor, who was seated at his desk facing the students. In his left hand he waved another pistol back and forth at the room full of seated students. Cameron's pulse rate and the adrenalin-fueled, fight-or-flight instinct almost exploded. The man with the pistols appeared to be in his late twenties or early thirties, and wore old, torn jeans, a dark grey sweat shirt and sneakers. His face was twisted into a ruthless scowl, and his movements were nervous and jerky as he held the class at gunpoint. Cameron noted that the gunman had chained both rear doors.

"Drew," Dekker whispered, "I think we have . . . what do you call it in English? . . . a hostage situation or armed seizure of classroom? I read about gun violence at Virginia Polytechnic . . . and University of California at Santa Barbara."

Just then, the gunman screamed, "I told you to stay in your seats or I'll kill you. I may kill you all if any of you give me a hard time! Do you understand?! I have enough ammo to kill you all, and I'm a trained killer. You will be lucky if I don't kill all of you, starting with the big know-it-all professor." He stuck the barrel of his pistol in the instructor's ear. "You're all a bunch of rich, spoiled-rotten punks. Isn't that right?" The students sat silent, grim-faced, pathetic, and frightened, one to the point of nausea. Several sobbed aloud and looked as if they would faint at any moment. Receiving no response to his question, he screamed, "Isn't that right?" and waved the pistol across the captive classroom as if contemplating which student to shoot first as punishment for not answering. Then he raised his aim and fired a shot straight into the ceiling. Pieces of plaster fell and dust slowly drifted from the ceiling onto the seated students, as the gunman grinned and reset his aim on the head of the instructor. Firing the pistol inside the classroom had created a painful, deafening noise, causing all the students to jump, some to scream or cry, and left all of them with a loud ringing in their ears.

At this point, Cameron remembered that during his first several weeks as provost, he had considered it thoughtful of Holly to insist that he give her his University-issued cell phone for an hour so she could program it to speed dial various important numbers on and off campus. *Did she include the ASU Police Department?* he thought to himself. Stepping back from the curtain, he touched the "Contacts" icon, which produced a long alphabetical list of names. He scrolled down to the letter "U," looking for University Police, but found only names such as "Undergrad Studies." Scrolling back up to "P" he found "ASU Police" and touched the green telephone icon at the bottom of the phone.

On the second ring, he heard "University Police Department," to which he stage-whispered, "This is Executive Vice President Andrew Cameron. We have an emergency. An armed man has seized room three-zero-five, the old auditorium, in Miller Hall, and is holding the students captive. The gunman has fired his pistol once, but I don't know if anyone was hit. We need immediate police intervention. He has chained the main classroom doors shut so officers will need to break through the doors to get in. 305 Miller Hall."

"Is he alone, Dr. Cameron? Is there just one gunman?"

"I think so, but I'm not sure."

"I have dispatched all available officers to the scene, Dr. Cameron. I'm also alerting SWAT. Miller Hall? Room 305?"

"That is correct."

"They should arrive in three minutes or less. Are you in immediate danger, sir?

"No. I am with a job candidate, and we are hiding in the new lab, behind a wall. The gunman doesn't know we are here."

"Do not try to intervene, sir. Stay hidden and remain quiet. Officers are on the way. I am also alerting New Cambridge Police, who will be on the scene very soon. Just stay on the line with me until they get in and capture the perpetrator. Is anyone hurt?"

"I don't think so, but I'm not sure."

"Okay. Just stay calm. How many students are in the classroom?"

"I'd guess fifty, maybe more."

Dekker appeared out of the dark by Cameron's side and whispered, "Police?"

"Yes. They're on the way."

"Good. Where is the switch to control the lights in the classroom?"

Two more deafening pistol shots exploded. Cameron looked through the slit in the curtain, backed away and spoke again to the Police Dispatcher, "He fired two more shots, and there is a student lying on the floor in the back of the classroom. I'm pretty sure the student's been shot, but I didn't see it happen."

"Okay, sir. Remain calm and quiet. Officers and emergency medical are on the way."

"Can we control the lights in the classroom from here in the lab?" Dekker asked.

"I think so. There's a master switch for both parts of the old auditorium — classroom and lab— inside the lab control room, right over there. By the elevator door we came in."

The two walked across the dark lab, careful not to make a noise, and entered the control room, a small glass-enclosed room within the lab that housed the file server and various control panels with many buttons and switches. The control room was illuminated only by the many green, red or yellow lights on the computer and related pieces of equipment, indicating that they were on, off or in standby mode.

"There it is," Cameron whispered, pointing to a small lever at the end of the control panel desk.

Dekker grabbed the spool of electrical wiring and a pair of wire cutters left by electricians working on the new lab. He cut off a piece of wire about a yard long and stuck it in his pocket. Then he handed the loose end of the wire on the spool to Cameron. "You stay here by this master light switch. Hold this wire in your fist. Wait until I signal you by jerking the wire twice, then turn out all the lights in that classroom," Dekker ordered. "We won't be able to see each other in the dark, and I can't speak to you across the lab without being heard in the classroom. So this is the only way I can signal you to turn out the lights. Do you understand?"

The gunman's threatening ranting continued in the classroom.

"Yes, I do. No, wait. I don't. I don't understand what we're doing. Do you have some kind of a plan?" Cameron asked. It occurred to him that they both had PhDs and had spent their entire careers doing bureaucratic white collar work seated at a desk — hardly qualifications to do dangerous police work. Yet Dekker was calm and confident, and seemed to have a plan, while Cameron felt nervous and confused. He simply repeated the Police dispatcher's message: "Wait, Axel. The University Police are on the way. They should be here any second."

"Dekker stared hard at Cameron and said, "Just do as I ask, Drew. Please. We must act now. That man could kill many of your students in the next minute, before the police arrive."

Then he made his way to the right-hand side of the stage, unwinding the wire from the spool as he walked about ten yards to the edge of the curtain. Cameron could see only a slight reflection of light from the side of Dekker's face as he looked into the classroom through the one-inch space between the curtain and the stage wall. Dekker could not see Cameron in the control booth.

Motionless, one student lay on the floor near the back of the room. The gunman, still waving both pistols, was circling around the room pointing them at various students and raging with anger about the injustices he had experienced at the hands of Alpha State University and cursing the arrogance and privileged status of ASU students. Over a minute had passed. Still no sign of the police.

"It's time for justice," he screamed and waved one pistol at the students and pointed one at the instructor, who still sat cringing at his desk. "Justice means you will pay for your sins. Your sins of being rich, spoiled, self-centered, lazy cowards. You never faced the Taliban during Kandahar, you never . . . ."

During the gunman's rant, Cameron felt the electrical wire tug at his fist twice in rapid succession, whereupon he flipped the master switch to "off." Even the various colored indicator lights on the computer equipment blinked off, leaving Cameron in the control booth, Dekker behind the curtain, and the students and armed man in the classroom, all in total darkness.

What happened next, in Cameron's memory, is unclear. His only distinct memory is feeling fear and helplessness. Deprived of any light, he had only his sense of hearing to rely on. All the sounds that he thinks he remembers seemed to be occurring at the same time. There were several more gun shots, maybe four or five, a lot of screaming and noises that suggested chairs turning over and scraping the floor, then several more gun shots, then for about half a minute complete chaos overcame the classroom. He was unable to see that a few students were trying to make calls on their cell phones, some were praying, some lay on the floor, others were trying to escape through the back doors, a few were attempting to hide in the corners of the dark room, a few just sitting in their chairs in clinical shock, and weeping. But Cameron heard no voice on a bullhorn saying "Drop your weapons and come out with your hands up."

Dekker appeared out of the darkness in front of the control booth, carrying a limp, unconscious man in his early thirties, whose face, neck and shirtfront were covered in blood. Dekker ordered, "Hold this man. Now, do as I say. You must trust me. Listen. Listen to me and do as I say." He laid the limp body on a table, stared hard at Cameron and held both his shoulders. "*You* subdued and disabled this man. We were here in this lab checking the new software to see how it works. While we were here, *you* heard the armed man yelling and the pistol shots and the students' screams and realized there was a classroom takeover. *You* called the University Police, then turned out the lights and went into the classroom to disarm the man. *You* attacked him in the dark, took his guns, and during the scuffle; *you* hit him in the face and choked him until he was unconscious. Do you understand?"

Cameron looked at the unconscious man lying on the table. He lay still, his nose still oozing blood. His hands were tied behind his back with electrical cord. Dekker turned his back to Cameron, revealing a pistol in each of his back pockets. "Take these, Drew. The safeties are on. Can you carry him back out to the front of the classroom?"

Cameron stuck one in each of his back pockets. "Yes, I think so," Cameron said, rising and feeling a little more self-confident, but still in state of wonder about this man Dekker.

"*I* never left this lab. *You* went into the classroom alone and subdued the man. Do you understand?" Dekker demanded. "*You* did this . . . *alone*. Now take him back out to the classroom, and I'll turn on the lights for you."

Cameron was dumfounded. "Okay, I see. Okay, Axel," he said.

Dekker went back to the control room as Cameron picked up the still limp body and half dragged him out of the lab, through the narrow space between the two-by-fours where the last sheetrock panel would go, through the curtain, and into the corner of the still dark, chaotic classroom. As Cameron lay the gunman's limp body on the floor, Dekker turned the classroom lights back on and joined Cameron in the classroom. Stunned by the lights, the students grew somewhat quiet and wondered if Cameron was a second gunman. But when they saw their captor lying unconscious on the floor with his hands bound, they realized they were safe.

Then a new, well-organized form of disorder exploded into the classroom. Both doors on the left side burst open, and half a dozen well-armed officers in black uniforms behind black, bullet-proof shields entered and dispersed throughout the room. A loud voice through a bullhorn commanded, "Drop your weapon and put your hands up. Lie on the floor or we will shoot to kill." At the same time, four officers dropped on ropes commando-like from ceiling to floor, one in each corner of the classroom, through four rectangular holes in the ceiling created by removing ceiling panels during the earlier chaos. All the students either sat at their desks with their hands up or lay prone on the floor.

Cameron raised his arms to demonstrate his innocence and said to the lead officer, "I am Andrew Cameron, Executive Vice President for Academic Affairs and Provost of the University. On the floor here," pointing to the captured shooter who was beginning to stir, "is the man who took over the classroom, and shot several students, I think. Here are his pistols," he said, turning around to allow the officer to take both from his back pockets. "And this is Axel Dekker. He is here interviewing for a position with the University."

About that time, Chief Redden came through the classroom door and recognized his boss. After a quick survey of the classroom, Redden returned his pistol to his holster and said to the officer to his left, "Captain Farmer, the man standing there," pointing to Cameron, "is our executive vice president. He's okay. Take charge of the crime scene." Captain Farmer ordered two officers to secure the prisoner, who had awakened from his unconscious state and was trying to wipe the blood from his face against his shoulder. The officers replaced the electrical wiring that secured the gunman's hands with handcuffs and read him his Miranda rights. The prisoner seemed too dazed to understand or to care.

Cameron smiled at the Chief, and said, "I guess you want to know what happened?"

"Yes. But first, are you alright?"

"There was a student down in the back of the class room, a young man shot I think," Cameron said.

In fact, there were four students with serious gunshot wounds whom the paramedics were already tending to. Two emergency physicians and two nurses from University Hospital had rushed into the classroom and started to work on the four serious cases. Officers and paramedics began taking names and organizing the students for debriefing and, in several cases, for psychological counseling. It appeared that several other students had minor injuries. One coed had fallen on her face while trying to run away in the dark and was still bleeding. An older male student, whom later official interviews revealed to be a veteran of the war in Iraq, had taken a bullet in the forearm but was calm and lucid. He had used his handkerchief as a tourniquet above the wound to minimize the loss of blood until the medics discovered him and initiated standard emergency procedures. There were a couple of bloody split lips and a dislocated finger caused by falls. Many still sat at their desks — immobile, stone-faced, eyes glazed over. And at least half a dozen were convulsing with hysterical sobbing.

"Dr. Cameron, tell me, are you alright?" Chief Redden said, and motioned for a nurse to examine Cameron.

"Yes, Chief. I'm fine. A little shaky but no worse for the wear."

"Are you up to an official police interview now?" the chief asked. "Or we can wait until after the nurse examines you if you'd be more comfortable."

"Now's as good a time as any." As he answered the chief, he wondered what he would and should say, because the only facts he knew were those he had been told, and he knew they were fabricated.

"Captain Farmer," Chief Redden called. "I will take the initial statements of these two witnesses. We'll be in the front office on the first floor. The crime scene is yours."

The two secretaries in the first floor office greeted the uniformed Redden with gratitude and tears of joy. The three men took seats at a table in the back room, and Redden closed the door.

"How did you two get into that classroom when my officers had to blow the door hinges off with RDX to get in?" the chief asked, as he placed his voice-activated recorder on the table.

Dekker looked at Cameron, who said, "We came in the back door, during the rainstorm, and took the service elevator to the third floor to see the new computer lab. What used to be the auditorium in that building has been partitioned into a large classroom in the front and a small lab in the back. The new wall is complete except for about a two-foot gap on one side. When the shots and yelling started, the only way to enter the classroom was through the gap in the new wall." The chief listened. Dekker remained quiet.

"So then you called University Police and reported what was happening?" Redden asked.

"Yes, I did."

"And then what did you do?"

After a few moments of hesitation, Cameron answered with studied vagueness, "Subdued the gunman."

"Sir, if I may," Dekker interrupted, "I turned out the lights in the classroom so Dr. Cameron could get into the room without being seen and surprise the man shooting the gun."

"So you went in there in the dark, Dr. Cameron, and then what did you do?" Chief Redden asked.

"I knew where he was, but he didn't know I was there. So I hit him in the neck as hard as I could, then . . . ." Cameron stopped and glanced at Dekker for some gesture of guidance. Detecting only a passive expression, Cameron continued, "Then I hit him in the face with my forearm. He dropped to the floor. I tied his hands behind his back with electrical cord. About that time, you and your officers came in."

"I see you have blood on your shirt and tie and probably on your jacket. Is it yours or his?" the chief asked.

"It's his. I don't have a scratch. At least I don't think I do."

"What about you, Mr. Dekker?" Can you add anything?" Redden asked.

"No sir," Dekker added. "It all happened very fast."

"Gentlemen, both of you can add to or amend your statement later, for the permanent record, if you think of anything else relevant. I have your statement recorded. Thank you both very much. Dr. Cameron, I'll be in touch."

As they rose to leave, the chief added, "Drew, I know the local media always monitor our police radio, so I'd bet there's half a dozen reporters trying to get into the crime scene right now. If you walk out the front door, they'll be all over you. You might want to slip down the corridor to that back door where you first came in. Your car is there?"

"Yes, it is. Thanks, Charlie. We will do exactly that."

They walked down the first-floor corridor to the rear entrance. Cameron called Holly on his cell phone to report that they were safe and on their way back to the office, and asked her to call Vanessa for him. Once back in the car behind the building, they stared at each other for a few moments in silence. As they drove toward the Admin Building, Cameron asked, emphasizing each word, "Axel, what just happened back there?"

"You did very well, Drew. A brief, lucid, credible report."

"Answer my question, Axel. I'm serious."

"Alright. Need to know, I suppose. You must promise me that you will never repeat what I am about to tell you. Do I have your solemn promise to that effect? I must," Dekker requested with urgent authority.

"Yes, I guess," Cameron said, with no idea of what Dekker was about to say.

"When we first met in Prague, I told you that after I had finished college at University of Leiden, I served in the Dutch Army for the minimum term, and then took a desk job as an entry-level white-collar bureaucrat with the European Union. For the next twenty-five-years, according to my résumé, I worked for the EU in several administrative positions, in several European locations, received promotions, retired on a nice pension just three years ago, and enrolled in the Charles University doctoral program, which I finished late last summer. Some of that is not true."

"So, what is the truth?" Cameron demanded.

"After college, I served in the Dutch Army for two years and then I was appointed to a joint task force of NATO and the EU — in reality, a special forces unit, on assignment to do whatever needed to be done by military force, mostly dealing with European security threats and military incursions in the Middle East and Africa."

"So you had a military career?" Cameron asked.

"Yes and no," Dekker answered. "After a few years in the joint special forces unit, I spent some time in California. I completed Navy Seal training, in San Diego. Then I was transferred back to an intelligence unit in the EU-NATO task force, and spent the next decade in various locations around the world doing mainly espionage work. I retired and enrolled in graduate school a little over three years ago."

Cameron stared into space for almost a minute and then asked, "So you decided to use some of your professional experience in Miller Hall?"

"That's about it," Dekker replied. "But you can never reveal this to anyone. Anna doesn't even know. You see, when I retired, they gave me a completely new identity and erased all public records of my real previous life. If my real identity were to become known, enemies of the EU and NATO would probably want to extract information from me. You see, I know a lot of state secrets, military and governmental, that would be valuable to our enemies. Or, they might just want to kill me."

"So you had to make me the hero of this incident rather than telling the police the truth?"

"It is the best way. It is now up to you to preserve the secret. If the truth becomes public, it could do severe harm to NATO and EU strategic interests. And to me."

"And what about the media? "Do you have any advice?" Cameron asked.

"To be plausible, it must be simple, concrete, and consistent."

Cameron found Dekker's explanation only a little reassuring but said, "Axel, thanks for the advice. And thanks for putting your life on the line to save the lives of our students. What you did took courage, selflessness, and expertise, and you seem to be loaded with all three. So, on behalf of all those students, Alpha State University, and me, thank you very much."

"I'm just glad it worked," Dekker said, with typical modesty.

"Nonetheless, you've put me in one helluva position," Cameron said as he slipped the University car into gear and drove toward the Admin Building.

As they rode, Dekker called Anna Zezulka on his cell phone to let her know all was well, in case she were to hear a news report about the violence on campus. As they pulled into the parking lot, almost dry by now, Cameron answered a cell phone call from Holly. "You probably want to avoid your office right now. We've got reporters all over the waiting room. Is Dr. Dekker okay?"

"Yes. We are both fine. Send the reporters to Chief Redden. Call Faust and tell him what we know so far. Tell him that I recommend that he ask Margaret Benedict to set up a press conference for . . . four o'clock this afternoon. He should preside. Make sure Chief Redden is there. I'll answer questions then and maybe that will put the media to rest. Meanwhile, I will be at home or at the Renaissance Hotel with the Czech delegation. I'll call Vanessa to let her know," Cameron said.

"By the way," Holly said, "we've received memos from almost everybody on the search committee. All of them really like Dr. Dekker a lot and want you to hire him."

"Thanks, Holly. I think we can do that. Prepare that letter ASAP," Cameron said as he drove toward the interstate to go home. "And by the way, Axel, Holly says the search committee likes you a lot. Do you want a job at Alpha State?"

"I do, of course."

"Then consider it done. Holly is drafting your offer letter now."

As he and Dekker navigated the interstate traffic, Cameron ignored his advice to his children about cell phone use while driving and placed a cell phone call to Vanessa, explaining what had happened. She was horrified at the thought of gun violence on campus, but relieved that Cameron was okay. As they traveled to suburban Bedford to enable Cameron to change clothes, he and Dekker discussed the forthcoming press conference. Dekker briefed him on how to reconstruct the events of the classroom shooting and how to answer questions about it. Cameron was grateful for Dekker's remarkable grasp of even the most subtle nuances of the English language. He changed into fresh clothes and made a pot of tea and some tuna salad sandwiches for the two of them while they continued their preparation for the press conference. By two o'clock, Dekker was satisfied that the provost would answer media questions quite well.

"I think I am prepared to deal with any questions the media can ask, Axel, thanks to you. What I am not prepared to deal with, to live with, is lying, deceiving the media and my colleagues at Alpha State University, and, most of all, lying to Vanessa."

"I think you will do fine, Drew," Axel responded. "But let me give you a different perspective on what I must ask you to do. I am a statistician, and I know that several academic fields, especially economics and policy analysis, use cost-benefit analysis to help them make a decision or to determine a proper course of action. All things considered, revealing my role in the Miller Hall incident would cause more trouble for more people than whatever good it might produce. Keeping it secret incurs some intangible cost. In the case of your conscience, significant cost. But the net benefits are greater. Don't you agree?"

After a long pause, Cameron responded, "I get your point. I am not at all sure I agree, but okay. I'll tell the 'medicinal lie' as well as I can. But please understand, I will probably get a lot of credit I don't want, for something that I didn't do, for something that you did. That's wrong and I don't like it."

"Think of the greater good. And remember, I am grateful to you. It is the right thing to do in this case. But let me add one provision. I understand your difficulty in not telling Mrs. Cameron the truth, so let me offer this concession. Allow five years to pass, and then tell her the truth," Dekker said.

Cameron thought a minute, then asked, "Are you sure that won't get you or your EU agency into trouble?"

"I think it will be okay," Dekker said, "because by that time, my agency will have changed all its codes. Now, I think I should take a taxi back to the Renaissance to join the Czech trade delegation. We return to Prague tomorrow."

"No," Cameron answered, "I'll take you. I want to say 'goodbye' to them, especially to Anna, and thank them for their good work. So, let's go."

9

"Good afternoon. I am Margaret Benedict, Vice President for Public Information. Thank you for coming. Let's get straight to the business at hand. President Faust?"

The auditorium in which Cameron had been introduced as the new provost just about six months prior was again full of news media representatives. All the TV cameras capturing the event were transmitting live across the entire country. The excitement of such a dramatic and important news event was shrouded with anxiety about its tragic reality.

"Thank you, Margaret," Steve Faust began as he took his place behind the mike and followed the text that Margaret Benedict had prepared for him. "We thought that by calling a press conference, we could provide the public with all the information we have at this time. Margaret's staff is finishing a press release that we will give you before you leave. I have asked ASU Police Chief Charles Redden and Executive Vice President for Academic Affairs and Provost Andrew Cameron, to brief you and to answer your questions. On behalf of all of us at Alpha State University, I want to say how very sorry we are for the four wounded students and their families, and for all the students and the instructor in the class who were subjected to this horrendous incident. We will do all we can to ensure that justice is done and that this kind of incident never happens again on Alpha State's campus."

"We mourn the tragedy of the incident, and are grateful that it was no worse than it was. The University will continue with its final exam schedule, except for the students in this statistics class. We will offer each of them a variety of options with respect to a final grade, and special clinical counseling for those who want it. President Faust looked up from his notes and announced, "Now, University Chief of Police, Charles Redden."

The Chief cleared his throat, adjusted the mike, and looked at his prepared text. In his almost three decades of police work, Charlie Redden had never addressed such a large crowd of media representatives, local, state, and national, with multiple TV cameras covering him live and reporters taking notes of every word he uttered.

"The details of what we know and can release at this time will be included in Ms. Benedict's press release, as soon as it arrives. This morning at approximately nine o'clock," Redden said, "the suspect, Holden R. Parks, a white male, aged thirty-one, carrying two loaded firearms and over four hundred rounds of ammunition, entered a classroom of fifty-nine students and one instructor in Miller Hall on our campus. He chained the doors closed from inside and held the students hostage for approximately thirty minutes. During that period, he fired fourteen rounds with two Glock 20, ten millimeter, automatic pistols. He wounded four of our students. Unknown to Mr. Parks, Executive Vice President Cameron and a candidate interviewing for a job at Alpha State were inspecting some new software in a temporary computer lab adjacent to the classroom. Dr. Cameron heard the shots and called University Police. After he called but before we arrived, he used the master switch in the computer lab to turn off the lights in the classroom, rushed into the dark classroom and subdued Mr. Parks from behind. This tactic was possible because at that time of day, the pitch-black clouds and heavy rain made it seem almost like night.

"Alpha State police and a New Cambridge SWAT team arrived, with a response time of seven minutes, broke through the chained doors and through the ceiling to enter the classroom, and took custody of the suspect without firing a shot. In fact, Dr. Cameron had already tied the suspect's hands behind his back with electrical cord. Dr. Cameron's actions no doubt prevented further shooting and any deaths. We owe him a huge debt of gratitude. It is likely that by subduing the suspect in the dark, he saved the suspect's life, too, because SWAT team procedure, when freeing hostages, calls for immobilization of an armed suspect by any means if he poses an immediate and deadly threat to civilians. It was luck that put Dr. Cameron in the adjacent lab during the classroom takeover, but it was quick thinking that enabled him to call University Police and both courage and skill that enabled him to subdue the suspect."

Upon hearing Chief Redden's account of the incident, almost certain to become the public and official account, Cameron experienced a sudden and frightening sensation of nausea.

"Dr. Isaac Goldman and two other emergency physicians," Redden continued, " and several nurses and paramedics from University Hospital — I don't have their names — accompanied the SWAT team and administered first aid to the four gunshot victims, and transported them to University Hospital for further medical attention. Six other students suffered minor injuries, such as bruises and abrasions, and in one case, a broken finger, mainly due to falling in the dark during the chaotic incident. These students also received emergency treatment."

Turning toward Margaret Benedict, Chief Redden asked, "Margaret, do we have time for questions?" She nodded, and he continued, "I will try to answer questions now if you have . . ." but even before he could finish his sentence half a dozen reporters blurted out questions, and momentary chaos filled the room.

The question that prevailed was, "Does the press release include the names of the wounded students?"

"No," Redden responded. "Their names are being withheld until the university attorney clears it with their parents."

"What's the name of the shooter again? Is that in the press release?"

"The suspect's name is Holden R. Parks."

"What can you tell us about him? Where does he live?"

"His driver license shows his permanent address to be in Franklin, Illinois, a suburb of Chicago."

"Is he a student at ASU?"

"No, not now. He moved to New Cambridge four years ago to attend the University, was registered as a student for two years, and then dropped out."

"Where is he now? Is he in New Cambridge central lockup?"

"He is in custody but not in central lockup. During the incident this morning, according to Dr. Goldman, the suspect suffered a broken clavicle and a broken nose. He has been transported to a secure location that can accommodate those injuries until his arraignment. As soon as the doctors approve, we will transport him to New Cambridge central lockup."

"Chief, what happens next?"

"The suspect will be arraigned and, I suppose, go to trial, as soon as the county prosecuting attorney is ready. The New Cambridge police detectives and several of my officers are continuing to investigate, taking statements from every student in the class and the instructor, to make sure we have all the facts that are relevant. All the physical evidence we have is in the hands of the New Cambridge police lab ."

"Has the shooter asked for an attorney?"

"Not as far as I know. We read him his Miranda rights at the scene. If he doesn't have a lawyer, the court will assign one to represent him."

"Does he have a prior police record?"

"No, not in this state, or in any other state, or with the Feds. Before he enrolled as a student here, he served in the U.S. Army and spent one tour of duty in Afghanistan. Later he received a general discharge."

"How do you compare the Alpha State shooting with the massacre at Virginia Tech or UCal Santa Barbara?"

"I don't. I'll take one more question now."

"Does Dr. Cameron have any special training that enabled him to stop the shooter?"

Chief Redden paused, looked at Cameron, and said, "I think Dr. Cameron can answer that question better than I can, so I will turn the podium over to him."

Cameron rose and walked to the microphone. "No," he said, "I have no special training."

"Could you, Dr. Cameron, reconstruct the dramatic narrative for us as it unfolded during this bloody shooting of innocent college students by a crazed gunman?"

Cameron recognized the man asking the question. He was one of the better known national network reporters who occasionally serves as anchor for the evening news. Cameron also recognized the well-known reporter's blatant attempt to emotionalize and sensationalize the news report with such phrases as "dramatic narrative," "bloody shooting," and "crazed gunman." He wondered if university schools of communications teach student journalists to do that, or if the networks and stations put aside objectivity in their quest for higher ratings.

Cameron took several minutes to reconstruct the events of the incident as Dekker had prepped him to. His reconstruction was clear, logical, credible and consistent with Chief Redden's account.

"How does it feel to be a hero?"

"I don't know."

"How do you feel?"

"Uncomfortable. And sad for the students and their families."

"What motivated you to subdue the shooter?"

Cameron paused for a long time to take several deep breaths as the feeling of nausea continued. "Fear, and the need to protect what we do here. Our students. Our mission."

"How soon after the gunman seized the classroom did you enter the room and subdue him?" asked a reporter from the NBC TV affiliate. "Was it before or after the first shots were fired?"

"After the first couple of shots. Maybe two or three minutes after he took over the classroom. I'm not sure. I . . . ." Cameron trailed off as if deep in thought or falling asleep.

CNN's reporter barked out, "Have you ever had any hand-to-hand combat training or anything like that?"

"No." Then he stopped, in part from nervous exhaustion from the events of the day but more because of the painful effect of perpetrating a gross lie.

"With your permission, please, I'd like to end my statement now. I am . . . exhausted. I would appreciate it if you will allow me to get some rest." He smiled and walked back to his seat to gather his belongings.

Seasoned media reporters are known to be worldly to the point of cynicism. They have been everywhere and seen everything. Yet, all of them stuffed their note pads and mikes under their arms and applauded as he left the stage. There was the old school connection for those who were ASU graduates, but most of them had studied journalism at other universities and had come from all over the country. They felt an almost spiritual gratitude to the fates for placing Andrew Cameron at the right place at the right time — and they felt deep respect for a person who risks his own life to save the lives of others, especially when he succeeds. As their various emotions subsided and their ovation ended, they felt a mild sense of embarrassment at having lost their professional journalistic neutrality.

Before Cameron could leave the podium, Chief Redden stood, placed his hat back on his head, saluted his boss, and then extended his hand for a formal congratulatory shake. Cameron looked dazed, feeling guilty for reasons that only he and Dekker knew. This scene and the cheers and applause that it induced were recorded in video, audio, and print that were to appear every day on television, radio, newspapers, magazines, and social media across America and the world for the next week.

Margaret Benedict stood and said, "If we end this news conference now, those of you who want to get your stories on evening news will have enough time. Otherwise, you might not make your deadlines. So, thank you for coming. The University's full press release, all the facts as we currently know them, is on the table in the back of the room."

The various TV camera operators repositioned their cameras to capture their reporters' final, improvised remarks. Mona Richards, reporting live to a national network audience through her New Cambridge station WDJD, concluded, "America has seen quite a few classroom takeovers by armed gunmen during the past ten or fifteen years. Almost all of them resulted in the injury and death of one or even many innocent students. Today, we witnessed another such violent incident at ASU. But today, only four students were wounded and none was killed. When he learned of the takeover, ASU Vice President Andrew Cameron broke into the locked classroom through a back door and subdued the gunman, even before police arrived. Today, he no doubt saved the lives of sixty students who were there to take their final exam. In contemporary America, we almost worship fictional comic heroes like Iron Man, Hulk, Spider-Man, and so on. But we don't need them. We have a real live hero — Andrew Cameron. Here in New Cambridge, in early December, I think we can say that Dr. Cameron has brought us a Christmas miracle. Reporting live from New Cambridge, for WDJD TV, this is Mona Richards.

Cameron had left through the back door to avoid further contact with the press and walked back to his car in the Admin parking lot under an overcast sky before anyone could get to him. Pulling out onto University Boulevard, he speed-dialed Holly. "Yes, Dr. Cameron? Are you alright?"

"I'm fine, Holly. But I'm going straight home unless we have an emergency."

"You have had all the emergencies you need for one day. See you . . . when I see you. Get some rest."

As he turned onto the Interstate, the only energy, the only motivation he had to continue was from his thoughts of Vanessa, and the comfort she would bring. He felt old, tired, and nauseous. His mouth, throat and eyes were dry and scratchy, and the back of his head and neck ached. First, he thought, a hug with Vanessa, second, two Tylenol. But none of this could erase the fact that he was deceiving her about such an important matter. Vanessa, of all people. He would simply have to think of something. Deceiving her just would not work. It would be so unfair to her, and he would feel guilty and depressed about it the rest of his life. He knew it might come to that, since there seemed to be no honorable exit. Cameron thought to himself, *Socrates drank the hemlock rather than live a lie.*

He could tell from the lights in the house that Vanessa was already home from work. The front porch light was shining and several interior lights were on. He drove his car into the garage beside Vanessa's and entered the kitchen through the garage door. As soon as he stepped onto the kitchen tile, he saw Vanessa sitting in the living room sipping a cup of tea, and seated across the room was Axel Dekker! For a moment, the surprise of seeing Dekker seated in his living room overcame his deep feelings of exhaustion and guilt. *What,* he thought, *could Axel Dekker be doing in my house now, talking to Vanessa?* Vanessa and Dekker stood and faced Cameron as he walked in.

"Come in. Let me fix you a cup of tea," Vanessa said as she walked to him and gave him a tight hug and a kiss. "Axel and I have been getting to know each other better and the result should lighten your burden."

"Hello, again, Drew," Axel said. "We think we have some good news for you, but I want Vanessa to tell you."

"Drew," Vanessa began, "in brief, Axel has hired me as his legal counsel on retainer, effective this evening. He came to me with a personal and professional problem that has resulted from the classroom seizure this morning. Of course, I redefined it into a legal problem. After we signed a contract, he shared with me, in confidence, his recollection of the events of this morning in Miller Hall." Cameron noticed that both Vanessa's choice of words and her rhetorical inflection had shifted from conversational to the style of an attorney answering a judge's question.

"My professional responsibility is to provide legal representation to Dr. Dekker in the event of any future repercussions from the Miller Hall incident, such as suits initiated against him by the university, students present, their parents, the suspect, or others. My role is to ensure that any such suit remains confidential within the judge's purview and is ruled non-justiciable. As a result, you are free to assume that I know all the relevant facts about the Miller Hall incident. I am bound by my oath as an attorney, as confirmed by the U.S. Supreme Court in *Upjohn v. the U.S.* in 1981, not to reveal any facts given to me by my client, Dr. Dekker, that are relevant to his reason for retaining me as my attorney. Attorney-client privilege. It is sacred."

The painful weight of guilt and exhaustion began to lift, and a smile came to Cameron's face. "I think I see what you two have done," he said. "And I am grateful far beyond my ability to express it. You just could not believe it."

"I think we could, Drew. I think we could," Dekker said, and Vanessa nodded, almost overcome with emotion at the miraculous solution that she and Dekker had just revealed. All three sat in silence for a minute, with moist eyes, and very grateful.

Finally, Dekker broke the silence when he placed his teacup back into the saucer and rose. "It's time for me to go. Thank you, counselor. Thank you, boss," and grinned. "As soon as Anna and I can get our Prague affairs in order, early in the New Year, we will return to New Cambridge to start our new lives. We both look forward to that."

"Our future here, especially mine," Cameron answered, "will be brighter because of you, Axel. I can never thank you enough for all you have done — underline all."

"You flatter me, Drew. I am the lucky one. I am lucky to have met you in Prague, lucky to be invited by you for a job interview at ASU, lucky to get your offer to work here. As we say in Holland, '*Vriendschap is in wezen een partnerschap.*' Sorry, but I originally learned that in elementary school. In English, 'Friendship is essentially a partnership.' By the way, it's a quote from Aristotle."

"Drew," Vanessa said, "maybe you hired him because of his academic training but you also got intelligence, integrity, and a big helping of charm," and gave Dekker a very affectionate hug.

"On that note, I say 'thank you' and take my leave." At that moment a car pulled into the Cameron's driveway. A security agent for the Czech delegation was driving their rental car. He stepped out and waited for Dekker to join him. It was cold and dark as Dekker drove away, but Cameron and Vanessa did not even notice. They did not talk about the events of the day any more. Each knew quite enough and their love filled in the few blank spaces.

That night, all New Cambridge TV news broadcasts featured coverage of the classroom shootings and the press conference, the outcome of which they dubbed, "The Christmas Miracle," adopting the label that TV reporter Mona Richards had given the incident. The national networks' evening news shows also used her label and devoted about five minutes of their half-hour to Alpha State University's terrible incident, in part because it could have been so very tragic but was not. Most of them described Cameron as a courageous but modest hero who saved the lives of many students. Vanessa and Cameron watched none of it nor read the article under the banner headlines, "ASU Classroom Shooting," in the next morning's *New Cambridge Morning News*. It was a night and a weekend of warmth, love, thankfulness, and peaceful rest for both of them.

"Good morning, Provost's office," Holly Nabisco said early on Monday morning. My goodness, Dr. Cameron, it's good to hear from you. Did you have a good weekend?"

"I did. You are in early, as usual," Cameron said a little before seven on his cell phone as he entered the Interstate in Bedford traveling toward New Cambridge. "I thought I should call to find out if I start the day in the office or have something off-campus first. I haven't talked with you since late Friday."

Holly did not mention that she had sent him an email attachment documenting his complete schedule for the day. Rather, she began, "After your day Friday, I'm surprised you are coming in to work at all, let alone at seven in the morning. Your first appointment is in your office at eight-thirty. There is nothing that requires any prep time until this afternoon. I moved some appointments around to make your day a little easier."

Elsewhere in the Admin Building, Ms. McInerney said, "Good morning, Mr. Speaker. How can we help you, sir? Yes, he's in. I will transfer you now." After a pause, "Speaker Clements on line two."

"Thank you, Ms. McInerney. Shelby, good morning. What's going on with you?" President Faust asked.

"You guys at Alpha State had one helluva Friday, didn't you," the Speaker of the state House of Representatives asserted. "Are those four wounded students going to be okay?"

"I think so, but it was a bad Friday, for sure."

"I want to get your full report on that terrible incident soon, Steve, but right now I have some good news and a small favor to ask of you."

"Where do you want to start, Shelby?" Faust asked, working hard to sound cheerful rather than curious.

"First, the good news. This weekend I had a three-way phone conversation with our new state senate majority leader, Hudson Neuberger, and Senator Broadbent in Washington. I think Hudson's gonna be a team player. Anyway, we cleared up the whole logjam on appropriations and some of it's important to you. We moved a little more money into state economic development so now you have all you need to buy out the Wolfe-Otis facility and do most of the renovations you wanted to do. We'll get this to you in writing early next week so you can start requesting bids on the work."

"Shelby, that's great news. Thanks for making it happen," Faust said but cut short any further expression of gratitude, remembering that Shelby was going to ask a favor.

"The rest of the good news is that Earl Broadbent said he's got about a half-million dollars left in end-of-year monies for the state to fund anything that benefits children and it's okay to push some of it your way for some R and D. So, you can count on that as long as you use it to support research or development projects that help kids, anything from," and here he paused to look at his notes, "pediatrics to early childhood education — some money to reward friends and neighbors, you know. Be sure to give Earl credit when you dole out the projects."

"Thanks for more good news, Shelby. We'll put the money to good use," Faust responded.

"Now, I need your help. My son, Patrick, finished his last final exam during the middle of last week, and he saw the grades for his history class posted on the professor's door Saturday morning. Anyway, he got an "F" in British History," and he paused again to look at his notes, "History 370, section two, the first semester of British History. Patrick's majoring in pre-law and wants very much to be a lawyer, just like his dad, and both semesters of British history are required in the pre-law major. He's had some issues in college, now and then, and his grades don't really reflect how bright he is. This 'F' will make it impossible for him to get into law school. A 'C' would keep him afloat. So, what I want to ask you to do is to . . . you know, look into it."

"Shelby, sorry this happened. I will look into it and see what can be done to help," the ASU president said. "Unless you hear from me by tomorrow at noon, the problem has been solved. Okay?"

"Thanks, Steve. When we work together, good things happen," the House Speaker said and hung up the phone.

President Faust sat for a moment, wondering how to deal with this problem. "Ms. McInerney, get me Rachael O'Brien, in Admissions and Records."

Seconds later, "Good morning, President Faust," Rachael said in her cheeriest voice.

"Rachael. Got some personal business for you, okay?" he said.

"How can I help you?" she said, recognizing the meaning of the code word, "personal business."

"We need to . . . adjust a transcript, bypassing the ad hoc grade appeals process. Patrick Clements, in this semester's History 370, section two. Grade of record must be C."

"I've got it. Record change by mediated adjustment?" Rachael asked.

"No. C will just be the grade of record. Thanks, Rachael."

Final exam week continued as always. By mid-December, students had taken and faculty had graded the exams, and turned in final grades. Some distinct changes did occur, however, during the next few weeks into the New Year. But this year, both state and national media gave an extraordinary amount of attention to the "Christmas Miracle," and especially to Drew Cameron, whom they covered with adulation. He received even more attention than Coach Paul Sylvester, whose football team lost to Michigan in the national championship game. And, he received more attention than President Faust, who, in private meetings, began to share with individual members of the Board of Trustees his irritation with some of Cameron's actions, in particular his secret investigation and subsequent firing of Zachary Kilgore. That investigation had revealed that Vice President Kilgore had falsified several of the statistics used by *American News Report* to rank public universities, thus eliminating Alpha State from breaking into the top thirty public institutions and, therefore, kept them from receiving a large bonus appropriation from the state legislature next year. Faust, several members of the Board, and at least two big alumni donors began to change their attitudes toward Cameron from warm and supportive to cold and critical.

At the same time, faculty attitudes also began to change, but in a favorable direction. At most universities, when a provost has been in office for almost a year, about one-third of the faculty thinks he or she is doing a good job, one-third thinks he is doing a bad job, and one-third maintains a comfortable isolation from anything about the provost. After the faculty became aware of the media accounts of how Cameron's courage and quick thinking saved a classroom full of students, their judgment of his value to the institution improved. Faculty support for long-term planning and for curriculum reform strengthened in every college. They began to appreciate his openness and candor with regard to University problems and issues. And, they acknowledged the value of his efforts on behalf of international exchange programs and even his key role in facilitating New Cambridge's rapid transit plans. In short, Cameron's new aura of modest heroism translated into faculty support.

On the last day of December, Axel Dekker and Anna Zezulka left their positions in Prague, he from Charles University and she from the Ministry of Trade. They arrived at New Cambridge International Airport early in January. When Axel called his new boss to check in, he reported that Anna would also begin a new job on February 1 as director of international trade relations in the Czech Consul General's Office in New Cambridge. Both were elated.

In late January, Holly overheard conversation among several ASU faculty members in the cafeteria as she waited in line to pay for her take-out lunch. She picked up on, "He's got a big majority of the faculty interested in curriculum reform," and "He's the first administrator in my thirty-five years at ASU to initiate a rational planning process," and "Did you hear, he's persuaded New Cambridge to start a rapid transit system."

A professor of nursing added, "But he earned everybody's good will with his heroics. I still do ER rotations in University Hospital, and I saw the records of the four students who were shot. In another five minutes, two of those students would have bled out and died. Plus, how many more might have been killed or wounded?"

"I think that was basically luck on Cameron's part," a geologist said, "but he's getting the reform and planning done with smarts and persistence, and for that he's okay."

As an additional cashier opened a second line, Holly moved forward and could no longer hear the conversation as she paid for her chicken salad sandwich and diet soda. She took care to remember who said what, and later that afternoon, watched Cameron blush as she recounted the conversation for him. "Also," she said, "we are beginning to develop a backlog of invitations for you to speak to organizations. And you're getting more from out-of-state. We can either set up some decision rules and I will respond to the invites in terms of those rules, or you can review every one and tell me how I should reply."

"Starting February first, let's do only local organizations. Tell the others 'maybe later' in so many polite words. This thing has gotten out of hand," he said.

Last summer, few students were even aware that ASU had hired a new provost. But after the Miller Hall incident, Cameron became their hero. For the first few weeks of the spring semester, the frequency of IHGOW in their text messages and on Facebook exceeded that of even LOL and OMG. As a result, IHGOW became chiseled in granite as the standard abbreviation for an enthusiastic, "Is he great or what?"

After losing the championship bowl game in mid-January, Coach Sylvester took two weeks of very well-paid vacation, and then plunged into the rigors of recruiting high school players for next season. Coach always said that recruiting good players was difficult work, requiring extensive travel, endless meetings day and night, persuading seniors and their parents that ASU would be the best place for their sons. The Department of Athletics owned two Lear jets for this purpose. Recruiting high school football players from southern Florida each year was very important to the team's success. And every year it required two or three weeks of work in south Florida. In January.

Cameron's life in the second semester continued as usual, except for his unwelcomed fame. After consulting with the Westerveldt Chair selection committee, he invited each of the four nominees to his office to announce to them that he was appointing Carolyn Anthony, novelist in the creative writing program, to the position, effective at the beginning of the fall term. She responded with a self-effacing smile, quick substitution of a hearty handshake for the hug she almost gave Cameron, and a profuse expression of gratitude. The handsome public historian, Alexander Robertson, immediately responded that he would be leaving ASU to take a "very attractive" offer from the University of Virginia. The strange financial economist, Emile Kupchinski, sat dumfounded, muttered something about "political decision," then stood and left the office. The biochemical engineer, Timothy McNathan, expressed gratitude at being considered as a candidate, shook hands with Cameron, and left. Later in the day he sent his sincere congratulations via email to the winner, Carolyn Anthony. Cameron also asked Holly to put a note in the file to remind him that he must find a way to recognize and reward Timothy McNathan. He and the committee had agreed that Anthony and McNathan were equal in value to the university. In secret, Cameron had broken the tie between them by flipping a coin, with Vanessa as his witness.

The next morning, President Faust answered his private cell phone to hear a very jovial "Steve, we've done it again! You and I and Earl Broadbent. Have you seen today's paper?"

"Not yet, but I get the feeling that I should read it right away."

"Indeed you should," Wolfe replied. Wolfe-Otis stock has jumped over sixteen dollars per share in the last two days. ASU has netted well over a million dollars in two days!"

"I thank you for the good advice you gave me earlier," Faust responded.

"And I thank you for lending the name of your famous Dr. Novak and ASU's reputation to our efforts, which almost guaranteed that the FDA would give us a green light. Money in the bank."

"Great. Alex," Faust said. "You and I and Earl are a pretty tough combination. Do you realize what an impressive record we have when we meet to devise a plan and drink sherry at the Renaissance Club? The next step is for Earl to announce the federal money that's coming to the state, to ASU, and then you. Then you announce that you are building a whole new headquarters and production facility in New Cambridge rather than in China. And then I announce that ASU is buying your headquarters to start a new satellite campus."

"And we're all heroes."

"I've gotta run, Alex," Faust said. "I have to be on a plane in about an hour."

"Your two o'clock with the Peace Corps assistant director is cancelled, Dr. Cameron. He has the flu. And you had a slightly irritated call from Dr. Osterman in Sociology. She wants to see you ASAP and it's not about curriculum reform. She says that's going well. She wouldn't tell me what it's about. She's available for the next hour or so."

"Get her in, then. Let's see what's on her mind."

A few minutes later, Osterman came bustling into Cameron's office carrying several folders of computer printout, followed by two other people whom Cameron thought he recognized as faculty members. Her vocal tone conveyed a mixture of angst and anger as she said, "You'll never believe this one. I hope you didn't have anything to do with it."

"And what might that be, Melinda?" Drew asked.

"You know last June, right before you became provost, the state Higher Ed Council put a freeze on all salary increases in the university system?" she asked.

"I do. They were following the legislature's direction."

"Oh, excuse me, do you know Betsy Cannon and Jim Simpson?" Melinda said. Without waiting for an answer, she continued, "They're colleagues. Betsy's in the Law School and Jim's in the Business School." Each of them shook hands and exchanged greetings with Cameron. Betsy, with a warm smile, short brown hair, and big hazel eyes exuded confidence and gratitude for being included. Simpson's shaven head, his confident smile, his inquisitive brown eyes, and a soft-spoken baritone voice gave him an impressive theatrical aura.

"I asked them to come with me to see you because of what's going on in their schools. Thanks for meeting with us. So, if there's a statewide freeze on higher ed salary raises, does that mean that nobody at any public higher educational institution in this state can be awarded a salary increase until the state freeze is rescinded?"

"That's my understanding," Cameron said, as the Law and Business faculty members nodded in assent and the four took seats.

"And are you also familiar with the concept of the "forgivable loan"? Before Cameron could respond, Osterman continued, "Let me tell you about it. It's called a loan, but the recipient does not have to pay it back, ever, as long as he or she remains on the faculty. So it's not really a loan but a salary bonus!

Three months after the state freeze, the University awarded forgivable loans to the deans of the School of Business and the School of Law. Did you know that? Do you know how much each of their forgivable loans is for? Each one is for a half million dollars!" Osterman stopped her exposé to let the amounts sink in, then continued, "Betsy happened to get wind that her dean got a 'forgivable loan' in November." Osterman spit out the term "forgivable loan" as if it caused a foul, caustic taste in her mouth.

"It's a potential salary issue," Associate Professor Betsy Cannon intervened, "so I brought it to Melinda's attention as chair of the Faculty Senate."

"So we put Betsy's legal expertise to good use by filing an open records request to identify use of funds from the Law School Foundation over the last four years. We discovered that a total of twenty law professors have been awarded 'forgivable loans' during that time. The current assets of the Law School Foundation total $121 million," Osterman said, and Betsy Cannon nodded.

"So we got Jim Simpson in Business to join Betsy and me to file a similar open records request for information on the Business School Foundation. They currently have $152 million in assets. And they awarded sixteen 'forgivable loans' in the past four years."

"That strikes me as a bad practice whether there is or isn't a freeze on salary increases," Cameron volunteered.

"And here's the *coup d'etat*," Osterman said. All thirty-six of the 'forgivable loans' were given to white males. So I'm bringing this to you in private first rather than kicking the hornet's nest in public in the Faculty Senate."

"Betsy and I did some checking on law and business schools around the country," Associate Professor Jim Simpson stated, "and we found out that their foundations can avoid some disclosure requirements by making these loans. They argue that these loans are necessary for the business or law school to remain competitive among their top-tier competitors. Moreover, they give these loans only to people in order to recruit them to the faculty or to retain them against the risk of their leaving for another job."

The radical feminist sociologist, Melinda Osterman, beamed as she handed Cameron a folder containing their documentation. "God, how I love it when a plan starts coming together," she said.

"Thanks Melinda, Betsy, Jim. I'll look into this case right away. We have been looking at compensation practices at Alpha State in terms of long-term planning and our curriculum, as Melinda knows. You are suggesting that we should also make sure that our policies and practices are . . . not illegal or immoral. I agree. And I thank you all three for bringing it to my attention."

"Dr. Cameron," Simpson added, "Betsy and I are not doing this because we want raises or think we are underpaid. If you give us more money we won't turn it down, of course, but that's not our point. Our point is that if 'forgivable loans' can be justified for white males, they could be justified for women and people of color, and for faculty in other colleges and schools. I think these loans weaken the market's ability to match actual supply and demand. Betsy thinks they work against 'equal protection of the law.' We're glad you seem to agree."

"Okay, let's go. Thanks, Drew. We will keep in touch. Tell us if you want us to do anything," Osterman said as the three walked toward the door. Cameron heard her say to Jim and Betsy as they neared the main office exit to the elevator, "I told you he was the people's provost, didn't I?"

Although Cameron did not welcome yet another problem, he was grateful to learn about ASU's use of forgivable loans. He marveled again at the essential functions of academic disciplines and their practitioners. Melinda Osterman, sociologist, looked at forgivable loans and saw structural dysfunction that necessitated overthrow of the ruling elite. Betsy Cannon, the legal scholar, saw disregard for legal principles of equity and pronounced a guilty verdict. James Simpson, economist, saw inefficient resource allocation as market failure that required regulation.

Holly entered Cameron's office saying, "That newspaper reporter called again. He wants to meet you somewhere, not in your office. He finally gave me his name, Curtis, but I'm not sure if that's his first or last name. He won't tell my why he wants to meet with you, only that it is urgent."

"Holly, just tell him I am too busy, make up some excuse, out of town a lot, capital campaign, etc., and get rid of him. If he had a good reason to meet, he would come to the office," Cameron said.

"I've been trying to set up a meeting for weeks, so I'm happy just to pull the plug on him. You also just had a call from that nice channel eleven reporter, Mona Richards. She wants you to return the call. You have thirty minutes before your next appointment. Do you want to answer some calls now?" Holly asked.

"Sure, let's do it," Cameron replied, as he began skimming a report from the School of Nursing on the state's need for certified nurses over the next decade, along with the dean's request to increase the nursing faculty by two fulltime positions each year, for ten years.

"Mona Richards on line two," Holly announced.

"Hello, Mona," Cameron said.

"Do you remember me, Dr. Cameron? We talked at a couple of the press conferences. I'm with channel eleven."

"Of course, Mona. What's on your mind?"

"First, let me thank you for what we in the media call the 'Christmas Miracle.' You have become quite a celebrity. Now, to business. I have some information to give you and a request," she said. Without waiting for a response, she continued, "I am aware that Curt Barnes has been trying to set up a meeting with you, for several months. Do you know who he is?"

Cameron remembered numerous calls and even a letter from a newspaper reporter asking for a meeting, and Holly's reference to a 'Curtis' just moments before. "He's a newspaper reporter, isn't he?" Cameron asked.

"A former newspaper reporter. He was nominated for a Pulitzer Prize early in his career, ran into some bad luck, and then sort of dropped out of the journalism profession. We went to college together as journalism majors at Vanderbilt. Both of us took our first jobs in Los Angeles. I was a writer for a TV station and he worked for the *LA Times*. He's still one of the best investigative journalists I've ever known. Right now, he wants very much to meet with you. I'd like to arrange that, if I may. He said I could even join the two of you if you'd feel better about that."

Cameron's curiosity overcame his suspicion and he said, "I suppose we could meet. But what's the agenda, Mona?"

"I realize, Dr. Cameron, that we hardly know each other, so this might seem strange. But, may I ask you to keep this information confidential?"

Impatience joined suspicion and curiosity, but he agreed to keep the confidence. "Okay. What's this about?"

"Curt tells me that he has quite a lot of information, evidence he calls it, about ASU's football coach, Paul Sylvester, and the football program. He wants you to know what it is and to tell him what he should do with it," Mona said. "That's about all I feel comfortable saying."

"Mona, are you doing a favor under duress for an old friend or are you telling me that I should assume that Curt Barnes' call is a serious matter? Level with me."

"Both," she answered.

"Okay, hang on a second," Cameron said, as he put Mona Richards on hold and buzzed Holly.

"Holly, get on line one with Mona Richards and set up a meeting time with her and Curt Barnes. She may ask for a meeting at a strange time and place, but within reason, agree. I'll do it."

"Mona, Holly Nabisco, my administrative assistant, will come on the line next and set up a meeting for you, Barnes, and me. I look forward to meeting him. Thank you for the call." Soon Holly buzzed him for the next call and so on until other business called him away from the phone. More meetings, more phone calls, more emails, more reading reports or their summaries, but fewer speeches about the Miller Hall incident filled the next few days for Cameron.

• • •

On the following Monday, three men in their forties, dressed in their best vested suits and ties, one of them carrying a manila folder of documents, exited the elevator on the fourth floor of Wolfe-Otis Pharmaceuticals, walked into the outer office of CEO Alexander Wolfe, and took their seats on the dark brown leather couch. Inside his plush office, Wolfe was finishing a phone call but already looking forward to his next meeting. As soon as the light on her phone blinked, the receptionist looked at the three men and announced, "You may go in now; he's expecting you."

Wolfe always enjoyed conversations with his people from the third floor — much more than conversations with the people from the fifth floor. Fifth floor people wore lab coats and spoke what he termed "foreign languages" — chemistry, pharmacology, computer programming, and biology. Third floor people wore tailored suits and spoke "Wolfe's language" — product distribution, branding, advertising, market share, and profit margin. Wolfe trusted them because they, too, had MBAs, theirs in marketing, his in management.

"Come in, fellas. Good to see you," Wolfe said.

"Thank you sir. Good to see you, too." Have you had a chance to read our proposal?"

"I have. Excellent recommendations." Wolfe stopped here because he knew how much they enjoy telling him about their marketing study, and he wanted them to lead the discussion.

"Mr. Wolfe, we propose beginning with periodic surveys of a random sample of six hundred physicians in the major markets, plus a few of our friends from past trials, and then add others as we proceed."

"It worked well last time, Peter, so I like it," Wolfe said.

"We are sorry that the budget goes a little over your initial recommendation. Is that okay, or do you want us to cut it back?"

"You boys remember that we have to spend money to make money. We did last time, didn't we? So, I'm approving your proposal. Get it started, today. This will be big for the company, and for you and me. Besides, accounting will allocate almost the whole cost of your marketing plan to research and development's budget anyway. Makes us look good."

Wolfe's approval brought instant smiles to the faces of the three marketing specialists. Their proposal had pleased their boss. They showed themselves out, working hard to constrain their glee.

Back in his office on the third floor, Peter asked his secretary to produce and mail letters to the six-hundred-plus physicians and then placed a call to his former graduate school classmate, Olivia Akers at Akers Opinion Research. "Olivia, how's the second best Wharton MBA of all time?"

"Peter, Peter pumpkin eater, what is on your mind? A contract, I hope."

"Exactomundo, you blithe and beautiful blond," Peter bantered with his old friend. "The propacricin deal is a go. The old man just approved it. So, I'm sending you the specs for your part of it as an email attachment."

"That's good news, Peter. Does it still include two years of quarterly interviews with the sample of docs?"

"Right. Look at the questionnaire and let me know if you want to make any changes. I defer to your superior skills in protocol design. Do stick to our list of physicians and private phone numbers we've included. It's our usual 'random sample'. Really a 'purposive sample'."

"Peter! Don't tell me that stuff. Unlike some people I know, I have ethical obligations," Olivia said with a grimace.

"Whatever. Just thank me in various seductive ways for getting Akers Research a sole source contract for all our survey work."

"Okay. Thank you. Now, send the specs over. We'll get to work," Olivia stated with finality, and hung up.

Olivia Akers assigned the project to one of her survey project managers, who, in turn, called a late Friday afternoon meeting of the twelve she picked to work on the project. One of them was an Alpha State sociology doctoral student, Diana Callahan, who was doing a six-credit internship with Akers Opinion Research. She listened to the manager's briefing, asked a couple of questions, stuffed her copy of the Wolfe-Otis specs into her briefcase as the meeting concluded, and left for home as the clock showed five-thirty.

As she drove home in her eleven-year-old Corolla, she found herself "twiddling" her hair below her right ear with her right hand, an habitual gesture, she had noted, when she was worried. Taking stock, she had to admit that she was happier now than at any other time in her life. Growing up in a family of very high standards, she was expected always to make straight As in both high school and college, the same college her parents, both physicians, had attended. And she did, because that's what they expected from her. As a biology major, she was required to take only one social science course, and she chose introductory sociology, mainly as a scheduling convenience. She was surprised to discover that she enjoyed it and was excited by it. The scientific study of the causes and consequences of human social interaction, in small groups and in societies, allowed for plenty of mathematical analysis, one of Diana's strengths, as well as social criticism, a penchant of hers since junior high. ASU's doctoral program in sociology required six hours of internship, which she had postponed until all her course work was finished. She had chosen this internship with Akers Opinion Research to strengthen her skills in survey research, and was happy that her first assignment was a health care project. After the internship was to come the dissertation, titled, "Social Roles and Social Networks in Five Hospitals."

She realized that for several minutes she had been sitting in her car, its engine still running, parked in front of her apartment, still "twiddling" her hair. Once inside, she yelled to her roommate, "I'm home," but got no answer. Her roommate, Meg Hartley, was a doctoral student in neuropsychology. They had planned to stay at home this Friday night to get some rest. To that end, they had decided to watch a double feature on the movie channel, but with her distracting case of the "twiddles," Diana couldn't even remember what movies they had planned to see, starting at seven o'clock. Meg Hartley soon arrived, grocery bag in hand. "Hi, Diana. I stopped by the Quickie-Mart and picked up a six pack and some popcorn for the movie," she said. "How was your day?"

"Good, Meg. I made us a salad. Let's eat. The movie starts in thirty minutes. By the way, what movie did we say we're watching tonight?" Diana asked.

"Don't you remember, it's Michael Douglas night — a double feature of his *Wall Street* films!"

"Oh, yeah. 'Greed is good,'" Diana said.

Promptly at seven, swigging a lite beer and eating popcorn by the handsfull, both women were soon lost in a dramatic world of power, money, greed, and exploitation in the absence of ethical constraints. Yet Diana's" twiddly" feeling continued. Near the end of Oliver Stone's 1987 film, she leapt to her feet, knocking her beer off the table and spilling half a bowl of popcorn, and screamed, "I knew something was wrong! I knew it!"

"Whoa, girl. What's wrong? It's a great movie."

"Not the movie, Meg. The research protocol, the pharmaceutical company's so-called clinical trials protocol that I'm supposed to start working on soon. The team manager briefed us on it today. Damn!"

"I don't get it. What?" Meg asked.

"Did you ever take Epstein's seminar in bioethics? Or Collander's seminar in medical ethics?"

"No. Neither one.

"But you understand the research procedures involved in experimental clinical trials."

"In my sleep," Meg answered. She had studied the methods of and participated in the design and management of scores of clinical trials using electroencephalography, magnetic resonance imaging, magneto-encephalography, and other brain-imaging techniques that even Diana had a hard time pronouncing. In fact, fellow doctoral students had nicknamed her "MEG" to reflect her obsession with experimental research on MEG or magneto-encephalography.

"As you know, real clinical trials require random assignment of subjects to treatment and control groups, use of placebos, and blind or even double-blind administration of treatments. That's real research. When you do that, you know the results are valid and reliable. You know the drug is either effective or not, it's safe or not."

"Yeah, Diana. The second film is about to start."

"But what Wolfe-Otis has asked Akers Research to do is not a clinical trial, although that's what they call it. It's nothing but a 'seeding' trial."

"Okay. Quick tell me what a seeding trial is before they finish running the credits for the second movie," Meg said, with more impatience than curiosity.

"A seeding trial is a marketing device, pure and simple. They're using six hundred doctors who have had no experimental research training as far as we know. They were not randomly chosen. They are paid to recruit subjects, their patients, to take this new drug, propacricin, for up to two years, during which time they become more familiar with the drug and more apt to prescribe it later. Patients are glad to sign up because they trust their doctors and they think they have been selected to be part of a national scientific study. But, they are just being used by Wolfe-Otis to promote and market their drug."

Meg looked at Diana and said, "Oh, yeah, Diana. 'Greed, for lack of a better word, is good'," quoting Gordon Gekko from the movie they'd just seen, after which they turned off the second Wall Street film and discussed the ethics of seeding trials until almost 1 AM.

10

Cameron found a parking place near the address at the dark end of a strip mall in a working-class neighborhood. He couldn't find his umbrella, so he jumped out and took several quick steps to reach the sidewalk sheltered by the overhanging roof. The car blinked its headlights and emitted a "chirp-chirp" as he walked about twenty yards toward the light shining from a hazy window. The sign on the window said, "Rusty Bucket."

He took a seat at a table in the corner in the Rusty Bucket, and tried to be patient but found himself looking at his watch — the fourth time at nine-fifteen. Holly had told him that the rendezvous with Curtis Barnes had been set for 9 PM. He had watched half a dozen men enter, remove their coats and hats and wipe the rain drops from their foreheads as they walked to the bar and ordered either a beer or a whiskey. Seconds before a self-conscious and impatient Cameron rose to leave, someone stepped through the door wearing dark glasses and a black hooded raincoat. The person glanced around the room for a few seconds and then walked toward his table. *It must be the mysterious Curt Barnes*, Cameron thought to himself.

He couldn't have been more wrong. Mona Richards shook the rain off her coat, removed her hood and lifted her sunglasses. "Dr. Cameron, sorry I'm late. And thanks for agreeing to meet."

"That's okay, Mona. Glad you're here." They shook hands and she took a seat.

She removed her cell phone from her purse, placed a call, and said, "It's okay, Curt. He's here," and returned her phone to her purse. "That was Curt. He's a little shy. A little eccentric. He was afraid you wouldn't show."

For the third time, the peevish waitress approached his table oozing with condescension. "Now do you want to order something, since your lady friend's here?" she asked.

"Go ahead, Dr. Cameron. This is on me," Mona Richards offered.

Cameron assumed that the quality of wine served at the Rusty Bucket would match either the waitress's attitude or the bar's décor, so he ordered a bottle of beer. Mona said, "Make it two." Then to Cameron, "I need to tell you a couple of things, Dr. Cameron, before Curt gets here. In confidence, if you agree," Mona said.

"Sure," Cameron agreed. "What is it?"

"Maybe you've never heard of Curt Barnes until a few weeks ago. Where to begin. He is a member of Mensa, a certified genius. He studied journalism at Vanderbilt. He's always been a little eccentric. He took his first job with the *LA Times* when he finished at Vandy and within four years was nominated for a Pulitzer Prize. But he had some . . . health problems and dropped out of journalism. He was, he still is, a superb investigative reporter and writes like a modern Hemingway. He's a trust fund baby, so since he quit the *Times* he's just written an occasional piece for a magazine or paper, including the *New Yorker* and *Atlantic*. Otherwise, he just keeps to himself. He wants to talk to you about the . . . oops, here he comes now."

Out of the cold, rainy night, Curt Barnes walked into the Rusty Bucket wearing neither coat nor hat and came straight to Mona. They shook hands and exchanged friendly greetings. "Dr. Cameron, I presume?" he asked, and took a seat.

"Hello, Curt. Drew Cameron."

"Thanks for meeting with me, Dr. Cameron. And thanks, Mona, for arranging it," he said, his face conveying more discomfort than politeness.

Barnes' demeanor changed from sheepish to serious in just a few seconds as he looked at Cameron. "Sir, I'm a journalist — an investigative reporter. I have a news story and I want to give it to you first, in hopes that you will know what to do with it. My good friend Mona tells me that I can trust you, that you will do what is right. It should be published but maybe that's not all."

"I am flattered. But why me? I read the papers but I don't know anything about the technical or literary aspects of investigative journalism," Cameron confessed.

"Why you? Because you are the Executive Vice President of Alpha State University, and the story centers on ASU, on the football program," Barnes said. "Because Mona said I can trust you."

"Well," Cameron responded, "winning national championships deserves media attention, so you should be talking with Coach Sylvester, and with President Faust and our vice president for public information, Margaret Benedict. But I thought you said you are an investigative journalist, not a sports reporter."

"When the situation calls for it, I am both. I have been both for four years. Let's get to the main point. If I give you indisputable evidence that Alpha State University football has been involved in corruption, unethical and immoral practices, and serious violation of a lot of NCAA rules, what would you do with it?" Barnes asked.

Barnes' expression indicated that he was serious, so Cameron answered in kind. "If it's credible, I would first seek to verify it. If I found it to be factual, I'd have no choice but to give the evidence to the proper authorities. My professional obligation would be to use my office as Executive VP to see that justice is done and then to ensure that our sports program regains its integrity — and its winning tradition, if that's possible," Cameron said, feeling a slight uneasiness at the path their conversation had taken. "So what are your allegations, Curt?"

"Remember," the Pulitzer nominee answered, "that a coach has to accomplish four things to win games. He has to get good players, keep them eligible, keep them happy and coach them. Coach Sylvester violates recruitment rules to get his players, he arranges for unearned grades to keep them eligible, and he pays them to keep them happy."

As Barnes and Mona Richards awaited Cameron's response, he thought about the potential consequences if any or all of these general allegations were true. Visions of national, even international headlines whirled through his head. Who could forget the NCAA's imposition of the death penalty on SMU in 1987 for paying players? Or Southern Cal's loss of ten scholarships and the right to play in post-season for two years, plus forcing Reggie Bush to give back his Heisman Trophy in 2011 because his parents were provided with a home in suburban San Diego? And Oklahoma's punishment for eighteen NCAA violations and an arrest for selling cocaine to an undercover FBI agent in 1989? Or Ohio State's players trading Buckeye memorabilia for tattoos in 2011, their coach denying he knew of it when he did, and his shameful resignation. Or the academic cheating scandal that forced Florida State to vacate twelve victories in 1987. The list goes on. Not to mention the more recent scandals at Miami and Penn State. The potential consequences were frightening. Coaches, athletic directors, and high-level academic administrators fired or forced to resign in disgrace, careers besmirched or even ended. University enrollments and tuition revenue suffer. Football ticket sales plummet. Booster club enthusiasm diminishes. Big donor gifts drift away. Alumni support weakens.

"Your allegations are serious. So I need serious proof before I can proceed. Where's the evidence?" Cameron asked.

"I have to go," Barnes said, and got up to leave.

"You'll get no help from me until I get help from you," Cameron said in a threatening tone.

"Mona will contact you with a time and place. And you will have your evidence, Dr. Cameron." Barnes stood and walked toward the exit, and left.

Cameron and Mona Richards sat without speaking for a minute, staring into space and thinking their separate thoughts. "All I can tell you, Dr. Cameron, is that even though he's in his late thirties, he's an old school reporter. He's a certifiable genius who knows right from wrong and always defends the good guys and goes after the bad guys. Okay, he's a little eccentric, but he has always been driven by facts, not by the need to create a dramatic narrative to sell newspapers. The trust fund that he lives on is big, and he hasn't worked for pay in years, so it's not money that drives him. It's ethics, and his idealized conception of professional journalism. He told me that he has been investigating the ASU sports program for four years. Earlier, he had a little alcohol problem, but he did a stint in rehab and has been clean and sober ever since. I made a few calls to check that out before I called you, and it's confirmed. You probably noticed that he didn't order anything to drink tonight."

"We'll see," Cameron said, as Mona motioned to the waitress to bring the bill. "Call me when he's ready with proof. Otherwise, my hands are tied. Without evidence, I am not about to raise the question. It would be both disloyal to the University and suicidal for me."

By 10 AM, as Cameron drove home from the Rusty Bucket, stars had replaced clouds and drizzle in the sky. Nonetheless, his ambivalent feeling about the former *LA Times* journalist had not cleared away. He asked himself, *Is Barnes a delusional trouble-maker or a legitimate muckraking journalist?* He'd just have to wait and see if Mona Richards calls to set up another meeting.

Two nights later, Vanessa and Cameron were cleaning up the kitchen after a quiet dinner at home when the phone rang. Vanessa dried her hands and took the call. "Hello," she said in a neutral tone. Then, "Oh, my God, Barb, so good to hear from you!" She covered the phone and said to Cameron, "It's Barb Corcoran!"

They exchanged the usual introductory pleasantries between two good friends who worked together in the same law firm in Albany. Then Barb said, "The reason I'm calling, Vanessa, is a strange one. Your old firm's home office in New York City is representing Northeastern Health Systems, Inc. that is being threatened by a buyout from Hofstadter-McManus, the big private equity firm. The Albany office assigned me to go to the City office and work with a junior partner on the case."

"So," Vanessa teased, "having brunch with Woody Allen in a Central Park deli every day, are we, Barb? And closing the Blue Note every night?"

"Don't I wish. Anyway, in the pre-trial maneuvering, each side asked for a ton of data from the other side. I've had a couple of long meetings with the

Hofstadter-McManus data systems guy to get the data we need. I got the impression that I couldn't trust him, so I asked our staff investigator to run a background check on him. I just got his report about a half hour ago. By the way, I'm calling on my cell in a taxi as I go back to the hotel. Anyway, what he turned up was that this guy used to work at Alpha State University, but there's nothing about his position there. Not even dates of employment."

A long silence ensued, Barb waiting for the information to sink in with Vanessa and Vanessa waiting for some clue as to why this is important. "So I wondered if your dear hubby knows him and, if so, what's his evaluation of the guy. My detective said he had worked for Hofstadter-McManus only since December 1 and the position of Data Manager was created just for him in late November. With a very nice salary of $300,000 a year! His name is Zachary N. Kilgore. The other strange thing is that the previous managing partner of Hofstadter-McManus was Steven Faust, who is, as you know, the current president of Alpha State."

"Barb," Vanessa said, with a puzzled look on her face, "I think I'd better give the phone to Drew."

Vanessa turned to her husband and said, "Drew, Barb has some questions about someone I believe you know.

After the exchange of friendly greetings, Vanessa heard Cameron say, "Who? Are you sure? I find myself in a very strange position. All I am able to say, Barb, is that he was employed by the University for three and one half years. His last official day was December 31 of last year."

Barb, an experienced attorney, recognized Cameron's response as part of a legal termination agreement. No information about a terminated employee, just an acknowledgement that he was employed there and the dates of his employment. "Okay, Drew," Barb responded, "I hear you. That tells me what I need to know. My cab just pulled up to the hotel, so I'd better ring off. My love to both of you. Come back and see us in Albany."

As soon as Cameron hung up the phone, he said, "Vanessa, as soon as we caught Kilgore hacking into the police computers, Chief Redden said to me, 'I wonder if Kilgore altered the data just because he wanted to or because someone ordered him to do it.'"

After they shared what Barb Corcoran had told each of them, they sat in stunned silence. "Alright, Drew. What do you think is going on here?" Vanessa asked.

"Okay, I have a theoretical explanation that fits the facts, but I have no proof, of course. Kilgore altered the data because Faust asked him to. Faust asked him to because lower crime stats and higher graduation rates would help to boost Alpha State into the top thirty public universities in America, and that would get the legislature's million-dollar award. When we caught Kilgore red-handed and fired him, he must have told Faust that if he didn't get him another job, far away from Alpha State, he would tell the authorities that Faust had ordered him to do it. So, Faust made a call to his old private equities firm in New York City and got him a new position. Does that make any sense?"

Vanessa said, "Maybe. But why did Kilgore agree to commit fraud in the first place?"

"Because, somehow Faust discovered that Kilgore had falsified his résumé when he applied for the VP position in Admissions and Records and threatened to reveal it and fire him if he didn't falsify the data. So Kilgore did as he was ordered. But we found out and I fired him."

'You sound like a great prosecuting attorney, Drew."

"It doesn't feel so great."

"So what are you going to do about it?"

"Without evidence, proof, it's all circumstantial, as you attorneys would say. And you'd be right." Cameron answered.

"But Drew, for all practical purposes, there is no statute of limitations on this alleged offense, so I recommend you document everything you know about this situation, sign it, and put it away in a safe place. Meanwhile, be receptive to any information that might bear on this case. Meanwhile, here's a hug to make you feel better", which he appreciated. Neither one of them slept well that night.

Over the next few weeks, approaching midterms, life at ASU seemed smooth and routine. A majority of faculty members had come around to support curricular reform, including general education requirements for all students aimed at developing skills of communication, critical thinking, and complex analysis. Most of them, including department chairs, favored modernizing their own majors and minors. Likewise, a growing majority was beginning to see long-term planning as a way to improve their performance. Cameron's two highest-priority proposals appeared to be headed for success. He continued to be something of a folk-hero among ASU students, faculty, and alums because of his aura of bravery in the Miller Hall shootings.

Meanwhile, he continued to worry about what might come to pass as he attended or conducted countless meetings including the President's Council, his own office staff, the Deans Council, alumni groups, and the Chamber of Commerce, and kept appointments with countless individuals seeking information, permission, more funding, exception to a rule, approval, and so on. Cameron worked hard and long hours to keep the University's business flowing but also, in part, to avoid thinking about Miller Hall.

Diana Callahan also worked hard and long hours during the next month or so but not just on assignments at Akers Opinion Research. She was driven by her anger at pharmaceutical firms, namely Wolfe-Otis, for using a marketing device — seeding trials — and calling it scientific clinical research, to sell their product. She reasoned that if Wolfe-Otis would do that to maximize profits on their new diabetes drug, then maybe they faked all or some of their actual "clinical trials" that they had submitted to the Food and Drug Administration to get it approved. She racked her agile brain for a way to get a copy of the proposal they submitted to FDA. She called on one of the friends, a medical student, that she had made when she took the seminar in biomedical ethics last semester. Because the FDA had just given its approval to propacricin, the Medical School's research librarian moved their copy of the proposal from "classified" to "restricted." It could be checked out by full-time faculty and students in medicine but not removed from the library premises.

Diana called in sick at Akers early on a Friday and met her medical school friend at the library. He checked out the file containing all the clinical trials — hundreds of pages — and sat and read a transplant hepatology textbook while Diana examined the files. It took her most of the day to scan and record the entire set of studies. Using amazing stealth, she photographed each relevant page with her I-phone, not even stopping for lunch, and was never caught by a library official. She and her friend had agreed that she could "read" the studies until four, at which time he returned and checked them back in at the main desk. On the steps of the library, she thanked her accomplice and gave him a friendly kiss.

It took the whole weekend just to study the result. At every available moment over the ensuing days, she used her considerable methodological skills to evaluate the validity and reliability of the propacricin clinical trials. She persuaded her roommate, Meg Hartley, to help. They made three important discoveries. Right away, they discovered that ASU's own Dr. Edward Novak, Professor of Medicine, was listed as the principal investigator of the studies.

"Diana, this is big," Meg said. "ASU's med school is linked to the clinical trials. If they're faked in any way, our soon-to-be *alma mater* is implicated."

In the middle of another long night of critical investigation, they discovered a second lead. "Meg, one of these trials treats one group with propacricin and treats the other with the old line prescription drug, Receedren. Would you get on the web and see what Receedren's side-effects are?" Diana asked.

A few minutes later, Meg read aloud the list of Receedren's side-effects. When she came to, "turns urine dark yellow, almost brownish," Diana screamed, "You got it, girl! In trial number eight, they list Receedren's side effects, four of them, but not a word about brown urine. Those bad boys didn't administer the regular dosage of Receedren to the control group as they claim. If you give a very small dose of Receedren or a placebo to the control group and a regular dose of propacricin to the experimental group, the experimental group will, of course, look better. I think we've got 'em!"

"I've got just one idea," Meg said, as she glanced at the clock showing 3:15 AM. "Several of the early trials were done in *La Ceiba*, Honduras, in the *Centro Médico Regional*. Remember hearing me mention Jorge Ramon, the grad student in architectural engineering I dated for a while? He's from Tegucigalpa, Honduras. I guess I could ask him to make a couple of phone calls and see if he can learn anything about those trials. It's a long shot."

"But it's a possibility. Do it. In the meantime, thanks old friend," Diana said to her roommate and best friend. "I appreciate you more than you know. Now, I'm worn to a frazzle. I assume you are, too, so let's get some rest," Diana said. They retired, encouraged by what they had found so far.

The next day, Meg called Jorge, who in turn called his father, a wealthy landowner and builder with significant interests and influence in northern Honduras near *La Ceiba*. Jorge's father contacted a practicing physician he knew in *La Ceiba*, a city of over one hundred seventy-five thousand, and inquired about the recent *studios de investigación sobre la diabetes*. In three days, which seemed like a month, Jorge called Meg with a report. "My father called his doctor friend in *La Ceiba*, who told him that, in his memory, nobody had done diabetes research there. The doctor said he sits on a human subjects committee for the whole region, and if anybody had done any diabetes drug research in the last six years, he would certainly know about it. He said that he had never heard of the three doctors whose names you gave me, the ones who assisted in the clinical trials at a *La Ceiba* clinic, nor had management at the clinic ever heard of them. Sorry I have such bad news, Meg."

"Jorge," Meg almost sang, "that's the best bad news I've ever heard. *Muchas gracious, amigo.* You're the best."

Meg called Diana at work on her cell phone. "Diana, you won't believe it. More very good bad news." And without explaining that strange expression, she reported what she had learned from Jorge's father in Honduras.

"So," Diana responded, "if the evidence so far shows the trials to be questionable, we have to do something about it. And, if the principal investigator is an ASU professor of medicine, maybe first we need to take our case to someone in authority at ASU."

After almost a minute of silent concentration, Meg spoke up. "What about the new provost? Remember, he's the one who stopped that classroom takeover and saved the students from the gunman?"

"Okay, we'll go see him," Diana said. "First, let's write up our findings in a nice report. Then maybe we can make an appointment to see him. See you at home tonight."

Mid-morning the next day, Cameron and Dekker sat in the inner office and discussed the very favorable set of recommendations from the curriculum reform committee. Holly's familiar buzz resonated from Cameron's phone. "Yes, Holly."

"President Faust on line three."

"Steve. Good morning."

"Good morning to you, Drew. You may not have such a good morning when I tell you why I have called," Faust said.

Cameron's expression changed from cheerful to anxious, then back to cheerful as he listened to President Faust's question. Then he smiled and said, "I'm very sorry to hear that, Steve. But, no problem. We can survive without her for three days."

When their conversation ended, Cameron said to Dekker, "Steve Faust wants to 'borrow' Holly for three days. Ms. McInerney needs some time off to relocate her mother from Indiana to a residential care facility in New Cambridge. He has some key donors, individual and corporate, flying in to meet with him on those days, so he needs somebody who can approximate Ms. McInerney's omniscience. Wait a second; I need to tell Holly so she can designate her replacement."

As he returned and resumed his discussion with Dekker, Holly's buzz sounded again. "Mona Richards on two," she said.

"Mona, good morning,"

"Good morning, Dr. Cameron. Right to business. Are you free to meet tomorrow afternoon at four at Meridian National Bank? It's at the corner of Central Avenue and Noble. Curt Barnes will meet you there and get the bank to open his lockbox. That's where he keeps his evidence."

Cameron asked, "Will you be there?"

"Yes, he wants me there."

"Good. I can make it, but would it be okay if I bring my wife along? Another pair of eyes to help me remember what I see when I am thinking about what to do later."

"I'll ask him. If you don't hear from me by tomorrow morning, then it's okay," Mona said.

In the mid-afternoon, Cameron left the office to go downtown to a couple of meetings, and then returned to his office. As he left for the day, Holly handed him his schedule for the next day and remarked, "I have you booked for an eight o'clock with two doctoral students. They want to talk with you about some important research being done at the University. Is that okay?"

"I guess. So much business, so little time. But discussing research with doctoral students will be a welcome change of pace," he said.

When he returned the next morning at 7:15 AM, the first thing he saw was two well-dress young women sitting in the outer office. *Funny*, he thought to himself, *they don't look like two female graduate students. They are well dressed, their hair is immaculate, their shoes are medium heels rather than sneakers, they are sitting erect in their chairs, and they are even wearing make-up.*

"Good morning. I'm Drew Cameron. Are you here to see me?"

'Yes, sir. We are. Diana Callahan from Sociology and Meg Hartley from Psychology. Thank you for agreeing to see us this morning."

"You're welcome. My assistant is out for a few days, so we three are on our own. "I'm going to fetch myself a cup of coffee. Can I get either of you some?"

Both women refused, saying that they had already drunk too many cups of coffee this morning. When Cameron returned, they accompanied him into his office and took seats.

Diana began, "Dr. Cameron, we have a problem. We think . . . we are pretty sure . . . straight to the point. We have reason to believe that the clinical research studies on Wolfe-Otis Pharmaceutical's new drug, propacricin, are seriously flawed. The trials were supervised by an ASU medical professor."

"In fact," Meg continued, "we have reason to believe that the research was falsified. We believe it may be a fraud. And yet, it was the set of clinical trials that got FDA approval for propacricin, the new diabetes drug."

For the next half hour, the two graduate students detailed their findings and in the process demonstrated their strong skills in experimental research methods, which Cameron appreciated. They emphasized that in the clinical trials, all the patients who were treated with the alternative drug, Receedren, should have had the side-effect of brownish urine but did not; that nobody at the clinic in *La Ceiba*, Honduras ever heard of the three physicians who, according to the research, had conducted several of the propacricin clinical trials in that clinic; and, that Dr. Edward Novak, Professor of Medicine at ASU, was the principal investigator of the clinical trials. Then they handed him a folder containing their well-footnoted evidence and answered a couple of his questions. He thanked them for their concern as they left.

Later that afternoon, both Camerons entered Meridian National Bank and spotted Mona Richards seated in the reception area. Cameron introduced Vanessa to Mona. Then Mona explained, "Curt has gone into the vault and is waiting for us. He asked us to sign in at the vault desk and joint him."

They found Curt Barnes, sitting at a long conference table deep in the cavernous vault, arranging six or eight neat stacks of materials. Without even turning toward them, he said, "Here is my evidence. It's proof. Is your wife with you?"

By the time Cameron answered and Vanessa extended her hand, Barnes had already returned to his arrangement of the evidence. "As you can see, the evidence is overwhelming. It represents four years of my life." As if delivering a lecture to a large audience, Barnes pointed to each stack as he recited his case. "I have photos, recordings, my notes from interviews with eye witnesses and participants, copies of telephone bills, copies of airline tickets, and copies of hotel and restaurant receipts. My interviews include ASU Eagle Club members, graduate assistants, restaurant and hotel employees, several enterprising young women, two former assistant coaches, several former ASU football players, two professional football agents, and a history professor, to name a few."

What specific violations do they document?" Cameron asked.

"They will document," Barnes said, eager to answer this question, "Coach Sylvester's sexual exploits with a prostitute in a swank Miami hotel, academic cheating, paying players, recruitment violations including too many phone calls, campus visits and nights in a hotel for high school seniors, paying graduate students to write papers for team members, and offering ninety-seven hours of independent studies courses in history with oral finals for eighteen players and awarding almost all As."

"Some of those allegations describe what they do to keep players eligible once they're on the team. What else do they do? I'm referring to academic matters, now," Cameron said.

"Let me give you an example," Barnes said. "Are you aware of the 'independent studies' major? Approximately half the football team is majoring in 'independent studies', whatever that is. It allows them to take pretty much only courses taught by a few bad-apple professors who are under the control of the Athletics Department. They can cherry-pick the courses that require almost nothing and have almost no standards!"

Cameron was nonplussed. Even Vanessa, accustomed to maintaining a serious courtroom demeanor, almost gasped when she heard Barnes' list of alleged transgressions. "For starters, what do you mean by 'paying players,'?" she demanded.

"I mean," Barnes answered, "paying the players — with money or services. First, during the school year, they paid them money, several hundred dollars at a time, sometimes in bags, sometimes in envelopes, according to Eagle Club members and several of the former players themselves. It's documented here. During the summer, they paid them with summer jobs provided by alums who required no work, just that they show up to collect a nice paycheck. They paid them with the services of prostitutes on call; they referred to it as the 'stable'. They also paid them with elaborate parties and free nights at ritzy hotels, all kept very private and secret. Now remember, the university did this for members of its football team. Their admission test scores indicate that sixty percent of them can read only at or below the level of an eighth grader."

"And you can document all of those charges with this evidence?" Vanessa asked.

"Yes, I can," Barnes said and turned to Cameron and repeated, "Yes I can. Who, what, where, why, when. It's all in there, including evidence that your president intervened with the New Cambridge police to arrange for them not to arrest that great defensive back two years ago on charges of possession and sale of crack cocaine. They just let him walk. The chief has a VIP box, you know. The NCAA likes to convey the image that they are supervising their member schools and conferences by the book and that all is well and good. So if you present this evidence, all will not be well or good, to say the least."

"So why isn't the NCAA doing its job?" Vanessa asked.

"It's all about the money, Mrs. Cameron. Do you know how much money Coach Sylvester made last year? Over six million dollars in salary and almost two hundred thousand more in various perks. His assistant coaches made between four hundred twenty thousand and seven hundred fifty thousand. Three years ago when they won the national championship, they recorded almost eighty million dollars in total revenue and reported a fifty-five million dollar profit. If you look at all of college football last year, they generated a net profit of well over one billion dollars. The teams that played in a bowl game last year averaged more than one million dollars in revenue per game played during the season. It's all about the money."

Hearing this description of a college sport from a credible source while sitting in a windowless vault with a sixteen-foot ceiling created an overwhelming sense of ironic surrealism. Somewhere between the original Greek Olympic ideal, a healthy mind in a healthy body, and contemporary college football, something strange had evolved. Cameron and Vanessa spent about half an hour examining many of the documents, taking notes and commenting to each other about potential strengths and weaknesses of the material.

"Thank you very much, Curt, for your hard and professional work in assembling this information and for meeting with us to share it. Thank you, Mona, for connecting Curt with me. We appreciate your effort, Curt, in recording and assembling all these documents. Let us think about where we go from here, and we will get back to you. Through Mona?"

"Yes, Dr. Cameron. Get in touch with me through Mona," Curt said.

As Cameron, Vanessa, and Mona Richards walked toward the bank's main reception area, Curt started replacing the documents in the steel box to be locked in the vault. Standing outside the bank, Mona said, "Thanks again. And if it means anything, I know he is a little eccentric, but there's nobody in the business with more integrity and professionalism than Curt. I have to believe him."

"But why," Vanessa asked, "do you think he has done this, for four years?"

"I'm not sure, Mrs. Cameron, "but I think it might have something to do with his older brother, Al. As I understand it, years ago Coach Sylvester was Al's coach at a small university where Al played linebacker. There's something about Sylvester insisting on Al playing several games in his senior year even though he had had one or more concussions, and the team physician had recommended against it. Within a few years after finishing college, he developed various symptoms normally associated with Parkinson's and Alzheimer's. For the past few years he has been in a long-term care institution. Now, Al doesn't even recognize Curt, his own brother, and he's still in his forties."

"That's terrible. Anyway, thank you, Mona. We won't keep you any longer. We'll be in touch," Cameron said, as they shook hands. Cameron and Vanessa then left in their separate cars.

Later at home, Cameron asked, "Well, counselor, are we going to take the case or not?"

"The question is, 'What kind of case do you want to make?' I saw enough evidence to convince the NCAA to investigate. If one rather talented and persistent newspaper reporter can uncover this much evidence, half a dozen NCAA investigators could open the floodgates, if they choose to."

"Yes, but what should we do with what we know?" Cameron said.

"Assuming that all the NCAA rules are fair and appropriate," Vanessa began, "we shouldn't think like a prosecutor or a defense counsel. We need to think like a judge, determining what happened and what to do about it."

"You mean 'justice?'" Cameron asked.

"Yeah, your job is to determine what is just," Vanessa answered.

"I agree. In that case, assuming that even half of Barnes' allegations are accurate, we have no choice. We have to turn the evidence over to the NCAA. No, my job is to take it to Steve Faust. It's his job to bring in the NCAA. By the way, thanks for coming with me today, counselor. I may just decide to keep you on retainers. For a long time."

"That's good. Because if you don't, I'll have to sue you," Vanessa said with a wry smile.

They decided to eat a light dinner, ham and cheese sandwiches, while discussing Cameron's predicament. To that end, Cameron played a Bill Evans CD, one of their favorites.

"So here's your situation as I see it," Vanessa began. First, the vice president you fired for altering official university records now works in your current boss's old investment firm in New York City. Even Inspector Clouseau could see potential wrongdoing in that. Or maybe it's just labor supply and demand. Second, and maybe more troublesome, we have seen evidence of football wrong-doing that I'm pretty sure a judge would assess as meriting a grand jury hearing. So, what can, should, and must you do?"

"Vanessa, there are two more problems I should tell you about. This afternoon, two doctoral students came to my office and told me they have evidence that one of our medical school professors served as PI on a series of clinical trials of Wolfe-Otis Pharmaceutical's new diabetes drug and that the research was falsified in order to get FDA approval. The evidence they showed me is enough to require further investigation."

"Say it isn't so! A grand slam of problems. At least this last one is in my field — health care law," Vanessa said.

"There's a fourth one and it is also in your field of expertise. You've heard me speak of Melinda Osterman? She brought me documented evidence that the deans of Business and Law have been submitting requests to their foundation boards for big bonuses — they call them 'forgivable loans' — for some of their faculty members — up to a half million dollars — even though the legislature last year put a freeze on all raises until further notice. The dean of Law even requested a bonus for himself. Both the Business and Law Foundations awarded the money."

Vanessa squinted. "They'll claim that they only want and deserve the salary they would be making if they were in private practice or in a corporate business instead of working for a university."

"That's what Melinda Osterman said. But if her allegation is true, I will inform Faust and then fire both deans. I can't revoke tenure without spending a bundle on court costs for each one and it takes forever. But I can relieve them of their deanships and maybe get the money back," Cameron said.

"What do you plan to do about the other three problems?" Vanessa asked.

"They are not in my field of expertise, but they are in the field of expertise of someone else in my office."

"Who is that?"

"Axel Dekker. He knows a little about criminal investigation as well as statistics," Cameron answered, forcing a smile.

11

Returning to his downtown Los Angeles hotel at 10:30 PM, tired and a little tipsy, Steve Faust felt good about the night. He had treated a new donor and his wife, Mr. and Mrs. Elliot Benton, to a celebratory dinner at an excellent Italian restaurant. The Bentons had just pledged a corporate gift of several million dollars from their import-export firm to Alpha State. Both were ASU alums. He felt exhausted as he turned on the lights to his room and tossed his briefcase on the desk. For several days he had traveled across three time zones, caught early flights, and attended late meetings. Faust had also consumed three Scotches at the cocktail party, an excellent beaujolais with dinner, and a Drambui afterwards.

He turned on the desk lamp, turned off the overhead light and set up his laptop on the desk to see if he had received any important email messages. Tomorrow he would call the office. He yawned and rubbed his eyes as he scanned through about twenty email messages but found only two that required an immediate response. First, he emailed his newly revised schedule to Holly Nabisco, who was filling in for Mrs. McInerny for a few days. Elliot Benton had insisted that Faust stay an extra day to meet a banker friend who might also be interested in supporting Alpha State. Second, he sent a brief answer to Zachary Kilgore's rather histrionic and peevish email message from New York, and that took longer than expected. Yielding to his exhaustion, he turned out the light and fell into bed at 11:15 PM local time, 1:15 AM in his head.

Promptly at seven the next morning Holly began her third day substituting for Ms. McInerney as President Faust's executive assistant. She had experienced two good days. Nothing had gone wrong. The office staff was friendly, in a formal sort of way, and quite competent. Still, she looked forward to completing her final day as a substitute. Her first email message of the morning came from President Faust. He told her that he would be delayed one extra day and asked her to reschedule his appointments. She made the necessary changes and wrote notes to herself to notify the affected parties. Her second email also came from President Faust and was sent only a few minutes after the first one. As she read it, she knew that the message was intended for someone else. The salutation made that clear. Reading just the first paragraph confirmed her suspicion. Her jaw muscles tightened, her throat constricted and her pulse rate increased. She sat stunned, considering which of a dozen things to do while knowing full well the one thing she must do.

As Cameron walked, coffee in hand, through the outer office and past Holly's desk, Sue, substituting for Holly, looked up and greeted him with, "Dr. Cameron, good morning. Call Holly right away," and handed him a pink telephone note. And here are some other calls. Tell me which ones you want me to return."

"Thanks, Sue. Good morning to you. To start, call Holly," and gave her back the pink slip with Ms. McInerney's number.

"Dr. Cameron?"

"Holly, good morning. It's me. We sure have been missing your competence and charm over here."

Holly's typical answer would have shown polite embarrassment at receiving the compliment. But this time there was a long delay while she walked from Ms. McInerney's desk in the outer office to President Faust's inner office and closed the door behind her. "Dr. Cameron. I need to talk with you, ASAP. Alright?"

Sensing the seriousness in her tone, Cameron said, "Time and place?"

"Are you busy for the next half-hour?"

"No."

"I'll be right there. And I am coming to your office because you called me over to find an important file that you need and can't find. Okay?" Without waiting for an answer, she was gone.

No more than two minutes passed before Cameron heard the familiar knock as Holly entered, closed the door and looked straight at her boss, which gave Cameron a moment of bewildered discomfort. Then, almost in slow motion, she unbuttoned the top button of her blouse, then the second button, and reached into her bra. She retrieved a sheet of paper folded into the size of a wallet photo, then re-buttoned her blouse. "I'm sorry to act like a James Bond character, but it's the only thing I could think of. Here, please read this email from President Faust." Her face reddened and her hand shook as she handed him the sheet of paper. "He sent it to me but I'm pretty sure he didn't mean to."

"Sit down a minute, Holly. Are you alright?"

"Just read it, Dr. Cameron. And you know I've always been loyal to you. And I always do what I think is best for the University. You know that, don't you?"

"Yes, Holly. I do. Now, sit down and relax, please. I'll read it."

> Zachary,
>
> I received your message. I've been in California for three days. One more day in LA, then home. Sorry things are not going well for you in NYC. Regarding salary, $300K should be enough for a year but I do remember the cost of living in NYC. And you will meet some friendly people in time. It's harder there, but you will. Be patient. I'll talk with my people at Hofstadter-McManus. Rest assured that I do appreciate your continuing cooperation. As our VPAR you took some risks at my request. Don't worry. I will take care of you and your family as soon as I get back to New Cambridge.
>
> Steve

Cameron read the email message three times, but he still found it difficult to believe what he read. "Holly, you did the right thing coming to me. This may be nothing, but if there are any repercussions, I will make sure you are secure," he said. "Go back to Faust's office, resume your work, and say nothing about this to anybody. Let me worry about it. You did the right thing." Seeing how shaken Holly was, Cameron then violated one of his cardinal rules of administration and gave his administrative assistant a quick hug. The hug seemed to restore some of her natural composure.

She smiled, stood tall, and said, "Okay. I will be back at my desk tomorrow, by noon at the latest," and walked out the door.

Cameron's schedule was full, but easy, until six that evening. Vanessa called to tell him that her firm's case against a big insurance company in St. Louis was heating up and that the senior partners thought that she should go there to help the firm's two young attorneys who were fulltime on the case. She said she would be going to St. Louis for two or three days.

Between meetings he asked Sue, Holly's substitute, to call Dr. Dekker for him. She responded, "He is at a brunch at the Dutch Consul General's office. He said he'd be back in the office by eleven."

"Good," Cameron said. "Have him come by the office when he gets back."

When Dekker came by the office later, Cameron shared with him some details about several of ASU's serious problems. He described journalist Curt Barnes' evidence and allegations about Coach Sylvester and the ASU football program; the two graduate students' evidence of wrongdoing by an ASU medical professor and Wolfe-Otis Pharmaceuticals, Inc., whose CEO is chairman of the ASU Board of Trustees; and the email message that President Faust sent to Holly by mistake. At the end of fifteen minutes of uninterrupted description of these problems, Cameron asked, "So, Axel, you've had relevant training and experience. What do you think I should do?"

Dekker took about a minute to think, then answered, "Drew, the highest priority is, in my opinion, the fraudulent or flawed drug trials. We don't know for sure, but it is possible that if the two graduate students are right and the trials are not valid, and the FDA approves the drug for use, an innocent party who takes that drug might become ill or even die as a result. That requires immediate attention. Second priority is the potential football scandal. Accept the evidence that you saw in the bank vault and assure your newspaper reporter Barnes that you will take it to the NCAA for full investigation. Are those the right initials?" he asked.

"Right, National Collegiate Athletic Association.

"Lowest priority, in my judgment," Dekker continued, "is the potential problem with your former Vice President Kilgore. The clear implication in the email message is that President Faust asked Kilgore to submit invalid crime records to the government. With that one, I'd advise caution because it involves your immediate superior who happens to be the CEO of the University. You cannot ignore the evidence. But waiting a while to act on it won't result in further harm. But, it is clear that because President Faust seems to be implicated in a fraud, you can't very well go to him for help in solving the other two problems."

"As usual, Axel, your values and logic are impeccable. Based on what the two grad students told me," Cameron said, "we have three points of attack with respect to the drug trials. First, we get a copy of the report on the trials submitted to the FDA and examine it for evidence of fraud. Second, we can determine with certainty whether a La Ceiba, Honduras medical clinic hosted ASU's Medical School and get their perspective on the study."

"Sounds like a plan, Drew. Is there anything I can do to help," Dekker said, conveying his eagerness to bring some justice to the perpetrators.

"How many languages do you speak, Axel?" Cameron asked.

"Uh . . . several, as you know."

"Right, and among them is fluent Spanish," Cameron asserted. "So, how would you like a quick secret trip to Honduras to find out if anyone ran diabetes drug trials in La Ceiba?"

"La Ceiba it is. First, I will find out everything we know about it, from a copy of the study itself and from the two graduate students," Dekker said.

Cameron buzzed Sue in the outer office and asked her to get the two graduate students into the office as soon as possible and indicated that they would understand why. Sue reached Diana Callahan at work and Meg Hartley in the Psych Lab and they agreed to meet with Dr. Cameron at five-fifteen.

Meg was a little early and Diana a little late in arriving at the meeting with Cameron and Dekker. After a few minutes of conversation, Cameron indicated to them why they had been asked to meet. Although both of the young women maintained a serious composure, it was easy to see that they were almost giddy at the prospect of using their expertise to do justice. Dekker explained that he would travel the next morning to La Ceiba to visit the medical clinic and collect documentary evidence that Wolfe-Otis did or did not conduct experimental propacricin drug trials there. Just as Cameron was explaining the need to get a copy of the whole study, Diana interrupted and said, "Dr. Cameron, excuse us but we have a plan. I think you'll like it."

Cameron and Dekker looked at each other, not knowing whether to be surprised or pleased. Cameron said, "Okay, what's your plan?"

Diana began, "Meg's specialty in psychology is neuropsychology, and within that specialty, she has developed special expertise in tomography, you know, brain scans. Her dissertation is on . . . . Meg, it's your baby, you explain it."

"My dissertation," Meg announced, "compares the results of several standard methods for brain scans. My major interest is in the incidence and effects of cortical atrophy. We discovered in small samples that there's a strong interaction between hypertension and diabetes. When subjects have both diabetes and hypertension, we find cortical atrophy or degeneration of brain cells. When there is diabetes but no hypertension, we find no cortical atrophy."

"I think I understand you so far, Meg. Axel?" Dekker nodded a tentative yes.

"So, Meg continued, "what we thought we'd do is go see Dr. Edward Novak, the PI on the propacricin trials, and ask him to allow us to see the whole study, the one that's in the Med School library but can't be checked out. We figure since he's the PI, he either has a copy himself, with the data compendium, or he could tell the library to let us have it for a day or two. He studied a diabetes cure, and I have been studying what brain scans can tell us about brain cell deterioration and diabetes. We need to know whether propacricin remedies diabetes by reducing cortical atrophy or by eliminating symptoms of diabetes. I'll tell him that my dissertation advisor will call him if he has any doubt. That way we can get our hands on the actual data for reanalysis."

"I'm impressed, Meg, Diana. If you get access to the whole study, what's your plan," Cameron asked.

"We are both strong in statistics," Diana answered, so we want to do some reanalysis to see if the data justify their conclusions."

"If you need any help with the statistical end of it, you can consult Dr. Dekker," Cameron said. "He has a doctorate in statistics."

"Then I think we can do a proper reanalysis, Diana said." They left the office, sworn to secrecy, and elated to be able to help solve what appeared to be a serious problem of academic integrity and possible fraud.

The next day, Dekker flew to Nicaragua. He had flown into and out of Tegucigalpa's Toncontin Airport before and remembered that it features short runways located on a small plain surrounded by high mountains on three sides and a drop-off into the ocean on the fourth side. Landing there requires pilots to undertake aerial maneuvers with their large passenger planes that resemble those of a small fighter jet in combat. They must touch down early, reduce speed as much as possible, and manage to stop before the runway ends in a precipitous one-hundred foot drop into the ocean. Although Dekker, in his earlier career in European national security, had often bailed out of planes, been picked up on a ladder by helicopters and survived two crashes, his recollection of landing at Toncontin was more discomforting. But this flight landed without mishap, except for several passengers pale with nausea and paralyzed with fear.

In Tegucigalpa Dekker rented a car, drove the one hundred eighty miles to La Ceiba on the northeastern Honduran coast of the Gulf of Mexico, and checked into a local guest house. Early the next morning, he met with the director of *Centro Médico de Regional La Ceiba* and several other senior physicians, each of whom had worked there nine years or longer. All of them said the same thing. Nobody had been to their facility to conduct clinical trials on diabetes since they had been there. The director signed the statement that Dekker had prepared to that effect. Dekker did learn that almost three years prior, an American man who spoke no Spanish and his wife who did speak Spanish, had brought their daughter to the clinic with symptoms of food poisoning. They had been on vacation for a week in Roatán, a small island north of La Ceiba within easy ferry distance. The physician had treated the girl, kept her overnight and released her the next morning. The father paid cash. On the various registration and check-out forms, he had signed his name as Layton Covington and given a New Cambridge address.

Dekker thanked the clinic staff, drove back to a small inn near Toncontin Airport, and caught an early flight the next morning back to New Cambridge. He felt confident that he could verify that no trials had been conducted in La Ceiba. He also felt grateful that the pilots maneuvered the large plane down the runway full throttle, fast enough to lift off, and banked hard to the left, around the bowl where Toncontin Airport is located, and up just high enough, soon enough to avoid the surrounding mountains.

The next morning, he was at work in his office in the Provost's suite when Cameron came in at about seven thirty. Both men were glad to see each other and eager to share new information. "Drew, I think we can prove the Honduran trials were faked," Dekker said.

"Let's go back to my office," Cameron said, "to show and tell." When they closed the door, he said, "You first."

Dekker summarized his finding at the clinic in La Ceiba and made one quick reference to his arrival and departure at Toncontin Airport.

"Excellent," Cameron replied. "I think that evidence alone will enable us to persuade the FDA to put a hold on propacricin. Diana and Meg also reported some good findings. They talked with Dr. Novak, the PI on the propacricin trials, and persuaded him to let them have a copy of the trials, data compendium and all, on an extended basis. They're working on it now. He also gave them a copy of a manuscript he submitted for publication in *Diabetes Quarterly*, which has already been accepted for their next issue. Diana and Meg are looking for evidence of error or fraud there, too. Finally, they came away from the meeting with Dr. Novak with the distinct impression that he did not know much about the contents of the drug trials or his forthcoming article in the *Diabetes Quarterly*, so they're suspicious."

"So far," Dekker commented, "everything we have seen points to some kind of faked research. That's serious."

"You are right, of course, but Axel, I'm an academic administrator, not a law enforcement investigator. I am not comfortable doing what we are doing. And yet, as I think about it, we discovered too much incriminating or at least suspicious evidence to ignore it. But going to President Faust or to law enforcement without convincing evidence about the Wolfe-Otis drug trials or Coach Sylvester's football program or Faust ordering Kilgore to alter data would bring great embarrassment to Alpha State, and damage to its reputation. Anyway, before I got in the office this morning, Diana had left this with Sue. It's a copy of the write-up of the drug trials." Cameron placed the one-hundred-page document on his desk for Dekker to see.

Dekker's eyes lit up as he pointed to the title page listing the PI and co-authors of the research. "Layton Covington is listed here as one of the co-authors of the research. I see that he is a staff researcher at Wolfe-Otis. Now that's curious. When I was in La Ceiba, I learned that he was on vacation with his family in Roatán three years ago. His daughter had food poisoning, so they took her to the closest clinic, in La Ceiba. Now what do you make of that?"

"Either it's a coincidence and has no relevance or Layton Covington was there, learned about the clinic, and when they needed to make up some trials to say whatever they wanted to say, he picked that clinic as the site of the imaginary trials. Because it does exist but it's in a remote town, in a distant third-world country, he figured nobody would bother to check it out."

"Drew, maybe you are an academic administrator, but you also have rather good instincts as a criminal investigator."

Both men returned to their administrative work, Cameron to an appointment with officers of the Student Government Organization concerning the possibility of a new student union and Dekker to meet with French Professor Jean St. John concerning international graduate student exchanges. At about ten-thirty that morning, someone knocked at Cameron's office door and opened it. Holly and Sue came in and Holly announced, "Ms. McInerney is back and I am back and Sue is finished here, Dr. Cameron. Changing of the guards." Cameron welcomed Holly back and thanked Sue for filling in so well for three days, then all returned to work.

At about five-thirty that afternoon, Diana and Meg showed up unannounced at Holly's desk and asked to see Dr. Cameron. Unaware that these two students were on assignment for her boss, and being put off by their bloodshot eyes, tousled hair, and the rumpled clothes they had worn for thirty-six hours, and since it was already past 5:00 PM, Holly insisted that they make an appointment for another day. Fortunately, Cameron came out on his way to the water fountain in the hall and discovered the pair with Holly.

"Holly, these two are working with me. I should have let you know. They have access just about any time," Cameron said. "Call Dekker and have him join us if he's free."

Diana and Meg came into Cameron's inner office, one carrying a laptop computer, the other several manila folders, soon followed by Dekker. Diana began, "We rechecked the data in six trials and re-ran the analyses," as she turned on the laptop and typed instructions into the keyboard. "When the sample size was big enough, we also did a statistical power analysis on the coefficients. Each trial included only certain kinds of subjects, you know, like people between the ages of sixty and seventy-five, or children, or people with certain complicating health factors, or people already on some medication for another reason, and so on."

Meg chimed in, "In each trial, the subjects were randomly assigned to the control group, which received no diabetes medication, or to an experimental group that receive propacricin, or an experimental group that received the current leading diabetes drug, Receedren. The research given to the FDA shows that symptoms were reduced by thirty to eighty percent in the propacricin group as opposed to the other two groups in all twenty trials. The report says that the differences between the pairs of groups were all significant at the 0.01 or better.”

Then Diana added, “We re-ran them all and found no significant differences.”

“Here, look at this trial,” Meg said, as Diana brought up the figures on the computer screen. “Plus, the sample sizes in two of the trials were too small to be significant at 0.01, as they claim it is. It’s mathematically impossible unless everybody in the experimental group recovered from diabetes, and none of the controls did. This stuff was all made up!”

“Sounds like you two did a good job. Questions, Axel?” Cameron asked.

After several minutes of answering Dekker’s technical questions to his satisfaction, Diana went on. “Two more things you ought to know, Dr. Cameron, and Dr. Dekker, the article Dr. Novak wrote summarizing the trials for *Diabetes Quarterly* uses the exact same flawed data and analysis we found in the original reports. There are lots of FDA investigations and court cases showing that famous doctors get paid in the millions for conducting experimental drug research for Big Pharma but don’t enroll any patients in their studies but fake the data and conclusions. Then they publish the results in medical journals. That may be what we have here, with Dr. Novak.”

“Sad but true,” Dekker admitted. “May I add that my visit to the clinic in La Ceiba confirms that no diabetes trials have been conducted there in the last ten years. Again, evidence that the study reports data created out of thin air.”

“Diana, Meg, I think we can now make a strong case that the research on propacricin is either flawed or fabricated. In either case, it’s invalid,” Cameron asserted, looking at Dekker.

“I agree,” Dekker responded. “What do you plan to do now?”

“First, I plan to send these two home to get some rest. You two look like you’ve been up all night.”

“Yes, sir,” Meg said, “two nights, to tell the truth.”

“Thank you very much for excellent work. Now, go home. You’ve earned some rest. That’s an order from your Provost! We will be in touch,” Cameron spoke, giving them the same advice that he would give to Tom and Char in similar circumstances. Diana folded up their laptop and Meg placed three folders of print-out on Cameron’s desk as they left, tired but proud and happy.

Once the door closed behind them, Dekker said, “Drew, maybe ASU’s Dr. Novak committed the fraud. Or maybe Wolfe-Otis just paid him to agree to be listed as PI as a way to tap into his big professional reputation when, in fact, their own Layton Covington faked the study. We must find out before we proceed.”

It was already past seven o’clock. Even Holly was gone, so both men left for home. Cameron very much looked forward to seeing Vanessa after her three days in St. Louis. They should arrive at their home at about the same time. On the way, he called Holly on his cell and left a message: "Holly, I apologize for bothering you on a Friday night, but I don't know how to get hold of Ms. McInerney at home and you do. Could you please call her and set up a meeting for me with Faust, first thing on Monday? Two things on the agenda: forgivable loans and a possible problem with Dr. Novak and the Wolfe-Otis research on their new diabetes medicine."

Fifteen minutes later, just as he was greeting Vanessa in their kitchen, Holly called. "Dr. Cameron, Ms. McInerney has it set up for eight-fifteen Monday morning. Also, Chief Redden won't be in Monday all day. He is attending the funeral of a friend, out of town."

Thanks, Holly," Cameron said. "Have a great weekend."

One of the aspects of Steve Faust's work as a university president that contrasted with his executive career in private equities at Hofstadter-McManus in New York, and one that he did not especially like, was working outside the office on Saturdays. At ASU he spent many Saturdays at some public occasion. Most of these obligations involved alumni affairs, capital campaign fundraising, one of the sports programs, or a speech for some civic or business organization. This Saturday, however, was free. By midmorning, he had finished reading the *New Cambridge Daily News* and wandered into his study to read the *Wall Street Journal* on-line. First, out of habit, he checked his email messages. He scanned down the list until he saw one from Ms. McInerney. When it appeared on screen, he discovered that his Monday schedule now included an eight-fifteen with the Provost to discuss two items: possible fraud in Wolfe-Otis drug trials and forgivable loans. Although he did not know what the first item was about, it didn't sound good. The second item, forgivable loans, rang a very familiar chime in his head and he knew it was not good. He wondered why the academic types almost never understand the financial realities of running a large, corporate organization in a competitive market.

He placed a call to Alex Wolfe's cell phone with the thought of finding out about the Wolfe-Otis drug trials.

"Hello, Steve," Wolfe answered, seeing Faust's name on his cell phone screen.

"Alex, good morning. Something's come up and I need you to fill me in on it. I've been in LA for three days. Drew Cameron has set up a meeting with me Monday morning to discuss what he calls fraud in Wolfe-Otis drug trials."

After a long pause, Wolfe growled, "Damn, Steve, I told you a year ago that we shouldn't offer the job to Cameron. I told you he'd be trouble and here it is. I can't meet with you today, I'm at the FDA in Silver Spring, Maryland. You caught me between two meetings. We're finalizing the propacricin approval process. And we expect to celebrate with Earl Broadbent at dinner tonight."

"Okay, Alex, when are you coming back to New Cambridge?"

"I'll fly back tomorrow morning. I'll get in to New Cambridge at about twelve-fifteen," Wolfe answered.

"Then how about Renaissance House tomorrow at one o'clock for lunch?"

"Gotta go, the final meeting is about to start. I'll be there," Wolfe said. The phone went dead.

On Sunday, Alex Wolfe's plane from Washington landed early at New Cambridge Airport. He took a taxi straight to the Renaissance House where the *maitre d'* escorted him to a table in the private dining room where Steve Faust was waiting. As was their habit, when they met for lunch or dinner they did not discuss business until they had finished eating. When the waiter served coffee, Wolfe said with a broad smile, "The good news is, FDA indicated final approval for propacricin. The director will sign off on it Monday. Then we're in business."

"I hope I don't have the bad news, Alex," Faust said, as he stirred his coffee, "but while I was in Los Angeles, Cameron scheduled a meeting with me for Monday morning to discuss something about fraud in some of your drug trials. So I need to know whatever you can tell me before I meet with him. What the hell is he talking about?"

Alexander Wolfe's expression changed from happy to indignant. He glared at his friend and said, "Dammit, Steve, here we go again! I told you Cameron wouldn't be a team player!"

"What's the problem, Alex?"

"Are you sure you really want to know?"

"Let's have it, Alex," said Faust.

"Maybe I'm jumping the gun, but the problem may be that a very big deal I've worked on for several years is coming unglued. You remember we sat with Senator Broadbent right here in the Renaissance almost a year ago and planned for Wolfe-Otis to move into a brand-new production facility and headquarters here in New Cambridge?"

"Yeah, Alex. Your rumor that Wolfe-Otis was planning to build its new facility in Asia rather than in New Cambridge started the ball rolling. You and I and the senator designed the plan for you to deed your facility over to the university as soon as Earl could arrange for a nice set-aside from Congress for the university to buy and renovate your vacated facility as a remote-site campus. It's a sweet deal."

"Right," Wolfe confirmed, "and the City of New Cambridge agreed to use its power of eminent domain to acquire the forty acres on the outskirts of town, and then they gave the property to Wolfe-Otis to build the new facility there — with no property taxes for ten years. And, with a promise to extend high-speed rail to our front door, which they are now doing."

"The city sure didn't want to lose the tax revenues that Wolfe-Otis's payroll gives to the area," Faust said.

"So, "Wolfe continued, "the state kicked in some more money to help you buy our old facility and land, Steve, and gave us some state tax breaks for the same reason."

"Both Wolfe-Otis and you personally have been very helpful to the governor and mayor when they faced election campaigns. Earl Broadbent, too," Faust added. "And Earl put some pressure on the FDA for us."

"But you, Steve, are the magnet that holds this complicated deal together," Wolfe said. "When you agreed to take on the present facility that Wolfe-Otis is vacating, and to allow one of your medical professors to serve as the PI of our clinical research on propacricin, you put ASU — education and winning football — at the center of it. That made it almost inevitable that the others would fall in line."

"Which brings us to the reason we're here, Alex — the propacricin drug trials," Faust said.

"Steve, like any other pharmaceutical manufacturing firm, we hired a big drug development company to take care of the clinical trials on propacricin. We contracted with PDRI – PharmaDynamics Research, Inc. – a firm in Baltimore. They have a huge success rate with the FDA. We paid them over a million dollars to do the work," Wolfe said, with a mixture of pain and pride.

"But is there some kind of fraud involved in their work product?" Faust asked.

"Steve, these guys have done clinical trials for drug companies all over the world for almost thirty years. They're among the best there is. Fraud? I doubt it, but how the hell should I know?"

"So what am I supposed to tell Drew Cameron on Monday," Faust asked.

"Nothing, Steve. It's none of his damned business. And all I can tell you is to be alert to opportunities. Look for signs of life in your Wolfe-Otis stocks. Check in with what's-his-name in the Foundation, Gibbs, now and then. Okay?"

Wolfe rose and said, "If there's nothing else, Steve. . . ."

"That's about it. Stay in touch."

"One more thing, Steve. We need to figure out a way to bring down the curtain on Cameron. We hired a new provost last spring to help us, not cause us trouble. This guy . . . . Think about it."

"Maybe you're right. We'll see," Faust said, as he, too, rose and walked toward the door. Driving away from the Renaissance House, he felt more than a little uneasy about their conversation.

At eight on Monday morning, Holly buzzed Cameron's phone and announced, "Acting Vice President Madrigal on two."

Cameron picked up and said, "Sylvia, it's good to hear from you. What's going on?

"Dr. Cameron, I am sending you a full report through campus mail this morning, but I wanted you to know that we have completed round one of awarding the scholarships to low-income applicants. We had almost seven hundred qualified applicants, so we had a good crop to pick from."

"That sounds encouraging, Sylvia."

"Among those we awarded, we had high SATs and ACTs, A-minus/B-plus high school grade averages, and lots of extra-curriculars. I think you will like the group," Sylvia said.

"Thanks for the information. I look forward to reading the full report," Cameron said.

"Great. Thanks again for giving me the chance to work on this project," Sylvia said, "and in this job."

"You are welcome, Sylvia."

At that moment, Cameron heard Holly's familiar knock and his office door opened. It's time for you to get over to the President's office, Dr. Cameron," she said.

Ms. McInerney escorted him right in. Steve Faust remained seated behind his desk while exchanging greetings with Cameron rather than taking another seat on one of the leather chairs or couches that he used for such meetings.

"Good morning, Steve. How was your trip to California?" Cameron asked.

"Elliot Benton and his firm came through for us. We will soon have our Benton Import-Export Institute for the Business College, and we can add some frills as we go on."

"Good news. You've hit a lot of homers in this game of fund-raising," Cameron said. "Sorry to bring you a grey cloud, but I have two problems to discuss. While you were away, I discovered that the Business and Law deans approved some rather large forgivable loans, quarter million to half-million dollars, for a select few of their faculty members and themselves, from their own colleges' own foundation accounts. I talked with each one of them last week and they didn't seem to understand what they'd done."

"Interesting," Faust responded. "What did you say to them?"

"First, I said that it's a blatant violation of the specific ruling of the legislature and the State Commissioner of Higher Education for this fiscal year, and second, it's unfair."

"So, what do you proposed to do about it," President Faust asked.

"Take their deanships away from them and demand that they return the money."

"I'm half-way with you, Mr. Provost," Faust said. "I'd agree with taking their deanships away, but demanding that they return those loans? You'd better talk with the university attorney first. That could be tricky. You realize, don't you, that their constituencies and the alums around New Cambridge will raise hell with you about this. The Colleges of Business and Law are not like Arts and Humanities or Social and Behavioral Sciences. They've got plenty of clout and money. Canning their deans will not make them happy."

"I'm glad you agree with my decision," Cameron said, ignoring Faust's warning. "I'll take care of it today. Second item: based on the evidence I've seen, it seems pretty certain that Wolfe-Otis Pharmaceuticals' clinical trials on their new diabetes drug are either flawed or fraudulent. ASU has two connections to that research. The PI of record for the clinical trials is Dr. Edward Novak in the Med School, and the CEO of Wolfe-Otis is, of course, the chairman of ASU's Board of Trustees. Is this a problem for us?"

"Not in the least. First, Dr. Novak has academic freedom. Maybe he screwed up. If so, the Med School will deal with him, and maybe even the AMA will. Second, the subject of those propacricin clinical trials has never been on the agenda of a Trustees meeting, never been mentioned even once, by anybody. It's no concern of ours, and we have no liability in the matter."

"Still, Steve, I have an uneasy feeling about it. I think I'll have a talk with Dr. Novak and see what he says."

"Don't waste your time, Drew. Get back to the big issues that really matter to our university. You have been making real progress on a planning process and on reforming our curriculum. Don't always be so suspicious."

President Faust's phone buzzed, interrupting their tense conversation. "I'm having a meeting with the Provost, Ms. McInerney, and we're not through. Can it wait?" Faust asked. He listened, then said, "Alright, put him through."

"Steve," ASU Foundation Director Gibbs said to Faust, "I just got off the phone with our brokerage firm and they said that Wolfe-Otis shares have doubled just since the market opened this morning. And they're still rising."

"Hold a minute," Faust said to Gibbs. "Drew, I have to take care of this and it may take some time. Can we continue later?"

"Sure, Steve. Later." Cameron returned to his office, disturbed by the feeling that his relationship with Faust had just crossed the line from positive to negative.

"Okay, what's going on, Avery?"

"What do you want me to do, Steve?" Gibbs asked.

"I want you to sell off the Wolfe-Otis stocks, today. Could you prepare me a short analysis of how we did? Just a one-pager."

"I think I can do that, Steve," Gibbs said. "Mid-to late afternoon, probably."

"Just don't fax or email it to me, Avery. I'll send somebody to your office to pick it up, okay?"

"Sure. It'll be here when you're ready."

Back in his office, Cameron said, "Holly, get me brief meetings with Dean Farnham in law and Dean Bellson in business, today if possible."

By late afternoon, Cameron had met with each of the two deans in question, relieved them both of their positions, effective at the end of the month, and explained that the salary of each would revert to the amount they made as full professors. Each of the two soon-to-be former deans became angry when informed of the decision. Each claimed that Cameron had no right to fire them. Each threatened dire consequences.

Cameron countered with, "That would force my hand, but ASU could pay its court costs from the illegal salary we just retrieved from you." Later that day, he appointed the senior associate dean of each college as the acting dean until permanent deans could be installed.

Word spread fast around the campus. The two deans and other faculty members who had received forgivable loans that year then had them taken away were outraged. Almost everybody else on the ASU faculty thought justice had been done, condemned the culprits, and applauded their provost. Cameron reflected on the fact that some years ago law and business school curricula included a required course in professional ethics. Now, in both curricula ethics is often relegated to a tiny section of the syllabus of a single, often elective course.

"It's only ten after four, but after the day you've had, Dr. Cameron, you should go home while you can," Holly Nabisco said, after her customary "knock and enter" routine.

"No. Holly. I do need to get out of the office for a minute though, so I'm going downstairs to talk with Gibbs in the Foundation," Cameron said. "I'll be right back."

Moments later at the ASU Foundation front desk, "I'm sorry, Dr. Cameron," the receptionist answered. "He's not back yet from his meeting downtown with Federal Bank and Trust people. Do you want me to call you when he returns?"

"Well, who's in charge while he's out?" Cameron asked. "I just need some information."

"His assistant, Mr. Wheeler, is here," she said as she buzzed him. "Dan, could you come here a sec. Dr. Cameron needs something."

Dan Wheeler came out of the Foundation maze of cubicles and greeted Cameron. "What can I do for you, Dr. Cameron?"

"I need some information on our Wolfe-Otis stocks."

"Sure, Dr. Cameron. I made only one copy. Do you want to take it up?"

"I'll take care of it, Dan. Thanks," Cameron answered, not sure what had just transpired.

Wheeler returned from his inner office in half a minute and said, "Here you go," as he handed Cameron an envelope.

"Thanks, again, Dan."

As he walked by Holly's desk on the way to his own office, her phone rang. "Provost's office. I see." Covering the mouthpiece, she asked Cameron, "Do you want to talk with Acting VP Madrigal? She sounds really serious."

"Sure, I'll take it." Holly handed Cameron her phone and he said, "Sylvia, what's up?"

Holly watched her boss as he listened to his acting VP for Admissions and Records. His expression changed from cheerful to dismayed, and he looked up at Holly and shook his head as if to convey the receipt of bad news. "No, Sylvia, come on over right now. I have some questions and I want to make some decisions."

In just a moment, Sylvia Madrigal opened the outer door to the Provost's suite and spotted Holly standing inside Cameron's office. "Tell her to come in, Holly."

As she approached them, Sylvia said, "I'm sorry, Holly, but maybe I should speak with Dr. Cameron alone about this business."

"It's alright. Holly knows everything I know," Cameron responded. "What's the problem?"

"Today," Sylvia began, "I determined that Rachael O'Brien, a senior clerk in my office, changed an undergraduate student's grade from F to B, without my permission or knowledge, and without any appeals process. I called the student's professor and he confirmed that he had given the student an F. Just five minutes ago I confronted Rachael, and she admitted it. When I asked her why, she said that it was okay because President Faust asked her to do it."

"That's a strange response, Sylvia. She has violated the rules, but it's not the end of the world. I'm sure you can handle it," he said, trying to calm her down. "You are the VP of Admissions and Records. You don't need my help."

"Yes I do. Dr. Cameron. It's worse than you think. Look at the student's name on the transcript. It's 'Patrick Clements', the son of Shelby Clements, Speaker of the State House of Representatives."

"Sylvia," Cameron said, "you did the right thing in coming to me. We'll work together to solve this problem. Is Rachael still in the office?"

"She was there when I left five minutes ago."

"Go back to your office, Sylvia, and if she knows you came to see me, tell her that I was not available. Otherwise, just tell her that she should not change any more grades unless a request has passed a regular appeals process. You and I will deal with this later when we have more information."

"Fine with me, Dr. Cameron."

"Sylvia, please call me Drew."

"Very well, Drew. *Muchas gracias.*"

"*De nada,*" Cameron replied.

When Sylvia Madrigal left, Cameron opened the envelope given to him a few minutes earlier by Dan Wheeler in the Foundation and studied it. Then he put it and several other items in his briefcase and prepared to leave for the day. Holly handed him his schedule for the next day. "Holly, go home. I'm leaving."

"I will, Dr. Cameron. See you tomorrow."

Thoughts flashed in and out of his mind as he entered the Interstate for the commute home. One thought, a tentative conclusion, kept repeating itself: several of my problems appear to lead back to Steve Faust and Alex Wolfe. Cameron had discovered that neither the Law School nor the Business School foundation can award a forgivable loan unless the request is signed by both the appropriate dean and the president. President Faust's email message to Zachary Kilgore that he by mistake sent to Holly instead of Kilgore, and Rachael O'Brien's claim that Faust asked her to change the grade of the Speaker's son, certainly implicate Faust in the violation of federal law and university rules. Both Coach Sylvester and the Athletic Director report straight to President Faust, not through the Provost. Extreme nonfeasance could account for the fact that Faust has remained unaware of the football program's habit of violating university and NCAA rules, or malfeasance in the case of complicity. Given Alpha State's net annual income of almost two million dollars per football game, it is unlikely that Faust has delegated all responsibility for oversight of the program. Furthermore, the university is tied to Wolfe-Otis Pharmaceuticals through the friendship between Faust and Wolfe, and through Wolfe's position as chairman of the ASU Board of Trustees. That seems to suggest the possibility of a connection between Faust and the fraudulent clinical drug trials for propacricin. He remembered that Dekker had advised that he focus first on the drug trials because real and irreparable harm might be done if the trials had been faked and the drug were to go on the market. Finally, last fall the University had invested several million dollars in Wolfe-Otis stock and sold it today for almost triple the original price per share. Most of the gains came right after a mysterious leak to the press that the FDA was giving approval to propacricin.

As he pulled into his driveway, his spirits began to lift a little, knowing that he was home and would soon be with Vanessa. They exchanged the usual kiss and embrace and brief information about how their days had gone — hers well, his not. Both were weary, a light dinner went fast, and bedtime came early.

When Cameron awoke the next morning, somewhat refreshed after the rather discouraging day he'd had the day before, he showered, shaved, dressed, and went to the kitchen to make coffee, without waking Vanessa. Fortified by a cup of bold, dark roast, he proceeded to the middle of his driveway to pick up the newspaper. Once back inside, he found Vanessa pouring herself a cup of coffee. "Good morning, love, here's some news," Cameron said, as he handed her the *New Cambridge Morning News*.

She laid the newspaper on the table, unopened, and announced, "No, Cameron, I think I already have the news," she said. "You may not like it. I probably don't either. I thought about it all night," she said, glancing at her watch.

"What?" Cameron said, puzzled.

"You've been Executive VP and Provost for less than a year and you've discovered several horrendous problems that nobody else even knew about or that nobody cared about. They look to me like problems brought about not by neglect or incompetence or bad luck, but rather by careful planning and stealth. Each one brings more money and power to the already rich and powerful. Am I wrong so far?"

"No," Cameron said. "I think not."

"Fraudulent alteration and reporting of official university records to get higher rankings," Vanessa continued; "countless violations of NCAA and university rules in pursuit of millions in profits from winning football; the whole forgivable loans thing is unforgivable; and a drug trial mess that has all the signs of an even bigger problem! Not to mention that less than six months ago you had to deal with a classroom seizure and shootout!"

"Vanessa, I think I know where you're going with this line of reasoning, and I'm not sure I like it."

Vanessa thought long and hard before she responded. "You like historical analogies. Try these two. Once England ruled America, taxed them heavily and gave them no representation. George Washington accepted the challenge to right the wrongs. He led numerous battles for several years against superior military forces. As a result of his sacrifice and his military victory, America won the war and he became president. But also remember that once England ruled France. France's Joan of Arc accepted the challenge of freeing her nation. She led French troops in several victorious battles against the British. Then the British captured her and burned her at the stake."

Cameron sat in silence for a moment, digesting the implications of Vanessa's discussion. She spoke first. "I think you may be in a Joan of Arc situation rather than a George Washington situation. The cost to you, to us, of freeing this university from nefarious forces may be just too high. It may be impossible, even for you."

"So what are you saying, Vanessa? Spell it out for me."

"Bottom line. It's time to calculate one of your wonderful risk-reward analyses. Time to decide whether the fight can be won, and if it can be won, can you survive the victory? George Washington or a Joan of Arc?"

12

The reality of Cameron's second semester at Alpha State University had been so distressing that he had not noticed the transition from a cold, grey winter to a sunny, mild spring. Nor did he realize that final exam week had begun that Monday morning. Streams of students walked the sidewalks across and around the large quadrangle, rematerializing every hour along with the Riedel Tower chimes. Birds celebrated late spring with cheerful song, but students, under the duress of final exams, did not notice. The smaller number of A students walked alone, tired but confident, while the large number of B and C students trudged across campus in small clusters, almost as if hesitant to reach their destinations. Their look of resignation, smiling through their angst, was interrupted by a few expressions of dark humor and forced laughter. The D and F students followed paths between hope and despair, alone, slow, quiet. All of them soldiered on to confront their adversary — an important, difficult, two-hour exam. Uniformed crews continued to manicure the attractive landscape of lawn, flowers, shrubs, and trees, including a healthy oak outside the east window of Blackburn Alumni House.

As he stared through his office window at the students below, Cameron wondered how many of them had anxious thoughts of the Miller Hall incident that occurred during the last round of final exams. *Are they thinking that about five months ago, students were sitting in their chairs waiting to take a stat final and that an armed gunman seized the classroom, locked the students in, held them hostage, waved guns at them, screamed at them, shot four of them?* The legal maneuvers and counter-maneuvers between the New Cambridge County Prosecutor's Office and defense counsel, including psychiatric testing and observation of the alleged shooter, had consumed the better part of five months. Just last week, it had all come back to Cameron in great detail, because the *New Cambridge Morning News* had featured several lengthy articles in its Sunday edition, in which they analyzed the incident in historical context. The articles discussed and quoted him at some length. In addition to that, he had been required to appear in the Prosecutor's Office last week to sign the official papers detailing the events of the incident. Holden R. Parks, the alleged perpetrator, had been judged to be unfit to stand trial due to a mental disorder. By judicial order, he was to be confined to the state maximum security mental institution for continued observation and treatment. In three more months, he and his attorney would appear in court again for a determination of his ability to stand trial.

Returning his attention to his desk, Cameron buzzed Holly and asked, "Is Dekker on campus this morning?"

"Yes, he came in early, as usual," Holly answered. Then she asked, "Did you notice anything different in the outer office today?" as she looked up and around.

"Wait a second," he answered, and walked into the expansive outer waiting room. Failing to see anything different, he said, "I don't get it. Is there something different?"

"Yes. Except for the New Cambridge clock, all of the wall clocks have been reset and labeled for different cities around the world. I happened to mention to Dekker this morning that it was about time to change the cities and times of our international clocks, so I asked him to do it. I hope it's alright." Cameron remembered how fascinated Holly had been with his idea to place half a dozen large, round clocks around the outer office wall, each one labeled for a different world city and set to its time — a subtle message to students and faculty alike that globalization is real and important.

"I see," Cameron said to Holly, and thought to himself, *So it's time for a change.* "I approve. It's a nice change. You two picked some nice cities."

"A lot of faculty and students have noticed it. They talk about it while they're waiting for an appointment, and some of them have mentioned it to me," Holly said. "In fact, Dr. Aiken in Physics said he really appreciates the clocks because to him, as a physicist, they represent time and space," she added, beaming.

"It's working then. Can you get Dekker in to see me as soon as he's free?"

"Sure," Holly said.

At that moment, 8:00 AM, Chief Redden entered Cameron's outer office and said, "May I have a brief word with you, Dr. Cameron?"

Chief Redden stood almost at attention in his full-dress uniform, silver pistol belted to his right hip, hat held under his left arm, his tone and demeanor indicating that this was a serious professional visit. Cameron was not sure how to respond but said, "Sure, Charlie, come in."

Chief Redden remained standing as Cameron took a seat. "Dr. Cameron, I am here to give you a very important package of materials to examine. Friday, I attended the funeral of an old friend in Carlton, about four hours from here by car. He had written in his will that, when he died, his attorney was to give me this package, because I 'would know what to do with it', his note said." The chief handed the large brown envelope to Cameron. "So, I'm giving it to you."

"Charlie, what is it?

"The funeral I attended was for my predecessor at ASU, the former Chief of Police, Douglas Wood. The package contains the official records pertaining to the death of the coed in one of our dorms almost a year ago and Doug's private investigation of the death — the coroner's report, DNA tests, lab reports, images of the perpetrator entering the dorm and walking down the victim's corridor, and Doug Wood's report to President Faust on the results of his own private investigation."

"Charlie, shouldn't these documents go to some appropriate office in the City of New Cambridge"?

"No, sir. I have spent the whole weekend reading them, over and over. The bottom line is, President Faust reported to the media and the university community that the incident was a death due to natural causes when in fact, he knew that was incorrect. The coed was raped and murdered, by one of our own former students. DNA tests confirm the perpetrator's identity. The physical evidence documented in this envelope is overwhelming!"

For a few moments, Cameron was speechless. He tasted both anger and fear and felt a strong fight or flight impulse. "Charlie, I know you wouldn't say that unless you were convinced that it's true. So . . . I don't know what to say. What do you see as the next step?"

"Sir, I have only two choices. I can make sure that justice is done or I can resign."

"I understand, Charlie. I'll consider your two options and get back in touch soon. First, this matter must remain our secret for now. Second, allow me some time to read all this and put a response in place. Just a few days. Agreed?"

"Yes, sir, Redden responded and proceeded to exit.

About fifteen minutes later, Dekker knocked at Cameron's open door and entered, saying, "*Goedemorgen, mijnneer.* Did you want to see me?"

"I think you just said 'Good morning, sir,' in Dutch, and *Ja wel,* I do want to see you," Cameron said. "Close the door and have a seat, Axel. I want to tell you what I'm thinking at this point about the several ugly problems we have at this university right now, including one you don't even know about yet. You're official job title is administrative post-doc but let's be realistic." Cameron lowered his voice almost to a whisper and said, "With your years in

European security, you know more about solving a problem and accomplishing a mission than just about anybody else I know."

"Oh, my, Drew. You are upset about something."

"First, I want to tell you what I learned yesterday about the University and Wolfe-Otis Pharmaceuticals. I got a report — never mind how I got it — from the ASU foundation showing that they invested eight million dollars in Wolfe-Otis stock on November second of last year. That's almost a half million shares at $17.85 per share. There was basically no change in that share price until right after the leak to the media that the FDA was going to approve the new Wolfe-Otis diabetes drug, propacricin. That's when Wolfe-Otis stock started rising fast, about a week ago. The Foundation sold off those shares three days ago for a little over $50 per share. The ASU foundation almost tripled its investment in six months! Did somebody in the foundation buy the Wolfe-Otis stock as a routine re-investment of available funds or did we get wind that FDA would approve the Wolfe-Otis diabetes drug months before that information was public? Astute financial management, blind luck, or insider trading?"

On hearing Cameron's latest news, Dekker's eyes showed a change from curiosity to anger as he said between clenched teeth, "*En dan de duivel dook.*"

"Give me the English version."

"It means, 'And then the devil popped up.'"

"Correct. And now you know everything I know — except what I learned just a few minutes ago. Here's the short version: Chief Redden just gave me a package of documents that, he says, prove that the coed who was found dead in her dorm room during spring final exams last year, right before he and I started our jobs at ASU, died not from natural causes, as President Faust announced, but was raped and murdered. And, Faust knew it soon after her death."

The two sat for several minutes, just staring at the floor. "What is our plan?" Dekker asked.

"I am going to document what I know and the evidence that supports it concerning our main problems," he said, and counted on his fingers as he mentioned them — "the football program, the University's involvement in what appears to be a federal drug scandal, possible insider trading, the fraudulent alteration and reporting of official University records, and covering up a rape-murder. I am going to prepare a dossier on each problem, combine them in a single report, and secure it in a bank vault downtown."

"Then what?"

"I don't know what I am going to do with the dossiers. I have to weigh all the risks and rewards of two courses of action: doing nothing, or making one or more of the dossiers public."

"Your grasp of the public interest, the common good, in the long run, is unerring, Drew. You will make the right decision," Dekker said.

"If I make the dossiers public, it would lead to punishment of the guilty parties but do great harm to the University for years to come. The state legislature, Congress, and our corporate and individual donors would turn their backs on us. Students and their parents would not want to be associated with corruption or losing football or a school that hides the murder of one of its students. Enrollments would decline. Tuition revenues would shrink. Law suits could cost millions. Many innocent people would suffer, and it would take the University years to recover, if it ever did."

"I don't want to interfere," Dekker said, "but if there is any way I can help you, just ask."

"Thanks. I have to figure out what you statisticians would call an 'optimal solution' to the problem," Cameron said, forcing a smile.

"Right. Maximize the positive value within given constraints. You could use the von Neumann's asymptotic minimax theorem."

"That's almost funny," Cameron said with a wince, knowing that his friend was just trying to lighten the moment. "But I will prepare the dossiers and keep thinking about the problems and what, if anything, to do about them."

"Call if you need me. I'm at your service," Dekker said as he turned to leave.

"What we need is half an hour with Aristotle. He always seemed to have the right answers to ethical questions," Cameron said with equal parts frustration and humor. "I think he would tell us that ASU is being corrupted by greed, the root of all evil."

Dekker nodded agreement and left. Cameron buzzed Holly and said, "Holly, get me an hour with Faust as soon as he can make it," and then he began assembling his dossiers.

Within only a few minutes, Holly reported, "Ms. McInerney says he can see you first thing in the morning, seven-thirty or eight."

"Make it seven thirty," Cameron said. And get me an appointment with an officer at Meridian National Bank, at 5:00 PM today. I have some business with them."

At four-thirty he said goodbye to Holly and left the office. At a little before five, he paid for one year in advance to rent a lock box at Meridian National Bank, placed one copy of his dossiers in the box, and left with his key. By five-twenty, he was home. Vanessa was still at work, so he sat alone, in the den.

Cameron tried to think positive thoughts, about daughter Char coming home from study abroad in London, about son Tom getting married soon, about the strong majority vote the ASU faculty had given last week to both the curricular reform and long-term planning proposals he had initiated, about how well Vanessa had been received as a new colleague in the law firm, and even about the beautiful spring that had enveloped New Cambridge. But his thoughts returned to tomorrow's meeting with President Faust. Feelings of dread and anxiety throbbed in his temple.

When Vanessa arrived home, Cameron told her about the latest revelation on campus – the rape-murder case reported by Chief Redden. Vanessa found it hard to believe. They ate dinner and turned in early. The forces of exhaustion and anxiety battled over Cameron's mind and body, and for a couple of hours he thought he would never get to sleep. Near midnight, unconsciousness crept into his brain and claimed the sleep center for itself. Early the next morning, he awakened to the rich aroma of bacon frying. Vanessa was already up and preparing a tasty breakfast to get him off to a good start for what might be a difficult day.

Half way through breakfast, however, about six-thirty, the phone rang. Char called from London. "I have my plane ticket to New Cambridge on May 22. I arrive at 11:15 AM at terminal two, gate twelve. Can you pick me up?"

"Of course, one or both of us will be there," Vanessa said, "and we can't wait to see you!"

"I got honors in all my courses, so I don't have to sit for any final exams!"

Vanessa and Cameron were ecstatic and so was Char.

Later that morning, Ms. McInerney seemed to be in an upbeat mood rather than her usual somber, all-business state of mind. "Good morning, Dr. Cameron," she said with a smile, as she opened Faust's office door. "Go right in. He's expecting you."

President Faust looked up from his desk, glared at Cameron over his reading glasses and said, "Executive Vice President Drew Cameron, do you have any idea what you've done? Do you understand it at all?" Without waiting for a response, which Cameron did not have anyway, he continued, "In less than one year, you have taken actions that will bring this great university to the edge of chaos!"

Cameron assumed that Faust had somehow discovered that he had prepared the various dossiers of evidence against the university. He lost a few seconds but not his composure as he thought about how to respond. "And what chaos are you referring to?" he asked, to consume more time while he thought about it.

"Do you realize what it will do to this university?" Faust asked.

"It will have a profound and lasting impact," Cameron said, assuming that Faust's remarks constituted the preliminaries to a charge of disloyalty and a demand for his immediate resignation.

"Correct. I had to fire the last provost because he couldn't get it done in three years and you've done it in one."

Cameron struggled to think fast and to conceal his bewilderment in the face of Faust's remarks.

"So congratulations, my good man," Faust said. "I read the summaries of both committee reports — curriculum reform and long-term planning — and you have generated considerable faculty enthusiasm for both efforts. Believe it or not, the faculty seems happy! Even Melinda Osterman, who hasn't spoken a civil word to me in years, called a couple of days ago and said some very nice things about you and even hinted that I might not be totally evil — a big change of opinion from her."

"The chaos you referred to," Cameron asked, "is approval of the long-term planning and curriculum reform proposals?"

"Yes," Faust said with a big grin, "and I'm going to tell the trustees that you not only subdue armed psychopaths in the classroom and save students' lives but you also charm hostile and old-fashioned faculties into modernizing their product and their organization. You did your job, and you did it well."

Without pause, Cameron said, "That's why I'm here, Steve. To do my job and do it well, I must tell you what I know about several very serious problems we face as a university."

Faust's immediate surprise was evident as his facial and vocal expressions changed from jovial to solemn as he stared at Cameron. "What problems?"

"Okay. A few days ago when you were in Los Angeles, you intended to send an email message to Zachary Kilgore in New York City. By mistake, you sent it to Holly Nabisco. She received the message and showed me a copy." Cameron stopped here, waiting for Faust's response.

"Look, Cameron, that's a privileged communication. You have no damned right to it," Faust said. "But anyway, it's time you grow up and learn what universities do, and must do. Kilgore was on our team. He changed a few statistics now and then, with my approval. Every university does that. Every one of them. We joke about it at the annual college presidents' meetings. We were closing in on qualifying for the state legislature's bonus for getting into the top thirty public universities, but you had already blown that when you had Kilgore arrested. I tried to ignore it and to pretend you just didn't know any better but would learn in due time. Now one of our state competitors will probably get the annual million dollar legislative award." Faust shook his head and asked, "Don't you get it?"

"But it's a form of corruption! It's cheating!"

"Wake up and smell the coffee, Cameron. You're an Executive VP now. You need to start acting like one. Those news magazines that rank universities every year are not exactly as pure as the driven snow. The rating criteria they use, the weights they attach to each criterion, their heavy reliance on subjective rankings by college executives, the whole damn thing is somewhere between absurd and unscrupulous." Faust's face reddened, as he continued, "Do you know how many copies of their lamebrain magazine that tripe sells each year? Tens of thousands."

"Okay," Cameron said, almost as if conceding to Faust's sarcastic arguments, "let's move to problem number two. I have seen hundreds of documents — detailed, dated, authentic evidence, including pictures — from credible sources, that indicate that our football program, including their alumni support group, has for years violated dozens of NCAA regulations, our own rules, and even state and local laws." And then, before he thought, Cameron blurted out "Surely you were aware that Coach Sylvester and even Athletic Director Payton were doing this stuff."

"What stuff? Just exactly what stuff?"

"Prostitutes for players, paying players, making more phone calls to potential recruits than allowed by the NCAA, paying for many more nights in hotels for potential recruits to visit ASU than allowed, erasing the police record of a player caught selling crack cocaine! Shall I go on?" Cameron said, daring his boss to ask for more.

"You really don't get it do you? There was a time when ASU's state legislative appropriation covered two-thirds of the University's expenses and tuition covered the rest. Last year the legislature covered less than a fourth of our expenses, and tuition covered just ten percent. How the hell do you think we pay the bills and keep growing? Research grants and contracts pay fifteen percent. The rest of our revenues, about half, we earn in the market as business entrepreneurs. And you know who does a large part of that? The football program, that's who. Our big corporate donors are impressed by our winning football program, not by our philosophy department."

"Are you going to tell me that every university looks the other way when its sports programs break the rules?" Cameron asked.

"Yes! Every public university that has, or aspires to, a position in the national market," Faust answered. "Think about this! As a result of winning the championship bowl game three years ago, I renegotiated our franchise agreement on ASU vending machines and concessions at all our sports games. Guess what? To get the contract, FlavorStream offered nearly double the old contract, an additional million or so per year for years to come. You already know we made a killing selling the naming rights of the football stadium to Universal-Lifeguard Insurance. What you don't know is that late last week Millennium Real Estate agreed to pay twenty-five million a year to name our basketball arena. We'll announce it to the public in a few days. Are you getting it now?"

"Those are legal arrangements, Steve, and . . . . But ASU should not have to violate rules, should not have to cheat to win sports events, in order to be a good *academic* institution. The bad publicity from cheating could ruin us for decades if the NCAA discovers it and punishes us."

"Look at the facts, Mr. Executive VP. The NCAA does not like to hand out <u>major</u> punishments on a <u>major</u> university in a <u>major</u> conference, even for <u>major</u> violations. They always negotiate it down to a tolerable punishment that doesn't hurt the program. Just in the last few years, the NCAA has punished Alabama, Southern Cal, Oklahoma, TCU, Purdue, and UT Austin, to name a few, for so-called 'major' violations. Those punishments didn't kill their sports programs or their reputations, or their annual revenues. Universities accept an occasional NCAA slap on the wrist as a badge of success in sports. Even when the coach is fired or resigns, the university hires another good coach and the seats stay full."

"Okay, there's more, Steve," Cameron interrupted.

"You just don't know when to quit, do you?" Faust said, no longer concealing his anger. "Maybe Alex Wolfe was right. Okay, what? Make it quick!"

Cameron realized that his boss was about to tell him to leave, so he went straight to the heart of his third item. "The Foundation gave me a copy of their report on their purchase of Wolfe-Otis stock last fall and the sale of that stock last week. We made millions in just a few months. We need to be able to explain that, to show that it was market smarts and good luck and not insider trading."

The anger dominating Faust's demeanor changed to a reddened expression of anxiety and he opened his mouth as if to speak but said nothing for several seconds. "Look, Cameron, you have no business with that report in the first place. It is privileged information. You have no authority over the Foundation. But even more important, you still don't get it."

"Get what?" Cameron demanded.

"That most major, so-called state universities have been privatized. We are forced into the position of a private corporation that has to live by the rules of the market — make a profit and grow, or go out of business. We survive and grow because, as I just, dammit, got through telling you, we are self-supporting. The state legislature doesn't give me enough money to run a decent lemonade stand! Since 1980, the higher ed percent of the state budget has fallen from ten percent to under six, while the percent to fund prisons has risen from three to eleven percent. We used to be a state university but now we are barely a state-assisted university. So, we please our constituents who give us money, we invest it to make more money to meet payroll — we do our job and live another day. It's that simple. And, yes, every university does it, or stagnates! And if you're not growing, you're dying!" Faust paused, glared at Cameron, and shook his head in disgust.

"I think maybe I'm beginning to understand it, Steve," Cameron confessed. "I don't feel good about it. Not yet, anyway, but I see your point. I guess I . . . I should thank you for being so . . . straightforward with me. Thanks." As he stood to leave, he said, "Alpha State is really a private university, not public. It's not a public agency but a business corporation. We operate under the rules of the economic marketplace. Our primary goal is to maximize profit. If we fail, we go out of business."

"Then maybe you do get it, Drew. So act like it! And remember, we give a lot of young people an opportunity to learn some skills and have a better life." Suspecting that his Executive VP still harbored serious doubts, maybe even the intent to go public, Faust said, "So what's your next move?"

Cameron decided not to mention the problem of concealing a campus murder. "Well, I guess I will think hard about the facts you have given me about these . . . situations, and the perspective you take on them, and . . . decide how I can best operate from that perspective."

"Then we have an understanding," Faust said, somewhat relieved. "That's good, because if you don't, the party's over. Now, you tell me if there's anything you want me to do to speed up the curricular reform and planning projects."

"Thanks. I'll keep you informed," Cameron said as he left Faust's office.

Holly greeted him with her usual cheerfulness, but her every word, gesture, and facial expression revealed overwhelming curiosity about what had happened in the meeting. "Is everything alright, Dr. Cameron?

"Sure, Holly. Everything is fine." Then he realized that her question referred to what she interpreted as a major confrontation between her boss and Faust. "Come in a second." When she stepped into his office and closed the door, he said, "We had some differences of opinion about university policies. We aired them. He gave me some new facts, a new perspective to consider, and I am doing that. So, we'll see."

"Good. When you were gone almost two hours, I began to worry. I rearranged most of your schedule for the rest of today by postponing a lot of it until tomorrow. Is that okay?" And without waiting for an answer, Holly continued, "Did you forget, you have your annual physical with Dr. Li at 3:00 PM. Here's my strong recommendation. After you go to lunch, go straight to your Dr.'s appointment, and then go home. Her office is closer to your house in Bedford than it is to the University, so just go home from there."

Cameron thought about it for a moment, then said, "Holly, as usual, your advice is good. I'll do it."

At about four-thirty, he pulled into his driveway, the earliest he had ever arrived home from work since he joined Alpha State. He collected the mail from the mailbox and took a seat in his favorite chair in the den. He noticed that one of the pieces of mail was a first-class letter addressed to Vanessa, from the State Bar Association. *It has to be good news*, he said to himself. *Vanessa passed the Bar exam. It's gotta be!*

Receiving the letter from the State Bar Association served as the playwright's cue in the Cameron family drama because at that moment Vanessa pulled her car into the driveway. Cameron's energy level increased and his heart was practically racing. As soon as she opened the door, he exclaimed, "Vanessa, darlin', look what came in the mail today!" and gave her a kiss. "Here, you open it," he said.

Vanessa tore off a quarter inch of one end of the envelope, blew into the open end, and removed the letter. As she read it, a confident smile spread across her face and she said, "Well, I passed the bar exam. I'm legal."

Cameron gave her a congratulatory hug and said, "I'm so glad for you — for us. I'm so proud of you. But there was never a doubt. I knew you'd do it."

"Thanks, love. I do feel better about things now. How did your day go?" Vanessa asked?

"First," Cameron responded, "I'm pouring us a glass of wine to celebrate your success." They took their bottle of chardonnay and two glasses to the patio. For over an hour they talked, reliving old times of Vanessa studying to take the bar exam in New York State almost twenty years ago.

As Cameron swallowed the last sip of his second glass, alternate waves of relaxation and anxiety swept over his mind and body. It was then that Vanessa said, "You never told me about your day, Drew. How did it go?"

"Not well."

For the next hour and a half, Cameron and Vanessa prepared and consumed a dinner salad, cleaned up the kitchen, and discussed his disturbing meeting with President Faust. "So what are you going to do?" she asked.

"I'm not sure, Vanessa. But I don't think I have many options."

"What do you see as your options?"

"I could resign and get a different job. Maybe not work for a university. Maybe do something in a research or consulting firm."

"Or you could go public with your dossiers of evidence and nail Faust and the rest of them to the wall," Vanessa counseled.

"Or, I could accept the way things are in the academy, play by the prevailing rules, and make Alpha State even more . . . ."

"More what?" Vanessa interrupted.

"To be honest, it's the way, the only way, for me to follow my own career ambition. You know, Vanessa, we've talked about it. I still hope to step into a university presidency someday. If I blow the whistle on Faust for any of these problems, it will cause a tsunami, and the first thing to get blown away will be my career."

"It's late, and I can tell you're dead tired," Vanessa said. "Tomorrow's another day. And besides, you know how to make decisions. Sleep on it and see what you think tomorrow."

"You know, Vanessa, I've been in school, on one side of the desk or the other, since kindergarten, and a faculty member for over two decades. I've seen a lot of big changes in universities during my career – new discoveries and developments in different academic fields, and the computer revolution has been huge. But now I'm beginning to see an even bigger change. We've been corporatized. Our main purpose is pursuit of profit and power."

"You're exhausted, Drew. Let's put it to rest for now."

They did go to bed and Vanessa was surprised when Cameron's breathing and perfect stillness revealed that he had fallen into a deep sleep in only ten minutes. Grateful that he was getting some much-needed rest, she took one last look at the clock, 10:35 PM, turned over and soon drifted off to sleep.

At about one o'clock, she was awakened by what she thought was Cameron asking her a question. She waited a moment then answered, "What is it, Drew?" He grunted, moved his legs as if he wanted to walk fast, and made more sounds, some of which resembled words. She listened and waited for several minutes. He began moving his legs and arms again and speaking louder and with more clarity. Vanessa was very sleepy and wondered whether she should awaken him so he could get relief from his apparent nightmare and return to peaceful sleep.

She decided just to listen to what he was saying or trying to say, because he seemed to be repeating certain words and phrases with considerable emotion and volume. She reached into the bedside table and grabbed paper and pen and turned on a small flashlight. With a litigator's interest in testimony as evidence, she became her own court reporter and began to record his words so she could tell him about it in the morning. Most of it made no sense. His random declarations and the jerking motion of his legs continued for another five minutes or so, and then he became still and quiet. Vanessa turned off her flashlight and soon fell back to sleep.

When the morning sun invaded their bedroom, they awoke with a start, having forgotten to set an alarm. As they rushed to get dressed to go to work, Vanessa said, "Cameron, sweetheart, you had a long and terrible nightmare last night. Did you get any sleep at all?"

"Uh, nightmare? I don't think so," and his expression changed from the reality of the moment to a distant gaze of incredulous recollection. "I do remember something about . . . walking for a long time . . . with some other people . . . and talking and listening . . . and we walked around a big house, with columns, I think and . . . . But I must have slept pretty well. I feel fine."

"Just out of curiosity, I wrote some of what you said on a legal pad, the parts I could understand. Maybe it'll help you remember what was going on in your unconscious or subconscious or whatever." Vanessa picked up the sheet of paper and read to Cameron: "'I see um nick oh monkey an ethnics doctor nova mean.' You said that or something like that three or four times."

Cameron looked at her notes and spoke his apparent words or sounds several times. "I said that? I have no idea what I was saying, or what those words mean. It's all Greek to me. Anyway, Vanessa, I'm sorry I woke you up."

Because they were running late, they skipped breakfast and drove away to their jobs in New Cambridge. Without really knowing why, as she left for work Vanessa grabbed her page of notes of Cameron talking in his sleep, rolled it into a small scroll and stuck it in the outside pocket of her briefcase.

As soon as Holly spied Cameron entering the outer office, she jumped and ran to get him his morning coffee, something he had told her was not in her job description. "You had such a bad day yesterday," she said, "that this is the least I can do. But you look rested and ready to go, now."

"Thank you, Holly,' he said. "Vanessa passed the bar, so we are elated,"

"Wonderful, but nobody's surprised. Drink your coffee. I need to brief you on your first commencement at ASU. It's only ten days from today. This year, President Faust has arranged to hold graduation in the basketball arena. Ms. McInerney said we could find out why later, if we're interested. Here's a prelim copy of the program. I have noted your parts with yellow marker. Senator Broadbent is giving the commencement address, so a lot of important people will be there. It's also his fiftieth college reunion. Remember, we're giving him an Honorary Doctorate of Humane Letters."

"Yes, I'll study it, Holly." Then he thought to himself, *President Faust wants to hold graduation in the basketball arena because that's where he wants to announce his selling of the arena's naming rights.*

The ten-day period between the end of final exams and commencement at Alpha State University was quiet, as it is in every institution of higher learning in America. Students were gone. Faculty members were either at home grading the last final exam papers or resting or doing their own research. Riedel Tower's hourly chimes went unheard. Administrators tried to get caught up with reports, meetings, and preparations for summer school and fall enrollment.

Almost every day Cameron tried to think about the problems he had discussed with Faust and their growing estrangement. What should he do with the dossiers? Should he attempt reconciliation with Faust? Should he offer his resignation? He realized that the longer he waited, the less freedom of decision he would have.

Char came back from study abroad at Oxford, and Tom and his fiancée, Anne, drove to New Cambridge from graduate school in Washington. Their timing was perfect, so that week both Cameron and Vanessa took off two full days and two half days, to spend time with the kids. All three had learned a lot as students and had matured as human beings during the past several months. Hearing them talk about it was pure joy for Cameron and Vanessa, not to mention the obvious fact that the love and respect between Anne and each member of the Cameron family grew stronger.

At the pre-commencement briefing for all faculty and staff participants, the event managers discussed procedures in detail and answered many questions. Forty or fifty administrators in full academic regalia would sit on a raised platform at one end of the arena facing east. Directly in front of them, but on the arena floor, the university wind ensemble would sit. Graduates' chairs were also located on the arena floor facing the platform. Visitors would sit in the raised arena seats around three sides of the students, where basketball spectators sat during games.

In the briefing, Cameron learned that his role was to be small. After the graduates, faculty and administrators marched in to the university wind ensemble's rendition of *Pomp and Circumstance*, President Faust would make some welcoming remarks. A Jesuit priest would bless the occasion with a prayer, and the ensemble would play a brief classical piece. Cameron would make a short statement about the significance of bestowing formal academic degrees. Then Faust would introduce Senator Broadbent, who would deliver the commencement address. As their names were called, each degree-recipient would march from his or her seat on the arena floor, across the stage to be handed a document that looked like a diploma (the real one had to be picked up at the bookstore later), and proceed back to his or her seat on the arena floor, all at a fast pace. Then President Faust would introduce the chairman of the state board of higher education, who would make the degrees official. At that point, bedlam would ensue, because this year, ASU was holding only one large commencement for all degree recipients rather than a smaller one for each college. In addition, media representatives would be there — televising, interviewing, taking notes, shooting snapshots of all the relevant sights and sounds of this important event.

On Commencement morning, Char, who had not yet adjusted to the seven-hour time difference between London and New Cambridge, rose much earlier than her mother or Tom and Anne. Her father had already left for work. Mother soon joined daughter in the kitchen and they enjoyed breakfast rolls, juice, coffee and, most of all, mother-daughter togetherness. They took their second cup of coffee to the study to sit in the easy chairs. Vanessa proceeded to tell Char that her dad had discovered some major problems at the university that had resulted in a serious confrontation with President Faust.

"That sounds pretty bad. He's not in danger of losing his job, is he? Or resigning? What's he going to do?" Char asked.

"I don't know, and I am not sure he knows either," Vanessa answered. "But even if he were to get fired as provost, he's tenured in political science. He can always be a professor again."

"How's he taking all this?" Char asked.

"I'm not sure, but the night after his confrontation with President Faust, he had a dream, a nightmare I think, and talked in his sleep for what seemed like half an hour, very unlike your dad. I actually wrote down some of what he said. Weird stuff. The next morning, he had no idea what it meant or what he was saying." She handed Char the sheet of paper on which she had recorded Cameron's dream-induced utterances.

Char first read Vanessa's version aloud: "'I see em Nick. Oh monkey. And ethnics. Dr. Nova Mean.'" Then she asked, "Has Dad become a modern poet? This has many of the characteristics of twenty-first century poetry — free-style, not at all lyrical, full of metaphors, witty, no rhyme whatsoever. But it lacks despair," she said with her blend of cynicism and satire.

As they sipped their coffee, Char continued to read the nonsense syllables, trying different combinations of sounds, emphases and cadences. On the fourth time through, she tried "'I see 'em. Nick oh mockey and ethics. Dr. Nova Mean.'" Then she repeated that particular interpretation several times.

After another thoughtful pause, Char set her coffee mug down hard and almost screamed, "Mom!" I know what this is, what it might be. It's got to be. Dad said it. In a dream. Who else would say something like this?"

"Well, Oxford scholar, what did he say?"

"Listen, Mom, while I read it," and held the paper so her mother could see it as she spoke the words, "'Lyceum. *Nichomachean Ethics*. Doctrine of the Mean.' Dad was dreaming about Aristotle! The Lyceum is the name of the school Aristotle founded in Athens. While he was there, he wrote a book called *Nichomachean Ethics*. It's about how people can achieve virtue and happiness, as individuals and as a society. The last thing Dad said doesn't refer to a doctor named Nova Mean. It's Aristotle's doctrine of the mean - moderation. That was the theme of Aristotle's book. He defined virtue as choosing to avoid the vices of excess and deficiency and always choosing the mean - moderation," Char said, and mugged a cute smirk of accomplishment.

Vanessa was stunned. First, that their daughter, only nineteen years old, could provide such a profound, classical interpretation of what appeared to be gibberish. Second, that Cameron would recite lines from Aristotle in the middle of the night, although she knew that he had been a philosophy major in college. "How on earth do you know that, Char?"

With a heavy, upper-class British accent and a twinkle in her eye, Char said, "I took a course in Ethics and Political Philosophy at Oxford this spring, Mummy dear, and we commenced our studies by reading and discussing Aristotle's *Nicomachean Ethics.*"

"That's gotta be it, Char. Your dad was dreaming about Aristotle. You, young lady, are one fine student and one fine daughter. Thank you."

"Thank you for paying a gazillion dollars so I could do a semester abroad, Mom."

"Money well-spent, kiddo," Vanessa assured her. She glanced at her watch and said, "Come on. We've got to wake up Tom and Anne and get ready to go. We have a 10:30 AM champagne brunch to attend at the university. And then commencement."

As she showered and dressed, Vanessa's thoughts shifted from Char's hard work and academic success to Cameron's dream. She reasoned to herself, *If Drew, who almost never dreams, had a big dream of any kind, and his dream focused on Aristotle's ethical principles, and he recited what he was dreaming, the dream must have been triggered by anxiety about the serious ethical problems at the University. Therefore, if he said he felt good when he woke up, it's because he had, in his subconscious, decided what to do — or what to choose, as Char put it.*

In early June, New Cambridge weather can be hot and humid or cool and rainy or just plain beautiful. On this Commencement day, it was just plain beautiful. To take advantage of the weather, President Faust had asked his staff to arrange the champagne brunch in the courtyard of the president's residence. About twenty years prior, the wealthy Lawrence family had given the Noble-Lawrence Museum of Fine Arts building, on the edge of campus, to the university and moved their art collection to a new, larger building in the arts district downtown. After renovation, the old museum facility became a posh, presidential residence. Steve and Ruth Faust used the first floor and grounds for formal social events, and lived on the second and third floors.

Two hundred invited guests attended the brunch to celebrate the culmination of the university's academic year. High-level university administrators, a few senior faculty, big donors and potential big donors, high-level government officials, and important alumni mingled and socialized as they sipped champagne and munched on scrumptious *hors d'oeuvres*. Cameron's main responsibilities were to work the crowd and to introduce people outside the university to university people they would relate to and appreciate. He wanted to introduce Steve Faust to Anna Zezulka and the visiting Czech Ambassador to the U.S., but hadn't found him in the crowd yet. At a distance, he spotted Margaret Benedict, who was always involved in planning and facilitating important university social functions.

"Margaret, hey, good morning. Where's Steve Faust?" he asked her.

"I haven't seen him. He's supposed to have been here at least half an hour ago. I tried his landline and cell phone and got nothing. Oh, there's Ms. McInerney," Margaret said, relieved. As they approached her, Margaret said, "Good morning. Have you seen President Faust?"

"No. Margaret. Not today."

"Neither of us has seen him, either," Margaret replied.

"It's still early, he'll be here, I'm sure, any minute now," Cameron said, and Margaret smiled and nodded.

Just then, Ms. McInerney's cell phone rang. She looked at the small window that revealed the number of the caller. "It's not President Faust's number, but it's a University cell phone number." She answered, "Hello," and as she listened to the caller, her facial expression changed from curious to bewildered. She said, "Yes. Change of plans. I see. Yes. He's standing right here beside me. Of course." Then she handed her cell phone to Cameron and said, "It's Sgt. Brown, you know, President Faust's security assistant. He wants to speak to you."

Cameron furrowed his brow, took the phone, and said, "Drew Cameron," then listened for several minutes. Mrs. McInerney looked confused. Margaret Benedict looked curious.

Cameron said, "I see. Yes, sir. Yes, we will. Thank you for the call. And please thank Sgt. Brown. Goodbye."

"Who was it, Drew? What did they say?" Margaret asked.

Cameron stared into space for a moment, then demanded, "Margaret, how much time until we should be in our seats in the arena?"

"Forty minutes."

"It's a five minute walk to the arena. Come on. I'll tell you what I just found out as we walk," Cameron said. He saw Vanessa and the kids on the far side of the patio next to the eggs Benedict station, in a conversation with the managing partner of another downtown law firm and the new acting dean of the ASU Law School.

When he caught her eye, he pointed to his watch, signaled with his hands that he had to go and blew her a kiss. She responded with a nod and a smile.

"Well, Drew, what did Sgt. Brown say? What's going on?" Margaret said.

"I'll tell you as we walk. Let's go."

As soon as they could conduct a private conversation, moving among the clusters of people walking from Noble-Lawrence House to the arena, Cameron said, "Alright, here's what I know." Margaret and Ms. McInerney were itching with curiosity. "President Faust won't be here for Commencement."

Both of Cameron's walking companions gasped in disbelief. "Where is he? Is he okay?" Ms. McInerney asked.

"He's okay. He's fine." Cameron said.

"Where is he, then?" Ms. McInerney demanded.

"He's in Washington."

"Well I hope Senator Broadbent is not in Washington. Where is he? He's supposed to be with President Faust, and they're both supposed to be here," Ms. McInerney said, revealing both disappointment and confusion.

"Senator Broadbent died last night . . . of a heart attack. Governor Portman requested that Steve Faust fly with him to Washington early this morning in the Governor's private plane," Cameron said.

"That's terrible. Senator Broadbent was a good man. He was such a good friend to the University," Margaret said, sad from news and somewhat breathless from walking so fast. What are we going to do now, Drew? We have fifteen thousand visitors and two thousand students and faculty waiting for commencement to start in about thirty minutes!"

"Hold on a second. There's more. While I was speaking with Sgt. Brown, who was in Washington with President Faust, I also spoke to Governor Portman. The Governor said . . . ." Cameron paused and frowned. "Governor Portman has appointed Steve Faust to fill-out the remaining two-and-a-half years of Senator Broadbent's term in the U.S. Senate. Senate leadership assured him that they will swear Steve in as a U.S. senator later this afternoon, to make it official. They risk being one vote short and losing a Senate vote on some big appropriations bill on Monday unless the state replaces Senator Broadbent by tomorrow morning. So, the Governor acted fast."

"So, if my boss has gone to the U.S. Senate, who will take his place here and run ASU? Did the Governor tell you that, Drew?"

"As a matter of fact, he did, Margaret. He said that appointing an acting university president is in the hands of the Governor and the Commissioner of Higher Education. Governor Portman has appointed me the Acting President. Ms. McInerney, Margaret, you have ten minutes to help me make whatever changes we need in the Commencement program, given that we have lost our president and our keynote speaker. Here's entrance D. Let's go in and do our jobs." Cameron called Vanessa and Holly by cell phone to let them know what had transpired.

13

To the strains of Sir Edward Elgar's *Pomp and Circumstance*, about fifteen hundred undergraduate students had marched onto the arena floor and stood in front of their seats arrayed in countless rows, followed apace by students receiving graduate credentials - masters, doctoral, and professional degrees. Last came a procession of faculty leaders, administrators, and honored guests marching down the middle aisle and up to their seats on the large speaker's platform. On cue, two thousand academic participants, all clad in caps and gowns, took their seats, surrounded by about fifteen thousand family members and friends in the regular arena seating. The vivid hues of the students' tassels and the faculty's doctoral hoods, against all their black robes, resembled hundreds of colorful ducks swimming on a black lake. As the wind ensemble finished playing, Cameron reflected on Elgar's 1901 composition. *He wrote it as one in a collection of several military marches and borrowed the terms "pomp" and "circumstance" from a line in Shakespeare's Othello. Elgar said he wanted to represent both aspects of war, thus Pomp, the military pageantry and Circumstance, the death and destruction. Why do we always play such a tune at a college graduation?*

As Riedel Tower chimed a single, sonorous gong, Cameron walked to the podium and introduced Fr. Allen Dyson, who offered an invocation. Next, he introduced Professor Karen Green, a tall, Julliard-trained soprano in ASU's Music Department who, accompanied by the wind ensemble, sang ASU's alma mater. Her performance was beautiful. She sang with great artistry and technical skill, in spite of the fact that she had told the ensemble conductor during rehearsal that she found both the words and the music "singularly uninspiring."

Returning to the podium microphone, Cameron stood motionless and speechless for almost ten seconds. He looked across the arena and spotted

Vanessa, Tom, Anne, and Char sitting in the section reserved for University employees and their families. He smiled and felt encouraged by their presence. Then he refocused on his entire audience and began his introductory remarks.

"Good afternoon and welcome to Alpha State University's annual spring Commencement. My name is Andrew Cameron. I serve as the Executive Vice President and Provost of the University. President Steven Faust is supposed to be here today to preside over this ceremony, but he cannot be here." Cameron paused again, dreading having to say what he knew he must say next. "And U.S. Senator Earl Broadbent, who was scheduled to deliver today's commencement address, also will not be here. It saddens me to announce that we learned about one hour ago that Senator Broadbent, an ASU alumnus, passed away last night. May we now observe one minute of silence in his honor."

Students and visitors alike were shocked by the news and sat in respectful silence, most with closed eyes and bowed heads. Then Cameron continued, "Late last night, when Governor Portman learned of Senator Broadbent's passing, he called ASU President Faust and both of them, accompanied by their wives, flew to Washington. The governor informed me this morning by phone that he has appointed President Faust to Senator Broadbent's unexpired term, and thus President Faust has resigned his position as president of Alpha State University, effective this morning."

Cameron paused to allow his audience of students, faculty, visitors and some media representatives to assimilate still more disturbing information. It is customary for so many people in a large arena to produce a constant din of coughing, whispering, babies crying, feet shuffling, and young kids talking out loud. But when Cameron announced the death of long-serving and much-respected Senator Earl Broadbent, the background noise ceased. All eyes focused on Andrew Cameron, all ears concentrated on every word he uttered, as if his words could relieve them of their growing discomfort. As Cameron paused and looked at his audience, he was almost overcome by sensory deprivation - the virtual absence of sound and movement of the many people in front of him. The news he had just reported had, for a moment, frozen this mass of breathing, animated people seated in the arena into a giant, three-dimensional still-life painting, *Audience at the Commencement*. Cameron overcame his momentary dizzy anxiety to continue.

"This morning, Governor Portman appointed me as Acting President of the University. That is why I am presiding over today's Commencement. And that is why, with your forbearance, I will take this opportunity to make a few brief remarks, to our students who are about to enter a new and important period in their lives."

Looking at the sea of black on the arena floor, Cameron began, even though he had only a vague theme in mind for his remarks, but had prepared nothing. "In every American generation, each graduating class faces serious challenges. The class of 1929 faced the Great Depression. The class of 1940 faced World War II. Many classes from 1960 through 1989 faced the threat of nuclear holocaust during the Cold War. Since the 1990s, experts in such matters have debated whether bioterrorism, global pandemic, or climate change is America's biggest threat. All are horrifying and deadly challenges, to be sure." Every student sat at attention, eyes, ears, and thoughts focused on Cameron's words.

"However, I am persuaded that your generation faces a threat that is even more complex and harmful than those I have already mentioned. Most of our past challenges posed an external enemy that threatened us in some way. The new threat I refer to reminds me of a quote from a famous American philosopher . . . Pogo." Cameron paused. "Pogo said, 'We have met the enemy, and he is us.' It is our own changing values and behaviors that are causing this serious threat and, if unabated, will cause our downfall. The leaders of America's economic institutions have substituted the ravenous pursuit of profit as their primary goal in place of the supply of a quality good or service at a fair price. The leaders of America's political institutions have substituted the predatory amassing of power as their purpose in lieu of promoting democracy and solving national problems. To make matters worse, when the U.S. Supreme Court rules that money is speech and that there are no limits to the amount of money that a person may give to a political action committee, a PAC, economic power and political power merged, enabling corporate and government leaders to collaborate in establishing a far more <u>imperfect</u> union — a government of the people but not by and for the people — in short, a plutocracy." The commencement audience — students, university personnel, and guests — sat in shocked disbelief.

"Now, we find that profit and power have become driving forces in the academy. Even Alpha State University, your alma mater, often pursues profit and power for itself rather than providing enlightenment for students and society. For example, at ASU and elsewhere, the football program has become the tail that wags the dog. In this program, we exploit our students and violate our own rules, and even the law, in order to generate millions in revenue every year. With our athletic programs, ASU is the largest single producer/supplier in this state's entertainment market."

The sudden shuffling of feet and movement in the audience represented more than just the release of tension and anxiety. But Cameron was unsure whether it symbolized disagreement or a more positive response.

"With similar effect, often when an Alpha State University researcher makes a patentable discovery that earns thousands or even millions of dollars in the market, he or she and the university share the profits, even though the researcher's salary and research expenses are paid by the taxpayers; that's you. The university then uses some of the profits to pay other researchers to produce more patentable and profitable discoveries and inventions. Sometimes, the university and the researcher and a corporation are in collusion to share the profits, even though the taxpayers pay the bills."

"In the fifth century B.C., Aristotle wrote a book about ethics in which he discussed how a virtuous person confronts an ethical or moral challenge." On hearing her father mention Aristotle, Char touched her mother on the arm to get her attention and share a smile. As she did, she noticed tears gathering in her mother's eyes. "According to Aristotle's 'Doctrine of the Mean', when we face a serious challenge," Cameron continued, "we could have an excess of confidence, but that would cause us to act in a reckless manner. Or we could have a deficiency of confidence, but that would cause us to act in a cowardly manner. However, if we choose Aristotle's counsel of moderation, we will have an appropriate measure of confidence, which is . . . courage. And that is virtue."

"So, graduates, you will soon be our leaders. Don't be reckless. Don't be cowardly. Be courageous. Use your positions of leadership to help restore the proper purpose in the polity, the economy, and the university— serving the legitimate needs of mankind rather than stockpiling power and money. If you do, you will be proud, society will be the better for it, and history will honor you and your generation for its virtue and greatness. I pledge to you to do everything I can, as long as I am able, to ensure that your alma mater stands for its original, authentic purpose — enlightenment — the moderate and virtuous position between ignorance and arrogance."

"If you and I use our leadership positions to reform our institutions in this way, I expect that our lives might be turbulent or even hazardous. Aristotle never promised us that achieving individual virtue or the good society comes easy. Good luck to us both. As of this moment, your degree is now official. Congratulations. We stand adjourned." As he returned to his seat and replaced his cap, the wind ensemble started playing Brahms' *Academic Festival Overture*, and Acting President Cameron led the platform party off the stage toward the middle aisle into the black lake of students seated on the floor of the arena.

As he entered the center aisle the students stood and began to applaud and cheer in an almost rowdy display and to toss their caps high into the air, both to emulate the tradition and to symbolize their acceptance of Cameron's challenge. At the same time, most of the gallery of several thousand visitors also stood and broke into thunderous, sustained applause. The celebratory din in the arena was so loud that no one could hear the ensemble playing Brahms' romantic piece. The cheering and applause continued for well over two minutes, until the platform party disappeared through the tunnel on the far end of the arena. That cued the commencement marshal to direct various sections of students to exit double-file down the aisle and disappear into the tunnel as they had been instructed.

Cameron's family high-fived and hugged and cheered and applauded with tears of pride. When the cheering diminished and the Brahms overture became audible again, Tom said, "Dad is a hero!" to which Anne and Char shouted their agreement.

Vanessa smiled and nodded assent but said to herself, *Yes, he's a hero. But is he George Washington or Joan of Arc?*